Adventures in the
Ancient World: 5

Adventures in the Ancient World: 5

Belshazzar

H. Rider Haggard

Adventures in the Ancient World: 5
Belshazzar
by H. Rider Haggard

Leonaur is an imprint of Oakpast Ltd

ISBN: 978-0-85706-162-1 (hardcover)
ISBN: 978-0-85706-161-4 (softcover)

http://www.leonaur.com

Publisher's Notes

The views expressed in this book are not necessarily
those of the publisher.

"In that night was Belshazzar the
King of the Chaldeans slain."

Dedication

Dear Cowan Guthrie,
You, a student of that age, persuaded me to write this tale of
Belshazzar and Babylon. Therefore I offer it to you.
Sincerely yours,
H. Rider Haggard
A. Cowan Guthrie, Esq., M. B.

CHAPTER 1

Ramose and His Mother

Now when by the favour of the most high God, Him whom I worship, to whom every man is gathered at last, now, I say, when I am old, many have urged upon me that I, Ramose, should set down certain of those things that I have seen in the days of my life, and particularly the tale of the fall of Babylon, the mighty city, before Cyrus the Persian, which chanced when he whom the Greeks called Nabonidus being newly dead, Belshazzar his son was king.

Therefore, having ever been a lover of letters, this I do in the Grecian tongue here in my house at Memphis, the great city of the Nile, whereof today I am the governor under Darius the Persian, for it has pleased God after many adversities to bring me to this peace and dignity at last. Whether any will read this book when it is written, or whether it will perish with me, I do not know, nor indeed does it trouble me much, since none can tell the end of anything good or ill, and all must happen as it is decreed. Man makes a beginning, but the rest is in the hands of fate; indeed his life itself is but a beginning of which the end is hid.

Now today when he is almost forgotten, I can say without fear that I am a king's son, for my father was none other than the Pharaoh Uah-ab-Ra, whom the Greeks called Apries and the Hebrews Hophra. Nor is my blood all royal, seeing that I was not the son of the wife of Pharaoh, but of one of his women, a Grecian lady named Chloe, the daughter of Chion, an Athenian by birth, of whom the less said the better for my mother told me that being a spendthrift and in want of money, he turned her beauty to account by giving her to Apries in exchange for a great present. I know no more of the matter because she would seldom speak of it, saying that it was shameful, adding only that her father was well-born; that her mother had died when she was an infant, and that before she came to the court at Sais, they saw many changes of fortune, living sometimes in wealth, but for the most part humbly and in great poverty which in after years bred in her a love of rank and riches.

Here in the palace of Sais during the little time that my mother was in favour with Pharaoh, I was born, and here I lived till I was a young man grown, being brought up with the sons of the great nobles and taught all things that one of my station should know, especially the art of war and how to ride and handle weapons. Further I got learning because always from the first I loved it, being taught many things by Greek masters who were about the court, as well as by Egyptians; also by a certain Babylonian named Belus, a doctor who was versed in strange lore concerning the stars. Of this Belus, my master and friend but for whom I should long ago be dead, I shall have much to tell.

Thus it came about that in the end I could read and speak Greek as well as I could Egyptian, which was not to be wondered at, seeing that I learned it at my mother's breast. Also I mastered the Babylonian or Chaldean tongue, though not so well, and with it the curious writing of that people.

Of my father, the Pharaoh, I saw little for he had so many children such as I, born of different mothers, that he took small heed of us, he upon whom lay this hard fortune, that from those who were his queens according to the law of Egypt, he had no offspring save one daughter only, while from those who were not his queens he had many. This was a heavy grief to the Pharaoh my father, who saw in it the hands of the gods to whom he made great sacrifices, especially to Ptah-Khepera the Creator and Father of Life, building up his temple at Memphis, and praying of him a son of the pure blood. But no son came and an oracle told him that he who loved the Greeks so much must to the Greeks for offspring, which was true, for all his sons were born of Grecian women, as perhaps the oracle knew already.

****

On a certain day I and other lads of my age were running races after the Grecian fashion. In the long race I outran all the rest, and fell panting and exhausted into the arms of one who, followed by three companions, stood wrapped in a dark cloak, (for the time was winter,) just by a wand that we had set in the ground to serve us as a winning-post.

"Well run and well won!" said a voice which I knew for that of Apries. "How are you named and who begot you?"

Now I rose from the ground upon which I had sunk, and pretending that he was a stranger to me, gasped out,

"Ramose is my name, and as for that of my begetter, go ask his of Pharaoh."

"I thought it," muttered Apries, considering me. Then he turned to the first of his councillors and said,

"You know of what we were talking just now; this lad is straight and strong and has a noble air; moreover I have a good report of him from his instructors who say that he loves learning. Why should he not fill a throne as well as another? The double crown would look well upon his brow."

"Because his skin is too white, Pharaoh," answered that councillor. "If the Egyptians learned that you purposed to set a Greek to rule them after you, they would cut his throat and perhaps tumble you into the Nile."

I remember these words very well, because although spoken at hazard, they must have been inspired, for they were in fact a prophecy, seeing that in the after years Apries was tumbled into the Nile whence Amasis who had usurped his throne, rescued his body and gave it royal burial.

After this Pharaoh spoke to me for a while, but not until he had bidden one of his councillors to lift the cloak from his shoulders and throw it round me, lest I, who was hot with the racing, should take cold. So there I stood, wrapped in the royal cloak of Tyrian purple, while those King's Companions muttered together, thinking that this was an omen and that one day I should sit upon the throne. Yet it was none, for it was not fated that any of the blood of Uah-ab-Ra, or Apries, should reign after him. That cloak I have to this day, though I do not wear it because of its royal clasp, for Pharaoh does not take back his gifts, or even that which he has lent for an hour. Yes, I have the cloak but not the crown, though this in truth I never sought.

Well, he searched me with his shrewd eyes that at times could look so fierce, and asked me questions as to my studies; also what I wished to be, a priest or a scribe or a soldier.

"What Pharaoh pleases," I answered, "though if I had my will, I would be all three, a priest because he draws nigh to the gods; a scribe because he gathers learning which is strength, and a soldier because he defends his country and wins glory. Yet most of all I would be a soldier."

"Well spoken," said Pharaoh, like one who was astonished at my answer. "You shall have your way if I can give it to you."

Then he held out his hand to me to kiss and left me, muttering,

"Would that his mother had been Egyptian and not Greek."

Here I must tell that before this time my mother, Chloe, who long ago had been succeeded by others in Pharaoh's favour, no longer dwelt at the court in Sais. For Apries, wishing to do well by her, had given her in marriage to a wealthy Egyptian named Tapert, who was one of his officers at Memphis where he filled the place of a judge and overseer of revenues. This Tapert, a kindly-faced, grizzled little man, had fallen in love with my mother's beauty while he was at court making report to Pharaoh on matters at Memphis, and especially as to the rebuilding of the temple of Ptah in that city, with which he had to do. Noting this, as he noted all, when the time came for Tapert to return to Memphis, Apries asked him if he desired any gift of Pharaoh whom he had served well. Tapert made no answer but let his eyes rest upon my mother who, with other women of the royal household, sat at a distance broidering linen with Grecian patterns, as she loved to do.

Apries thought a while, then said,

"Take her, if she will go. For you are a good man, if ugly, and as your wife she may be happier than here—as nothing. Ask her. You have my leave."

So he asked as it was made easy for him to do, and in the end, although she loved the pomp and pleasures of the court, my mother listened to him, knowing him for a very rich and honest man of good blood and station, one, too, whom she could rule. So it came about that while she was still a young and beautiful woman, for the Greeks do not wither as early as do the Egyptians, by the permission of Pharaoh my mother was married according to the full custom to the Count Tapert, a man of many offices and titles who settled wealth upon her should he die. Thus it happened that she went to live with him at Memphis, while I stayed behind at Sais.

Our parting was sad, although after my childhood we had met but little, because the laws of the court kept us apart.

"Hearken, my son," she said to me. "I make this marriage for a double reason. When I was but a child I was delivered into the hands of Pharaoh, who soon forgot me in favour of others who came after, but because I had borne him a son, treated me honourably. Now while I am still fair I have opportunity to leave this cage with golden bars, and to become a free woman as the wife of a rich and honest man who loves me, one by whom I shall be cherished, and I take it thankfully who, if I stayed here, might one day find myself thrown into the street. Yet not altogether for my own sake, because it means that we must be parted; also, if I am loved, I do not love. Know, my son, that what I do, I do for you more even than for myself. Here in the palace you are highly placed; the Pharaoh looks upon you with favour; there are some who think that in the end he will make a prince of you and, having no lawful heirs of the royal blood, name you to follow after him. It may be that this is in his mind. But if so I am sure that it could never come about while your mother, the Grecian slave, remained at court to remind the great ones of Egypt that you are base-born of a woman whose people the Egyptians hate, whereas if I go away this may be forgotten, though I fear that your skin will always tell its own story.

"Nor is this all. As Tapert has whispered to me, Pharaoh is rich; Pharaoh is powerful and under him the people have prosperity, the arts flourish and their gods are better served than they have been for many an age, all of which comes about because Egypt is guarded by the Greeks whom Pharaoh hires. Yet he says that they hate those guardians, they who will not protect themselves, and it may well happen that from this hatred trouble will come, bringing with it the fall of Pharaoh and of those of his House. Therefore, should that chance, I would make ready a refuge for you, my son.

"Tapert is very rich, as he has told me, one of the richest men in Egypt, although few know it, and henceforth all he has is mine, and what is mine is yours, for I do not think that I shall ever bear him children. Therefore, in the hour of trouble remember always that there is a place where you can lay your head, my son of the royal blood of Egypt, whose throne you still may win by help of the wealth that I can give you, and thereby make me, a Grecian slave bought for her beauty, the mother of a king."

Thus she spoke and as she did so I read her heart, who although I was so young had knowledge of the court ladies and their ways. She went because she thought it no longer safe to stay near to Pharaoh who was weary of the sight of her and of her importunities for gifts and honours, and might at any time cast her out. Still I was sad, for I who had no one else to love, loved my mother however vain and foolish she might be.

So she departed and became the wife of Tapert, Pharaoh making many gifts to her. But I stayed on at court and grew in strength and stature, also in favour with Pharaoh. Hence it came about that I was advanced beyond my station and made a Count of Egypt and a Companion of the King with other offices and titles, seeing which all men bowed down to me, thinking that in days to come, although I was base-born and half a Greek, I still might sit where Pharaoh sat. And so it might have chanced had it not been decreed otherwise and had not Hathor, whom the Greeks call Aphrodite, lit a flame of love within my heart that burned me up and well nigh brought me to my death.

It happened thus. The King of Babylon had attacked certain peoples in Syria of whom the chief king was named Abibal, an old man. Now in the fighting the Babylonians were driven back, or rather had retired purposing to return at their own season with a larger army—it might be next year, or the year after, or the year after that, as it suited them, to burn the cities of Abibal and his allies and to slay their peoples or take them captive.

Now in this fighting the old king Abibal was wounded with an arrow in the thigh, which wound festered so that in the end he died. Before he died he determined to seek the aid of Apries, the Pharaoh of Egypt, against the Babylonians. Therefore since he trusted no one else, he left command that a young wife of his named Atyra, whom he had married in his age, the daughter of another Syrian king, should go in person to the court of Egypt and lay the cause of her country before Pharaoh, so that he might send an army to defend it from the Babylonians. For this old king cared nothing of what might happen to his young wife after he was dead, or who should take her, but for his people, and the other peoples who were his allies, he cared much.

So he bound the Queen Atyra by a solemn oath to do his bidding, calling down the curse of his spirit and that of his gods upon her if she failed therein, and she who was youthful and desired to see new lands, and above all Egypt, swore all that he wished readily enough, after which he died and was buried. When he had been sealed up in his tomb Queen Atyra, a woman of great beauty who had been brought up in statecraft, with a voice so sweet and a mind so subtle that she could win any man to her will, started upon her journey in much pomp and bearing many gifts, leaving her dead lord's successor seated upon his throne.

At length having passed all dangers and escaped from a troop of the Babylonians that was sent out to capture her, she came safely to Egypt and encamping at a little distance from Sais, despatched messengers to Pharaoh to announce her and ask his safeguard for herself and her companions. As it chanced I, Ramose, now a young man in my twentieth year, was the captain of the guard that day; therefore it fell to me to receive these messengers and bring them before Pharaoh and his officers.

He listened to their tale of which already he knew something from his spies and those who served him in Syria. Then, having consulted with his councillors and scribes, he beckoned to me and when I came and bowed before him, said,

"Ramose, take an escort with you and ride out to the camp of this lady Atyra, and say to her that it is too late for me to answer her prayer today when the sun is already near to setting, but that I will consider of it tomorrow. Talk with her yourself, if you can, for she will suspect no guile in one so young, but at least spend the night at her camp learning all that you are able concerning her and her business, and tomorrow at the dawn return to make report to me."

So I went clad in the Grecian armour that Apries had commanded the guard to wear, thereby giving much offence to the Egyptian generals and soldiers, taking my newest cloak and mounted on a fine horse of the Arab breed. Indeed, having heard through the messengers that this lady was young and beautiful, I desired to look my best, for to tell the truth, like many youths of my age I was somewhat vain and wished to please the eyes of women. Moreover this was not altogether strange, seeing that all thought me comely, who was tall and well-shaped, having clear-cut Grecian features that I inherited from my mother, brown hair that curled upon my head and large dark eyes, the gift of my Egyptian blood. Further, I was ready of speech and could talk of anything, though in truth as yet I knew little, all of which I do not shame to write now when I am old. Lastly I must add this, though it is not to my credit; that I was too fond of women and made love to them when the chance came my way, which was often at the court of Sais. Or perhaps they made love to me—I do not know; at least none of them had really touched my heart, or I theirs.

Thus, full of youth and goodliness and the lust of life and all the gifts that the gods give us when we are young, of which we think so little until we have grown old and they are gone, followed by my escort I galloped forth proud of my mission and hoping for adventure. For little did I know that I rode into the arms of terror and of sorrow.

CHAPTER 2

The Cup of Hathor

An hour later, guided by the messengers, one of whom had gone on ahead to warn this lady Atyra of my coming, I caught sight of her camp set upon the sand at the edge of the cultivated land, and noted that it was large. The tents were many, dark in colour, most of them, for they were woven of camel hair after the Arab fashion, but in their midst was a great white pavilion dyed with stripes of blue and red, over which fluttered a strange, three-pointed flag which seemed to be blazoned with stars of gold.

This banner, I guessed, must mark the resting-place of the lady Atyra who called herself a queen. What sort of a queen was she, I wondered. Thick-made and black probably, though these Syrians whom in my ignorance I believed to be swarthy folk, thought her fair, as indeed all queens are fair according to those who serve them.

Whilst I was musing thus we came to the camp and must pass between two lines of camels, many of which were lying down chewing their food. Now like most horses, mine, a spirited beast, hated the sight and smell of camels and growing restive, took the bit between its teeth in such fashion that I could not hold it. Rushing forward it headed straight for the great pavilion with the coloured stripes. Soldiers or servants sprang forward to stay the beast, but without avail, for it overthrew one of them, causing the rest to fly. On we went, till at the very door of the tent my horse caught its feet in a rope and fell, hurling me straight through the open entrance. Over and over I rolled and though my bones were unharmed, for the sand was covered with thick carpets, the breath was shaken out of me, so that for a while I sat gasping with my helmet all awry like to that of a drunken soldier.

The sound of laughter reached me, very gentle laughter that reminded me of water rippling over stones. Also there was other coarser laughter such as might come from the throats of slaves or eunuchs or

14

of serving-girls. It made me very angry, so much so that being half-stunned, with what breath I had left I said words I should not have uttered, adding that I was Pharaoh's envoy.

"And if so, Sir, is this the fashion in which Pharaoh's envoys enter the presence of those whom it pleases Pharaoh to honour?" asked a silvery voice, speaking in the Grecian tongue though with a soft and foreign accent.

"Yes," I answered, "if they set stinking camels to frighten their horses and lay ropes to snare their feet."

Then the blood went to my head and I suppose that I fainted for a while.

When my sense returned I found myself stretched upon a couch and heard that same voice giving orders both in Greek and in the Babylonian or Chaldean tongue of which I knew something through the teaching of my tutor, Belus, also in others that I did not know, all of which talk concerned myself.

"Take that helm from his head," said the soft voice, though not softly. "O daughter of a fool, can you not see that you are pressing the edge of it upon the bruise? Away with you! Let me do it. So. Now re-move the breastplate—that is easy for the straps have burst—and open the tunic to give him air. What a white skin he has for an Egyptian. Any woman would be proud of it. By the gods he is a noble-looking youth and if he dies, as he may for I think his neck is twisted, those who tied the camels there and left the ropes lying shall pay for it. Now, wine. Where is the wine? Lift him gently and pour some down his throat. Nay, not so. Would you drown the man? Hand me the cup. Has that old leech been found? If not, bid him get himself back to Syria as best he may—"

Just then I opened my eyes to the lids of which leaden weights seemed to have been tied. They met the glance of other eyes above me, very beautiful eyes that were neither blue nor black, but some-thing between the two. Also I became aware that a white arm was supporting my head and that the fair and rounded breast of a very beautiful woman who was kneeling beside me, touched my own.

"I am the envoy of the Pharaoh Apries, King of the two Lands and of the countries beyond the sea. The Pharaoh says—" I began in feeble tones, repeating the lesson that I had learned.

"Never mind what the Pharaoh says," answered she who leant over me in a rich, low voice. "Like most of his messages of which I have had many, I doubt not that it will serve as well tomorrow as today. Drink this wine and lie quiet for a while—that is, if your neck is not broken."

So I drank and lay still, thankful enough to do so for I had fallen on my head and been much shaken, having clung with my hands to the reins of my horse as I had been taught to do in the military school, instead of stretching them out to protect myself. The wine was good and warmed me; also it seemed to clear my brain, so that soon I was able to look about me and take note.

I saw that the pavilion in which I lay was finer than any that I had ever known, being hung all round with beautiful mats or carpets that shone like silk wherever the light fell upon them. Also there was a table at its end set with vessels of gold and silver, and round it folding stools made of ebony inlaid with ivory and piled with cushions, and a brazier that stood upon a tripod, for the desert air was chill, wherein burnt wood that gave out sweet odours. Moreover there were hanging lamps of silver that presently were lit by a swarthy eunuch, for now night was closing in, which burned with a clear white flame and like the fire gave out scents.

The eunuch, clad in his rich apparel and head-dress of twisted silk, glanced at me out of his oblong eyes and went away, leaving me alone in that perfumed place. Lying thus upon my soft, cushioned bed, a strange mood took hold of me, as it does at times of those whose brains reel under the weight of some heavy blow. I seemed to lose all sense of time and place; I seemed to be floating on a cloud above the earth, looking backwards and forwards. Far away behind me was a wall or mass of blackness out of which I crawled, a tiny, naked child, into the light of day. Then came visions of my infancy, little matters in my life that I had long forgotten, words that my mother had murmured into my baby ears, her caresses when I was sick; the softness of her cheek as she pressed it against my fevered brow, and I know not what besides. And all this while I, the infant in her arms, seemed to be asking this question of her,

"Mother, whence came I and why am I here?"

To which she answered, "I do not know, my child. The gods will tell you—when you are dead."

The stream of time flowed on. Yes, it was a stream, for I saw it flowing, and on it I floated, clutching day by day at sticks and straws wherewith I built me a house of life, as a bird builds its nest, till at last I saw myself falling from the horse and for a moment all grew dark. Then out of the darkness there appeared shadowy shapes, some beautiful, some terrible, and I knew that these were the spirits of the future showing me their gifts. They passed by and once more before me was a black wall such as that whence I had seemed to come in the beginning, which wall I knew was Death. I searched to find some opening but could discover none. I sank down, outworn and terrified, and lo! as I sank there appeared a glorious gateway, and beyond it a city of many palaces and temples in whose courts walked gods, or men who looked like gods.

My vision passed and I awoke, wondering where that city might be and if within it I should find any habitation.

It was a foolish dream, yet I set it down because I think it told me something of the mystery of birth and death. Or rather it set out these mysteries, revealing nothing, for who knows what lies beyond those black walls that are our Alpha and Omega and between which we spell out the alphabet of Life. Also it was not altogether foolish, for even then I knew that the shapes of terror which seemed to wait upon my path were portents of advancing woe—and trembled. . . .

It must have been the dead of night when I awoke thus out of my swoon, for now there was no sound in the camp, save the tramping of the sentries and the howling of distant dogs or jackals smitten of the moon. In the pavilion the scented lamps burned low or had been shaded, so that the place was filled with a soft gloom, in which shadows seemed to move, caused no doubt by the swinging of the lamps in the draught of the night air. Yet one of these shadows, the most palpable of them all, did not move; indeed it seemed to stand over me like a ghost that waits the passing of one whom it has loved. I grew afraid and stirred, thinking to speak, whereon the shadow turned its head so that the light of the lamp fell upon the beautiful face of a woman.

"Who are you?" I asked in a whisper, for I seemed to fear to speak aloud.

A sweet voice answered,

"O Ramose, Pharaoh's son and envoy, I am your hostess Atyra, once a queen."

"And what do you here, Queen Atyra?"

"I watch you, my guest, in your swoon."

"A poor task, Lady, more fitting to a leech or slave."

"I think not, Ramose, son of the king, as I have been told that you are by your escort and others. There is much to be learned from those who sleep by one who has the gift of reading souls."

"Is it your gift, Lady?"

"I have been taught it by wise men in Syria, *magi* the Persians call them, and as I think not quite in vain. At least I have read your soul."

"Then, Lady, you have read that which is worth nothing, for what is written upon so short a scroll?"

"Much, Count Ramose, for our life is like the chapters of a book, and already at our birth Fate has stamped the titles of those chapters upon its clay, leaving it to Time to write the rest. Your story, I think, will be long, if sad in part. Yet it was not to talk of such things that I have come here alone at night."

"Why, then, did you come, Lady?"

"First to see how you fared, for your fall was heavy, and secondly, if you were well enough, to hear your message."

"It is short, Lady. Pharaoh bids me say that he will answer your requests tomorrow, since today it is too late."

"Yet it was not too late for him to send you, Count Ramose, charged with words that mean nothing. I will tell you why he sent you; it was to spy upon me and make report to him." Thus she said, resting her chin upon her hand and looking at me with her great dark eyes which shone in the lamplight like to those of a night-bird, but I remained silent.

"You do not answer, O Ramose, because you cannot. Well, your office is easy, for I will tell you all there is to learn. The old king, Abibal, whose wife I was in name, is dead, and dying left a charge upon me— to save his country from the Babylonians, calling down the curse of all the gods upon my head in life and on my soul in death, should I fail by my own fault to fulfil his dying prayer. Therefore I have come to Egypt, although the oracles warned me against this journey, for the case of these Syrians is very hard and desperate, and in Egypt lies their only hope who alone cannot stand against the might of Babylon. Tell me, Son of the king, will Apries help us?"

"I do not know, Lady," I answered, "but I do know that least of all things does he, or Egypt, desire a war against Babylon. You must plead your own cause with him; I cannot answer your question."

"How can I plead my cause, Count Ramose? I bring great gifts of gold and silks and spices, but what are these to him who holds the wealth of Egypt? I can promise allegiance and service, but my people are far away and Egypt seeks no war in which they can be used."

Again I answered that I did not know, then added,

"Yet your nation could have found no better envoy, for Pharaoh loves a beautiful woman."

"Do you think me beautiful?" she asked softly. "Well, to tell truth, so have others, though as yet such favour as I have, has brought me little joy—" and she sighed, adding slowly, "Of what use is beauty to her who has found none to love?"

"I know little of such things, Lady. Yet, perhaps for you the search is not finished."

18

She looked at me a while before she answered,

"My heart tells me that you are right, O Ramose. The search is not finished."

Then she rose and taking a cup of wine gave me to drink of it, afterwards drinking a little herself as though to pledge me.

This done, she poured the rest of the wine upon the ground, like to one who makes an offering before some god, bent down so close that her scented breath beat upon my brow, whispered to me to sleep well, and glided away.

I think there must have been some medicine in that wine, for presently all the pain left my head and neck and I fell fast asleep, yet not so fast but that through the long hours I seemed to dream of the loveliness of this Syrian queen, until at length I was awakened by the sunlight shining in my eyes.

A servant who must have been watching me, noted this and went away as though to call some one. Then an old man came, one with a white beard who wore a strange-shaped cap.

"Greeting, Sir," he said in bad Greek. "As you may guess, I am the court physician. Most unhappily I was absent last night, seeking for certain plants that are said to grow in Egypt, which must be gathered by the light of the moon, since otherwise they lose their virtue; indeed, I returned but an hour ago."

"Is it so, Physician?" I answered. "Well, I trust that you found your herbs."

"Yes, young sir, I found them in plenty and gathered them with the appropriate spells. Yet I would I had never learned their name, for I hear that my mistress is very wrath with me because I was not present when you chanced to roll into the tent like a stone thrown from a catapult, and may the gods help him with whom she is wrath! Still I see that you live who, I was told, had a broken neck. Now let me see what harm you have taken, if any."

Then he called to the eunuch to come within the screens that had been set round me, and strip me naked. When this was done, he examined me with care, setting his ear against my breast and back, and feeling me all over with his hands.

"By Bel, or whatever god you worship," he said, "you have a fine shape, young lord, one well fitted for war—or love. Nor can I find that there is aught amiss with you, save a bruise upon your shoulder and a lump at the back of your head. No bone is broken, that I will swear. Stand up now and let me treat you with my ointments."

I stood up, to find myself little the worse save for a dizziness which soon passed away, and was rubbed with his aromatics, and afterwards washed and clothed. Then I was led out of the pavilion to where my men were camped, who rejoiced to see me living and sound, for a rumour had reached them that I was dead. With them I ate and a while later was summoned to the presence of the Queen Atyra.

So once more I entered the pavilion, to find this royal lady seated in a chair made of sycamore wood inlaid with ivory. I bowed to her and she bowed back to me, giving no sign that she had ever seen me before. Indeed she looked at me with her large eyes as though I were a stranger to her, and I looked at her clad in her rich robes over which flowed her black abundant hair, and marvelled at her beauty, for it was great and moved me.

I will not set out all our talk; indeed after these many years much of it is forgotten, though that which we held at midnight I remember well, when we were but man and woman together, and not as now, an envoy and a foreign queen discussing formal matters of state. The sum of it was that she grieved to hear of my mischance, and prayed me to accept a stallion of the Syrian breed in place of my own which had been lamed through the carelessness of her servants, but rejoiced to know from her physician that beyond a blow which stunned me for a while, I had taken little harm.

I thanked her and delivered Pharaoh's message, at which she smiled and said that it told her nothing, except that she must wait where she was, until it pleased him to send another. Meanwhile she hoped that I would be her guest as the physician told her I was not yet fit to ride.

Now as this plan pleased me well, for to tell truth I longed for more of the company of that most lovely woman, I summoned the scribe who was amongst those who rode with me, and wrote a letter to Pharaoh, telling him of what had chanced, which letter I despatched in charge of two of my guard. They departed, and at evening returned again, bringing an answer signed by Pharaoh's private scribe, which bade me stay till I was able to travel, and then accompany the Queen Atyra to the court.

So there I remained that night, being given a tent to sleep in near to the pavilion. In the evening also I was bidden to eat with the queen and certain of her councillors, when, as she alone knew the Grecian tongue, the talk lay between her and me. Indeed as soon as the meal was finished she made some sign whereat these men rose and went away, leaving us alone.

The night was very hot, so hot that presently she said,

"Come, my young guest, if it pleases you, let us leave this tented oven, and walk a while beneath the moon, breathing the desert air. No need to call your guard, for here you are as safe as though you sat in Pharaoh's palace."

I answered that it pleased me well, and calling for two of her women to accompany us, we set forth, the queen wearing a hooded, silken cloak that the women brought to her, which covered her white shape and glittering jewels like a veil. I too was wrapped in a cloak, since I wore no armour, and thus, we thought, the pair of us passed unnoted through the camp.

At a distance on the crest of a sandy hill, stood the ruin of some old temple overlooking the cultivated land and the broad waters of the Nile. Thither we wended followed by the two women; at least at first we were followed by them, but later when I looked I could not see them any more. Still of this I said nothing who was well content to be alone with this gracious and beautiful lady. We came to the temple and entered its hoary courts whence a jackal fled away, as did a night-bird perched upon a cornice, telling me that here there was no man. At the far end of the court there remained a statue of Hathor, one of a pair, for the other had fallen. That it was Hathor might easily be known for she wore the vulture cap and above it horns between which rested the disc of the moon. Near to the feet of this statue in the shadow of a wall, Atyra sat herself down upon a broken block of alabaster, motioning to me to place myself at her side.

"What goddess is this," she asked, "who carries the horns of a beast upon the brow of a fair woman?"

"Hathor, goddess of Love," I answered, "whom some call Mistress of the gods."

"Is it so? Well, by this title or by that she is known in every land, and well is she named Mistress of the gods and men. Strange that amidst all this ruin she alone should have stood through the long centuries, an emblem of love that does not die. How beautiful is the night! See the great moon riding in yonder cloudless sky. Look at her rays glittering on the river's face and hark to the breeze whispering among the palms beneath. Truly such a night should be dear to Hathor, so dear that—"

Here she broke off her dreamy talk, then said suddenly,

"Tell me of yourself, Prince Ramose."

"Do not give me that title," I exclaimed. "If it were heard it might bring trouble on me who am but a Count of Egypt by Pharaoh's grace!"

"Yet it is yours, Ramose," she answered, "and in this place there is none to hear save Hathor and the moon. Now speak."

21

So I told her my short tale, to which she listened as though it had been that of the deeds of a king; then said,

"But you have left out the half of it all. You have left out Hathor."

"I do not understand," I answered, looking down to hide my blushes.

"I mean that you have left out love. Tell me of those whom you have loved. Do you not know that it is of love that all women wish most to hear?"

"I cannot, Lady, for I have—never loved."

"If that be true, how deep a cup of love is left for you to drink, whose lips have not yet sipped its wine, Ramose. So here in the shadow of Hathor sit a pair of us, for to give you truth for truth, I tell you that though I am your elder, I too have never loved."

"Yet you are a widow," I said astonished.

"Aye, the widow of an aged man who married me because of my birth, my wit, my wealth, and the great friends I brought him, and whom I married to serve my people that were threatened, as his are today, by the giant might of Babylon. Abibal was to me a father and no more, if a beloved father whose commands I will execute to the death, which commands bring me upon a long and perilous journey to seek help from mighty Pharaoh who desires to give me none."

Now I glanced at her sideways, and said,

"You are very beauteous, Lady. You have the eyes of a dove, the step of a deer, the wisdom of a man and the grace of a palm. Were there then none who pleased your eyes about your court in Syria?"

"While my lord lived I was blind, as became a loyal wife," she answered.

"And now that he is dead, Lady?"

"Oh! now I cannot say. No more do I seek a husband who am a queen and would remain free, the slave of no one, for what slavery is there like to that of marriage? Yet it is true that I desire love, if I may choose that love. Come; let us be going, for yonder Egyptian Hathor of yours casts her spell over me and brings thoughts that for long I have forbidden in my heart. I think that this is an evil-omened place; its goddess tells of love, but its hoar ruins tell of death. Doubtless did we but know it, here we sit above the shrouded dead who, staring at us from their sepulchres, mock our beating hearts which soon will be as still as theirs. Come; let us be going, who yet are young and free from the webs of Hathor and of death. Death, I defy thee while I may. Hathor, I make a mock of thee and thy calm, compelling gaze. Dost thou not also make a mock of Hathor, Ramose?" and turning, she looked at me with her great eyes that seemed to glow in the shadows like to those of an owl.

"I do not know," I answered faintly, for those eyes drew the strength out of me. "Yet it is dangerous to mock at any goddess, and most of all at Hathor. Still, let us go, I think it very wise that we should go; the scent of your hair overwhelms me who have been ill. My brain rocks like a boat upon the sea. Hathor has me by the hand."

"Yes, I think that Hathor has us both by the heart," she answered in her low rich voice, a voice of honey.

Then our lips met, for there in her temple we had drunk of Hathor's cup.

CHAPTER 3

The Counsel of Belus

We rose; her face was like the dawn, her eyes were dewy, but I trembled like a leaf, I whose heart for the first time love had gripped with cruel hands.

I thought I saw a shadow flit across a pool of moonlight that lay within the temple's broken pylon, the shadow of a man.

"What frightens you?" she asked.

I told her in a whisper.

"Perchance it was a spirit of which this place must be full, for such, they say, look like shadows. Or perchance it was thrown from the broad wings of some fowl of the night," she answered lightly. "At least if it be otherwise, that watcher was too far away to have seen us here, seated side by side in gloom. Certainly he could not have heard our words. Yet, Ramose, Hathor's gift to me, I would warn you. Among those who sat with us at the board tonight, did you take note of one, a bearded man of middle age, hook-nosed, with flashing eyes like to those of a hawk?"

"Yes, Lady Atyra, and I thought that he looked askance at me."

"It may be so. Listen. That man was a councillor of Abibal's, a priest of his god also, and as such one of great power in the land. Always he has pursued me with his love, and now he would wed me. But I hate him, as hitherto I have hated all men, and will have none of him. Moreover," here her voice grew hard and cold, "when I am strong enough I will be rid of him, but that is not yet. If I can win Pharaoh's friendship and bring it to pass that he names me to succeed to the throne of Abibal, as his subject queen, then and not till then shall I be strong enough, for this Ninari has a large following and the half of my escort are sworn to him. Meanwhile, have no fear and be sure that in this, our first kiss, I pledged my heart to you and to no other man."

"I thank you, O most Beautiful," I answered. "Yet tell me, Lady, how can this matter end? You have been a queen and will be one again, while I am but Pharaoh's base-born son, one of many, though I think that he loves me best of all of them. Also I am young and un-proved. What then can there be between us?"

"Everything before all is done, I think, Ramose, if you will but trust to me who am wise and strong in my fashion, and being alas! older than you are, have seen and learned more. Already I have a plan. I will persuade Pharaoh to send you with me to Syria, there to be his eyes and envoy, and once back in my own country I will be rid of this Ninari and will take you as my husband, saying that such is Pharaoh's will."

"May that day come soon!" I muttered, who already was as full of love of this royal woman, as a drunkard is with wine.

Meanwhile we had left the temple, and were walking side by side but not too near, down the slope of sand towards the camp. As we went, from a clump of stunted sycamores appeared the two waiting-ladies whom Atyra chided because they had not followed her more closely.

They answered that they had seen a man who looked like a thief of the desert, watching them and being afraid, had taken refuge among the trees till he went away down towards the river. Then they had come out but could not find us, and therefore returned to the trees and waited, not knowing what else to do.

"You should have run back to the camp and fetched a guard," she answered angrily. "For is it meet that the Lady Atyra should wander unaccompanied in the night?"

Then she dismissed them and they fell behind us, but although I was young and knew little of women's tricks, the only thing I believed about that tale, was that they had seen a man, perchance the same whose shadow flitted across the moonlight within the broken pylon.

When we reached the camp and had passed the sentries in front of the pavilion, we met the councillor and priest Ninari, who seemed to be waiting there, doubtless for our return. He bowed low and spoke to the queen in a Syrian tongue which I did not understand, and in that tongue she answered him, somewhat sharply, as I thought. Again he bowed low, almost to the ground indeed, but all the while I felt that his fierce eyes were fixed upon me. Then with some courteous words to myself, thanking me for my company, she passed into the pavilion.

I, too, turned to go to my own quarters where my escort awaited me, when this Ninari stepped in front of me and said in bad and gut-tural Greek,

"Young lord from the Pharaoh's court, your pardon, but I would have you know that whatever may be the fashions of Egypt, it is not our custom for strangers to walk alone with a great lady at night, especially if she chances to be our queen."

Now there was something in the man's voice and manner which stirred my blood, and I answered, holding my head high,

"Sir, I am a guest here and Pharaoh's envoy, and I go where my hostess asks me to go, whatever may be your Syrian customs."

"You are strangely favoured," he said sneering. "Your horse which you cannot manage, hurls you like a sack stuffed with barley into the presence of our mistress. She doctors your bruised poll, and now takes you out walking in the moonlight. Well, well, I should remember that you are but a forward, cross-bred Egyptian boy, well-looking enough as bastards of your kind often are in their youth, just such a one as it pleases grown women to play with for an hour and then cast aside."

I listened to this string of insults welling like venom from the black heart of the jealous Syrian. At first they amazed me to whom no such words had ever been used before. Then as the meaning of his coarse taunts, hissed out in broken Greek, came home to me, being no coward I grew enraged.

"Dog!" I said, "beast of a Syrian, do you dare to talk thus to Pharaoh's envoy, a Count of Egypt?" and lifting my arm I, who was a trained boxer, doubled my fist and smote him in the face with all my strength, so that he went headlong to the ground.

At the sound of my raised voice men ran together from here and there—some of them those of my own escort whose tents were near at hand, some of them Syrians—and stood staring as this Ninari went backward to the earth. In a moment he was up again, blood pouring from his hooked nose, and came at me, a curved and naked blade in his hand, which I suppose he had drawn as he rose. Seeing this, I too drew my short Grecian sword and faced him, though there was this difference between us, that whereas I had no armour, being clothed only in a festal dress of linen, he wore a coat of Syrian mail. My men, noting this, would have thrown themselves between us, but I shouted to them to stand aside. The Syrians would have done likewise, but at some command that I did not hear, they also fell back. Thus we were left facing each other in the full moonlight which was almost as clear as that of day.

Ninari smote at me with his broad, curved blade. I bent almost to my knee and the blow went over my head. Rising, I thrust back. My sword-point struck him full beneath the breast but could not pierce his good armour, though it caused him to reel and stumble. Again he came at me, smiting lower to catch me on the body which he knew was unprotected, and this time I must leap far backwards, so that the point of his blade did no more than cut through my linen garment and just scratch the skin beneath.

Yet that scratch stung me, more perhaps than a deeper wound would have done, and made me mad. Uttering some old Greek war-cry, as I think one my mother had taught me as that of her father's House, I flew at the man and smote him full upon his helm, shearing off one side of it and causing him to stagger. Before he could recover himself I smote again and though the steel glanced from the edge of his severed helm, yet passing downwards, it cut off his right ear and sank deep into his neck and shoulder.

He fell and lay there, as it was thought, dead. The Syrians began to murmur for they did not love to see a noted warrior of their race thus defeated by an unarmoured youth. My men, fearing trouble, ringed me round, muttering such words as:

"Well done, young Ramose!" "You have lopped that cur's ear, Count, although he wore a collar when you had none." "Now if any other Syrian would like a turn—" and so forth, for this escort of mine, some of them Greek and some Egyptian, were all picked fighters of Pharaoh's guard, and rejoiced that their boy officer should have won in so uneven a fray.

The business grew dangerous; the friends of Ninari drew their weapons and waved spears. My escort made a ring about me in the Grecian fashion, their swords stretched out in front of them. Then I heard a woman's voice cry,

"Have done! Fools, would you bring Pharaoh's wrath upon us and cause our country's prayer to him to be refused? If this young Egyptian lord has done ill, let Pharaoh judge him."

"Queen," I broke in, panting between my words, "I have done no ill. This follower of yours," and I pointed to Ninari who lay upon the sand groaning, "for no cause bespattered me with the vile mud of insults, till at length unable to bear more, I felled him with my hand. He rose and although I wear no mail, sprang at me to slay me with his sword. So I must defend myself as best I might. There are many here who can bear witness that I speak the truth."

"It is needless, Count Ramose," she answered in a clear voice, "for know that I heard and saw something of this business and hold that you were scarcely to blame, save that you should have taken no heed of mad or wine-bred talk. Yet, lest harm should come to you and I and my people be put to shame, I pray you leave this camp now at once and return to Sais whither I will follow you tomorrow to seek audience of Pharaoh and ask his pardon. Let the horses of Pharaoh's envoy be made ready."

27

Men ran to do her bidding, but my guard who looked doubtfully at the Syrians, remained about me, save two of them who went to my tent and thence brought my armour which they helped me to gird on.

Meanwhile that same old leech who had tended me, had been busy with Ninari whom he ordered to be carried to his tent. Now he rose and made his report to Atyra.

"The Lord Ninari henceforth must go one-eared," he said. "Also the Egyptian's sword has cut through his mail and sunk into the flesh of his shoulder, for the blow was mighty. Yet by chance it seemed to have missed the big vein of the neck, so unless his hurts corrupt I think that he will live."

"I pray the gods it may be so," answered Atyra in a cold voice, "and that henceforth his tongue may remember what has chanced to his ear. Hear me all! If any lifts a hand against Pharaoh's envoy or his company because of this matter, he dies. Farewell, Count Ramose, till we meet again at Sais," and with one flashing glance of her great eyes, she turned and went, followed by her women.

A while later I and my guard rode out of the camp, I mounted upon the desert-bred stallion that the queen had given me in place of my own beast which was lamed. The Syrians watched us go in silence, except one fellow who cried out,

"You won that fight, young cock of Egypt, but it will bring you no good luck who have cropped the ear of the priest Ninari and earned the curse of his god."

I made no answer, but presently when we were clear of the camp and riding alone in the moonlight, I began to think to myself that this visit of mine had been strange and ill-omened. It began with the fall of my horse, which hurled me, as Ninari had said, like a sack of barley into the presence of her to whom I was sent, a mischance which even to this day I cannot remember without shame. Then came those hours when I lay half-swooning and in pain, and woke to find that most beautiful queen watching me alone, which in Egypt we should have thought strange, though mayhap the Syrians and the desert-dwellers had easier customs. At last she spoke and told me that she had come thus to read my soul while I slept. Why should she wish to read the soul of one who was unknown to her until that day?

Now I bethought me of what had passed between us afterwards in the ruined temple, and an answer rose in my mind. It must be because at first sight of my face this lady had been smitten with love of me, as I had heard sometimes chances to women and to men also. Could I doubt it with her kiss still burning on my lips? And yet who

28

knew—it might be that she did but play a part to serve her secret ends, which caused her to put out her woman's strength and make me her slave. Why not?

This love of hers, if love it were, had been most swift. Was it to be believed that she, my elder by some years, would suddenly become enamoured of a lad? Was it not easy (as indeed I knew) for a woman to feign passion? Was it not done every day on the street or elsewhere? What did a few kisses matter to such a one? Was I more than a young fool beguiled, and for this beguilement was there not good reason? I was Pharaoh's son whom he was known to favour in his fashion because I was well-looking, quick, and, in a way, learned. Also I was his envoy, one whose report he would accept. Further, this great Syrian lady desired Pharaoh's help. What more natural, then, than that she should strive to win that favoured son and envoy to her interests, and how could she bind him better to her than with her lips and wanton hair?

So this was the sum of it, that I knew not whether I were but a painted plaything or the jewel on her breast. All I knew, alas! was that she had taken my heart into those soft white hands of hers and that passion for her burned me up.

Truly it was an evil business and to make it worse I had quarrelled with and hewn off the ear of that jealous-hearted, foul-tongued priest-minister of hers, who doubtless hoped to wed her and thus win a throne. Oh! truly this had been an accursed journey from which no good could come, as that shouter of a Syrian had foretold. And yet—and yet, I was glad to have made it, for Atyra's kisses burned upon my lips and I longed for more of them when she came to Sais.

We reached the palace before the dawn and I went to my chamber and slept, for after all that had chanced to me this night I was very weary. Also there was time, since none might appear before Pharaoh until within two hours of midday, after he had made his offerings to the god and rested. When at length I awoke, the first thing that my eyes fell upon was the brown, wrinkled face of my master and friend, the learned Babylonian, Belus.

"Greeting, Ramose," he said. "I heard that you were returned and as you did not come to me, I have come to you. They are telling strange stories in the courtyards of your adventures yonder in the desert, stories that are little to your credit as an envoy, although they praise you as a man. At least I hear that your escort speak well of your swordsmanship. Now out with these tales, for they will go no further than my ears, and for the rest, perhaps I can give you good counsel."

So because we loved each other, I told him everything from the beginning to the end. He listened, then said,

"When I entered this chamber, Ramose, I smelt two things, the scent of a woman's hair and the reek of a man's blood; which was natural as you have neither bathed your face nor cleaned your sword. Or perhaps the spirit that is in me did this; it does not matter. Now what has chanced to you was to be expected, seeing that you are young and well-favoured, one of a kind that women will seek out, as butterflies seek the nectar that they love in the throats of certain infrequent flowers; one, too, whose hand is shaped to a sword-hilt. So the woman has come and the sword has swung aloft and now follows the trouble."

He paused a while in thought, then went on,

"As you know, Ramose, in the time that I have to spare from the writing of letters to Babylon and work or learning of the useful sort, I follow after divination according to our Babylonian methods by the help of stars and the shadows that these throw in crystals or in water, a foolish and uncertain art, yet one through which now and again peeps the cold eye of Truth. Last night at least it told me something, namely that you would do well to take a journey by Pharaoh's leave, say to Memphis to see your mother, until this half-queen, Atyra, has finished her business at the court and returned to Syria."

"I do not wish to leave the court at present, Belus," I answered awkwardly.

"Ah! I guessed as much. They say that though past her youth, this Syrian woman is very fair and doubtless those experienced eyes of hers have pierced to your heart and set it afire. Yet I pray you to go till she has departed back to Syria."

"You speak earnestly, Belus. Tell me, what else did the starlight show you in your crystal?"

"That which I liked little, Son—much, and yet nothing. That light turned to blood—whose blood I do not know, yet in the red mist I saw shapes moving and one of them was—yours, Ramose."

Now I grew afraid and that I might find time to think, bade him speak on.

"Hearken, Son. You have tasted a wine that some men desire more than any other and you would drain the cup. Yet the dregs of this passionate drink from nature's ancient cup are always bitter and often deadly or charged with shame. You would make that woman yours and perchance if she does not play with you, you may succeed, for I think that she too found the potion sweet. Yet I say that if so it will be to your sorrow and hers."

30

"Why should I not love her?" I broke in. "She is beautiful and wise, she is unwed. Though she be older than I am I would make her my wife and share her fortunes. May not a man take a wife who pleases him and whom he pleases?"

"A man may if he is foolish," answered Belus with his quiet smile, "but what is mere unwisdom for a man, for a lad is often madness. Moreover this lady lies like a bait in a snare-net full of policies, high policies that you do not understand. To meddle with her may bring about a war with Babylon, or perchance may throw the peoples whose cause she is here to plead, into the arms of Babylon and thus open Egypt's flank to Egypt's foes. If either of these troubles happened, do you think you would earn Pharaoh's thanks? I say that he would curse you and cast you forth, perhaps over the edge of the world into death's darkness.

"Indeed already one of them has begun. Because of her you have fought with a priest of her gods that are not your gods or those of Egypt, or even of the Greeks, black gods and bloody. You have cut him down and maimed him, even if he is not slain. Do you hold that this priest and counsellor will suffer those gods or their worshippers to forget such an outrage against their minister? Will he not lay that severed ear of his upon their altar and cry to them for vengeance. Already it seems the Syrians muttered curses on you as you rode away, and if they come to learn that you, an alien of another faith, are the favoured lover of their lady, the widow of their king, through whom since he has left no children, perchance one of them hopes to win his throne, what then?

"Lastly, I warn you that this business may end in terrors, or rather I pass on the warning that my spirit gives me. I pray you, Ramose, to heed my counsel. Let me go to Pharaoh and ask of him to send you hence till this embassy is finished. Indeed I would that I had gone already, as soon as I learned your tale."

Thus he spoke and watching him I noted that he was much in earnest, for his face had flushed and his hands quivered. Now, although my flesh rebelled, for I yearned to see Atyra again more than ever I had yearned for anything, my reason bent itself before the will of this master of mine, whom I loved and who, as I knew, loved me. I would accept his decree as though it were that of an oracle; if Pharaoh permitted, I would go to Memphis or elsewhere and if I must find a sweetheart, she should be one of a humbler sort upon whose favours hung no great matters of the state. Yet, having as it seemed, made conquest of so lovely and high-placed a lady, a victory of which I was proud indeed, it was very hard to leave her without reason given or farewell. Still it should be done—presently.

"Belus," I said, "wait a little while I bathe myself and change my garments, and eat a mouthful of food. I think that I will do as you wish, but you ask much of me and I would have a space in which to think. Be pleased, therefore, dear Belus, to grant it to me."

He studied me with his bright and kindly eyes, then answered,

"Take what you wish, for well I know the vanity of youth and that if I deny your will, it may turn you against my counsel. I will wait, though in this matter I hold that delay is folly. Be swift now, for with every minute that passes, danger draws more near.

So I withdrew and the black slaves who were my servants, for in all ways at the palace I was treated as a great lord and even as a prince, bathed me and clothed me in fresh garments and dressed my hair. While they did so I ate a little and drank a cup of wine that was brought to me. These things done I went into the anteroom where Belus walked to and fro with bowed head.

"What word?" he asked.

"Master," I answered, "I have taken counsel with myself and though it costs me dear, I bow to your will, knowing that you are wise, while I am but a lad and full of folly. Go to Pharaoh, lay all this matter before him, giving it your own colour. Then, if having heard, he thinks it well that I should depart, I will do so at once and see the Queen Atyra no more, though thus I earn her scorn, or even her hate."

"Well spoken, Son!" he answered, "though I would that you had been less stubborn and had found those words an hour ago. Still, such sacrifice is hard to the young and I forgive you. Now bide you here while I wait on Pharaoh in his private chamber to which I have entry as one whom he consults upon many secret matters, also on those of his health. Presently I will return with his commands."

As the words left his lips the curtains at the far end of the chamber opened and through them came a messenger, clad in the royal livery, who bowed to me and said,

"King's Son and Count Ramose, Pharaoh commands your presence, now, at once."

"I obey," I answered but Belus at my side groaned and muttered,

"All is spoilt! Too late! Too late!"

CHAPTER 4

The Fall of Ramose

I was led to Pharaoh's private chamber, Belus coming with me. Here I found him in a troubled and a wrathful mood, and guessed from his face and those of certain who waited on him, among them Amasis the General, he who was afterwards destined to become Pharaoh, that there was evil tidings in the wind. Here I should write that this Amasis, a fine-looking man though of no high birth, and a great soldier, was a friend to me to whom he had taken a fancy while I was still quite a boy. It was under his command that I had learned all I knew of matters which have to do with war, the handling of weapons and the leading of men.

"How shall we act?" Pharaoh was saying to Amasis. "There can be no doubt that the King of Babylon intends to threaten, if not to attack Egypt now that he has finished with those Hebrews. Moreover it is the matter of the Syrian tribes over whom Abibal was king that has brought the business to a head. Nebuchadnezzar, or whoever holds the real power in Babylon now that he is sunk in age, has heard of the embassy of the Queen Atyra to me, and purposes to be beforehand with us, fearing lest we should aid the Syrians. That is why he sends an army against Egypt."

"I hold that it is but a feint, Pharaoh," answered Amasis, "for as yet the Babylonians have not strength upon the frontier for so vast an enterprise. The best plan is to be bold. Do you send me with another army to guard our borders, and meanwhile speak this queen fair, lest suddenly she, or her Syrians, should turn round, make peace with Babylon and join in the onslaught. Then the danger would be great because those Syrian tribes are countless."

"Good counsel, or so I think," said Pharaoh. "Do you set about gathering troops, friend Amasis, and make all things ready, but as quietly as may be."

At this moment his eye fell upon me, and he said,

"So you are back, son Ramose. Now tell me what is all this tale I hear about you? First it seems you tumble off your horse and make yourself a laughing-stock to the Syrians, and next you quarrel with one of them, a dangerous fellow and a priest called Ninari of whom I have heard before, and crop him of an ear. I am angry with you. What have you to say?"

"Only this, Pharaoh," I answered. "It was my horse that tumbled over a rope, not I, and for the rest the Syrian insulted me, using words that you would not have wished your son to suffer; no, nor any gentleman of Egypt."

"Why did he insult you, Ramose? Had you perchance drunk too much of that strong Syrian wine?"

"Not so, Pharaoh. It was because at her own request I had led the Queen Atyra to the ruined temple above her camp, that thence she might look on the river by moonlight. This I did because Pharaoh bade me to win the friendship of the queen and learn all I could of her mind."

"Indeed, Ramose. And did you perchance learn anything else of her—let us say, that her eyes were bright or her lips soft?"

Now the blood came to my face while Amasis laughed in his rough fashion, and even Pharaoh smiled a little as he went on,

"Well, if you did, you will not tell me, so to ask is useless. Listen. I know this—for when I sent you on that business, I sent others to keep a watch on you—I say I know that this lady found you to her taste, or made pretence to do so for her own ends. Therefore I overlook your foolishness and purpose to make use of you. Presently she will be at the palace. I appoint you the officer in attendance on her with command to draw from her all you can and report what you learn to me. For now that I do not trust this woman who perchance is after all but a spy of Babylon. Do you hear me?"

"I hear, Pharaoh," I answered bowing low to hide the doubt and trouble in my eyes.

"Then understand this also: That I put a great trust upon you, Ramose. Play the lover if you like, but remember that your first duty is to play the spy. Above all, no more quarrels with Ninari or any other. Do nothing foolish. Speak warm words, but let your heart stay cold. Now opportunity is in your hand and if you fail me, it will be for the last time; aye, your life may hang on it."

"Spare me this task, Pharaoh," I muttered, "for it is one that may prove too hard for me. Give it to another, an older man like—like Belus."

Pharaoh looked at Belus who although not very old, already was bald and withered like to an ancient papyrus that for centuries has been buried in the sand. He was cold-eyed also and one who shrank away from women as though they were smitten by a plague, a man from whom wisdom and learning seemed to ooze, but whose history, heart and ends were hidden; somewhat sinister withal, save to the few he loved, perhaps from long acquaintance with dark secrets whispered by spirits in the night. Yes, Pharaoh looked at him and laughed.

"The learned Belus has his uses," he said, "as all know when they are smitten in body or in soul, but I do not think that the cozening of fair women is one of them. Each to his trade and part. But, Ramose, beware lest you betray the one and overdo the other. Take, but give nothing, and above everything be friends with all, even with this Ninari if he lives, praying his pardon and salving his hurt with gifts."

Then he waved his hand to dismiss me and once more fell into talk with the General Amasis.

I prostrated myself and went, followed by Belus, my tutor, who, when we had reached my quarters, sat himself down upon the floor like a mourner and wiped his brow, saying,

"Unless you are wiser than I think, son Ramose, all is finished and you are lost."

I stared at him in question and he went on,

"Do you not understand that Pharaoh has set you a terrible task? You, the hungry bee, must hover over the open flower but not taste its nectar; you, the dazzled moth, must wheel round the flame but not scorch your wings. You, the young and ardent, must play the part of the aged and the cold. Moreover, this he has done of deep purpose, to try your quality and to learn whether duty can conquer passion. I think that if you prevail in this matter, he means to lift you high, even to the footsteps of the throne. But if you fail, why then, farewell to you."

"I shall not fail," I answered wearily, "for my honour is on it. Now let me rest a while. I have been hurt, I have gone through much and for two nights I have had little sleep; also I have fought for my life."

Then without more words I threw myself down upon my bed and soon forgot all things, even Atyra.

When I awoke it was already late afternoon, so late that scarcely was there time before night fell for me to visit the chambers of the palace where the Queen Atyra and her servants were to lodge, and give orders for their preparation, as now I had authority to do. These chambers as it chanced, whether by design or by accident, adjoined my own, for I dwelt in some small rooms of that wing of the great palace that was used to house Pharaoh's guests. Therefore I had not far to go, only the length of a short passage indeed, and through a door of which I held the key.

Until it was dark and next morning from the sunrise, aided by chamberlains and other palace servants, I laboured at this making ready. All was clean, all was garnished, everywhere flowers were set. Beautiful curtains were hung up, vessels of gold and silver fit for a queen's use were provided; the garden ground that lay in the centre of this wing of the palace, having in it a little lake filled with lotus flowers, was tended so that if she pleased, the Queen Atyra might sit there beneath the shadow of palms and flowering trees, the eunuchs were furnished with fresh robes, and I know not what besides.

At length when all was prepared, I looked out from an upper window and saw the cavalcade of the Syrians drawing near to the palace. In its centre, preceded and followed by white-robed, turbaned men mounted upon camels, was a splendid litter which doubtless held the queen for it was surrounded by a guard of horsemen. Also there were other litters for her women, while last of all came one like that on which the sick are borne, whereof the bearers stepped very carefully, that I guessed hid none other than the priest Ninari, who to tell truth I hoped had gone to the bosom of Osiris, or of whatever god he worshipped. Belus who was by me, read as much in my eyes and shook his head, saying,

"Snakes are very hard to kill, my son, as I who have hunted one for years, know as well as any man and better than most. Be careful lest this one should live to bite you."

Then I hurried away to be arrayed in the festal robes of a Count of Egypt and to put about my neck the gold chain that marked my rank as the son of a king. Scarcely was I prepared when a messenger summoned me to the great hall of audience. Thither I went to find Pharaoh gloriously attired, wearing the double crown, with the gold ear-rings and other ornaments of state, and holding in his hand a sceptre. Round about him were the great officers of the court, at his feet crouched scribes, while just behind the fan-bearers stood his generals, some Egyptian and some Greek, all clad in armour, amongst whom I noted Amasis.

I advanced, followed by Belus my tutor, and prostrated myself before the throne. Pharaoh bade me rise and with his sceptre pointed to where I should stand among, or rather a little in front of, the nobles and king's sons, of whom there were several, my half-brothers born of different ladies, though I was the eldest of them. As I went, stepping backwards and bowing at each step, Pharaoh turned and spoke to Amasis and I think his words were that I was a young man of whom any king might be proud to be the father.

"Yes," answered Amasis in a hoarse whisper that reached me, "yet it is pity that he is so like to one of those statues that the Greeks of whom you are so fond, fashion of their gods. His mother has too much share in him, Pharaoh. Look at his curly head."

Then they both laughed and I nearly fell in my confusion.

At this moment trumpets blew, heralds cried aloud, and preceded by officers with white wands, the Queen Atyra appeared between the pillars at the end of the hall of audience. On her head she wore a glittering crown, jewels shone upon her breast, pearls were twisted in her looped and raven locks and round her white wrists, while her silken train was borne by fair waiting-women. Oh! seen thus, she was beautiful, so beautiful that as I watched her tall, imperial shape glide up that hall like a sunbeam through its shadows, my heart stood still and my lips burned with the memory of her kiss. A little sigh of wonder went up from the courtiers and through it I heard the jesting Amasis whisper once more,

"I wish that you had given me Ramose's office, Pharaoh," to which Apries answered,

"Nay, you are too rough, you would frighten this Syrian dove, whereas he will stroke her feathers."

"Dove! Dove!" muttered Amasis.

Then Pharaoh lifted his sceptre and there was silence.

Atyra drew near in all her scented beauty, with bent head and downcast eyes. Yet for one instant those dark eyes were lifted and I felt rather than saw them flash a look upon me, saw also the red lips tremble as though with a little smile. I think that Belus saw also, for I heard a groan come from where he stood near by in attendance on me. The queen mounted the royal dais and curtseyed low, though prostrate herself she did not because she was a majesty greeting a majesty. Pharaoh descended from his throne and taking her hand, led her to a seat that was placed near though slightly lower than this throne.

Then she spoke—in Greek which by now had become the courtly language among many nations that did not know each other's speech. An interpreter began to render her words, but Apries, waving him aside, answered her in the same tongue which he knew as well as he did his own, having learned it from my mother and others. This caused many of the Egyptians round him to frown, especially those that were old or wedded to ancient ways which had come down to them through thousands of years, who hated the Greeks with their new fashions, their language and all that had to do with them. Indeed I noted that even Amasis frowned and shrugged his shoulders and that the other Egyptian generals looked on him with approval as he did so.

As for the talk between Atyra and Pharaoh, it need not be set out. She made a formal prayer to him, reminding him of the ancient friendship between the Syrians and Egypt that more than once during the generations which had gone by, had been their over-lord, yes, from the time of the great Thotmes onward, though sometimes they had quarrelled "as a wife will, even with the husband whom she loves." Now she, the widow of Abibal who had been the head king of the Syrian peoples and who had died leaving his mantle upon her shoulders, came to seek renewal of that alliance, even though Syria must thus once more become the wife of Egypt and serve as a wife serves.

Here Pharaoh asked shrewdly if this wife sought to shun the arms of some other lover, whereon she answered with boldness, "yes," that this was so and that the name of that lover was Babylon, Egypt's ancient enemy and the one from whom she had most to fear.

Now Pharaoh grew grave, saying that this was a very great matter of which he must consider with himself and his councillors, after private talk with her. Then dismissing all such affairs of state, he asked her how it had fared with her during her long journey, from which he hoped that she would rest a while here in his palace at Sais, treating it as her own. She answered that she desired nothing better, who all her life had hoped to visit Egypt and acquaint herself with its wonders and its wisdom.

So this prepared and balanced talk went on, reminding me of a heavy weight swinging to and fro, and never going further or less far, till at length Pharaoh bade her to a banquet that night. Then, as though by an afterthought, he added,

"O Queen Atyra, the other day I sent Ramose, a young Count of Egypt in whom runs no mean blood, to your camp to welcome you in Egypt's name. I grieve to hear that while he was there a quarrel arose between him and one of your followers, and for this I ask your pardon."

"There is no need, Pharaoh," she answered smiling, "seeing that in every quarrel there is something to be said on either side."

"Then, Queen Atyra, if you can forgive him, would it please you that while you are here I should appoint this Ramose who stands yonder, to be your chamberlain to attend upon your wants and bear your wishes to me? Or would you prefer that I should choose some older man to fill this office?"

"I think that it would please me well," she answered indifferently, "seeing that I found the Count Ramose a pleasant companion and one with whom I could talk in Greek; also one who can instruct me in the customs and history of Egypt and in its tongue, all of which I desire to learn. Yet let it be as the Pharaoh wills. Whoever Pharaoh chooses will be welcome to me."

So saying, she turned her head to speak to one of her servants in her own language, as though the matter troubled her not at all.

"Count Ramose," said Pharaoh, addressing me, "for the days of her stay at our court we give this royal lady into your keeping. Let it be your duty to wait upon her and to attend to her every want, making report to us from time to time of how she fares. Know, Ramose, that we shall hold you to strict account for her safety and her welfare and that if aught of ill befalls her while she is in your keeping, you shall make answer for it to us."

Thus in formal, stately words was the lady Atyra set in my charge. I heard and bowed, while the other courtiers looked on me with envy, for this was a great duty and one that should bring with it advancement and rewards. Yet it is true that as I bowed my heart, which should have leapt for joy, seemed to sink and fail so that I could scarcely feel it beat. It was as though some icy hand of fear had gripped it by the roots. A great terror took hold of me, a shadow of woe to come fell upon me. Almost I determined to prostrate myself and pray Pharaoh to confer this honour on some other man, one with more knowledge and older. I even turned to advance to the steps of the throne and do so, although I knew that such a prayer would cause me to be mocked by all the court. It was too late, Pharaoh had risen; his decree was written on the rolls, the audience was at an end.

****

Now I will press on with the terrible story of Atyra which was to turn the current of my life and for aught I know, robbed me of the throne of Egypt. At least so Belus held, as did some others, though if so, that is a loss over which I do not grieve.

For a while all went well. I waited on the queen; with her officers I was her companion at her table; I instructed her as best I might in all she wished to learn, for to me alone she would listen and not to Belus or another. When she visited Pharaoh and his councillors I accompanied her, standing back so that I might not overhear their secrets. In short I did all those things I had been instructed to do, even to make report of everything I learned from the queen as I had been bidden.

One day she turned on me laughing and said,

"I thought you were my friend, Ramose, but I find that you are nothing but a spy who repeats to Pharaoh all I say. I know it because he used to me some of my very words, thinking that they were his own, which words could only have come to him through you."

Now I turned aside and hung my head, whereon she leant over me, whispering,

"Foolish boy, do not think I am angry with you, who know well that you must do your duty and therefore tell you nothing that you may not cry out from every pylon top. These matters of policy are between me and Pharaoh, or rather between Syria and Egypt. I and you have others to discuss that Pharaoh would think dull. Now tell me of your boyhood and of the woman that you first thought fair."

So it went on and ever as I drew back, so she came forward. At first I think that she was puzzled who could not understand why I resisted her and made search to find some other woman who had built a wall between us. Soon she discovered that there was none; indeed she drew this out of me. At last in a flash she guessed the truth—that I was under an oath, to my own heart or another, which, mattered not, to treat her as a queen who was Egypt's guest, and no more.

Then Atyra did what she should not have done, as doubtless she knows today. She set herself to make me break that oath. For nothing else do I blame her who, I know, loved me truly, boy though I was. But for this, how can she escape from blame? She knew that her witchery was on me, she knew that she had made me mad—indeed in those days of resistance I went near to madness, I who worshipped her as a thing divine, and yet she put out all her woman's strength to break my will and cause me to forswear myself.

At last the matter came to a head, as such do always. The feast was over, the guests had departed, I presented myself, as I must, to take my farewell of her for the night, and found that I was alone with her in the little ante-chamber where a single lamp burned dimly. She was standing at a window-place cut in the thickness of the wall, watching the rising of the moon, a figure clad all in white, but for some scarlet pomegranate blooms fastened upon her breast, for her maids had relieved her of her royal ornaments, save a girdle of gold about her waist.

Discovering her at length I advanced to inquire her commands for the morrow, bow and be gone.

"How quietly you walk, Ramose," she said. "I heard you not, yet I knew that you were coming. Yes, I felt your presence, as we do that of those whom we love—or hate. My orders? Oh! I have none to give you at the moment, young chamberlain. Why think of the morrow on such a night as this. Look at that great moon rising yonder out of the desert. No wonder that you Egyptians set your Isis in the moon, for it is a lovely throne fit for any goddess. Now of what does this one put me in mind? Ah! I remember—of that which rose over the waters of the Nile when you and I sat together in a ruined temple of the desert. Do you not remember it?"

I muttered some answer, I know not what it was, and half-turned to go, when with a swift and sudden motion she flung herself against me. Yes, from her foot to her shoulder I felt all the weight of her beautiful body leaning against me.

I never stirred, I did nothing, and yet I know not how, presently her lips were on my own.

She drew away, laughing low and happily, and asked,

"Now, Ramose, do you remember that night in the ruined temple when we looked together at the moon rising over the Nile?"

I fled away, and as I fled, still she laughed.

****

It was after this that for the first time I saw the priest Ninari among the other servitors of the queen, recovered of his wounds but wearing a cap with lappets that hung down over his ears. He greeted me courteously enough, but in his eyes was a fierce look that I could not misunderstand.

"We quarrelled once, young lord," he said, "but now that you are the appointed guardian of my queen, we are friends, are we not?"

"Surely," I answered.

"Then all is well between us, young lord, while you guard her faithfully, who otherwise may quarrel once more and with a different ending." And again he smiled upon me with those fierce eyes and was gone.

On the evening of my meeting with Ninari, I was in waiting on Queen Atyra in the garden of which I have written, and noted that she was troubled. Presently she led me to a seat beneath the palms in front of which lay the little pool where flowered the blue lotus lilies. It was a pleasant, secluded seat hidden from the rest of the garden and from the palace windows by a bank of flowering shrubs and of tall reed-like plants with feathery heads.

"What ails you?" I asked.

"Everything, Ramose," she answered. "All goes awry and I would that I were dead. My mission to Pharaoh is ended, and not so ill. To-

41

morrow at the dawn the Egyptian general Amasis, with a great force most of which has gone on before, advances to attack the Babylonians on the borders of Egypt. Tomorrow also I leave Sais to journey back to my own country. It was decided but an hour ago. Do you understand that I leave Sais?"

"I understand, Queen, though this sudden plan amazes me. Why do you go so swiftly?"

"I will tell you. Ninari has been with Pharaoh and has told him that news has come from my country that those who are left in power there, urged on by the people who are afraid, threaten to make peace with Babylon, and that one of the terms of that peace will be that we Syrians should join the Babylonians in the attack on Egypt. He has told him also that there is but one hope of defeating this treachery, namely, that I should return at once bearing Pharaoh's offers of alliance, and as the wife of Ninari who alone can control the priesthood, which is the real power in the land, and overthrow this plot."

"As the wife of Ninari," I gasped. "May the gods avert it!"

"The gods make no sign, Ramose. If there be any gods, these ask of men that they should carve their own fate upon the cliffs of Time. In this matter Ninari is the god."

For a little while we sat silent staring at the lotus blooms. Then she spoke again.

"Do you love me, Ramose?"

"You know that I love you," I answered.

"Yes, yet your love is to my love but as a dewdrop to the waters in that lake. Ramose, a madness has taken hold of me. I will tell you the truth. You are very young and as yet of small account in the world, while I am a queen who perchance will become the sovereign of a great country, if with Egypt's help we can overthrow Babylon, as may happen now that Nebuchadnezzar grows old and feeble and there is none to take his place. Still I say to you that you, the son of Pharaoh's woman, are more to me than all earth's thrones and glory. Here fate thrusts me on, not folly or passion, but fate itself with an iron hand. I will have none of Ninari. Rather than that accursed priestly hound should creep into my chamber, I will die, or better still, he shall die who knows not with whom he has to deal. Yes, here and now I pronounce his doom."

Thus she spoke in slow, cold words that yet were full of fearful menace, then suddenly went on in a soft, changed voice.

"Let us talk no more of this foul Ninari. Hearken! If you will play the man I have plans that shall make of you a great king and give to you one of earth's fairest and most loving women as a wife. But I, who perhaps have said too much already, dare not speak them here. Always I am watched, the very air seems to play the spy upon me, and even now I feel—" and she shivered. "Moreover my women wait to tire me for Pharaoh's farewell feast and I must be gone. Ramose, you have the key of the door that leads to my chambers. In the first of them I sleep quite alone, for I will have no one near me in my slumbers and the guards and eunuchs are set far away beyond. Come to me at midnight and I will tell you all. Will you come, knowing that if aught miscarries, your life hangs in it?"

"My life," I answered sadly. "What is my life? Something of which I think I should be well rid could I say goodbye to it with honour. I have not been happy of late, Queen Atyra. Pharaoh laid a charge upon me and, forgive me for saying it, it seems that always you have put out your strength to cause me to break my trust. By Amen I have fought my best, but alas! I am weak with love of you. When your eyes shine upon me I grow dizzy and at your touch my purpose melts like wax in the midday sun. What you command, that I must do and if death waits at the end of your road, may Thoth, the weigher of hearts, be merciful and give me sleep that I may forget my shame."

She looked at me and there was pity in her eyes. Then the pity passed and they burned with the light of passion.

"I grieve for you as I grieve for myself, whose danger is greater than your own," she said. "Yet for me the choice lies between you and madness. Know, Ramose, that without you I shall go mad, and ere I die work woes at which the world will shudder. Think! is such a love as mine a gift to be lightly cast away?"

"I will come, I have said it," I answered.

Then she rose and went.

****

Pharaoh's feast that night was very glorious and at it none was merrier than the Queen Atyra. Indeed she was so beautiful in her royal apparel that she drew all eyes to her and every man bent forward to watch her and hear her words, yes, even Pharaoh's self. Yet to me it seemed a feast of death and even the scented cup I bore to her wherein she pledged her country's future fellowship with Egypt, smelt of the tomb.

At length it was over. The dancers ended their dancing, the music faded away. The lovely queen bent before Pharaoh and he kissed her hand. She departed with her company. The lamps died out.

****

It was midnight. I unlocked the passage door; I crept to her chamber like a thief, for now all my doubts were gone and I was aflame. Its door was ajar. I entered, closing it behind me. In the chamber burned a hanging lamp of which the flame wavered in the hot night-wind that came through the open window-place. There upon a couch she lay clothed all in white, a thing of beauty, her black locks flowing about her. I went to her, I knelt down to kiss her lips, but she did not stir, she said nothing. I touched her brow and lo! although her shape stayed still, her head rolled towards me.

Then I saw that her neck was severed through and through. She was dead!

I rose from my knees, smitten with a silent madness. From behind a curtain appeared Ninari, a red sword in his hand.

"Young Count of Egypt," he said in a soft voice, "know that I heard all your talk with this traitress, for I was hidden in the bushes behind you in the garden. Now, that our queen might not be shamed, I have executed the decree of my god upon her, and go to make report of what has been done to the people over who she ruled. I bid you farewell, Count Ramose, trusting that you who are young and were sorely tempted, will have learned a lesson which cannot be forgotten."

My strength came back to me. I said no word. I sprang at him as a lion springs. He struck; I caught his arm with such a grip that the sword fell from his hand. I closed with him and in the might of my madness I broke him like a stick. At least suddenly he sank together in my hands and his head fell backwards.

Then I hurled him through the window-place. I took his sword and set its hilt upon the pavement, purposing to fall upon it. Already I bent over its point when it was struck away. I looked up. There by me, white, wide-eyed, stood Belus.

"Come!" he said hoarsely, "come swiftly, for your life's sake!"

44

Chapter 5

The Flight to Amasis

In the doorway of the chamber I glanced back. By the wavering light of the lamp I saw the white shape of her who had been the Queen Atyra and my love, lying still and dreadful on the couch, her head turned strangely as though to watch me go. On the floor from beneath a rug and a splendid garment which she had worn at the feast, crept the red stream that told of murder, and near by it lay the sword of Ninari. Some jewels glittered upon a stool and among them was a flower, one which that afternoon I had given to her—yes, she had taken it from my hand, kissed it and set it in her girdle. The moon shone through the open window-place out of which I had hurled Ninari. Such was the picture, a terrible picture that in every detail must haunt me till I die.

I wished to turn back to recover that flower, but Belus thrust me before him and closed the door. We passed down the passage to my apartment. This door also Belus closed and locked. We stood face to face in my chamber.

"What now?" I said drearily. "Give me one of those drugs of yours, Belus, that which kills so swiftly, for all is done."

"Nay," he answered, "all is but begun. Be a man and hearken. The woman is dead; by her lies the sword of Ninari. Who save I knows that you entered her chamber? Ninari is dead also; he lies broken at the foot of the palace wall for I saw you cast him from the window-place whence it will be believed he flung himself after doing murder, since he is untouched by knife or sword."

"I know, Belus, I know; and my face will tell the tale or I shall go mad and babble it."

He nodded his wise head.

"Perchance, Ramose. At least Pharaoh will kill you because she was in your charge. Or, if he does not, those Syrians will, guessing the truth. By this hand or by that, death awaits you here, sure death, and with it shame."

"I seek to die," I answered.

"You cannot, for it is written otherwise. Have I not read it in your stars? Listen. The General Amasis has departed to join the army that goes to fight the Babylonians on the frontiers of Egypt. Pharaoh does not trust this Amasis whom the soldiers love too well. He sends me to be his counsellor and to spy upon him, and I depart within an hour for the command is urgent. Disguised as my scribe you will accompany me. Foreseeing trouble already I have ordered all. Tomorrow you will be missed and perhaps it may be thought that some ill has befallen you. Do not young men wander out at night and meet with adventures that have been known to end evilly? Has not the Nile borne the bodies of many such towards the sea? Or may not the Syrians have murdered you, as they murdered the queen who was known to look on you so kindly? At best there will be much talk and Pharaoh will be wrath, but as you have vanished away the matter will be forgotten. If afterwards it is learned that, seeking adventure, you went to join Amasis, you may be forgiven—that is unless those Syrians know all and plotted this murder. Answer not, but come, bringing your sword and what gold you have."

A while later, it may have been one hour, or two, I forget, whose memory of that night is dimmed by a fog of wretchedness, two figures might have been seen leaving that part of the palace which was called Dream House because there always dwelt the royal astrologer. They left it by a small gate guarded by a single soldier who challenged them. Belus gave some password; also he showed a ring and spoke in the guard's ear.

"Right enough. All in order," said the man. "Belus the Babylonian and a scribe we were commanded to pass. Well, here is Belus the Babylonian whom we all know, for he tells our fortunes by the stars, and there's the scribe in a dark cloak with a hood to it. A very fine young man, too, for a scribe who generally are short and round-stomached, or sometimes, quite small and very like a girl, for many are named scribes who never served apprenticeship in a temple or a school. Magician Belus, I fear that I cannot let this scribe pass until I have called the officer to have a look at him—or her."

"What do you mean, man?" asked Belus coldly. "Is not Pharaoh's ring enough?"

"Not tonight, Master. Although you may not have heard it, there is trouble yonder in the palace. Something terrible has happened there.

46

Some great one has been murdered. Who it is I know not. Still word has come that all gateways are to be watched and none allowed to pass whose faces are covered or who are not known, even under Pharaoh's seal. Therefore I pray you stay a minute until the officer and his guard pass upon their round."

"As you will," said Belus, "and while we wait, friend, tell me, how is that little daughter of yours whom I visited two days ago in her fever?"

"Master," answered the man in another voice, a trembling voice, "she hangs between life and death. When I left to come on guard at length she had fallen asleep and the wise women said that either it is the beginning of the sleep of death or she will wake free of the fever and recover. Tell me, Master, you who are wise and can read the stars, which she will do. For know, I love this child, my only one, and my heart is racked."

With the staff he bore Belus made a drawing in the sand. Then he looked up at certain stars and added dots to the drawing, which done, he said,

"Events are strangely linked with one another in this world, my friend, nor can we understand who or what it is that ties them thus together. Who for instance would have dreamed that your daughter's fate hangs upon whether I and this scribe of mine, whom perchance you guessed rightly to be a woman, though a tall one such as are loved by small men like myself, pass at once upon our business, or wait until it pleases some officer to wander this way upon his rounds. If we pass, the stars say that your daughter will live; if we wait, while we are waiting she will die—yes, before the moonlight creeps to that mark, she will die. But if my departing footstep stamps upon it, she will live."

"Pass, Magician Belus, with the girl disguised as a scribe," said the man, "for such I see now she is, though at first the moonlight deceived me. Pass."

"Good night, friend," said Belus, "the blessing of the gods be upon you, and upon that daughter of yours who will live to comfort your old age."

Then with his foot he stamped out the pattern on the sand and we went on.

"Will the child live?" I asked idly, for this sight of the grief of another seemed to dull my own.

"Yes," answered Belus. "My medicines have worked well and that sleep is a presage of her recovery. Surely she will live, but what will happen to her father when it is learned that he has suffered some veiled traveller to pass out, I do not know."

"Perchance he will keep silence upon that matter."

"Aye, but when the light comes our footprints on the sand will tell their own tale, that is, unless a wind rises. Still by that time we shall be far away. Run, Scribe, run. The horses and the escort, men who are sworn to me, await us in yonder grove."

****

Eight days later we came to the camp of Amasis upon the borders of Egypt. An officer led us to the tent of Amasis whom we found in jovial mood, for he had dined and drunk well, as was his custom.

"Greeting, learned Belus," said Amasis. "Now tell me on what business Pharaoh sends you?"

Belus drew out a roll, laid it to his forehead and handed it to Amasis, saying,

"It is written here, General."

He undid the roll, glanced at it and cast it down.

"It is written in Greek," he exclaimed, "and I, an Egyptian, will not read Greek. Repeat its contents. Nay, it is needless, for I have heard them already by another messenger who has outstripped you, one of my own captains whom Pharaoh did not send. The writing orders that I must make report daily, or as often as may be, of all that passes in this army, through you, Belus the Babylonian. Is it not so?"

"Yes," answered Belus calmly, "that is the sum of it."

"Which means," went on Amasis, "that you are sent here to spy upon me and all that I do."

"Yes, General," replied Belus in the same quiet voice. "Pharaoh, as you know, is jealous and fears you."

"Why, Belus?"

"Because the Egyptians love you, especially the soldiers, and do not love Pharaoh who they think, favours the Greeks too much, and in all but blood is himself a Greek."

"That I know. Is there no other reason?"

"Yes, General. As you may have heard, like other Babylonians I have some skill in divination and in the casting of horoscopes. Pharaoh caused me to cast his, and yours also, General."

"And what did they say, Belus?" asked Amasis leaning forward.

Belus dropped his voice and answered,

"They said that the star of Apries wanes, while that of Amasis grows bright. They said that ere long where shone the star of Apries, will shine the star of Amasis alone, though first for a time those two stars will ride in the heavens side by side. That is what they said though I told Apries another tale."

"Do you mean the throne?" asked Amasis in a whisper.

"Aye, the throne and a certain general wearing Pharaoh's crown."

For a while there was silence, then Amasis asked,

"Does Pharaoh send you to poison me, as doubtless you can do, you strange and fateful Belus, who like a night-bird, have flitted from Babylon to Egypt for your own dark and secret purpose?"

"Nay, and if he did, I, their servant, am not one to fight against the stars. Fear nothing from me who am your friend, though there are others whom you will do well to watch. Now, General, here in this camp I am in your power. You can kill me if you will, but that would be foolish, for I have not told you all the horoscope."

"Your meaning?"

"It is that if you kill me, as I think you had it in your mind to do but now, me or another, that star of yours will never shine alone, because my blood will call for yours. Am I safe with you and if I need it, will you protect me when you grow great?"

"You are safe and I will protect you now and always. I swear it by Amen and by Maat, Goddess of Truth. Yet, why do you turn from Pharaoh who has sheltered you ever since you escaped from Babylon?—for I have heard that you did escape on account of some crime."

"Because Pharaoh turns from me and presently will seek my life; indeed I think that he seeks it already. For the rest, the crime of which you have heard was not mine, but that of another—upon whom I wait to be avenged in some far-off appointed hour," he added and as he spoke the words, his face grew fierce and even terrible.

"Be plain, Belus, but tell me first, who is this with you who listens to our most secret thoughts? How comes it that I never noted him?"

"Perchance because I willed that you should not, General, or perchance because wine dims the eyes. But look on him, and answer your own question."

As he spoke, very swiftly Belus bent forward and unclasped the long cloak which I wore, revealing me clad as a soldier with an armoured cap upon my head. Amasis stared at me.

"By the gods!" he said, "this is none other than Ramose, Pharaoh's bastard and my pupil in arms whom I love well. Now what does this young cock here? Is he another of Pharaoh's spies whom you have brought to be your witness?"

"A poor spy, I think, General. Nay, like me he flies from Pharaoh's wrath. There has been trouble in the palace. A certain Syrian queen whom you will remember, for in truth she sent you here, has come to her end—a swift and bloody end—as has her minister."

"I have heard as much, for rumour of the death of great ones flies more swiftly than a dove, but what has that to do with Ramose? Did he perchance stifle her with kisses, as I would have done at his age?"

"Nothing, nothing at all, General. But Ramose was her guardian and chamberlain, and Pharaoh demands his life in payment for hers, so do her Syrians, or will ere long. Therefore he seeks refuge under the shield of Amasis, his captain."

"And shall have it, by the gods. Am I a man to give up one who has served under me, over the matter of a woman, even to Pharaoh's self? Not so, and yet I must remember that this youngster is Pharaoh's son and half a Greek and has heard words that would set a noose about my neck. Do you vouch for him, Belus?"

"Aye, Amasis. Listen. From boyhood this lad has been as one born to me and I, who now am—childless—love him. He has been drawn into trouble, and thereby, as I fear, embroiled Syria and Egypt. Therefore his life is forfeit, as is mine who have befriended him and aided his escape. Therefore, too, both of us have fled to you, and henceforward swear ourselves to your service, looking to you to shield us. Tell us, may we sleep in peace, or must we seek it elsewhere?"

"Yes, you may sleep easy, even from Pharaoh, for here in this camp I am Pharaoh," answered Amasis proudly. "Have I not sworn it already and am I a troth-breaker?" he added.

Scarce had the words passed his lips when from without came a sound of sentries challenging, followed by a cry of "Pass on, Messenger of Pharaoh." The tent opened and there appeared a travel-stained man clad in Pharaoh's uniform, who bowed, handed a roll to Amasis and at a sign, retired.

"Pharaoh sends me many letters," he said, as he cut the silk and undid the roll. Then he read, looked up and laughed.

"Your guardian spirit must be good, Belus. At least you two were wise to take that oath of me upon the instant. Hearken to what is written here," and he read aloud,

"Pharaoh to the General Amasis,

"The Syrians who came hither with the Queen Atyra who is dead, as the price of the friendship of their nation to Egypt, demand the life of the Count Ramose who was her chamberlain, because he failed in his duty and did not keep her safe; also because as they allege he murdered one Ninari. If he has fled to your camp disguised as a scribe, as is reported, put him to death and send his head to Sais that it may be shown to them. With it send Belus the Babylonian, that the truth of all this matter may be wrung from him.

"Sealed with the seals of Pharaoh and his Vizier."

"Now, Belus," went on Amasis, "tell me, you who are wise in counsel, what shall I do? Obey Pharaoh or my oath?"

I listened like to one in a dream, but Belus answered quietly,

"Which you will, Amasis. Obey Pharaoh, cause this lad to be murdered and send me to the torturers at Sais, and see your star set—as I promised you. Obey your oath, and see that star shine out above all storms, royally and alone. Yet, is it needful to urge Amasis to honesty by revealing what Thoth has written concerning him in the Book of Fate?"

"I think not," answered Amasis with his great laugh. "Do they not say of me in Egypt that never yet did I break troth with friend or foe, and shall I do so now? Young man, I see that you have scribe's tools about you; therefore be seated and write these words:

"From Amasis the General, to Pharaoh,

"The letter of Pharaoh has been received. Know, O divine Pharaoh, that it is not the custom of Amasis to kill those who are serving under him in war, save for cowardice or other military offence. If the Syrians have aught against the Count Ramose, let them come hither and set out their case before me and my captains. For the rest, Belus the Babylonian, whom the good god Pharaoh sent hither to watch me, is too weary to travel. Moreover, I keep him at my side that I may watch him."

When I had finished writing, Amasis read the roll, sealed it and summoning an officer, bade him to give it to the messenger to be delivered to Pharaoh at Sais. When the officer had gone he thought a while, and said in his open fashion,

"The quarrel between me and Pharaoh or rather between the Egyptians and his friends the Greeks, has long been brewing. It is strange that it should have boiled over upon the little matter of this young Count and his love affairs, yet doubtless so it was decreed. Have no fear, Ramose, Pharaoh is cowardly for otherwise he would not seek the life of his own son for such a trifle from dread born of Syrian threats; a tyrant also and when tyrants are taken by the beard, they grow afraid. Yet my counsel to both of you is, to keep out of the reach of Pharaoh's arm till this business is forgotten. If ever he speaks of it to me again, I will tell him to his face that he should thank me who have saved him from the crime of murdering his son, whose blood would have brought the curse of the gods upon him. Now drink a cup of wine, both of you, and let me hear this tale of the death of Atyra, if she be dead in truth."

So I told it to him, keeping nothing back. When it was done, he said, "I am glad that you threw that Syrian rat through the window-place, sending him to settle his account with Atyra in the underworld. Grieve not, young man. There are more women left upon the earth who will teach you to forget your trouble, and for the rest this ill-fated lady was one hard to be resisted. Now, go rest. Tomorrow I will find you a place in my bodyguard and we shall see whether you are luckier in war than you have been in love."

Thus he spoke though in the after years, when he had ceased to be a bluff general and had become a wily Pharaoh steeped in statecraft, he forgot, or pretended to forget all this story and asserted that Atyra had borne me a child before her death. But of this in its season.

****

That night ere I slept, for the first time I opened all my heart to Belus, showing him how great was its bitterness and woe. Moreover I told him that if I escaped the wrath of Pharaoh and the accidents of war, I had sworn an oath before the gods to have no more to do with women.

"I rejoice to hear it, Son," answered Belus, with his strange wise smile, "and I pray that the memory of the gods of Egypt is not too long. You say that you have done with women, but mayhap women have not done with such a man as you, nor because one has brought you sorrow, is it certain that another may not bring you joy. Now grieve no more over what cannot be mended nor for her who is dead because of you, but follow after Fortune with a brave heart, for such she loves. Only one thing I hope of you, that you will suffer me, your master, to stay at your side through bad weather and through good, until perhaps I am drawn away to fulfil the purpose of my life."

Then without telling me what was that purpose, he kissed me on the brow and I laid me down and slept.

CHAPTER 6

The Gift of God

Next day the march began. I saw and knew all, for Amasis, a man of his word in those days, appointed me to be an officer of his guard, also, because I was a scholar, one of his private scribes. Further he kept Belus in attendance on him, so that between us we learned all there was to know. Thus I came to understand how great was the power of Amasis, the beloved of the soldiers.

About him was none of the ceremonial of Pharaoh's court. His captains were his fellows; also he drank, jested and bandied stories, some of them coarse enough, with the common soldiers round their fires. A man of the people himself, he talked to them of their fathers, yes, and mothers too. He asked no great reverence from them, nor that any man should bow to the dust when he passed by and to many a fault he was blind. If one off duty drank too much, or broke camp to seek some girl who had looked at him kindly, he said nothing; but if such a one did these things when he was on duty, then let him beware, for he would be flogged, or even hanged. No man was promoted for lip-service or because his birth was high, but to those who were brave and loyal every door was open. Therefore the army loved him, so much indeed that he dared to defy Pharaoh in such a letter as he had written concerning Belus and myself, and yet fear nothing.

Some thirty or forty thousand strong not counting the camp-fol-lowers, we marched against the Babylonians, a great host of them un-der the command of Merodach, said to be a son of Nebuchadnezzar, who awaited us beyond the borders of Egypt. Or rather they did not await us for as we came on, they retreated. Then we discovered that we were being led into a trap, for Syrians by the ten thousand, were hanging on our flank waiting to cut us off. Belus learned this from spies whom we had taken, but who, it seemed, belonged to some se-cret brotherhood of which he was a chief.

For although Belus was willing to fight against his own people, I found that among them he still had many friends. This at the time I could not understand, for not until many years had gone by did I come to know that the Babylonians were divided among themselves, numbers of them hating the kings who ruled over them and all their cruelties and wars.

So Amasis separated his army. Half of it he left entrenched upon a range of little hills that encircled an oasis where there was water in plenty, beyond which hills the Babylonians had retreated, thinking to draw us into the desert on their further side. The rest, among whom were nearly all the horsemen and chariots, he sent to swoop down on the Syrians. Making a long night march we caught them at the dawn just as they were breaking camp. Until we fell upon them they did not know that we were near. Therefore, although they outnumbered us by three to one, our victory was great. Hemming them round in the gloom, we attacked at daybreak and slew thousands of them before they could form their ranks. Also we made prisoners of thousands more and took a great booty of horses and camels.

This done we returned to the low hills in a fortunate moment, for discovering that the half of our army was gone, at length the Babylonians had determined to attack. Night was falling when we reached the camp and therefore they did not see us advancing under cover of the hills. Some of us, I among them, pushed on and made report to Amasis of how it had gone between us and the Syrians, a tale that pleased him greatly. Moreover, having heard me well spoken of by those under whom I served for the part I played in that fray, he promoted me to be captain of a company of which the officer had been killed by an arrow. This company was part of what was called the General's Legion, appointed to surround him in battle and to fight under his own command. I knew it already, since from it was drawn his bodyguard, of whom I had been one until I was sent out against the Syrians.

Next morning at the dawn from the crest of our hills, far away upon the plain and half hidden by clouds of dust, we saw the Babylonians approaching, a mighty host of them. Indeed so countless were they and so vast was their array, that at sight of it my heart sank for it seemed as though for every man of ours they could count ten. While I stood staring at them, suddenly I found Amasis himself at my side wrapped in a common soldier's cloak.

"You are afraid, young man," he said. "Your face shows it. Well, I think none the worse of you for that. Yet take courage, since it is not numbers that make an army terrible, but discipline and the will to conquer. Look now at this great host. As its standards show, it is made up of many peoples all mixed together. See, it keeps no good line, for its left wing is far advanced and its right straggles. Also its centre, where is Merodach, the king's son, with his chosen guards, is cumbered with many wagons and litters. In those wagons are not food or water, but women, for these soft Babylonians soaked in luxury, will not move without their women even in war, and they must be protected. Therefore I say to you, and to all, be not afraid."

Then he departed to talk to others.

All that morning the Babylonian multitude came on slowly, till by noon they were within a mile of us. During the heat of the day they rested for some two hours or more, then once more they advanced, as we thought to the attack. But it was not so, for when they had covered another three furlongs again they halted as though bewildered, perhaps because they could see so few of us, for the most of our army was hidden behind the crest of a hill. At length officers rode forward, five or six of them, carrying a white flag, and reined up almost at the foot of the hills.

Amasis sent some forward to speak with them, among whom was Belus whose tongue was their own, disguised as an Egyptian captain, a garb that became him ill. They talked a long while. Then Belus and the others returned and reported that the Prince and General, Merodach, gave us leave to retire unmolested, also that he offered a great present of gold to Amasis and his captains, if this were done. Then, he said, he would retire to Babylon and make it known to the King Nebuchadnezzar that he had gained a victory over the Egyptians, who had fled at the sight of his army.

When Amasis heard this, he laughed. Nevertheless he sent back Belus and the others to ask how much gold Babylon would pay as a tribute to Pharaoh, and so it went on all the afternoon, till at length Amasis knew that it was too late for the Babylonians to attack, for night drew near. Then he sent a last message, demanding that the Babylonians should surrender and give hostages; also the gold that they had offered. This was the end of it.

Later Belus came and told me the meaning of this play. "Those Babylonians have no water," he said, "save what they carry with them. Tomorrow they will be thirsty and drink all, leaving nothing for the horses and the elephants, that they thought would drink at the springs of the oasis tonight. Truly Amasis is a good general."

All that night we watched, thought with little fear for there was no moon and we knew that in such darkness the Babylonians would not dare to attack. Now I thought that Amasis would fall on them at the dawn, as we had done on the Syrians. But he did not, who said that thirst was the greatest of captains and he would leave him in command. Still when he had seen that all our army was well fed and all our horses were well watered, he sent out a body of cavalry, five thousand of them perhaps, with orders to charge at the centre of the Babylonians as they began to muster their array, and then suddenly to retire as though seized with panic.

This was done. When they saw the horsemen coming the Babylonians formed up with great shoutings, and the elephants were advanced. As if frightened at the sight of these elephants, our men wheeled about and fled back towards the hills, though not too fast. Now happened that which Amasis had hoped.

The enemy broke his ranks and pursued the Egyptians. Elephants, chariots and clouds of horse pursued them all mingled together, while after them came the bulk of the host. The word went down our lines to stand firm behind the crest of the hill. We opened and let our horsemen through, to re-form behind us, which they did, having scarce lost a man. Then we closed again and waited.

The hordes were upon us; chariots, horse and elephants toiled up the sandy slopes of the hills, slipping back one step for every two forward. At a signal our bowmen rose and loosed their arrows, cloud after cloud of arrows. Soon the heads and trunks of the elephants were full of them. Maddened with pain the great brutes turned and rushed down the hill, crushing all they met. The horses also, those of them that were not killed, did likewise, while the sand was strewn with dead or wounded men. The charge turned to a rout and few that took part in it reached the great army unharmed. Still, so vast was it that those who had fallen with their beasts were but a tithe of its numbers, though now few of the elephants were fit for service and the chariots and the horsemen had suffered much.

At this repulse rage seized the Babylonians or their generals. Trumpets blew, banners waved, words of command were shouted. Then suddenly the whole host, countless thousands of them whose front stretched over a league of land, began their advance against our little line of hills that measured scarcely more than four furlongs from end to end.

Amasis saw their plan, which was to encircle and closing in from behind, to overwhelm us with the weight of their number. He divided our horse into two bodies and weary as they still were from their journey against the Syrians, commanded them to charge round the ends of the hills and to cut through those wings, leaving the breast of the great host like a bull with severed horns. This they did well enough, charging forward, and back again through and through those Babylonians, or their allies, till between the horns and the head there were great gaps; after which they changed their tactics and charged at the tips of the horns, crumpling them up, till from ordered companies they became a mob.

Meanwhile the breast advanced, leaving a reserve to guard the wagons and the stores and the plain below.

Wave upon wave of the picked troops of Babylon, they dashed up at us, like breakers against a reef, and the real fight began.

We raked them with our arrows, killing hundreds, but always more poured on, till they came to the crest of the hills and met the Egyptians sword to sword and spear to spear.

****

I had no part in that fight who stood behind in reserve, with the General's Legion that guarded Amasis and Egypt's banners. Yet I saw it all and noted that many of those who attacked, were wasted with thirst, for their mouths were open and their tongues hung out, while the hot sun beat down upon their helms and armour.

Amasis saw it also, for I heard him say, "I thank the gods that they have given me no Babylonian prince to be the captain of my life. Now, on them, Egyptians!"

We rose, we charged, we drove them before us in a tumbled mass, down those blood-stained slopes we drove them; yes, there they died by the hundred and the thousand. At the foot of the hill we re-formed, for many of us had been killed or wounded in the great fray. Then we charged at the heart of the Babylonian host where flew the banners of their general, the Prince Merodach, a dense array of fifteen or twenty thousand of the best of their troops, set to guard the general, the women and the baggage. We fell on them like a flood, but were rolled back from their triple line as a flood is from a wall of rock. We hung doubtful whose force after all was small, when suddenly at the head of about a thousand of his guards, whom he had kept in reserve, Amasis himself charged past us. We, the rest of that legion, would not be left behind. Leaving our dead and wounded we charged with him. How it happened I do not know, but we broke the triple line, we went into it as a wedge goes into wood, and it split in two.

Suddenly I saw the inmost body of horsemen that surrounded the Babylonian standards, wheel about and gallop off. A soldier cried into my ear,

"Merodach flies! Yes, he flies. Babylon is beaten!"

So it was indeed, for when the host saw that their general had deserted them with his guard of chariots and horsemen, the heart went out of them. No longer were they battalions of brave men, nay, they became but as sheep driven by wolves or dogs. They packed together, they fled this way and that, trampling one upon the other. They fought no more, they flung down their arms, each man seeking to save his own life. The Egyptians slew and slew until they were weary. Then the trumpets called them back, save the horsemen that for a while followed the wings of the army which, seeing what had happened, abandoned hope and joined in the rout.

What happened to that host? I do not know. Thousands of them died, but thousands more wandered off into the desert seeking safety and water, but above all water at the wells in their rear. I can see them now, a motley crowd, elephants, camels, chariots, horse and footmen, all mingled together, till at length they vanished in the distance, except those who fell by the way. Doubtless many of them reached Babylon and told their tale of disaster into the ears of Nebuchadnezzar the Great King. But he was aged and it was said distraught, almost on his deathbed indeed, and had heard many such before. Always his hosts gathered from the myriads of the East, were going forth to battle. Sometimes they conquered, sometimes they were defeated. It mattered little, seeing that there were always more myriads out of which new hosts could be formed. In Babylon and Assyria and the lands around life was plentiful and cheap, for there men bred like flies in the mud and sun, and wealth was great, and when the king commanded they must go out to die.

The victory was won! Now came its fruits, the hour of plunder was at hand. There were the great parks of wagons filled with stores and women; there were the pavilions of the royal prince, the generals and the officers. Amasis himself, riding down our lines his helmet in his hand, laughing as ever, shouted to us to go and take, but to be careful to keep him his share.

We rushed forward without rank or order, for now there was nothing to fear. All the enemy were fled save those who lay dead or wounded, swart, black-bearded men. I, being young and swift of foot, outran my fellows. We came to the pavilion of the prince over which the banners of Babylon hung limply in the still air. The soldiers swarmed into it seeking treasure, but I who cared nothing for golden cups or jewels, ran round to another pavilion in its rear which I guessed would be that of the women. Why I did this I was not sure, for I wanted women even less than the other spoil; but I think it must have been because I was curious and desired to see what these ladies were like and how they were housed.

Thus it came about that I entered this place alone and letting fall the flap of the tent, which was magnificent and lined with silk and embroideries, stared round me till my eyes grew accustomed to the shadowed light and I saw that it was empty. No, not empty, for at its end, seated on a couch was a glittering figure, clad it seemed in silver mail, and beside it something over which a veil was thrown. Thinking that this was a man, I drew my sword which I had sheathed, and advanced cautiously.

Now I was near and the figure of which the head was bowed, looked up and stared at me. Then I saw that the face beneath the silver helm was that of a woman, a very beautiful woman, with features such as the Greeks cut upon their gems, and large dark eyes. I gazed at her and she gazed at me. Then she spoke, first in a tongue which I did not understand, and when I shook my head, in Greek.

"Egyptian, if so you be," she said, "seek elsewhere after the others who are fled. I am no prize for you."

She threw aside a broidered cape that hung over her mail, and I saw that piercing the mail was an Egyptian arrow of which the feathered shaft was broken off, also that blood ran to her knees, staining the armour.

I muttered words of pity, saying that I would bring a physician, for suddenly I bethought me of Belus.

"It is useless," she said, "the hurt is mortal; already I die."

Not knowing what to do, I made as though to leave her, then stood still, and all the while she watched me.

"You are young and have a kindly face," said she, "high born too, or so I judge. Look," and with a swift motion she cast off the veil from that which rested against her.

Behold! it was a child of three or four years of age, a lovely child, beautifully attired.

"My daughter, my only one," she said. "Save her, O Egyptian Captain."

I stepped forward and bent down to look at the child. At this moment some soldiers burst into the tent and saw us. Wheeling round I perceived that they were men of my own company.

"Begone!" I cried, whereon one of them called out,

"Why, it is our young captain, the Count Ramose, who woos a captive. Away, comrades, she is his, not ours, by the laws of war. Away! and tell the rest to seek elsewhere."

Then laughing in their coarse soldier fashion, they departed and presently I heard them shouting that this tent must be left alone.

"Save her, Count Ramose, if such be your name," repeated the woman. "Hearken. She is no mean child, for I am a daughter of him who once was King of Israel. Now at the last I grow clear-sighted and a voice tells me to trust you whom my God has sent to me to be my friend. Swear to me by him you worship that you will guard this child, yours by spoil of war; that you will not sell her on the market, that you will keep her safe and clean, and when she comes to womanhood, suffer her to wed where she will. Swear this and I, Mysia, of the royal House of Israel, will call down the blessing of Jehovah on you and yours and all your work, as should you fail me, I will call down His curse."

"A great oath," I exclaimed hesitating, "to be taken by one who is no oath breaker."

"Aye, great, great! Yet, hearken. She is not dowerless."

She glanced about her wildly to make sure that we were alone, then from her side, or perhaps from some hiding-place in the couch, she drew a broidered bag, and thrust it into my hands.

"Hide it," she said. "These royal jewels are her heritage; among them are pearls without price."

I thrust the bag into the pouch I carried, throwing from it the water bottle and the food which it had contained. Then I answered,

"I swear; yet, believe me, Lady, not for the gems' sake."

"I know it, Count Ramose, for such eyes as yours were never given to a robber of the helpless."

Then, as I knew by the motion of her hands, she blessed me in a strange tongue, Hebrew I suppose, and blessed her daughter also.

"Take her," she said presently in Greek, "for I die."

She bent down and kissed the child, then tried to lift her but could not, being too weak to bear her weight. I took her in my arms, asking,

"How is she named and who was her father?"

"Myra is her name," she gasped in a faint voice. Then her eyes closed, she fell sideways on the couch, groaned and presently was dead.

Lifting the veil with which it had been covered when first I entered the tent, I threw it over the child which seemed to be drugged, or mayhap had swooned with fear, cast one last glance at the pale beauty of her dead mother, who looked indeed as though she sprang from the blood of kings, and departed from that tent which presently the soldiers plundered and burned.

Here I will say that of this lady's history I heard no more for many years. She declared herself to be a daughter of a king of Jerusalem, and I half believed the story thinking that at the moment of death she would not lie to me. Certainly such a captive when she grew to womanhood might well have been taken by a king's son as one of his household. Also the jewels which the lady Mysia gave to me, were splendid and priceless, such as kings might own, being for the most part necklaces of great pearls. Among these also was an emerald cylinder on which were graven signs and writing that I could not read, a talisman of power as I learned afterwards. But of this in its place.

****

Departing from the tent and skirting the great pavilion of Merodach, I passed through groups of soldiers, counting or quarrelling over their spoils. As night fell, I climbed the slopes of the little hills that were thick with dead, for by now after the cruel fashion of war, all the enemy's wounded had been slain. At length I came to the tent which I shared with Belus, laughed at on the way by one or two because of the great bundle of spoil which I carried in my arms.

Here I found that philosopher, who had put off the armour which became him so ill, clad in his own garments and engaged in eating a simple meal of bread and sun-dried fruits. When he had greeted me, which he did heartily rejoicing to see me come safe from the battle, for the first time in the dusk of the tent he noted the bundle in my arms.

"It is strange how the wisest of us may be deceived. I have watched you from boyhood and thought that I knew your mind, Ramose. Indeed I would have sworn that whatever your faults, you were one who cared little for spoil. Yet I see that you have been plundering like the commonest."

"Aye, Belus, I have been plundering and found a rich treasure, yet I think one of which no one will wish to rob me. Lift the veil and look."

He did so, while I turned to the door of the tent so that the last of the daylight fell upon me and my burden. Belus stared at the child who still slept or swooned. Then he stared at me, saying,

"Now I wonder what god is at work in this business, and to what end."

"The god of mercy, I think, if there be such a one which I find it hard to believe just now," I answered. Then I told him all the story.

"There are certain oaths that may be broken and yet leave the soul of him who swore them but little stained, and there are others of which even the stretching calls down Heaven's vengeance. Such a one, Ramose, is that which you took before the dying mother of this child, who by now doubtless has registered it in the Recorder's book beyond the earth. Henceforth for good or evil, she is your charge."

"I know it, Belus."

"Yet what is to be done?" he went on. "How can you remain a soldier who have a babe tied to your girdle?"

"I do not wish to remain a soldier, who have seen enough of slaughter, Belus."

"If you marry, your wife will look askance at this little maiden and perchance maltreat her, Ramose; for what woman would believe a tale of a babe found upon the battlefield?"

"I do not wish to marry, Belus. Have I not told you that I have done with women?"

"Yes, but—" Here a thought seemed to strike him for he grew silent and at that moment the child awoke and began to wail.

We quieted her as best we could and fed her with bread soaked in the milk of goats, or camels, I forget which, for of all these Belus had a store in the tent, till at last she fell asleep in my arms. Then I laid her on my bed and gave Belus the jewels. These he hid away among his charms and medicines where none would dare to search for them lest some spell should be loosed upon them. For all the Egyptians held Belus to be a great magician.

"They are the child's and holy," he said, "and therefore we need give no account of them to the tellers of the spoil."

To which I answered that this was so, and turned to gaze upon the gift that God had sent to me. As I gazed a great love of that sweet child entered my heart where it still lives today.

CHAPTER 7

Ramose Seeks Refuge in Cyprus

When I woke on the following morning the sun was up and save for the child Myra, I found myself alone in the tent. She was seated by me upon the rugs which, spread upon the sand, made my soldier's couch, looking at me with her large, dark eyes. When she saw that I was awake, she asked for her mother, speaking in the Babylonian tongue of which I knew much even in those days, having learned it from Belus. I told her that her mother had gone away, leaving me to watch her, and I think she understood for she began to weep. Then I took her in my arms and kissed her, till presently she ceased weeping and kissed me back, at which my heart went out to her who was an orphan in the power of strangers.

Presently Belus returned, bringing with him a woman called Metep, the widow of a soldier who had been killed by a fall from his horse at the beginning of our march. This Metep was the daughter of a peasant of the Delta, not well-favoured but kind-hearted, one, too, who had loved her husband and would have naught to do with the trollops of the camp, where she must stay earning her living as she could do till the army returned to Egypt. As it chanced she, who counted some thirty years, was childless; yet she loved children, as those often do who have none. Therefore we hired her to be the nurse of little Myra whom she tended well and watched as though she were her own, preparing her food and making her garments of stuffs that came from the spoils of the Babylonian camp.

Belus told me that he had visited this camp at the break of day, hoping to learn something of the lady Mysia, who while she was dying, had told me that she was the daughter of a Jewish king. In this he failed, for drunken soldiers had fired the tent after plundering it and though he saw a body lying among the ashes, it was so charred that he could not tell whether it were that of man or woman, also it wore no armour such as I had seen, of which perhaps it had been stripped by some marauder who, if it was silver, broke it up for melting.

Also both then and afterwards he questioned certain prisoners, but could learn nothing of this lady Mysia, who perhaps among the Babylonians went by some other name. Merodach, they said, had women in his train as had other princes and lords, but who these were they did not know, for after the Eastern fashion they were kept apart and when the host marched, travelled on camels in covered panniers, or sometimes in closed litters. But now death had taken those who led the beasts or bore the litters, and with them the most of the lords who owned the women, the slaughter having been very great. Therefore none was left to tell their tale, even if it were known.

So the beauteous lady Mysia and her history were lost in the darkness of the past, which even the eyes of Belus the diviner could not pierce.

****

Amasis summoned the army and made an oration. He praised it. He showed that its victory had been very marked over a mighty host that outnumbered it many times; that it had been won by discipline and courage, (of his own skill in generalship he said nothing) and this without the aid of Greeks, (here the thousands of his hearers shouted in their joy) those Greeks whom Pharaoh leant upon and thought necessary in war, holding as he did that they outpassed the Egyptians in all qualities that make a soldier.

When he had given time for these cunning words of his to sink into the hearts of his hearers, where as he guessed, they would bear fruit in the future among Egyptians who hated and were jealous of the Greeks that Pharaoh favoured, Amasis spoke of other matters.

He said that after taking thought and counsel with his captains, he had determined not to follow the Babylonians into their own country.

"That host," he declared, "is utterly destroyed. Few of them will live to behold the walls of the Great City, for thirst and the desert men will cut off many of those who escaped the battle. But the King of Babylon has other armies to fight us who are few and war-worn after two victories, and whose horses are wearied with heat and work. Lastly, friends, I have no command from Pharaoh, the good god our master, to pursue the Babylonians across the deserts but only that I should beat them back from the borders of Egypt and because of your valour this has been done. Now, therefore, with your leave, we will return to Sais and make our report to Pharaoh."

Once more the army shouted applause, for nothing did they desire less than to march into the burning waterless deserts, there to fight new battles against the countless hosts of Babylon, they who wished to return to their wives and children, having earned the plots of watered land that Pharaoh promised to his victorious soldiers.

This matter finished Amasis spoke of that of the booty which was very great, for the Babylonian camp had been full of riches, also thousands of horses and beasts of burden had been captured during and after the battle. This spoil he commanded all men to bring in, that his officers might divide it among them according to their rank. Next morning this was done, though not without many quarrels, for all who had captured anything, wished to keep it for themselves. Amongst others I appeared carrying the child, Myra, in whose garments were hidden the jewels that her mother had given to me. This I did, because the punishment of those who withheld anything, was death, also because I felt that my honour was at stake although this wealth was not mine, but the child's.

When I appeared before the officers bearing Myra in my arms, a great laugh went up. One cried out, "How shall this plunder be divided?" Another answered, "Let the little one be taken and sold in the slave-market." To which a third replied, "Who then will carry her to Sais?"

But the officer who acted as judge, behind whom stood Amasis watching all, asked of me,

"Do you demand this child as your share of the loot, Count Ramose?"

"Yes," I answered. "I saved her from the battlefield and I demand her and all that she wears upon her body."

"Strip her!" cried one. "Her shift may be of gold."

The officer hesitated, but Amasis said,

"By the gods, are we babe-searchers? If the Captain Ramose wishes for a child who he says that he has found upon the battlefield, let him take her and welcome, with all that is on her. Who knows? Perhaps he found her before he left Egypt!" he added laughing, as did the others. So that danger passed with a soldier's jest, and bowing, I went on.

On the second day from this of the dividing of the spoil, our return march began. The army being heavy laden and weary and having nothing more to fear, travelled slowly and in no close array. One of the reasons why Amasis was so beloved of the soldiers that afterwards they made him Pharaoh, was that he never oppressed them or forced them to hard tasks that were not needed, such as the fortifying of camps in an empty land. Hence each man went much as he would though none was allowed to straggle or to leave the host, and I was able to keep the child Myra close to me and often riding on my horse. Thus it happened that from the first she grew to love me and if we were separated for long, would weep and refuse her food.

So at last we came to Pelusium where to reach Sais the army must cross the mouths of the Nile. Here Amasis sent for me and Belus.

"I have bad news for you," he said. "Apries your father is in an evil mood; even our great victory over the Babylonians does not rejoice him overmuch; almost might one think that he would have been better pleased had we been driven back, perhaps because he thinks that a certain general is more talked of in Egypt today, than is Pharaoh's self. Nor is this all. As he can find fault with little else he is angry because I did not obey his order to send to him your head, Ramose, and with it Belus still carrying his upon his shoulders; for his spies have told him that you are with the army and have been promoted by me in reward of your deeds. Again he bids me fulfil his commands, saying that the Syrians have given him much trouble concerning you and demand your life continually."

Now I looked at him in question, but Belus asked outright, "Is such your purpose, General?"

"I do not know," he answered. "A man must think of himself sometimes and I cannot always be troubled by Pharaoh about a young Count and a certain physician and diviner. Such a matter would be a small cause over which to quarrel with Pharaoh, though it well may be that we shall quarrel ere all is done, as I think you read in your stars, Belus. Hearken. This war is finished and your service is over. There are many boats sailing down the Nile, some of them large ships bound for Cyprus and elsewhere, taking with them soldiers whose service is ended or who have been wounded and seek their homes; also merchants. Now here I set few guards and if tomorrow when I make public search for the Count Ramose and Belus the Babylonian, that I may deliver them to Pharaoh, they cannot be found, am I to blame? I have spoken."

"And we have heard," answered Belus.

Then Amasis shook us by the hand in his friendly fashion and thanked me for my small share in the war, saying that he had watched me and that I might make a good general one day, if I gave my mind to arms and ceased from dreaming like a lovesick girl. "Or," he added with meaning, "perhaps something higher than a general, you who have old blood in you."

To Belus also he said that time alone would show whether he were a true diviner, but that certainly he was the best of physicians, as many a sick and wounded man in the army knew that day. Nor was this all. As we were leaving the chamber, for we spoke together in a house, Amasis called me back and thrust into my hand a bag, saying that it was my share of the spoil which I might find useful in my wanderings, which bag I found afterwards was filled with Babylonian gold. The sight of that gold, I remember, made me feel ashamed when I thought of the priceless pearls that had been hidden from him, till I recalled that these were not mine, but little Myra's inheritance.

Thus I bade farewell to the great captain Amasis whom I was to see no more for years. Indeed I bade farewell for ever to the Amasis I knew, for when we met again and he had exchanged a general's staff for Pharaoh's sceptre, in many ways he was a very different man.

****

Next morning at the dawn a merchant and his assistant, for as such we were disguised, with their servant, a peasant woman and her child, having hired passages, sailed amidst a motley crowd upon a ship bound for certain ports along the coast and afterwards for the isle of Cyprus. To Cyprus in the end we came in safety and as I think, unknown of any, for all were intent upon their own affairs, moreover the sea being rough, in no mood for watching others. Also the most of them left the ship at the coast ports.

Reaching Salamis, the greatest and most beautiful city of Cyprus, we hired a lodging there in a humble street, giving out that we were strangers who had escaped from Tyre which was beleaguered by the Babylonians, and taking new names.

Here at Salamis we dwelt for many years, Belus, whom I called my uncle, the brother of my mother, practising as a physician, also in secret as a diviner, under the name of Azar, and I as a merchant who dealt in corn and copper and was known as Ptahmes. Nor did we labour in vain, for although we made no show during those years we grew rich.

The mean street in which we dwelt, one running down towards the sea at a point where the ships anchored, once had been a great thoroughfare inhabited by rich merchants. Now these had deserted it for other quarters where the high-born dwelt around the palace of their chieftain who was called King of Salamis, for in Cyprus there were many kings who, at this time, owned the Pharaoh of Egypt as their over-lord. Yet their stone and marble palaces remained, turned to seamen's lodges, marts where every kind of merchandize was sold to mariners, thieves' quarters, or even brothels.

67

The house to which we had come by chance, had been perhaps the greatest of these palaces. Built of white stone or marble, it contained many fine chambers surrounding a courtyard, and behind it was a large garden with a fountain fed from a spring, where grew some fig trees and an ancient olive, but for the rest covered with nettles and rank growth. This house, or rather palace, wherein at first we had hired but a few rooms, by degrees we bought for no great price, so that at length it was all our own. Leaving the front unkempt and dirty as of old, also those spaces and the portico where I bought and sold, thus to deceive curious eyes, and with them an outer lodge that once had been a shrine dedicated to the worship of some Cyprian god, in which Belus dispensed medicine or, in a back chamber, made divinations, I set myself to repair the rest of that great building.

By degrees with thought and care, by help of skilled artists of Cyprus and of Greece, I made it beautiful as it had been in the day of its splendour when it was the home of merchant princes. I scraped its marble halls and columns, I mended the broken statues that stood around them, or procured others of a like sort and perhaps by the same sculptors, to stand upon their pedestals; I dug the dirt from the mosaics on the floor and hired good workmen to relay what was lacking; to clean out the marble baths that had been filled with rubbish and set the furnaces in order; to repaint the walls whence the frescoes had faded, and I know not what besides. Lastly I restored all the great garden that had become a refuse heap, rebuilding the high wall about it, making paths and flower-beds and setting a summerhouse under the ancient fig and olive trees that happily none had troubled to cut down.

Thus it came about that, although no one would have so believed who looked at it from the dirty street where drunkards roamed at night, slatterns screamed and fought and children played or begged of the passer-by, within the discoloured front like to that of the temple of some forgotten god, lay a mansion well-ordered, white and beautiful, filled with willing servants sworn to us under the oaths of some order of which Belus was a chief; a home worthy to be inhabited by the great ones of the earth.

Why did I do all these things and why did Belus help in the work? For sundry reasons. First because then as now I loved all that is beautiful, all that lights the soul through the windows of the eyes; and secondly because I, who was a scholar when I ceased to be a merchant, needed calm and quiet and fit places in which to store my manuscripts, where I could study them in peace. Yet behind all this lay a deeper reason. I was a celibate, one who because of a terror that had struck me in my boyhood, had forsworn woman and determined to fill her place with philosophy and learning, also with the study of religion and of the nature of the gods and of men, and of how these may draw near to the Divine.

The arts of magic and divination, however, I left alone, having always held these to be unlawful, though Belus who practised them after the fashion of the Babylonians, the great masters of star-lore and of sorcery, thought otherwise. Yet when we reasoned about the matter, he confessed to me that these were two-edged weapons which often cut those who wielded them, also that the answers which spirits gave, for the most part might be read in more ways than one. Still at times he was a good prophet. For example when he foresaw that trouble would be brought upon me by the beauteous queen Atyra, and that the general Amasis would rise to Pharaoh's throne which then no one else so much as guessed, except perhaps Amasis himself, in whose mind Belus may have read it.

For the rest, these gifts of Belus were of great service to us, inasmuch as they brought us into the councils of the highest in the land, for these of Cyprus were very superstitious and would pay great sums for oracles and horoscopes, protecting those who furnished them from all harm, since such foreseeing men were looked upon as prophets favoured of Heaven.

Thus drawing gain from all these sources, trade, medicine, and divination, living under our false names, we grew both wealthy and powerful, though with politics and plottings we would have naught to do, and outwardly remained humble and of no account.

To tell all the truth, there was a further reason why I made that old palace which to the passer-by seemed a mere relic of past greatness, so beautiful within, filling it with everything that was perfect and lovely. Myra was that reason. From the beginning, as I have said, this child loved me as a father, aye, and more, seeing that even in early youth a maid will favour other men besides her own father, because Nature so teaches her. With Myra it was otherwise. She clung to me alone, though Belus she liked well enough, also she loved her nurse, Metep, in a fashion. And as she loved me, so I loved her; indeed she was my all, the eyes of my head and the heart within my breast. Had she died, swept off of some sickness, of which there were many in Cyprus especially in the hot season, I think that I should have died also, or perhaps have slain myself that I might follow her to the Shades.

Therefore my desire was that those sweet innocent eyes of hers should never look save upon what was gracious and uplifting, and that on the tablets of her mind should be written nothing that was not pure and holy. I was her tutor also; in the mornings and after my trafficking was done in the evening, we studied together, reading the Grecian poets when she was old enough, or sometimes the hieroglyphics of Egypt, of which I expounded the hidden lore.

Belus took a hand in this game also, teaching her the wisdom of Babylon, its writing and its tongue; showing her the motions of the stars and how the world moved among them; telling her, too, the history of Israel and other nations, and instructing her in figures. So this child grew learned beyond her years, for her mind was quick and bright, though at times she had her thoughtful moods. In body she grew also, tall and straight and very fair to see, dark-eyed yet with hair the brown colour of ripe corn which told, perhaps, of the intermingling of her Hebrew blood with some more western stock. Thus at last in that hot land, she came near to womanhood and her mind growing ever, ripened till, although more wayward, it was the equal of my own and in certain ways its master.

One day Belus came upon us seated side by side studying an old manuscript with the lamplight shining on our faces, and stood contemplating us with that strange, secret smile of his playing round his withered lips. Our work done Myra rose and went upon a household errand. When she was gone Belus said,

"You two make a handsome pair and look so much of an age, that some might think that you were not father and daughter, as it is given out you are."

"Nor are we," I answered with a start, "at least in blood."

Then I was silent, for the thought troubled me.

"Has not the time come," went on Belus, "when this maiden should be told how she fell into your keeping?"

"Perhaps," I answered. "Do you tell her, Belus, for I cannot."

Tell her he did, in what words or when I do not know. At least on the following evening at the hour when we were wont to work, Myra came and sat opposite to me, her chin resting on her hand, looking at me with her large eyes from which I think tears had flowed, for her face was troubled.

"So, Father," she said at length, "you are not my father. I am no one's child and all that Metep has said to me about my mother who died when I was born is false."

"Has Belus been speaking with you, Myra?"

"Yes. He has told me all, saying you thought I ought to know, now when I am no more a little girl. I wish he had been silent," she added passionately.

"Why, Myra?"

"Because if I am not your daughter you will cease to love me, while I cannot cease to love you."

"Certainly I shall never cease to love you while I live, Myra, nor after perhaps."

Her face brightened.

"Then all is not black as I feared, for if you ceased to love me—oh! what shall I call you?"

"Ramose, when we are alone, but Father as of old before others."

"—if you ceased to love me—Ramose—I think that I should die. So it is and so it will ever be."

Now I grew frightened, although my heart leapt with joy at those sweet words.

"Perchance a day may come, Myra, when you will learn to love someone better than you do me."

"Never!" she answered fiercely—"Never!" and she struck the table with her little hand. "I know what you mean. Do we not read of marriage in books and was not Metep once married? Do not say that you wish me to marry, for I will never marry. I hate all men, save you and Belus."

"They will not hate you, I fear."

"What does it matter what they do? I have seen them; it is enough. Tell me quickly that you do not wish me to marry."

"No, no, Myra, I wish that we should go on as we are—always."

"Ah! I am glad. That makes me happy."

Here a new and dreadful thought struck her, for she added with a gasp,

"But you might marry, you whom all must love; and that I could not bear."

"Be silent, foolish one," I broke in. "I shall never marry. On that matter I have sworn an oath."

"Oh! that is good tidings. Yet," she added slowly, "Belus says that it is not wise to swear oaths when we are young, since we seldom keep them when we are old."

"Let Belus be and by the gods I pray you to talk no more of marriage, for the word does not please me, nor as yet is it fitting for your lips. Come, Myra, we waste time. Let us to the deciphering of this old poem that tells us of dead days and beautiful forgotten folk."

"I come, Ramose. Yet first I would say that I do remember something of the past of which Belus spoke. The shape of a tall and lovely lady with dark hair and eyes often haunts my sleep. Was my mother thus and did she ride among hosts of men clad in silver?"

"I saw her but once, Myra, and then for a very little while in an hour of death and tumult, but so she seemed to me. Perhaps now at times she visits you from the underworld to watch and bless you. Dream on of her, Myra, and for the rest let it lie. The gods have sent you here to rejoice the world, how they sent you is of no account. Take what the gods give you and be thankful."

"I am thankful," she said humbly and yet with pride, "for whatever they have taken away, have they not given me you who saved me from death and are not ashamed to love a poor maid who is no one's child."

Then we began our reading of the Grecian poet, nor did we talk again of this matter for a long while. Yet from that day life was a little different for both of us, and became more so as Myra grew to full and fairest womanhood. She was innocent if ever a maiden was, yet Nature taught her certain things, as perchance did her nurse Metep, pitying her motherless state. Therefore no longer would she throw her arm about me as we worked, or press her cheek against my own. But from that day also in some subtle fashion we became more intimate, though this new intimacy was one of the spirit. Our thoughts leapt together towards an unknown end. Soon Myra discovered that I sought for more than learning; that I sought after Truth, or rather after God who is Truth, and could not find him. Here it was that she came to my aid, perhaps because of the blood that was in her, that of the Hebrews.

For months we had been studying the gods of sundry nations, those of the Egyptians, those of the Greeks, those of the Babylonians, and others, a search in which Belus helped us much, for though I think he believed in none of them, he knew the attributes of all and their forms of worship.

At last the task was done. There written on a roll were all the gods and goddesses that we could count, and against each name its qualities and powers, as its worshippers conceived these to be. It was a great list that caused the mind to reel. Myra gazed at it, winding up upon a rod the roll which she had written in her neat letters, so that god after god departed into darkness as though Time had taken them from the eyes of men.

"What of all these?" I asked wearily at length.

She made no answer but taking me by the hand, led me to a window-place whence she drew the curtain. The night was very fine and clear and the blue of the great sky was spangled with a thousand thousand stars.

"You see those stars?" she said. "Well, Belus, who is a great astronomer as the Babylonians have been from the beginning, tells me that everyone of them is a world, or perhaps a sun like our own, with worlds about it. Now, Ramose, you wise philosopher, tell me. Do all those worlds worship our multitude of gods, most of them made like men or women, only stronger and more evil, and named gods by this little land or that, or even by this city or by that?"

"I think not," I answered.

"Then, Ramose, must there not be one God, King of the Heavens, King of the Earth, whom we ought to worship, taking no count of all the rest?"

"That is what the Hebrews say, Myra."

"My mother told you that she was a Hebrew, and no mean one. Perhaps, Ramose, this is what she teaches when she visits me in my sleep."

"Perhaps," I answered.

Then we passed on to other lighter matters, and doubtless before she left me Myra had forgotten all this debate which sprang suddenly from her heart, and as suddenly passed away. But if she forgot, I remembered and considered and accepted, till in the end, rejecting all else, though as yet I knew him not, in my heart I became a worshipper of that one unknown God of whom she had spoken, whereof all the other gods were rays in so far as they were good, or perchance ministering spirits.

Thus then did the maid Myra find the answer to my questionings and first outline the faith that I hold today.

Often I discussed these great matters with Belus. That wise man who had sifted the truth so often that at last he came to believe in nothing, only smiled, shook his head and answered,

"What is this one new god that you have found, but he who is named Fate, whose decrees I read written in the stars, unchangeable from the beginning of the world?"

"Does that make him less a god?" I asked.

"No," he answered, "it only gives him another name. But what is God? What is God?"

"Perchance that which we search for in the heavens and at length find in our own hearts," I answered. . . .

****

News came to Cyprus and reached us very swiftly through its great ones who were our clients. Thus we heard how Adikran the Libyan, being oppressed of the Cyrenians had prayed Apries my father, the Pharaoh, to help him against these Greeks. Thereon it seemed, the Egyptian party at Pharaoh's court forced him against his will to despatch an army to destroy those of Cyrene. As it happened, however, these defeated that army with heavy loss, whereon there was a great outcry in Egypt, the people thinking that Apries who was known to love the Greeks, had made a plot that the Egyptian troops should be destroyed by them. Then, so went the tale, Pharaoh in his trouble turned to Amasis, the general under whom I had fought against the Babylonians, and sent him to the army which was in rebellion, to take command of it, thinking that he, whom the Egyptians loved, would bring it to obedience. Yet the result was otherwise, for the Egyptian troops, seizing Amasis, set a crown upon his head and declared him Pharaoh, thus fulfilling the prophecy of Belus.

Now Apries my father raised another great army of thirty thousand Greeks to fight Amasis. But in this as in all battles, Amasis proved himself the better general, defeating the Greeks and taking Apries my father prisoner. So he remained a prisoner for some years, being well treated by Amasis who was kind-hearted and indeed kept him to rule with him over Egypt. In the end Apries rebelled, and departing from Sais, began to raid Egypt with his Greeks. There followed more fighting and at last Apries was killed, some said by the Egyptians, and some by his own soldiers. At least he was killed in a boat upon the Nile, and Amasis, taking his body, embalmed it and gave it royal burial.

This then was the fate of Pharaoh my father whom I had seen last at that farewell feast which he gave to Atyra the Syrian queen. Yes, this was the end of all his greatness and his glory—to be butchered like a sheep in a boat upon the Nile, after Amasis, who had saved me from death at his hands, had cast him from his throne.

Such was the news that came to us from Egypt while, under our feigned names, we lay hid in the city of Salamis in Cyprus.

When we were sure that the Pharaoh Apries, who begot me, was dead and that Amasis filled his throne, Belus spoke to me, saying,

"Is it your wish, Ramose, to dwell here at Salamis as a merchant for all your days? Bethink you, you have no longer anything to fear from the wrath of him who was Pharaoh, for Amasis sits in his place, and Amasis is, or was, your friend and mine."

"Nay," I answered, "I would return to Egypt to learn whether my mother still lives."

For though we had been parted these many years I still loved my mother. Yet I had not dared to write to her, because I feared her busy tongue and lest she should whisper of my whereabouts and thus set Pharaoh's dogs upon my scent. Therefore I thought it wisest to leave her believing that I was dead.

"If so, let us return, Ramose. Where you and Myra go, thither I will go also who grow too old to seek new friends. We have wealth in plenty and can live together where we will—until my call comes."

I opened my lips to ask him of what call he spoke, then bethinking me that he must mean that of death, closed them again. Yet this was not so, as I learned afterwards.

Thus in few words we agreed upon this great matter, which I did the more willingly because it came to my ears that a certain high one in Cyprus whom it would have been hard to resist, had learned of the wonderful beauty of the maid Myra and was plotting to take her. Very quietly we sold all that belonged to us in Cyprus and transferred our wealth to those with whom we dealt in Egypt, honourable men who, we knew, would keep it safe until we came to claim it in the trade name of our Cyprian firm, though it is true that when I saw how great it had grown, I was afraid.

At length all was ready and the ship in which we must sail on the morrow, lay at anchor at the mole. We three sat, somewhat desolate, in our desolate home that was no longer ours, for we had sold it with the rest. The statues, the vases, the gems and all the priceless treasures that piece by piece I had gathered to please our eyes and to make the place beautiful were on board the vessel, together with the most of such of the household as had chosen to follow us, so that the chambers looked naked and unfriendly. Myra noted it and wept a little, saying,

"I have been very happy here in Salamis, Ramose, and I would that we were not going away. My heart tells me that trouble awaits us yonder in Egypt."

Now I was distressed and knew not what to answer, save that regrets came too late, for I could not tell her about the peril from that high lord. But Belus replied,

"It is natural that you should grieve, Myra, who have grown from infancy to the verge of womanhood in this place. Yet hearken. My heart or rather the stars tell me another tale. I seem to see it written on the book of Fate that whatever ills we may find in Egypt, those that are worse would overtake us if we lived on here. I tell you," he added solemnly, "that a curse and great desolation hang over Salamis. What it is I do not know. Mayhap it will be burned by the Babylonians, or other foes, but unless my wisdom is at fault, soon Salamis the beautiful will be no more."

Thus he spoke nor did we question him about the matter, for like all seers, when Belus had uttered his oracle he would not speak of it again.

The next morning before the light we embarked secretly upon our ship, which we had given out was sailing on a trading venture, and departed from the shores of Cyprus. Before ever we set foot upon the quays of Memphis, we learned that a great earthquake had shaken much of Salamis to the ground, burying hundreds of her citizens, and that among the streets destroyed was that in which we had dwelt, for a mighty wave following the earthquake had flowed over it, washing it into the deep.

When we heard this tale, Belus looked at us and smiled, but we said nothing, whatever we might think.

CHAPTER 8

At Memphis

At length we came safe to Memphis, for Apries being dead and the Grecian mercenaries and marauders who clung to him, slain, or scattered, or driven away, there was peace throughout Egypt under the rule of the new Pharaoh, Amasis the Egyptian. The gates of the cities stood open, the Nile was free to all who sailed upon it, the husbandman ploughed his field and none robbed him of its fruits. In those years, before the Persians fell upon her, Egypt rested unafraid, rich and happy beneath the strong hand of Amasis.

As soon as we came ashore in the early morn I made inquiry of a port captain whether Tapert the high officer still dwelt there, and learned that he had been some years dead. Then with secret fear, but as it seemed carelessly, saying that I had known him when I was a lad, I asked if any of his household remained and waited with a beating heart.

"Nay," was the answer, "he left no children, but the Grecian lady lives on, she whom he married and who once, as she declares, was the love of Apries the Pharaoh. Indeed she remains a fair and gracious lady, one of much wealth also, for Tapert left her all he had, which was not a little. She dwells alone in a great house in a garden, not far from the temple of Ptah, and is famous for her hospitality, for she spends the most of her substance on feasts and costly raiment, saying that she has none for whom to save."

Now when I heard that my mother lived I was glad, for though the man's words showed me that she was still vain and foolish, after all she was my mother who had given me life.

Leaving the ship and its cargo in the charge of the officers appointed to watch the goods of traders, and of our servants, I hired asses, also a guide. Mounting these beasts, the three of us, Belus and I and Myra, who wore a veil in the Eastern fashion to hide her face, rode through the mean suburb that lay without the wall between the banks of Nile and the city, to the gate, through which we passed unquestioned. The guide led us up a broad street on either side of which dwelt the richest of the citizens, till, not far from the enclosure of the great temple of Ptah, we came to a walled garden. Being admitted we rode on through this beautiful garden to the door of a large white house built round a courtyard, which he said was that of the widow of Tapert. Here servants in fine garments such as are worn in palaces, ran out asking our business, to whom I answered that we were strangers newly arrived at Memphis who wished to have speech with their mistress about a matter that would be of interest to her, and when, unsatisfied, they desired to learn our names, I gave those of Ptahmes and Azar by which we had been known in Cyprus. A man departed with this message and presently there came an old fellow who carried a wand which showed me that much state was kept in this house. Moreover, although he knew me not, I knew him, for when I was a child he had been one of the servants appointed to my mother at Pharaoh's court.

"Follow me," he said, bowing in the fashion that he had learnt there in his youth.

"We follow," I answered and I saw him start at the sound of my voice and look at me curiously, like one who searches his mind for something forgotten.

We crossed the courtyard and a narrow, pillared gallery by which it was surrounded, and entered a large chamber with open window-places that looked towards the Nile. Near to one of these, seated in a beautiful carved chair inlaid with ivory, sat a tall woman clad in white Grecian robes, engaged in stringing a necklace of gold and gems.

From far off I knew her for my mother. Although now her hair was darker and her features thinner than they used to be, there remained the same gracious form, the same quick movement of the delicate hands and the same large grey eyes with which she glanced at us, as always was her wont to do at strangers. That glance first fell upon me and so dwelt awhile; then as though she were puzzled, with a shake of the head it passed on to Belus of whom she made nothing for he wore an Eastern robe with a hood to it. Lastly it rested upon the maiden Myra who had thrown back her veil, while astonishment grew upon her face, doubtless because of the beauty that she saw. It passed and she motioned to us to be seated upon stools that had been set for us, then asked in her pleasant voice,

"What is your pleasure, strangers, with Chloe, who once was great in Egypt, but now is known as the widow of Tapert? Can she be of any help to you?"

78

I whispered to Belus to speak, because I was confused.

"Lady," he said, "for a certain reason we have come here, travelling from far, to ask you if you know what has chanced to a young man named Ramose, who was said to be the son of Pharaoh now gathered to Osiris, as you were said to be his mother."

She turned pale and let fall the necklace.

"Who are you?" she asked in a cold voice, "that you come hither to stir up bitter memories? Ramose my son is dead. Trouble came upon him through a high-placed Syrian harlot who bewitched him, handling him as such women do the young who take their fancy, and whose death was laid at his door, as though a lad would have wished to slay his lover. So, as I was told, he fled away with a Babylonian knave and sorcerer called Belus, who was his tutor and used to draw horoscopes and doctor the sick at Pharaoh's court—indeed be it admitted—whatever his horoscopes may have been, his doctoring was good for I have profited by it. They fled to Amasis, now Pharaoh, who at that time was general of an army which fought and defeated the Babylonians, and there, as I have heard, my son played a man's part in war. Then he vanished away, for though the battle spared him, Pharaoh sought his life because of the high-placed Syrian strumpet whose death had brought trouble upon Egypt, and all know what happens to those of whom Pharaoh seeks the life?"

Now Belus threw back his hood and looking at my mother, asked,

"Does the great lady Chloe find the medicine that the knave and sorcerer Belus gave to her amongst others, for the pain which used to strike her in the head above the eyes, still of service in the autumn of the year?"

My mother sprang from her chair, staring at him.

"By Zeus!" she cried, "you are Belus, and little changed, as would chance with a sorcerer. Oh! Belus, tell me of my son. What befell my son for whom I had such high hopes? If he died, why are you, who shared his sin, alive?"

"Because sorcerers do not die, Lady," replied Belus drily. "Others die, but they live on, else of what use is it to be a sorcerer?"

My mother made no answer to his mockeries, but still stared at him.

"One thing is certain," continued Belus, "that if I am a sorcerer and a knave, you are no witch, but only—forgive me—a fool."

"A fool!" she answered angrily. "Why so?"

"Because a wise woman would have made certain that he whom she loved was truly dead before she put on the veil of mourning."

"Your meaning?" she said haughtily.

"I have talked too much," said Belus. "Ask it of these others. Am I your only visitor, Lady Chloe?"

Now for the first time my mother looked fixedly at me, who was dressed in a plain merchant's robe and seated in the shadow beyond the shaft of light that flowed through the window place.

"Sir," she said in a hesitating voice, "do you know aught of this business of the death of my son who, had he lived, might now perhaps have been a man of your age, though not, I think, a merchant, for I will not hide that he had royal blood in him."

Now I drew my stool forward out of the shadow so that the light fell full upon my face, and lifted the merchant's cap from my head, revealing the brown hair that curled beneath.

She stared at me; oh! how she stared!—then muttered as though to herself, "Can this be Ramose whom last I saw as a lad? Nay, it is not possible, for had he lived Ramose who loved me as a child and for whose sake I tore myself away from the sight of him, would never have left me desolate all these long years, believing that he was dead. Yet— those eyes—that hair, yes, and the fashion of locking his fingers—! Oh, torment me no more. Are you Ramose, or another?"

"I am Ramose, your son," I said, and was silent, for words choked in my throat.

She uttered a little cry, then rose and threw herself upon my breast and lay there speechless. In the stillness that followed I heard Belus whisper, I suppose to Myra, who all this while had sat like a statue, or perchance to himself,

"A fool I called her, and rightly. For what else is a woman who does not know her own son?"

"Be quiet," answered Myra, "or I shall call you hard names, Belus."

And he obeyed her, for with him Myra could do what she would.

"Listen, my mother," I said gently, "and reproach me no more because I hid from you that I was alive. I did this knowing that if you learned the truth, others would learn it too, and soon I should cease to be alive, for the ears of Pharaoh are long. Also I was not sure till an hour ago whether you still dwelt in Memphis or anywhere upon the earth. Therefore, under a false name, I lay hid in another land until I knew that Pharaoh my father was dead, and that I could return to Egypt to seek you fearing nothing, for he who now is Pharaoh was my friend and saved me from doom."

"Who is this before whom you tell all your secrets?" asked my mother, pointing at Myra. "Is she your wife? Nay, she is too young. Your daughter then?"

"Aye, the daughter of my heart, one whom Heaven sent to me who am still unwed."

"Then let this daughter of your heart be welcome," said my mother, "and be sure that I shall ask no questions concerning her that you do not wish to answer. Yes, and Belus also."

****

Of that day of reunion after many years I need write no more. Before we sat down to eat at noon our tale was told, though whether my mother believed that part of it which had to do with the finding of Myra upon the battlefield, I do not know. Moreover, I had promised that the three of us would take up our abode in my mother's house which was large and stately, for she would not suffer that we should go elsewhere, though from the first Myra wished to do so.

Thus began our life at Memphis. It was a very happy life, yet it had its troubles, as have all lives. First, I who had been so busy a man, occupied for many hours of the day with my trading, now must be idle, which I found wearisome. To remedy it, having wealth at my command, I bought lands near to the city, and farmed them. I bred cattle and horses, the finest beasts, perhaps, that had been seen in Egypt; I tamed deer and wild animals and raised every kind of grain. Yet as this was not enough, with Belus and Myra I followed after all learning, till at last I was almost as wise as Belus himself and Myra lagged not far behind me.

At all this my mother stared, saying that poring over scrolls and calculations was no task for a lovely maiden, or for the matter of that, for a man still young who should be busy with great affairs. Even my breeding of beasts did not please her, for this, she said, was the business of farmers and such humble folk. At length I grew vexed and asked her what she would have me do, who already possessed more riches than I needed, not counting her own which were great.

"Do!" she answered. "Why, rise. Be a man, show yourself as a high lord in Egypt, become famous. Wage wars and win them, as your noble Grecian forefathers would have done. Are you Pharaoh's son, of the true royal blood of Egypt upon the father's side; indeed as I believe, his only son left living, for Amasis or his party, has blotted out all the rest? Are you not by rank a Count of Egypt; have you not wealth at your command as great perhaps as that of any prince or noble of Egypt? Have you not a mother who knows the ways of courts and can help you? Yet you spend your days tramping amongst swamps to watch the corn spring, or counting calves and foals, and your nights with a maiden and a philosopher, studying strange, ancient books or staring at the stars. So the precious years slip through your hands like water and soon you will be old, not leaving so much as one lawful child behind you because of some silly vow you have taken that divorces you from woman."

Thus my mother taunted me, for she was very ambitious and as I could see, desired that I should wipe out the stain upon my birth by rising to great station where she could glitter at my side. Aye, she desired more, though she never said as much in words, namely, that I should become Pharaoh of Egypt in place of one whom she called "the usurper" and the "murderer" of Apries who had been her lord and my begetter.

For she forgot that this father of mine had sought earnestly to put me to death because of the trouble about a Syrian queen, which had disappointed him in his policies, and that Amasis had saved me from his anger. But I did not forget these things and therefore would have nothing to do with such plots, who indeed had no desire to become Pharaoh, but sought only to lead a quiet, learned life, such as befitted a man of fortune who knew that our days are short and who looked onward to all that might lie beyond it.

Still, to please my mother who would not let me be in peace, I entered into the public business of the city, taking this office and that, and rising always to the leadership of men. For now—I think through her—it became known who I was, none less in fact than the only living son of the dead Pharaoh, also that I was one of the richest men in Egypt; for which reasons I was courted, not only by the common people, but by the nobles and even by the high priests of the temples of the gods. For, after her vanity and ambition, this was my mother's greatest fault—she could not keep silent.

Now if these things were bad, another was worse, namely, the jealousy which sprang up between my mother and Myra.

Since I had returned to her I was everything to my mother, who would never leave me if she had her way. But before I returned I had been everything to Myra who was the constant companion of my leisure hours and who, as I have said, from the beginning would look upon no other man with favour, except at times, on Belus. Thus these two crossed each other's path continually till at length if I were sitting with the one, the other would not enter, but departed saying she saw that I did not wish to be disturbed, or some such words. All of which vexed me much and caused Belus to smile.

Meanwhile, month by month Myra became more learned and

sweet in mind and more beautiful in face and form, till at last she was the fairest maiden that ever I beheld.

One day Belus asked me,

"Why do you not marry Myra, Ramose?"

I started at his words, and answered,

"Have I not told you that, like a priest of Isis, I am sworn to remain celibate? Also Myra is very young and before she turns her thoughts to marriage, she should see other men, young men of her own age, one of whom perhaps she might desire as a husband."

"And do you desire to give her to some such stranger?"

At this a sudden change took place in me and a pain shot through my heart. It was as though it had been gripped by a cold hand. It was as though I had come face to face with death.

"I desire Myra's happiness," I answered, looking down, "I who stand in the place of her father, and mother too."

"Would it not be well to ask her what she herself desires?"

"I do not know. Perhaps, when she is older—say in a year or two. Meanwhile she is happy in her state; let her remain so for a while."

"Many things happen in a year or two," said Belus drily.

Now it would seem that this same matter of marriage was troubling my mother's mind, only in another sense, for having found me after many years of separation, and being by nature somewhat jealous, she did not desire that I should marry and thus, as she thought, be taken away from her again, at any rate, not yet. Least of all did she desire that Myra should become my wife although she was so lovely and so learned, because she was sure that then one roof would not cover the three of us, however large it might be. In truth it was Myra whom she wished to see wed, but not to me, if indeed it were lawful that I should marry her. For she thought or tried to think that we who were as father and daughter, would never be happy as husband and wife. Also, although she had taunted me on the matter, in her heart she believed that having remained single so long, it would be best that I should continue so, satisfying myself with her love and company, with no other woman to come between us.

Therefore she began to talk to her friends of the great charm and favour of this ward of mine in such a way that many came to think that she was not my ward, but my daughter, as perhaps at times she did herself who wished that it might be so. Further, she gave feasts to the noblest of Memphis, at which feasts Myra was present and was made known to the guests as my adopted daughter. Soon that happened which she had foreseen.

Within a month young Counts and others were seeking after Myra, and within two, one of them, a very fine gallant, had asked her hand through my mother, who at once told Myra what had chanced.

Myra, it seemed, making no answer, rose and departed with angry eyes. That afternoon I was away from home, checking the cattle on my farm with my overseers. The business was long and the moon was up before I returned, entering the garden of the house by a side gate, as was my custom. Following a winding path I came to a clump of palms, the most secret place in all that large garden, where stood seats and a table which Myra and I often used when we worked together in the heat of the day, because there a breeze always blew beneath the roof of palm leaves.

Suddenly a figure appeared stopping my path and I sprang back, fearing thieves. Then the tall figure threw off its hood and the sweet voice of Myra said,

"Ramose, forgive me, Ramose, but I would speak with you alone."

"What is it, child? Cannot you always speak with me alone?"

"Nay, Ramose, not of late, for in this way or in that, it seems that the lady your mother hears all I have to say. In Memphis we are not as we were at Salamis the happy."

"Well, speak on, most dear," I said, seating myself upon the bench and pointing to her accustomed place.

She took it, and said presently,

"Ramose, I am wretched. Your mother does not love me. I think that she is very jealous of me because you—do love me, or did in past days. Therefore she makes plots against me."

"What plots?" I asked astonished.

"Plots to be rid of me that she may keep you to herself. Ramose, in secret she gives it out that I am your daughter, which you tell me is not true, and that it would rejoice you to see me wed to some man of station."

"Hush!" I said. "Child, you dream. It is possible that my mother may have thought that you were too lonely here and like other maidens, desired to be courted, but for the rest, I say you dream."

"Aye, Ramose, I dream so well that—" here she named one of the greatest in Memphis—"has asked me in marriage through her."

"What of it, child?" I said lightly. "He is a man well spoken of, wealthy and in the way of advancement, if somewhat loud-voiced and boastful to my fancy."

"Perchance, Ramose. Yet to me he is as a crocodile or a toad."

Now I laughed and answered,

"Then say him nay and have done."

"Aye, that I will, Ramose, but cannot you understand that there are others behind him, and that to me they are all—crocodiles and toads?"

"Then say them all nay, Myra, and remain as you are. Do you think that I wish to force you into marriage?"

"No, Ramose. If I did I should kill you, or rather I should kill myself. Swear to me that you will protect me against marriage, and against all men; unless you desire to see me dead."

"Aye, Myra, with my life if need be. Yet yours is a strange mood for one who is young and beautiful."

"Then let it be strange, but so it is. You have sworn and it is enough, for when did you ever break your word, O most beloved Ramose? Now I would ask something else of you, but having received so great a gift, this is not the time."

"What would you ask, Myra?"

"Oh! that we might go out of this fine house to that cottage near the river, you and I and old Belus, and be rid of all these great folk, the women in their silks and perfumes, and the lords in their chariots or on their prancing horses, with their mincing talk and false eyes, and there, with Belus, look upon the stars and hear his Babylonian wisdom and his tales of the past, and his prophecies of things to come, and be quite at peace, forgetting and forgotten by the world."

"I will think of it," I answered, "but my lady mother would be angry."

"Your lady mother is always angry—with me. But you are not angry, Ramose, and you have promised to protect me from those men. So what does it matter? Good night, Ramose. I told your lady mother, who has made a liar of me, that I was ailing and sought my bed, so thither I must go. Good night, good night, dearest Ramose," and she lifted her fact that I might kiss it, then kissed me back and fled away.

I think it was at this moment that first I began to understand that I loved Myra, not as a father loves his child, but otherwise. Oh! if only I had told her so and taken her then, how many terrors should we have missed!

CHAPTER 9

Pharaoh Comes to Memphis

On the morning following my meeting with Myra in the garden, I was awakened early by a servant who said that the head overseer of my farm desired to see me at once. I commanded that he should be brought to my chamber. There the man, who was so moved that he could scarcely stand still, told me that a prodigy had happened during the night, namely that one of the finest of my cows had borne a splendid calf, in giving birth to which it died. Here he stopped as though overcome, and I answered that I grieved at the death of this cow, but that the news of it might have waited, nor did I see that there was any prodigy about the matter.

"Lord, that is not all," he went on in an awed voice, "the calf, which is male, seems to have upon it every mark of the holy Apis bull, or so says a priest of the temple who chanced to spend the night with me, and has seen it. Indeed already he has returned to Memphis to tell all the other priests the glad and wonderful news which by tomorrow or the next day will be known throughout Egypt."

Now I bethought me that I wished that priest had slept anywhere save in my overseer's house, for something warned me that this beast, in which I had no faith, having sought a higher worship than that of animals, whatever god the vulgar might believe them to incarnate, would bring trouble upon me. But as such heresies must be hidden, I asked him what the calf was like. He replied that it was black as ebony with a square spot of white upon its forehead and the figure of a white hawk with outstretched wings upon its back. Also on its pink tongue—wonder of wonders—was the figure of a *scarabaeus* in black.

Now I affected to be much surprised and said that I would come to see this holy calf, which in my heart I hoped, being so holy, would soon follow its dam to the underworld, or be gored to death of its foster-mother. But this was not to happen, for whenever it took milk the legs of that cow were tied together until it became accustomed to the changeling; also its horns were held.

Presently I met Belus and noting that he looked weary, asked him how he fared.

"Not too well," he answered. "Last night I consulted the stars, especially those that rule the destinies of us three, and until the dawn I have been at work upon their message."

"What was it?" I asked idly.

"This, Ramose: That because of some prodigy, trouble awaits us. Those stars enter an evil combination that foreshadows danger to all of us—great danger. Yet be not cast down, for in the end they emerge from this house of perils, or so my calculations tell me, and ride on into that good fortune which will endure until the end."

Now, though it is true that some of his prophecies seemed to have fulfilled themselves, perhaps because these came, not from stars, but from out of the hidden wisdom of his own soul, I did not believe overmuch in the divinations of Belus, I who always held that the great planets, sweeping ever on their eternal journey through the skies, could scarcely trouble themselves with the petty fate of men and women, or even influence them. Yet I was disturbed when he spoke of a prodigy, for suddenly I remembered the birth of this Apis calf and my own fears. So I told Belus what had chanced yonder at the farm while he watched the heavens.

Now it was his turn to be startled, for he answered,

"I put little faith in Apis, who is but a priest-made symbol. Yet, Ramose, all the Egyptians think otherwise, for to them he is a god incarnate upon earth in the flesh of a bull."

"Then may this god soon be disincarnate in heaven or elsewhere," I exclaimed, which was not to happen, for, as I have said, the brute lived and throve like any common calf.

When we had eaten Belus and I, Myra also for she would not be left behind, whether because she wished to behold this wonder or for other reasons, mounted our asses and rode to the farm to look upon the new-born calf. As soon as we were clear of the city I beheld a strange sight, for the road was black with people all talking and gesticulating, who, too, were travelling to behold the new god, or the place where it had appeared.

Avoiding these as much as might be, we came at length to the farm where a great crowd was gathered, who were being thrust back by priests and soldiers from the shed in which the calf lay. These people recognised me, and one cried out,

"Behold Ramose, the blessed of Heaven, upon whose beast the spirit of the gods has fallen in lightning. Behold Ramose and his beautiful daughter," (for the most of them believed Myra to be my daughter).

Another answered,

"Aye, behold him, Pharaoh's seed who one day may himself be Pharaoh."

"Aye," called yet another, "for otherwise how comes it that Apis is born in his house? It is a sign! It is a sign!"

So these fools clamoured till I wished that the earth would open and swallow them; yes, and Apis too.

After this we were admitted to the shed and saw the calf, which, save for its markings, was as are other calves. But the markings were there, and not painted, and when it opened its mouth to bellow, we perceived the black *scarabaeus* upon its tongue. Moreover round the shed were priests of Ptah upon their knees, praying and making oblations of flowers.

Myra wished to go in and stroke the beast, but one of these priests sprang up and dragged her back with threatening looks, muttering that it was not lawful for a woman to enter there, and that if she had escaped a curse she would be fortunate.

So we went home as quickly as we could, and afterwards these priests removed the calf whither I knew not, without so much as paying me its price, to keep it until such time as it should take the place of the old Apis, which was so near to death that its sarcophagus was already fashioned and in its niche at the burying-place of bulls some leagues away.

When my mother heard the news she was much rejoiced.

"When I learned that you had become a farmer, my son," she said, "it grieved me more even than when you told me that you had been a merchant, for both these trades are those of common people and unworthy of your blood, which on one side is that of kings and on the other that of warriors. Yet now I see that in all these matters Zeus, or Athene, has directed you, seeing that out of the trade you have won much wealth, while through the husbandry it has come about that the great god of the Egyptians has manifested himself in your house, so that because of this you and I, your mother, will grow famous throughout Egypt."

Thus spoke my mother who since she had left Pharaoh's household, where for a while she was a great power, had never been able to fit herself into the narrow bounds of private life, which, although she was rich, were all that remained to her after the death of her husband, the judge and officer, Tapert. Continually she looked back to the pomp and ceremony of Pharaoh's court, the martial guards, the blowing of trumpets, the heralds, the golden furnitures, the thrones and the garments woven with the royal symbols. Yes, and in her heart she dreamed and hoped that a day would come when through me once more she would move amidst all this glory, no longer as the mistress of the king, but as his mother.

It was for this reason, amongst others I have set out, that she desired to separate me from Myra, hoping that if once she were gone I might find a wife, however ancient or ill-favoured, in whom ran some drops of the true blood of the Pharaohs of Egypt. Therefore she set herself to make known far and wide the sign of favour which the gods of Egypt had given me in the birth of an Apis among my herd, and, as I learned afterwards, even wrote or sent messages to old friends of hers about the court, who had been servants of Apries, to tell them what had come to pass and to vaunt my wealth and favour among the people.

Soon all this reached the ears of Amasis who now was Pharaoh, and caused him to think that it would be well if he journeyed to Memphis to make an offering to the new Apis, or rather to the temple in which the beast was being reared and to the priests who guarded it; also to make sure who the man might be that was spoken of as a king's son and concerning whom the soothsayers made prophecies. For Amasis never forgot that he was a usurper who had won his throne by force of arms and had put his old master, the rightful Pharaoh, to death, or allowed him to be slain. Therefore he was afraid of any one who could claim that the true royal blood ran in his veins and, knowing this, I had not presented myself to him on my return to Egypt.

So in the end Amasis the Pharaoh came to Memphis, sailing up Nile with royal pomp and ceremony, and was received in state by the nobles, officers and people of the great city.

I was amongst those who watched him land, and noted that he was much changed from Amasis the general under whom I had served and who had saved my life from the anger of Apries years ago. For time, the cares of state and as some said, the love of wine, had whitened his hair and carved deep lines upon his rugged face, though still his eyes were pleasant, if now somewhat shifty and fear-haunted, as those of usurpers who have won their thrones through blood must ever be. Putting aside all ceremony, as of old he greeted us in his bluff, soldier fashion, speaking to us, not as a master or a god, but as an Egyptian to Egyptians, and calling us "Friends," and "Brothers," saying too how glad he was again to visit Memphis after many years and to meet its lords and people.

Then he mounted in a chariot and was conducted to the old palace of the Pharaohs that had hastily been made ready to receive him. Here, later, he held a court, at which we of the Council of the City were made known to him, one by one. When my turn came, for I thought it best to appear before him boldly, and he heard my name, he glanced at me sharply, also at Belus who followed me, and started.

"Surely, Count Ramose, and you, Belus the Physician, we have met before," he said.

"Yes, Pharaoh," I answered, "though long years have passed since then."

"Is it true, Count Ramose, that Apis has appeared among your herds?" he asked.

I answered it was true that I had been so honoured of the gods.

Again he looked at me as though he would search my heart, and inquired where I lived.

I told him that being unwed I had made my home in the house of my mother, the widow of the King's Companion, Tapert, who once was governor of Memphis.

"Is it so, Count?" he said. "Then at sunset Pharaoh will visit you there without ceremony, and perhaps the lady your mother and you will give him a bite of food and a cup of wine, also without ceremony, asking none to meet him save those of the household."

I bowed, muttering that the honour was too great, whereon he waved me and Belus aside and began to talk to others.

As soon as we might I escaped from that court with Belus, and returned home in my chariot which I drove myself, Belus riding with me. At the door I sprang out and called to the running footmen to lead away the horses.

"Belus," I said, "I am troubled. Why does Pharaoh wish to visit me thus?"

"I do not know, Ramose," he answered, looking down. "Perhaps to talk about Apis, or perhaps to speak with us of what happened when we were younger and the wars of long ago when he was but a general, for they say that although his memory has grown weak, those days are still dear to him. Who can tell? We shall learn in time."

"Yes, Belus, and I pray that it may not be more than we wish to know."

Then I went in to tell my mother what had chanced. She heard and broke into rejoicings which vexed me.

"Pharaoh coming to this house!" she said. "Truly the honour is great. Every high lady in Memphis will envy me. I must make ready."

"You forget, Mother," I said, "that he who comes killed him who was my father and your lord."

"My lord, yes, who soon wearied of me—one light love among many—and gave me in marriage to another man. And your father, yes, who sought to put you to death for small cause, from which end you were saved by this Amasis, wherefore I forgive him all. Moreover, it is said that he had naught to do with the slaying of Apries whom the Egyptians killed without his knowledge. But I must be gone; the time is short, the time is very short and there is much to make ready," and turning, she fled away.

Such is woman, thought I to myself. One comes who seized the throne of her lord and her son's father and brought him to his end. Yet because he is Pharaoh she rejoices as though she were about to be visited by a god—and Belus who had been watching, nodded his head and smiled as though he read what was passing in my mind, which no doubt he did.

Then I retired to my own chamber and stayed there for the rest of that day, discussing problems with Belus, or reading histories, for the house was in a tumult, and when I sought her to continue our studies, even Myra was not to be found.

Servants flew here and there, messengers went out and returned laden with goods in baskets, the cooks gathered to themselves other cooks and worked at their business as though their lives hung on it, the steward of the household ran to and fro cursing at all he met by the names of evil gods, the butler drew ancient wines from the cellars and tasted them until his eye grew dim and his voice thick, gardeners brought in plants and flowers that they had grown or purchased, and set them about the rooms. All of these things I saw through my window-place, or the half-drawn curtains of my doorway, and grew more and more vexed and troubled. At length when I was no longer able to bear the noise and confusion and the sound of my mother's voice grown shrill and angry as she scolded the servants, telling them first one thing and then another, I fled away to that large upper chamber of the house where Belus slept and worked.

Here I found him calm as ever, studying a map he had made upon a papyrus sheet, of the stars, or of certain of them, and turning balls hung upon wires round a larger ball, which he said figured the sun and the planets.

"You seem disturbed, Ramose," he said as he checked the motion of these swinging balls.

"And you seem calm," I answered angrily.

"Yes, Ramose, because I study the stars which are very far away and very quiet, while you study the earth, which is very near, and to-day more noisy than is common. If you wish for quiet, fix your heart upon the stars and leave the earth alone."

"And what do your stars tell you, Belus?"

"Much that as yet I have found no time to interpret fully, but above all this—that soon you and I will make a long journey. I believe it is one which I have awaited many years," he added slowly and in a cold voice.

"Over the edge of the world?" I asked, staring at him.

"No—not yet, I think, but—"

Here the chamberlain rushed into the room and from below I heard my mother's voice,

"My lord!" he said, "my lord Count, the lady Chloe says that you must attire yourself in your best, not forgetting to put on the gold chain that the late good god who was Pharaoh, gave to you, and all your other marks of rank."

"The late good god!" I muttered. "The late good god whose throat was cut by butchers in a boat upon the Nile."

"But who afterwards was embalmed in the best fashion, wrapped in gold, and buried with great glory and all his household wealth by the present good god, which should console him for his many woes," interrupted Belus mockingly.

Then my mother's voice rose shrilly from the foot of the stairs, calling to the chamberlain who fled, as presently I did also to do her bidding and array myself. But as I went I said,

"Belus, hearken. Search out another house for you and me and Myra, for here I can dwell no more. And let it be far away."

"I do not think there is any need," answered Belus. "I think that we should not dwell there long because the stars have appointed one for us that is very far away. Still I will do your bidding."

As the sun began to set I went to the portico of the house, followed by Belus who was clad in the robes of a physician and wore the cap of an astrologer. Scarcely were we come there when the sound of chariot wheels and of trampling horses told us that Pharaoh was at hand. Then he appeared surrounded by a mounted guard. He was arrayed as a general, and wore no emblem of royalty save a small golden *uraeus* upon his helm.

Leaping from the chariot he ordered the officer in charge of the escort to depart with his men, and return at a certain hour. Then quite unattended he walked up the steps of the portico and greeted me who stood bowing before him, in his old jovial fashion. And yet there was something lacking; his voice did not ring true as once it did; I felt a change.

"See, Ramose, how well I trust you," he said. "Better indeed than I would most men who might hold that they had a blood quarrel with me. That is because we are old comrades in war and therefore there is a bond of fellowship between us. Rise, man, rise, for here we are not Pharaoh and subject, but two soldiers met to drink a cup of wine together."

As he spoke my mother appeared, still looking fair enough, though the wonderful grace and slightness of form which once were hers had departed from her.

"The lady Chloe!" he cried, catching her hand as she curtseyed low, and kissing it. "Surely, after all these years I know her again. Tell me, Lady, have you made a bargain with your own Aphrodite that defying time, you remain so fair and young, you whom I used to worship from afar at the court of Sais, wishing, to speak truth, that for your sake I stood in Pharaoh's sandals?"

Thus he went on, bantering in his bluff fashion, for never did Amasis lose his manners of the camp, while my mother reddened to the brow, muttering I know not what, till of a sudden he ceased and stared past her.

Turning to discover at what he gazed so fixedly, I saw that Myra had followed my mother, as no doubt she had been bidden to do. There she stood uncertain, swaying a little like a palm in the wind; Myra, yet a new Myra. For she was apparelled, as to my knowledge she had never been before, in beautiful silken robes, while round her throat and arms were fine jewels of gold and gems, with necklets of large pearls, those same priceless ornaments which were the heritage that her dying mother had given to me in the tent upon the battlefield. On her brow, too, was a circlet of gold set with pearls and rising to a point, while ropes of pearls were twined among the waving tresses of her brown hair, which was spread like a cloud about her shoulders and almost to her waist. Most beautiful she looked thus in her young loveliness, yet most splendid, like to a queen indeed. Never before did I know how beautiful she was. So it seemed Amasis thought also, which was why he stared at her, then asked,

"Who is this fair maiden, lady Chloe?"

"Myra," answered my mother, "known as the daughter of my son Ramose."

"And therefore a granddaughter of Apries and of the royal blood of Egypt," said Amasis aloud, but as one who thinks to himself. "Well, she is very fair, so fair that were I a younger man I think that I should ask her to draw near to the throne of Egypt, which as it is I shall not do. Worthy of a king, she is. Yes, worthy of a king!"

Now I bowed purposing to show Amasis that Myra was not my daughter, and to repeat to him the tale of her finding upon the battlefield, which doubtless he had forgotten, but as the first words passed my lips the curtains to the right were drawn and the chamberlain, appearing between them, cried out that all was ready.

"Good," said Amasis, "let us eat, for know, I starve, whose lips have touched nothing all this day of ceremony," and taking my mother by the hand he led her into the large chamber now seldom used, where Tapert, her husband, feasted the nobles when he was a high officer of Memphis.

Here a table was spread, made fair with flowers and cups of gold and silver, for it had pleased Tapert to collect such vessels. At the centre of this table was Tapert's chair of state, a gilded, cushioned seat that my mother had prepared for Amasis. In it he sat himself while the rest of us stood, behind him.

"What!" he cried, "am I to eat alone like a prisoner in his cell? Not so. Forget, I pray you, my hosts, that for an hour I fill Pharaoh's throne, and come, sit at my side and let us be friendly."

So we placed ourselves at the curved board, my mother on his right, Myra on his left, and I beyond my mother with Belus beyond Myra.

The feast began, a wonderful feast, since it seemed to me that from it was missing no luxury known in Egypt. Indeed, I wondered much how in a few short hours my mother had made so rich a preparation.

Amasis was hungry and ate heartily, praising each dish, as well he might, for he could have tasted no better at his own table. Also he drank without stint, of the strong old wine of Cyprus with which Tapert had stored his cellars, and grew merry.

"Where have you been all these years, Ramose?" he asked. "I remember that we parted at Pelusium after we had defeated Evil-Merodach—ah! that was a battle and one that went the right way for us. It seems a long while ago, and so it is, for since then Merodach sat for a little hour upon the throne of Nebuchadnezzar at Babylon and is gone wherever the Babylonians go when they are dead, and two more after him, the last of them but a boy who reigned three months and then I think was murdered. Now Nabonidus is king there, chosen by the people of Babylon to be their ruler, they say, because he hates the sight of a sword as they have come to do."

"What is known of this Nabonidus, Pharaoh?" I asked.

"To me little enough, Ramose, except that by birth he is not royal—like some other kings," he added laughing and pointing to himself.

"May it please Pharaoh, I know something of him," said Belus speaking for the first time, "for when we both were younger I was his friend. He comes of a great House that has grown wealthy by trade. His nature is, or was, kindly and gentle. He was very fond of learning also and especially of all that has to do with bygone kings and times, and written records and ancient temples. Lately I have heard from Babylon where there are still some who write to me, that he spends his days in studying such matters and in rebuilding the old shrines of the gods, leaving most of the business of the State to be dealt with by his son, the Prince Belshazzar."

"Belshazzar!" exclaimed Amasis. "I have heard much of this man, more than I wish indeed. What of him, Astrologer? Is he, too, learned and gentle?"

"Nay, Pharaoh. I knew him also in his youth when he dealt very wickedly with—a friend of mine. He is a fierce and cruel man, ambitious and violent, but one of ability when he can turn from his pleasures and his wine."

"So I have heard also, and further that being an old fool, Nabonidus trusts all to him, signing whatever his son Belshazzar puts before him. Yes, he does this even at a time when Babylon is threatened by Cyrus the Persian. Therefore through his councillors and in the name of Nabonidus the King, Belshazzar seeks an alliance with Egypt upon whom Nebuchadnezzar was wont to war, as we know. In earnest of it he offers his sister in marriage to me, and asks that a princess of the royal House of Egypt should be given to his father Nabonidus who is lately widowed, that she may be Queen of Babylon and all its empire, and take with her as a dowry the friendship of Egypt."

Here he paused to drink wine, then added more as though he were speaking to himself than to us,

"But I have no princess to send to him, and Apries who went before me, left no daughters save one who is already married, old and childless, for whom even the ancient Nabonidus would not thank me."

Then again he paused, looking about him. His eyes fell upon Myra who was seated by him leaning forward so that she might hear all.

"Beautiful," he muttered, "most beautiful."

A thought seemed to strike him for he started, then began to talk to Myra, asking her of her life at Memphis, and whether it would not please her to shine in a king's court.

95

"Nay, O Pharaoh," she answered, "I am very happy here where I follow after learning with Belus for my teacher, and for the rest occupy myself with simple things."

"What do you learn, maiden?" asked Amasis "The languages of other lands?"

"Yes," replied Myra with pride, "I know Greek and the tongues of Cyprus, that of Babylon also, and can write them all."

"Thoth, god of letters, led by the hand of Hathor and Bes, gods of love and beauty, must have attended at your birth, maiden," exclaimed Amasis in the voice of one who had drunk too much, as leaning forward, he patted her on the hand.

Now I looked at my mother who, fearing some folly on the part of Pharaoh and understanding that I wished her to be gone, rose from her seat, bowed and departed, taking Myra with her. Amasis waited till the curtains had swung to behind them. Then he looked round the room and seeing that we were alone, for at a sign from me the servants had left us, of a sudden he seemed to grow sober, as I remembered he could always do if he wished.

"Ramose," he said, "now that the women have left us I would have a word with you, which was why I came here. Nay, Belus, do not go; it is always well to have a water-drinker for a witness."

I bowed and waited.

"Ramose," he went on, "if I were wise, I think that I should cause you to be killed."

"That Pharaoh cannot do," I said, "having eaten of my bread. Yet why should he cause me to be killed whom in the past he saved from death?"

"Because times have changed and we change with them, Ramose. Because without doubt you are of the old royal blood of Egypt, if on one side only, whereas not a drop of it flows in my veins, and but little in those of my sons, for those wives of mine who are called royal were made so by decree rather than by birth. Because, too, this is known among the people who, as my spies have told me, treat you like a prince and in their private talk speak of you as one who in a day to come may sit in Pharaoh's seat. Lastly because an Apis has been born among your cattle which the vulgar take for a sign, yes, and the priests who are the real power in Egypt. Certainly therefore it would be wiser that you should die, or so I think, who desire to be the forefather of a great dynasty that shall rule for hundreds of years."

"I am in Pharaoh's hands," I answered coldly. "He has thousands at his command to do his will, whereas I am defenceless. If Pharaoh desires to mingle my blood with my wine, what more is there to say? Let him who slew the father, slay the son and make an end."

Now, whether by design or because it was so, again suddenly Amasis seemed to grow drunken and answered,

"Aye, why not? It would save many doubts and troubles. Belus here will bear witness that we quarrelled and that I killed you in self-defence," and rising he half-drew the sword which he wore with his general's armour.

Belus sprang up and slipping behind Amasis, began to talk into his ear. Although he spoke so low all he said, or the meaning of it, came to my sense made keen by danger. It went thus:

"Pharaoh forgets that in this quiet place his armies avail him nothing. Here he can die like other men. Let him look."

Amasis glanced over his shoulder, to see that there was a knife in the hand of Belus and that its point was very near his throat.

"If Pharaoh died," went on Belus, "would it not be easy to hide him away while some went out and declared that he had been gathered to Osiris and that the gods who had caused Apis to be born in his house, had appointed Ramose, the son of Apries, to fill his throne? And if this were done, would not Memphis listen, and what Memphis says, would not all Egypt say, and would not the army welcome Ramose with a shout?"

"Perhaps you are right," said Amasis, again sobered of a sudden. "Ramose, know that I do not wish to kill you if only I can be sure that you will not plot against me. Believe me, neither did I wish to kill your father. After the army had made me king, yonder in Cyrenia and against my will, I kept him to rule with me, but he plotted against me and at last came the end. They tell me that you are doing likewise, and now Apis has been born amongst your herds which Egypt will take for a sign. If I spare you, how can I be certain that you will spare me?"

"Because I have no wish to sit upon any throne, Pharaoh, I who having enough to satisfy my every want, desire only to lead a peaceful, learned life. Is it my fault that an Apis is born amongst my herd?"

"No, Ramose, but it is a sign sent by the gods; at least the people will so interpret it and therefore you must bear the blame. For the rest, you may change your mind. I had no wish to be a king, yet a crown was thrust upon me, which could not have happened if Apries had killed me first, as, had he been wise, he would have done. Still as a lad you were ever honest; so, asking no oaths I believe you, for what are oaths when it comes to grips? Indeed, what I said was but to try you, so let it be forgotten. Yet Belus has threatened me with a knife, why then should he not die, he, the threatener of Pharaoh, who, as any priest will tell you, is a god—no less?"

Now Belus, showing no fear, answered boldly,

"I think that I answered that question long ago, Pharaoh, in a certain general's tent upon the borders of Egypt, before a great battle against the Babylonians."

"I remember," said Amasis. "You said the stars appointed me to be king which has come true, though at the time the words seemed folly," and he looked at him not without awe.

"I said more than that, Pharaoh. As my life seemed to be in danger then, as it does now, I told you that those stars declared also that if you killed me, my blood would call for your blood and that you too would die. I repeat those words, for the stars do not change their story. If you are weary of life and rule, strive to bring death upon me who never harmed you."

Amasis stared at him and his ruddy face grew pale.

"I think that you have power, Babylonian," he said, "if of a different sort from mine. Fear nothing. You shall go safe from me, and your master also, so long as he does not try to plot against me, or to take my place."

"Pharaoh is very wise," answered Belus in the same cold voice, "so wise that I will tell him something that I wished to keep secret. Already by his threats he has earned much evil at the hand of fate."

"What evil, man?"

"This—that though he live out his life in peace and splendour, yet it shall not be so with him who comes after, the son of his body. Storm-clouds are gathering in the east, O Pharaoh."

"Have done, Babylonian," broke in Amasis. "I would hear no more of your evil-opened talk. Our pact is made—it is enough."

"As Pharaoh pleases," said Belus bowing, while with quick eyes he searched his face.

Then Amasis turned to me and asked,

"What happened to you after we parted years ago, Ramose? I remember that you went away with a little child about whom you told some idle tale, but who in truth was your daughter, that same maiden who dwells with you today."

"She was not my daughter, Pharaoh—"

Thus I began, but he stopped me with a wave of his hand and his rough, soldier's laugh, saying,

"Oh! deny it not, Ramose. Have we not all heard of you and that

98

beautiful Syrian queen, a very flower of love whose favour you had the luck to win as a lad, though you brought her none? Did not the whole camp believe that the child was your daughter born of this queen or another woman perchance, whom you carried with you from Egypt to save her from the Syrians, and is she not proclaimed here as your daughter by your own mother and all in Memphis, yes, your daughter and the grandchild of Apries, as indeed may be read in her royal air? So anger me no more with your denials, as though I were a priest to whom you must plead purity, for I will not listen to them, who hate liars. Tell me, what chanced to you after you escaped from the wrath of Apries your father?"

Then thinking it wiser not to cross his wild, uncertain mood, which I set down to the wine that he had drunk, over this matter, small as I held it, I told Amasis how I had journeyed to Cyprus and made my home there and grown rich by trade.

"And why did you not stay in Cyprus, Ramose?" he asked suspiciously.

"Because I desired to see my mother from whom I had been parted for many years, and being Egyptian born, to dwell in Egypt where I believed that now I should be safe as Pharaoh's friend. Also Belus warned me that disaster was about to fall upon the city where we dwelt, which indeed happened, for after I had left it, Salamis was shaken to the ground by earthquake and those who dwelt in the house that had been mine, were crushed."

"Belus again!" exclaimed Amasis. "By the gods I would take him for my soothsayer, were I not sure that of me he would always prophesy more ill than good, and being a physician also, could bring it to pass, if so he chose. Therefore I leave you Belus, praying you to guard him well, who swears, or so I understand, that his death and mine will not be far apart. To tell the truth I have no fancy to see Osiris out of his wrappings before I must, or to chat with Apries and others at his table. No, no, keep Belus and live at ease, Ramose, even if your cows bear an Apis once a year, and be sure of Pharaoh's favour and all that he can give you, so long as you leave Pharaoh in peace. And now that we have settled these matters, let us drink a last cup together in pledge of them, Ramose, of whom I purpose to make a viceroy in Kush or elsewhere, or perchance to send upon an embassy. For you are one who should be great in war and council, and not spend your life in breeding beasts and growing grain, like any mud-born thickhead who calls himself a noble and to prove it, flogs his slaves; yes, one who should serve Pharaoh and prop up his throne, to his vantage and your own."

Then having drunk, as Belus and I pretended to do also, he set down his cup and walked with us, somewhat unsteadily, to the chamber where my mother sat. Here at the doorway he bade Belus and myself discover whether his escort was in attendance, and if not, to wait till it came and then advise him, who meanwhile would talk with my mother and bid her farewell.

So we went because we must, for in such matters Pharaoh must not be disobeyed, and for a long while tarried in the porch. At length the escort came, and with it the chariot of Pharaoh.

We returned to make report. The curtains were drawn over the entrance of my mother's sitting chamber. Thrusting them apart I saw her seated on a couch with Amasis at her side. He was leaning forward talking into her ear, while from time to time she nodded her head, as though in ascent. Perceiving me between the curtains she laid her fingers on her lips, as though to teach him silence, then rose, calling to me to enter. I did so and bowing to Pharaoh, told him that his guard and chariot waited on his pleasure.

"So much the worse," he grumbled, "seeing that now after some happy hours in the fellowship of old comrades and fair ladies, like an ox harnessed to a water-mill I must get me to my work again. See, now what it is. There is the matter of the repair or rebuilding of these temples of Memphis to be considered, for it must be done cost what it may, to please the priests—I mean the gods with whom no Pharaoh dare be out of favour. I am minded to put you in charge of that business, Ramose, because having been a merchant as well as a learned man and a lover of what is beautiful, you would save me from being cheated by roguish architects and craftsmen. Next I must up Nile to Abydos to tend the ruined shrines of Osiris, and thence to Thebes on a like errand; also to make offerings at the sepulchres of the ancient kings, though where their mummies may be today none knows, for thieves have been at work with all of them. Then back here again, perchance to bury Apis that they say is dying, with fitting pomp yonder in the desert where those gods lie. After that away to Sais to deal with matters of state and to face the eternal Babylonian trouble, to say nothing of that of the Persians, as best I can, as well as the quarrels of the women of my own household which will pursue me, as I think, to the underworld.

"Oh! who would be a Pharaoh? Ramose, be guided by me, I pray you, and never seek to be a Pharaoh, even should a mother urge it in your ears, though, this I am sure the lady Chloe, being wise, would never do. Now farewell to all of you, and not least, my hostess, to that fair grandchild of yours, Ramose's daughter, whose beauty, were it seen, would set the world aflame and lift her to a throne. Farewell, my hosts, and farewell, too, Belus, shepherd of the stars, or by them shepherded—I know not which. Belus the far-sighted, to whom the gods unveil and who handles wisdom as a soldier does his knife,—or rather who handles both wisdom—and a knife. Farewell, all. Ho! slaves, summon the officers to conduct Pharaoh to his chariot."

Thus Amasis came, and thus, bewildering us and hiding his purposes with this long, rambling speech, as dust obscures a chariot, he went from my mother's house at Memphis. When he had staggered down the steps and departed, Belus and I looked at each other, saying nothing. Then I turned to seek my mother, but she too had gone.

CHAPTER 10

The Happy House

With pomp and ceremony Pharaoh Amasis departed up Nile to Thebes. Yet ere he went he laid various offices on me as one marked for his especial favour; high offices not to be refused, to fill which I must take public oaths, swearing by the gods to be faithful to him and his House under pain of death and the curse of heaven. Also he appointed me as overseer of the architects employed upon the rebuilding of sundry temples, and especially of the great shrine of Ptah in Memphis.

Thus it came about that soon I must work from dawn till dark as never I had worked before, scarcely finding leisure to eat, much less to read with Myra or even to talk with her, of whom now I saw but little. When I met my mother, however, which was not often for I was out before she rose, and for the most part returned only after she had sought her bed, I noted a change in her. She seemed to be full of mystery and to follow more than ever after foolish pomps, seating herself in a chair that was like to a throne, with servants who held fans standing behind her, and even wearing marks of royalty when there were no strangers there to see, such as a circlet of gold upon her head from which rose the *uraeus* snake.

The sight of this angered me, so much that at last I asked her sharply what it meant and if she wished to bring trouble on me, by aping a rank that was not hers.

"Not so," she answered smiling. "Yet may not she who has borne a son to him who was Pharaoh bear the mark of royalty, that is, when she has special leave so to do, from him who is Pharaoh?"

"I do not know what you mean, my mother, but I do know that if this were the law, there would be many women in Egypt wearing the royal *uraeus*," I answered bluntly, adding, "I pray you therefore to lay that ornament aside lest my head should pay the price of what you set upon your own."

102

Then growing angry, she rose and left me as one who might answer but who would not, nor did she appear again before me adorned like Pharaoh's queen or daughter. Indeed I saw her but seldom and when we met she would rarely speak to me.

****

On a certain feast day, that appointed to some god when none laboured, Belus said,

"You bade me buy you a house and I have done so out of your moneys in my hands," (for I trusted all my wealth to Belus). "Also with the help of Myra I have furnished it. Come now, and look upon your new home."

"Does my mother know of this?" I asked astonished.

"I have not told her," he answered. "Yet I think she guesses. At least she said to me but yesterday that perhaps it was as well that you should live apart because you no longer agreed together; moreover she held it that it would be more fitting to your new dignities that you should have a dwelling of your own."

So I went to see this new abode and found it very beautiful. It was an old palace outside the great wall of the city, and therefore surrounded by a large garden, of which, because of the narrow space, there were few within the wall. In the ancient days when the Pharaohs lived at Memphis, this palace, it was said, had been that of the heir of the king. In later times, however, it had become a private dwelling, also a home of priests; but now for a generation, save for caretakers, it had been deserted though still used as a store-house so that the roof and walls were saved from decay. Further, the gardens had been hired to a husbandman who grew in them fruit and vegetables for sale in the city, also beneath the palm trees green barley for fodder.

Now all this had passed by purchase to me and already Belus, having all my revenues at his command, had set numbers of the best artificers and artists in Memphis to work to make the place beautiful, and once more a fitting home for a great noble or a prince. Moreover Myra was in the secret and throwing her heart into the business, laboured joyously that our new home—for never for a moment did she doubt that it would be hers as well as mine—should be made even fairer than that at Salamis, one of the most perfect indeed in all Egypt.

To this end all the furnishings which I had brought from Cyprus, the statues, the inlaid and enamelled chests, the chairs and beds, the vessels of gold and silver, and I know not what besides, which for years it had been my pleasure to collect as the choicest wares and examples of ancient art from Syria, Cyprus and Egypt, were gathered from the places where they had been stored because my mother's house would not contain them. Here and there Myra said they should stand, even before the rooms were ready to receive them, so that they must be covered up with cloths for fear of damage by the artists and the plasterers.

Also through Belus, who was foolish where she was concerned and, like her old nurse, Metep, unable to withstand her smallest fancy, Myra bought in Memphis the loveliest that it had to sell of hangings and carpets and couches and silver swinging lamps, all of which she set about the chambers, especially in those that were to be allotted to me. Yet when I entered her own I found it with bare walls and but plainly furnished; a low bed of white wood, some stools and chairs with feet shaped like to those of antelopes, also of white wood and hide-seated, and three chests to hold her garments, painted with scenes of wild-fowl disporting themselves among lotus plants, or rushing in alarm through papyrus reeds.

"How is this?" I asked. "My chamber is as that of Pharaoh, while yours might be the sleeping-place of the daughter of a village sheik."

"Because I would have it so," she answered, tossing her head. "Moreover in time to come the walls shall be painted, when I have finished the design and Belus can find an artist who is not a fool."

"I have found one," said Belus.

"Who is that artist?" she asked.

"Yourself," Belus answered, laughing drily, then turned and fled before she could scold him.

Indeed I was the only one who did not laugh over all this business when in the end I found that it had cost me the quarter of my fortune, no less.

"What does it matter?" said Belus in reply to my complaining. "What does anything matter, especially when there is plenty left which gathers day by day; that is, if it pleases Myra?"

"You are right," I said, "nothing matters if it pleases Myra. Now she will have little left for which to wish."

"I am not so sure," said Belus, and went away before I could ask him what he meant.

At length we took up our abode in this fine new home, although as yet it was far from finished. My mother came to view it, borne in a chair such as was used by a wife of Pharaoh when she went abroad, and when she discovered that all had been planned by Myra, found much fault with every thing, saying that I should have done better to be guided by her own purer Grecian tastes.

"Still," she added, "the place is fine and the furnishings and decorations are of small account, for when your daughter Myra leaves it to become the consort of some mighty man, they can be changed."

"I do not understand you, my mother," I answered. "Myra does not wish to change her state; also, she is not my daughter."

"Then, Ramose, if she is not your daughter, why is she not your wife? Surely you would make nothing less of her."

Having shot this bitter arrow, she went away without waiting for an answer.

"What does she mean?" I asked of Belus, who had heard these words.

"What she says, or so I think. Hearken, Ramose. There is some plot afoot. I know not what it is, but it has to do with Myra. If you would keep her at your side, Ramose, let it be as your wife. Remember that your mother is right. If you give it out that she is not your daughter and she continues to dwell in your house with no other woman save an old nurse, although you forget it because she has lived with you from a babe, you will cast a slur upon her name."

Now hearing this I was much disturbed.

"Are you mad, Belus?" I asked. "Have we three not always lived together? And for the rest, is it fitting that I who am almost old enough to be her father and who for years have forsworn women, should wed this young maid?"

"Would it then grieve you so much to take her was a wife, Ramose?" asked Belus in his quiet fashion.

Now I felt the blood come to my face, as I answered,

"It would not grieve me at all; to tell the truth it would delight me more than anything on earth. It was not of myself that I thought, but of the poor child who, if I spoke to her of marriage with me, would take it as a command and obey because she held it to be her duty, for that reason abandoning all hope of a husband of her own years."

"I thought that not so long ago she might have pleased herself in this matter, and would not, Ramose."

"It is true, but because a woman turns from one man it does not follow that she turns from all. After all that count was an empty-headed coxcomb; there are better than he in Memphis."

"It is a strange thing, Ramose, that those who are wise in nine matters, are often foolish in the tenth, and those whose sight is so keen that it can note a lizard on a housetop, often cannot discern the pitfall that yawns before their feet, or the sharp stone that will lame them. Such, I hold, is your case, Ramose. Now I pray you, if you have any faith in what you call my foresight and my vision, put this matter to the proof and show me that I am wrong."

"How, Belus?"

"By asking Myra whether or not it would please her to become your wife. Ask her, and soon. Tomorrow Pharaoh returns from Thebes to bury the Apis that is dead, and then passes on at once to Sais."

"What has that to do with Myra and myself?" I asked angrily, because, to tell the truth, I knew that Belus never spoke without reason. Words that from another would signify little or nothing, on his lips were full of meaning.

"More than you think, perhaps, Ramose," he replied, adding,

"Do you promise to prove that I am wrong, if you can, not next year, or next moon, but this very day?"

"Yes. That is, how can I who must go at once to attend to matters in the city that cannot be postponed?"

"You return to supper, I believe, and after supper it is customary for Myra and you to read together. Do you promise?"

"To please you I promise, though I do not know why you should force me to give Myra pain and to bring shame upon myself."

"Perhaps ere long you will find out. However you have promised and it is enough, for when did you ever break your word, Ramose?"

Then he went, leaving me wondering where I had heard those words before. Ah! it came back to me—from the lips of Myra herself after that boastful fop had asked her in marriage, and she had made me swear that I would protect her from all men. How came it then that these two spoke as with one voice? Had they agreed together to ply me with the same flattery? Nay, that was not in the nature of either of them; they did but say what they believed. They had set me, a man full of weakness and of failings, like a statue upon a pylon or a pyramid, one to be admired as higher than others; one to be loved more than others. This I could understand in the case of Belus who with all his learning and gifts from heaven was but a fond philosopher who, being childless and with few friends in his exile, had cherished me from my boyhood.

But what of Myra who knew all my faults and follies and must suffer from my moods? Could it be that there was something in her heart which caused her to forgive these many imperfections and to gild my clay with the gold of love? I did not know, but as I had promised Belus, I would discover the truth before I slept that night. Oh! if it should prove that this sweetest of all maidens loved me, not as a child loves her father, but as a woman loves a man, then how blessed would be my lot. Nay, it was too much to hope and I must be on my guard; I must watch lest her kind heart, duty and a desire to please, should put on the mask of love.

****

I went about my business which was very urgent, for much must be made ready before Pharaoh returned upon the morrow, asking account of my labours under his royal commission. All day I worked in the heat of the sun, much vexed with those that had failed me and with the foolishness of a self-willed architect, and at last as it sank, wearied out, was borne to my new home.

Here I bathed and clad myself in clean garments of linen. Then led by a servant I went to the eating-chamber, a very fine room where once the royal princes of old Egypt had banqueted with their friends and women, that now cleaned and repaired, we used for the first time. This apartment, of which the walls were painted with scenes of feasting and of gay sports, somewhat faded perhaps, seeing that the artist who limned them had been dead for hundreds upon hundreds of years, opened on to a gallery that looked over the gardens and the intervening lands down upon the distant Nile. From this gallery or portico the room was separated by painted columns formed of heads of Hathor, goddess of love, between which columns hung rich curtains that the furnishers had placed there only that day, those that Pharaoh's sons had used having rotted many generations gone.

In the centre of this beautiful room, illumined by hanging lamps that we had brought with us from Cyprus, Myra had set a table of black wood inlaid with electrum, and on it cups of gold and silver taken from my store, and alabaster vases filled with flowers. Here at this fair table I ate my first meal in that house, Belus sitting at one side of it and I at its head. At its foot, in the place of the Lady of the House, was Myra who in honour of this event had been pleased to array herself in her richest garments and ornaments, such as she had worn at the feast my mother had given to Pharaoh. Thus with the lamplight falling on her she looked beautiful indeed, I think the most beautiful woman that ever I saw, except perhaps Atyra whose loveliness was of a richer order and more matured. It was strange to see that this Atyra's memory should rise up and refuse to leave me on that night when I did not desire its fellowship. Yet it was so; had her spirit been standing at my side, like the Double watching in a tomb, she could not have been more present.

Myra was in her merriest mood. She laughed and talked and jested, till at length I asked what made her so joyous.

107

"Oh! many things, Ramose," she answered, "but chiefly because tonight I am like a slave whose fetters have been struck off and whose lord has granted her freedom."

"When did you wear fetters, Myra?"

"Till yesterday, Ramose, yonder in your mother's house, where, though you knew it not, I was always watched. Here I am free—free! Belus, first of prophets, be kind. Use your skill, Belus, and tell me my fortune. Here is water into which you may gaze; without are stars— that is, unless the moon has devoured them; here is my hand covered with a hundred tiny lines. Gaze into the water, read the stars and the birth-writings stamped upon my flesh, and tell me my fortune. Tell me that I shall have many years of joy in this place. Do you know what was its ancient name? I have discovered it from an old man who works in the garden who had it from his grandfather. It was called the Happy House in the bygone days when it was the home of princes and great lords. Tell me that it will be the Happy House for me and for Ramose and for you too, dear Belus."

Now Belus shook his head, saying that his arts were needless because her words had already fulfilled her wish. Still she would not let him be, but went on teasing him till at length he said,

"Give me that little lily you wear upon your breast, O foolish maid, who cannot be content with the hour and its joys."

She obeyed. He took the fair white lily, warm from her bosom, and cast it into a bowl of rich-hued glass that was filled with water for the dipping of hands when the meals were done, muttered some words that I could not understand, and breathed upon it; after which he watched it for a long while. Now, growing uneasy for I shrank from this jest who doubted whether Belus could play the conjurer even when he tried, he who was filled with so strange and true a wisdom, I rose and looked over his shoulder into the bowl.

There was the lily floating, but as I watched it seemed to lose its shape as though it had been grasped and crumpled; its whiteness also. The water, too, though this may have been fancy or because of the colour of the red Eastern glass, to my sight grew first to the hue of wine, and then to that of blood, so that suddenly I remembered the blood of murdered Atyra that lay beneath the robe upon the floor of her chamber at Sais, and shivered.

I glanced at the face of Belus and noted that it was not that of one who played a trick to please a girl. Nay, it was strained and anxious and on his brow appeared beads of sudden sweat. I was about to speak, or overthrow the bowl, but divining it although I stood behind him, he held up a finger and checked me. For a minute or more he went on watching, covering the most of the bowl with his hands, so that I could no longer see within it. Then his face changed and once more became quiet and impenetrable, also he sighed, a sigh of relief, such as is uttered when a great danger has passed by ourselves or one we love.

Removing his hands from the edge of the bowl, he said, "Look."

I did so and behold! there floated the little lily as white as it had been when it was gathered, in water as pure as when it was drawn from the well. He took the flower and gave it back to Myra, saying,

"Press it in a book, child, and cherish it all your life; nay, set it between two plates of crystal as a talisman."

"Oh! my lily," she cried, "how fair you are and how sweet you smell; although so small your fragrance perfumes the room. Ramose, you shall make me a present. You shall order the jeweller to enclose this little lily in a tiny shrine of crystal, hung upon a golden chain, such as I can always wear. That is, you shall do this tomorrow, tonight I will keep it for myself. But I forget! What did my magic flower tell you, Belus? Nay, do not shake your head. Speak, I command you, and truly. In the name of the Truth we worship, speak truly."

"Being thus adjured, it seems that I must obey," said Belus slowly. "Your magic lily told me that your wish will be fulfilled and that in this abode which is named the Happy House you will spend many years of such joy as is given to those who wander upon earth."

She clapped her hands rejoicing.

"Those are good words," she laughed; "those are most fortunate words."

"Yes, Myra, they are good and fortunate, wherefore forget them not when good fortune seems far away. You have not heard the end of them, Myra, which since you commanded me to speak all the truth, I must declare to you. Between this night of joy and those years of joy to come lies a space of fear and black doubt, such as crushes the hearts of mortals. Steel yourself to bear them, Myra, as others must who love you, as I did but now when I saw the white lily blacken in the cup and the water on which it floated turn to a pool of blood. Remember always, even when hope seems gone, that the lily will once more grow white and fragrant, and the water once more be pure."

"I will remember," she answered quietly and very gravely, who suddenly understood that this was no child's game, but something that the strength of Belus had wrung out of the clenched hand of Fate, something she could not understand, and perhaps that he himself did not altogether understand.

Belus rose and went; the servants came and did their office swiftly enough who were well trained, having been with me in Cyprus, leaving us alone.

"The place is hot," I said, "nor can we go to the chamber chosen for our studies, for it is not prepared, all is in confusion there. Come, Myra, let us sit without and watch the moon rise up on the Nile."

"Yes," she said, and led the way between the curtains to the portico or colonnade that was built along that front of the old palace which faced towards the Nile. Here were ancient marble seats and on one of these, that nearest to the corner of the house where a wall was built across the roofed-in colonnade, we sat ourselves down in the shadow.

"What did Belus mean, Ramose?" she asked, awaking from her silence. "Do you believe in these prophecies of his?"

"I am not sure, Myra. Sometimes I believe and sometimes I do not. Certainly some of them seem to have come true; but this may be by chance, for a wise physician who watches all things and has great knowledge of the hearts of men, cannot always read the future wrong, whether or not the stars reveal it to him. At least this last oracle of his is one of good omen, so let us accept it and be content."

"I am content, Ramose, now that we three are alone together as we were in Cyprus. Yonder I was not, for it seemed to me there, in your mother's house, I was like a bird in a cage or one about whom a net was being drawn."

"Why should my mother wish to play the spider to you?" I asked disturbed.

"I do not know, Ramose. Perhaps because she is jealous of me; perhaps because she wishes to use me who am called your daughter—always of late she speaks of me as your daughter when there are any to listen, as she did to Pharaoh—to advance your fortunes and her own. I say I do not know, but believe me, so it was; also that at the last she would have prevented me from coming here, aye and might have done so had it not been for Metep who outwitted her, how I will not tell you now for the tale is long. It is enough that tonight at last I am free and once more with you and Belus as we were at Salamis. Yet I pray you, Ramose, set a guard about this house that free I may remain, and near to you."

"Do you then desire always to remain near to me, Myra?"

"Aye, Ramose."

110

"You know that you are not my daughter, Myra, and indeed no kin of mine, whatever my mother or others may say."

"Aye, Ramose, I know it."

"Do you know, also, Myra, that it is hard for a man to dwell with such a one as you are who is not his daughter, and not to wish that she were even more than his daughter? Yes, that it is very hard, though it may chance that in years he might almost be her father?"

Myra sat up upon the seat, gripping the edge of it with her hands and glancing at me sideways, which things I could see in the twilight.

"Why is it hard? What do you mean, Ramose?" she asked in a low voice.

As she spoke the great moon appeared from a bank of cloud, her rays making a path of silver across the broad waters of the Nile and the cultivated land, flooding the pillared portico and striking upon the beautiful girl who sat at my side, her beast heaving, her lips parted. I gazed at her and of a sudden passion took hold of me. Yes, passion in its strength, and I knew that above all earthly things I desired her no longer as a daughter and a friend, but as my wife; yes, to be all my own.

"I mean, Myra," I answered, "I mean that I love you."

"This you have always done, Ramose."

"Aye, but now I love you in another fashion. Do you not understand?"

"I think I understand, Ramose."

"I suppose that it has been so for long, Myra. But to be plain I have been ashamed to tell you so, who was a man grown when you were but a babe. I have feared, Myra, lest if I did, you should hold it to be your duty to give yourself to me, not because of the hunger of your heart, but because it was I who asked it of you, to me, a man whose hair begins to grow grey upon his temples."

She smiled a little; the moonlight showed it; a somewhat mysterious smile such as is to be seen upon the carven faces of sphinxes, which told of secret thoughts hidden behind her eyes.

"You who are so wise, in some ways were ever foolish, Ramose," she answered and once more was silent, words that left me wondering, though in substance they did but repeat what Belus had said that morning.

Thrice I tried to speak, and thrice I failed, while still she watched me with that dreaming smile upon her face. At last in poor, bald syllables the common question broke from my lips.

"Myra, though I have seen some eight and thirty summers, can you love me as your husband?"

Very slowly she turned her head and now I saw that her cheeks glowed and that her wonderful dark eyes swam with tears. She strove to answer and in turn, failed. Then she took another road, sinking upon my heart and lifting her lips towards my own.

It was done. My arms were about her, her head rested on my shoulder.

"Oh! Ramose," she sobbed, "for all these years since I became woman, how could you be so blind?"

CHAPTER 11

The Burial of Apis

Of the rest of what passed between Myra and myself upon that night of joy nothing need be told. By degrees, stripped of all the trappings with which we mortals veil the truth, our love stood revealed in perfect beauty. It seemed that ever since she had come to womanhood Myra had desired to be to me all that woman can to man, and yet had so hid her secret that I guessed it not. It seemed, too, that as she loved me, so I had loved her and yet had buried that love beneath a hill of forms and self-deceiving falsehoods, pretending that I looked upon her only as a daughter and a ward given to me of heaven. But now the screens were down and behind them, pure and beautiful, appeared the naked truth.

At last we parted, but not before it was agreed between us that we would be wed at once; on the morrow if it might be, though this was doubtful, because for such a marriage formalities were needed, especially in the case of a man like myself upon whom many eyes were set, a man in whose veins royal blood was known to run. Moreover she who was to be my bride had been commonly reputed to be my daughter and as to this the truth must be registered by all of us before certain public officers, and in particular by myself, by Belus and by the old nurse, Metep, which matters would take time.

In truth they took longer than I thought, for stir as I would in the business three days went by before all was completed, because those who had to deal with them deemed it necessary to obtain the seal of a certain officer acknowledging that Myra was my ward, which officer was absent from Memphis.

I have named that night of betrothal and revelation a night of joy; yet it was not altogether so for the reason that nothing can be quite perfect on the earth. At length all was finished. We had told our tales, our last kiss was given and Myra had glided away to her chamber, turning again and again to look upon me. I stood alone in the portico leaning against a column and gazing upon the glory of the full moon shining over Nile. Of what did it remind me? Suddenly I remembered. It reminded me of just such a night as this when, long years ago, I and another woman seated amid ruined columns, had looked upon the moon shining over Nile and beneath her beams had kissed and clung. A shadow passed before me and to my strained sense almost it seemed as though it were the wraith of Atyra considering me with reproachful eyes.

If so, why should she reproach me who for all these years because of her had stood apart from woman, she who drew me into trouble when I was but a lad, and perished through the fierce jealousy of her ministers?

Oh! this was foolishness, yet the folly wore a cloak of fear. What if the new love told beneath the moon looking down on Nile, should also end in blood and terror, as did the old love told beneath the moon looking down on that same Nile? Nay, Belus had prophesied that it would not be so, and I put faith in Belus. Yet there the shadow moved, not beyond the columns, but in my heart, a shadow shaped of memories.

****

The forms were filled, the priest-lawyer from the temple of Thoth had written the marriage contract whereunder I settled the half of all I had on Myra, everything was prepared and Myra had left me. As she had no parents or other relatives from whom I could come to claim her as a bride, according to custom in case of maidens of high birth, she had been conducted with her woman, Metep the old nurse, to the temple of Hathor where she would spend the night in the care of priestesses. Here it was agreed, I must present myself at sunrise upon the following morning to name her my wife before the altar of Hathor and in the presence of the servants of the goddess.

She parted from me somewhat disturbed, reminding me that since she was an infant she had never slept away from the shelter of my roof, save when we were together upon a ship or in my mother's house, which was also my own, and that it seemed to her an evil thing that she should do so now.

I laughed away her fears, answering that on the morrow she would return and that thenceforward we should be together until death.

When Myra had gone I bethought me that I must ask my mother to be present at our marriage. Indeed it had been my wish to speak to her of this matter before, but when I said as much to Myra, she prayed me not to do so in such an earnest fashion that I let the business be. For the same reason I dismissed the thought which had come to me that instead of sleeping at the temple of Hathor, Myra should pass the night before our marriage at my mother's house. Yet now when she had gone to the temple in charge of the priestesses, to that house I went, knowing that it would seem strange if my mother were not present at the ceremony, also that she would be angry if she were not asked and think that Myra had wished to affront her.

Coming to the house, I entered, for the door was open, and went straight to the large chamber where my mother always sat. It was empty, nor could I find her in any other room. Thinking that she must be in the garden, I set out to search for her there, and on my way met an old woman who had been her servant for many years, from the time indeed when she dwelt at the court of Pharaoh Apries, my father.

"Where is the lady Chloe and where is everybody?" I asked.

"Oh! my lord Ramose," she answered, "I do not know where they are now, but some days ago the lady Chloe and the most of the household went away up Nile in a big boat, or perhaps they went in two boats."

"Up Nile! When, and what for?"

"I can't quite remember when, lord Ramose, for now that I am old my memory grows weak, but it may have been two days, or three; no, I think that it was four. As to why they went I am not certain, but it must have been for a great reason because they were all so finely dressed, the lady Chloe, my mistress, in beautiful clothes, such as she used to wear at the court of Sais; also the jewels and chains that Pharaoh Apries gave to her. Oh! she looked fine, lord Ramose, so fine that it rejoiced my heart to see her and made me think of the good days when she was the loveliest lady of the court and Pharaoh used to kiss her hand; yes, and her lips also."

"Have done," I said angrily. "Why did my mother go up Nile? Tell me, old fool, or it shall be the worse for you."

"Be not wrath, lord," she said, shrinking from me as though she feared that I might strike her. "I am but a slave who must do the bidding of my mistress and keep her secrets, lest it should be the worse for me."

"Nay, woman, you must do my bidding. The truth now, or you go to those who know how to wring it from you."

"Lord," she said in a great fright, "I will tell all I know; it is but little. Two mornings ago the lady Chloe and her servants sailed up Nile to meet Pharaoh who had summoned her and sent barges to convey her to him. Why she went to meet Pharaoh, I could not tell you, though you were to beat me with rods till I died."

When I saw that she knew no more, I left her and sought out other servants of my mother's on whom I wasted much time in useless questionings, for these seemed to know even less than did the old woman. So at last, weary and perplexed, I returned home and finding Belus, told him all I had learned, asking him if he could understand its meaning.

"It seems plain," he answered. "Your mother has gone to meet Pharaoh by appointment and to discuss certain private matters, but what these may be is known to the gods alone."

"Still, can you guess them, Belus?"

"Yes, I can guess that they have to do with Myra. Remember, Ramose, that it still pleases both your mother and Pharaoh to talk of Myra as your daughter."

"If so, what of it?"

"Only this: that then she is one who can be given in marriage."

"Not so, Belus; at least if she were my daughter I alone could give her in marriage."

"Pharaoh is the father of all and can give any in marriage to whom he will," answered Belus darkly.

Then he thought a while and added, "Save those who are already married, as Myra will be tomorrow. I would that it had been today, or better still a year gone, so that she held an infant in her arms. In this matter, Ramose, you have been too slow and lost time cannot be found again. Still, fret not, for tomorrow all will be righted."

Then upon some pretext or other he left me, as I felt sure because he did not wish to talk more of this matter. Often since that day I have wondered how much Belus knew or guessed of the calamity that overhung us.

I slept but ill that night, for the shadow of this unknown calamity lay dark upon my soul. Evil dreams came to me, in many shapes, yet the purport of each was the same—namely that I woke to find myself quite alone in the world. To and fro I walked in a desolate valley, stopping now and again to call on the name of Myra for whom I sought, but always from the cliffs which shut that valley in, echo repeated— Myra, Myra, Myra—and that was all.

Before the dawn I rose and dressed myself finely for the marriage. Then, accompanied by Belus and two running footmen, I entered my chariot and drove to the temple of Hathor. Leaving the chariot at the gate in charge of the footmen, we were admitted by priests who waited to lead us to the inner shrine. Here we stood a while, till presently we heard the sound of singing. Then from a side chapel appeared priestesses, eight or ten of them, accompanied by choristers and musicians who played upon harps and other instruments. In the centre of this throng, a veil thrown over her head and carrying flowers in her hand, was Myra, at the sight of whom my heart leapt.

She came, she stood at my side. The high-priest asked certain questions. Then at his bidding I took her hand and set upon her finger a piece of golden ring-money in token that I endowed her with my goods, announcing also that I took her to be my wife, as she too announced that she took me to be her husband. This done the high-priest blessed us in the name of Hathor and other gods, while a priestess was sent to the top of the temple pylon to call out to the heavens that we were wed.

Now all was finished and Metep, her old nurse, led Myra to the door of the sanctuary there to await my coming. I stayed a while to thank the priests and priestesses, and the musicians, also to direct Belus to double the customary fees, and make a special offering to the temple.

These things he did, taking the weighed gold from a bag which he had brought with him, slowly enough, as I thought. Then the treasurer of the temple, an aged, formal fool, must needs detain us while he re-weighed the gold and wrote an acknowledgement of my gift upon sheepskin.

At last when all was done, we parted from the priests with farewells and bowings and hurried to join Myra. At the gateway of the temple we found her waiting with Metep. She greeted me with a sweet smile, for now her veil was gone and she wore a long cloak over her bridal robes.

Yet there was that on her face which caused me to ask if aught were amiss.

"Nothing, husband," she said, hesitating at the word. "Yet, let us depart, for I see officers of Pharaoh's guard waiting beyond the outer gates and the doorkeeper has told Metep that they seek you."

"Well, what of it?" I said. "I have had much business with Pharaoh of late and doubtless he would learn something of me, though indeed I did not know that he had returned to Memphis."

So Myra and I entered the chariot, Belus walking by its side, and crossed the courtyard to the pylon gates which were opened for us. On the further side of them we were stopped by an officer of Pharaoh's guard, a man whom I knew. He saluted, saying,

"Well found, Count Ramose! I sought you at your home and was told that you were gone with your daughter to worship in the temple of Hathor at this early hour—" here he glanced at Myra who had hidden her face in her hood, and smiled.

I was about to answer that Myra was not my daughter, but my wife, when he stopped me, waving his hand.

"Your pardon, Count, but my errand permits of no delay. Pharaoh has returned to Memphis and being much pressed for time because of business that awaits him at Sais, has gone on at once to attend the ceremony of the burial of the Apis god at the tomb of the bulls, three leagues away, whence he departs this very night for Sais. Meanwhile he must see you and the learned Belus also, to hear your report concerning the works in your charge at Memphis, to give you certain instructions, and to consult with you upon other matters. I have horses here upon which you can mount, both of you."

"But I cannot come," I said angrily. "I have business that keeps me here."

Now that officer from some hiding-place about his person drew a gold ring and held it before my eyes.

"You are learned, Count Ramose," he said, "and can read the old Egyptian writing. Tell me, whose name and title are on this ring?"

I glanced at it. It was a signet of Amasis, the same, I think, that he wore himself, for I had noted it upon his hand.

"That of Pharaoh," I answered.

"Yes, Count, and how comes it that I, who am but an officer of the guard, bear Pharaoh's seal? I will tell you. It has been given to me to teach you that I speak with Pharaoh's voice. You must come with me and at once, likewise the learned Belus."

I stared at the man whom I knew to be no liar, and thought a while. The matter must be great and urgent that caused Pharaoh to summon me in this fashion. Doubtless he needed my counsel and that of Belus, upon some high business. Or it might have to do with the accursed Apis calf which had been born amongst my herd, that now would take the place of the old bull god they buried this day in the tomb of bulls. Or it might be something else.

With a pang of fear I remembered certain words which Amasis had spoken when he was, or feigned to be drunk at my mother's feast, threatening to make an end of me because in me ran the true royal blood of Egypt. What if he were decoying me into the desert purposing that thence I should return no more? A while ago the risk would not have moved me over much, a man who from year to year and from day to day strove to prepare himself to leave the world and enter some unknown house of Life, or if there were none, to dwell for ever in the abodes of Sleep.

But now, how could I dare it whose new-made bride stood by me clothed in love and beauty, making death terrible? I would not go. Surely I could escape from this man and flee with Myra. My chariot stood yonder drawn by horses as swift as any known in Egypt. We would leap into it and flee away to hiding-places I knew of, and thence pass to foreign lands beyond the sea.

Thus seized with panic, the shadow perchance of evils to come, I thought rapidly, but as I suppose, something of what passed within my mind wrote itself upon my face. At least that officer smiled and said,

"Look not at your sword, Count, nor at your chariot. You may kill me, but my men wait without; or you may flee, but you will be hunted down. Know that my orders are to bring you to Pharaoh alive or dead, and Belus the physician with you."

Now Myra, who all this while had been listening intently with a frozen face, broke in saying,

"Go, Ramose, lest a worse thing befall us. I will await your return in our home."

"Captain," I said, "we obey the command of Pharaoh, bringing this lady with us."

"My commands were to escort you and Belus to the presence of the king, but no other," he answered coldly.

Then Belus spoke for the first time, saying,

"None can fight against fate and what are Pharaoh's orders but the voice of fate? Also often we must reach our end by long and crooked paths."

Here he turned to Myra and added, "Be not afraid. That end will be reached. Remember what I saw some nights gone in the water of the bowl, and the words which my spirit then set between my lips, for I think that they are in the way of fulfilment. Look, the lily which once turned black beneath the spell, now lies white upon your breast embalmed in crystal. White it shall remain, Myra, white as your body and your soul. Do you understand?"

"I understand," she answered faintly in a voice that was full of tears.

I went to her, I kissed her, whispered that we should meet again unharmed, for God was good and Belus could not lie. Then I bade Metep her nurse to lead her to the chariot and bide with her day and night till I returned. They went and when they were gone I accompanied the officer like a man in a swoon, seeing nothing but the last glance of mingled love and fear that Myra gave me as the chariot vanished behind the temple pylon.

****

We mounted on horses and surrounded by an escort, rode through the gardens of Memphis and across the sands beyond, to the great necropolis where for thousands of years the nobles and gentlefolk of Egypt had been buried in the consecrated land. Passing through streets of their holy tombs we came at last to a temple that stood near to the mouth of the great caverns wherein are hid away the bones of the Apis bulls, outside of which temple flew the banner of Pharaoh surrounded by a guard of soldiers. We were led into this temple where a ceremony was in progress conducted by the priests of the god Ptah. It was very long, made up of rites which however gorgeous, to me were but mummeries, ending in a kind of sacramental feast whereat all of us from Pharaoh down, must touch with our lips a broth compounded from the flesh of the dead Apis, the smell of which broth—for taste it I did not—revolted me.

At last this rite was over and I thought that now I should be able to have speech with Pharaoh and be gone. Not so, however, for immediately a procession was formed in which a place was assigned to me as one specially favoured of the gods, because the new Apis had been found among my cattle. Accompanied by Belus I marched in it, preceded by Pharaoh, his great officers and the high-priests of Ptah and of Osiris, and surrounded by singers with other priests and nobles.

We entered the mouth of a mighty cavern and descended into the bowels of the earth, marching through stifling heat down lamp-lit passages hewn in the solid rock. Passing many walled-up chapels we came at length to one which was open. Here stood a huge sarcophagus that contained the mummied bones of the dead Apis. Now began more ceremonies which to me seemed to be without end, though what they were I cannot say, because from where I stood in the passage little could be seen of them; also the horrible heat of the place overcame me in such fashion that I could take note of nothing.

When all was finished Pharaoh, weighed down with royal and priestly robes and ornaments, marched past me, or rather was carried in a chair looking like a man asleep, and we followed him as best we might, till at length we struggled from that hole into the light and once more breathed the blessed air.

Now I asked to be led to the royal presence, but was told that this was impossible because Pharaoh was resting. Later I was told that

Pharaoh was eating and later still that he was asleep, being overcome with fatigue and wine. Then we were taken to a pavilion where food, that I could scarcely touch, was given to us, and afterwards night having fallen, to a tent where we must sleep. Here we lay down because there was nothing else to do and guards who tramped up and down without, made escape impossible. Thus, tossing to and fro, bewailing my fortune and unable so much as to close my eyes, did I pass what should have been my bridal night, racked with doubts and fears and, in my heart, cursing Apis as never god was cursed before.

The sun rose at length but even then we were not allowed to leave the tent, why I could not discover. At last came a herald who told me that Pharaoh had departed long before dawn, almost alone that he might avoid the heat and dust made by a great company, and that he bade me and Belus to follow after him.

Then I understood that for some unknown reason I was a prisoner.

We followed because we must, but it was not until we reached Sais after long days of journeying, that we were allowed to overtake Pharaoh. There on the following morning he received us in a private apartment of the palace, in which it seemed that he was wont to hide himself away when wearied with matters of the state, or with quarrels in his household.

We were led to this apartment and at its door I shrank back in horror, for it was the same in which years before I had seen the Queen Atyra lying dead upon her couch. Yes, although the furnishings were different, without doubt it was the same. There was the spot where her cloak had lain upon the floor hiding the bloodstain; there was the window-place out of which with the strength of madness I had cast that murderer, the priest Ninari.

My heart stood still, my limbs tottered so that I was like to fall. Why had I been brought to this place of evil omen? Was it a trick of Pharaoh's who knew what memories it held for me? Or was I led by the hand of fate that here, where had died the lover of my youth, I too must give up my breath? My mind reeled; visions appeared before me. I could have sworn that I saw Atyra in all her loveliness standing yonder waiting to receive me in her outstretched arms. Then I heard Belus whispering in my ear,

"Be a man! Out of this chamber once you passed from peril to freedom and happiness, and so you shall again. Come, Pharaoh waits us."

I found strength and comfort in these words, qualities that have ever flowed to me from the strong soul of Belus. My mind cleared, I was myself again. By the window-place looking out on the peaceful garden, sat Pharaoh Amasis with a table before him upon which were writings, a jug of wine with drinking goblets, and his sword which he had unbuckled, for as usual he wore the dress of a general. For the rest he seemed to be quite alone, though doubtless guards and others were waiting within call in the chamber through which Ninari had entered to wreak his vengeance.

Pharaoh looked up and saw us.

"Enter, Count, and physician—or magician—Belus," he cried in his hearty voice. "Enter; be seated without ceremony, and drink a cup of wine with me, for if I may judge by myself, you must be thirsty after toiling northwards in the summer sun."

We bowed and obeyed, seating ourselves upon two stools that had been placed for us, as I noted at a distance from the table. Then Pharaoh filled three of the goblets with wine and signed to Belus to take two of them, while he kept the third and drank a little from it, as though to show us that the wine was not poisoned. Yet, as I thought, this told us nothing, seeing that the venom might have been placed in our cups which after the Grecian fashion, were made of gold.

"Now," he said, "let us drink to better times, for know that these are bad indeed for Egypt."

So we drank who had no choice, I wondering whether presently I should feel my vitals twisting in agony. But this did not happen. Indeed the wine was of the best and heartened me.

"Ramose," went on Pharaoh setting down his cup, "I fear that you will be angry with me who have dragged you after me upon this long journey. Well, I did it because I must, who wished to speak to you privately and to Belus also, after I had returned to Sais and heard what the tidings were from the lands beyond Egypt. By all the gods they are dark enough. Cyrus the Persian has conquered Lydia and threatens Babylon where rules that old fool, Nabonidus, who thinks of nothing but the repairing of temples and the statues of ancient gods, which he drags from the cities that worship them to set them up in Babylon where he can see and prate about them. Still he is powerful, for there is his son, Belshazzar, that fierce man, and Babylon is yet mighty and a high wall built between Cyrus and his Persians and Egypt. Therefore it is necessary to make a friend of Nabonidus as he desires to make a friend of us, to which end I have made an offering that I think will please him."

He paused and Belus, eyeing him sharply, asked,

"Will Pharaoh be so gracious as to tell us what offering he has made?"

"Let the matter be," said Amasis waving his hand. "In this high

business it is scarcely worth mentioning further than to say that do-
tards like Nabonidus are pleased with trifles. Now I turn to a bigger
business, that of Cyrus who it may be in the end will conquer Babylon and become a mighty monarch whom Egypt must fear, lest he
should seek to seize her also. Therefore it is necessary that I should
learn the mind of this Persian. Do you not understand that it is most
necessary, Ramose?" he added, staring at me.

I bowed, answering that I did.

"I am glad," exclaimed Amasis, "for know that it is my purpose to
send you to the court of Cyrus to make inquiry into all these matters
and report to me?"

"Must I go as your envoy, Pharaoh? Or if not, in what condition?" I
asked, seeking to gain time while I weighed this command in my mind.

"I think not as my envoy, Ramose, for then Cyrus would suspect
you; also is not Ramose too well known as one of the royal blood of
Egypt openly to play this part? Nay, under some false name you might
travel as a great merchant trafficking between Cyprus and Egypt, as
indeed you have been, to make complaint to Cyrus of losses that
you have sustained through the conquest of Cyprus by Egypt, and to
sound his mind as to its seizure by the Persians after the conquest of
Babylon; yes, and that of Egypt also. But all this would be for his secret
ear. Publicly you would pretend that you were sent by me, Pharaoh,
to open trade between Egypt and Persian, or rather by my vizier from
whom you would hold letters of commendation which you must use
to cover your secret plottings against Egypt. Thus Cyrus may be led
into revealing secrets which having learned, you will return and tell to
me. Do you understand, Ramose?"

"I understand," I said, "who am no fool, but one acquainted with
the languages and the trade customs of the East. Yet pardon me, Pharaoh. For my own private reasons I do not wish to undertake this mission. Least of all do I wish to do so, not as an ambassador but in the
guise of a spy."

Pharaoh rose from his chair and stared at me.

"Count Ramose," he said, "you told me just now that you are no
fool, but I begin to think that in this you are mistaken, who do not
seem to know when you have received an order, or what is the penalty
of defying the command of Pharaoh. I hear that you have bought a
beautiful palace in Memphis, one which in the old days was inhabited
by princes of the royal blood. Do you wish to dwell in it, Ramose,
after a certain mission has been accomplished, or would you choose to
remain here and sleep at Sais—till the day of resurrection?"

Now understanding that I must submit or die, I made obeisance and said,

"Pharaoh's will is mine. What Pharaoh commands, that I do. But first I ask leave to travel to Memphis to settle my affairs and to bid farewell to my mother."

"It is granted," said Pharaoh, yawning as though he were weary of this talk. "For the rest my vizier and officers will instruct you in your mission and make provision. Remember, Ramose, that if you serve me well in this matter, after you return there will be few greater men in Egypt. Yes, you shall sit upon the steps of the throne."

We reached the door when a thought struck me. I turned and said,

"And what of Belus, O Pharaoh?"

"I spoke to both of you," answered Amasis, "knowing well that for these many years you have never been apart, that one of you completes the other. Also when two go forth upon a mission one may die and the other live to carry on the work; whereas if but one goes, all is finished with his passing breath. Farewell."

CHAPTER 12

Gone!

Twelve days had gone by when travelling in one of Pharaoh's ships, Belus and I drew near to Memphis which we hoped to reach that afternoon. For seven of those days we had been detained at Sais, though we saw Pharaoh no more. Indeed, perhaps that we might not do so, he quitted the city upon business or pleasure of his own, but commands reached us to await the visits of his vizier and other high officers, and from them to receive instructions with secret letters for Cyrus, the King of the Persians. Also preparations must be made for a long journey across the desert to the city of Susa where it was said that Cyrus dwelt when he rested from his wars.

Now although Belus and I pressed all these matters forward, they could not be accomplished quickly; almost it seemed to us as though Pharaoh's officers had orders to hasten slowly, so that only a little was accomplished each day or sometimes nothing at all. At length, however, when I was driven almost to madness, we were allowed to depart for Memphis where it was settled that all which was necessary should be prepared for our mission. For I must tell that during those days in Sais in truth though not in name, we were prisoners, confined to our quarters in the palace and visited only by the servants of Pharaoh.

But at last we drew near to the great city and within a few hours I hoped to clasp Myra my bride in my arms. Yet I was troubled, I knew not why. Dark fears took hold of me, of I knew not what, nor could I win any comfort from Belus who also seemed oppressed with gloom or forebodings. The journey which we had been forced to make to Sais was strange. Why could not Pharaoh have issued his commands to me here at Memphis, instead of drawing me after him for so many weary days that he might speak to me once in his palace at Sais? And why had he asked me nothing of the work that he had bidden me carry out upon the temple of Ptah? Were those works but a pretext to keep me where he could lay his hand upon me?

In the end, when I could contain myself no longer, I put these and other questions to Belus.

"Ramose," he said, "I cannot answer you. Yet I will tell you what is in my mind. I think that Pharaoh is afraid of you and for some reason of his own desires to be rid of you, which is why he sends you upon this distant and dangerous embassy."

"Then he might have caused me to be killed here in Egypt, Belus."

"Nay, that he could not do, for you have served with him and he has eaten your bread. On these matters Amasis may still have the conscience of a soldier and a guest. Moreover, your blood is known and if you were murdered, your death would look very evil and would bring trouble on him. For would it not be said that he had made away with you because you stood too near the throne? But on such journeys as that which lies before us many accidents happen, and if under a false name you died far away from Egypt who would trouble? Also consider this business. You are to go to Cyrus and play a double part, pretending to be an envoy from Egypt loyal to its king, and yet working against Egypt and its king, because of some private merchant's grudge which has to do with her conquest of Cyprus. Now when Cyrus discovers this, or it is revealed to him by other messengers, may he not grow suspicious and bring you to death or throw you into prison, especially if he learns that Pharaoh would not grieve if you returned no more?"

"It is so and I mistrust this embassy," I answered with a groan.

"Aye, Ramose, it is so. Yet I say to you, have no fear, for I am sure you will come safely through these troubles, as you have through others."

"That is good news, Belus. But what of Myra? How can I leave her at Memphis alone and unprotected?"

"You cannot, Ramose, she must accompany you, disguised if need be. Once out of Egypt there are other lands where we might shelter."

I remember no more of this talk, for just then we drew near to the quay and my burning desire to see Myra caused me to forget all else.

We landed and hiring a chariot drove swiftly to the Happy House where surely she would be awaiting me.

Now we were passing its gates and it seemed to me that there was something strange and unfriendly about the aspect of the place. There was the roofed and columned terrace where Myra and I had kissed as lovers, but it was empty. There were the large doors of sycamore wood, but they were shut, not open as they had been in the daytime since I owned that house. I knocked on them and presently heard them being unbolted by someone within. They opened and there appeared a man, a faithful Cypriote steward who had served me at Salamis.

"Where is the lady Myra?" I asked. "Bring me to her."

"I cannot, lord," he answered awkwardly, staring at me as though I were a ghost. "She has gone."

"Gone!" I gasped. "Whither has she gone? Speak, man, or by Amen I'll make you silent for ever."

"I do not know, lord. On that day when you went out at dawn, she returned early to the house with the woman Metep, saying that you had been summoned away and that she awaited you. Towards midday came the lady Chloe, your mother, and with her a number of men who wore Pharaoh's badge, also some women very finely dressed. The lady your mother and the men talked with the lady Myra apart, but what passed between them I do not know. The end of it was that she left the house with them, much against her will, I think, for she was weeping, and was driven away in a chariot accompanied by Metep. We, your servants, were angry and disturbed, and would have kept her by force, had she not said hurriedly that a command had reached her from you that she must obey your lady mother in all things, and therefore she went, though she liked the business little and of it could understand nothing. So she went, lord, and that is all, except that we heard afterwards that she had departed down Nile in great state upon one of Pharaoh's ship. No, not quite all, lord, for a lad whom I do not know, brought a letter which, he said, a woman called Metep had given him to be delivered to you if you returned to the house. Here it is," and from his robe he drew out a roll roughly tied up with a piece of palm fibre.

Like a man in a dream I undid the roll, saw that the writing within was in Greek and short and quickly penned. It ran thus:—

"To Ramose, my husband most beloved,

"I am being taken away down Nile, and as I understand to some distant country, by Pharaoh's officers. Your mother swears to me that this is by your wish and for my own good; also that you await me overseas, but I do not believe her. I would kill myself, were it not that Belus foretold to me that whatever troubles overtook me, all would be well at last. Fear nothing, for know that I will surely die rather than break my vows to you, because in death we shall meet again. Follow me, Ramose; the wisdom of Belus will teach you how, and find me, or my bones. I write this on the ship as we sail. Metep has found a messenger. Farewell, beloved Ramose; there is no time for more. Farewell.

"Myra."

I finished reading and gave the writing to Belus. Then in a cold voice that did not sound like my own, I said to the man,

"You are steward here, guard this place well, for it may be that I shall have to go upon a long journey. You have moneys of mine in your hands and more will be paid to you by my debtors and tenants as they fall due. Use them on my behalf. I trust all to you, but be sure that if you fail me, it shall go ill with you."

"I will not fail you, lord," he answered, the tears springing to his eyes, for he was a most honest and faithful man, "but oh! leave us not alone."

"That I must do for a while," I answered, and went.

"Where to?" said Belus as we entered the chariot which still stood at the door.

"My mother's house," I replied.

Soon, too soon, we were there.

"Would you not wish to see the lady Chloe alone?" asked Belus, who, I think, feared what I might say or do.

"No," I answered. "It seems that the lady Chloe cannot be trusted; therefore it is well that a witness should be present."

So he came with me unwillingly enough. We found my mother alone in her large chamber seated in a throne-like chair and very finely dressed. Indeed, she wore upon her beautiful head the little cir-clet of gold from which rose an ornament that might well have been an *uraeus*, that mark of royalty which she said Amasis had given her leave to bear, all of which showed me that she was expecting a visit from someone, though who it might be I never learned. Certainly it was not from me.

"Greetings, dear Ramose," she said confusedly. "I did not hope to see you. I—I understood that, that you had gone upon a journey on Pharaoh's business."

As she spoke she came forward as though to embrace me, but something in my face caused her to change her mind, for she shrank back and sat herself down again in the chair. I looked at her for a little while, thinking to myself that her words revealed that she knew the mind of Amasis as to my mission, which perhaps she had herself inspired.

"Why do you look at me so strangely?" she faltered.

"Where is my wife?" I asked slowly.

"Your wife! Have you a wife, Ramose? Surely you have not wed without telling me, your mother?"

"Where is my wife, Myra?" I repeated. "What have you done with her?"

"Oh! you mean your daughter, Myra, though you call her your wife in error. Why, as I thought you knew, she has left Egypt to become a queen. You must be very proud, Ramose, that your daughter should become a queen, as of course I am."

"Whose queen?" I asked.

"The queen of a very great king, perhaps the greatest in the world after Pharaoh—Nabonidus, Lord of Babylon."

"How comes it, Mother, that you have stolen away her whom you call my daughter, though you know well that she is not my daughter but my wife, to be forced into marriage with this old dotard of Babylon? Answer me and swiftly."

"I tell you that I thought you knew, Son. Also it was Pharaoh's will. The great king Nabonidus has sent one of his daughters to be wed to Pharaoh, as you will have heard, demanding in return a royal princess of Egypt to be his wife, the old queen of Babylon being dead, and Pharaoh wishes to make a close alliance with Nabonidus, so that Babylon and Egypt may stand shoulder to shoulder against Cyrus the Persian, should he threaten either of them."

Now in a flash all became clear to me, for I remembered the words of Amasis at Sais as to making a gift to Nabonidus, also how he had eyed Myra at the feast my mother made to him and asked her if she would not like to shine in a royal court. Lastly I remembered how my mother had slipped away up Nile to meet Pharaoh upon secret business. With a wave of my hand I stopped her talk, saying:

"Hearken while I set out this matter more clearly, I think, than you can do, Lady. Afterwards you can tell me if I have done so well. Does it not stand thus? Amasis, wishing to please Nabonidus and bind Babylon to Egypt, desired to send to him a royal princess to be his wife or woman. You may remember that he spoke of it at your table, grieving that there was no such princess who could be sent. Thereafter you and Amasis made a plot to rape away Myra, pretending that she was my daughter and that in her therefore ran some of the royal blood of the Pharaohs, although you knew well that she was not my daughter."

"I did not know, Ramose. I thought that you—lied to me on that matter, wishing to hide some sin of your youth."

"Who as you knew well was not my daughter," I repeated, "for often I told you so, as you knew that I took her to wife on that same day when owing to your plottings, Pharaoh dragged me after him to Sais, so that this woman-theft might be carried out in my absence."

My mother muttered something and began to wipe her eyes, while I went on,

"As soon as Belus and I were trapped after the marriage in the temple of Hathor, you loosed Pharaoh's dogs upon this defenceless girl, new made a wife; yes, you tore her, whom you hate, away and set her on Pharaoh's ship alone save for her old nurse."

"I deny it," she cried.

"Deny it if you will, but know that your spies did not watch her close enough. Here is the story in her own writing," and I held out the open roll.

Then my mother crouched down upon the seat, her elbows on her knees, her head upon her hands and listened, hiding her face from me.

"So she has gone," I said, "she, my wife whom I have reared from childhood, she whom I love better than all the world, better than my life, better than my soul; she has gone to become the plaything of an Eastern king—nay, to death, for that she will never be, it is written here," and I tapped the roll. "You have murdered her, as you, my mother, have murdered me, for be sure that if I find her dead, swiftly I shall follow after her to where there is justice, or sleep."

"Spare me, Ramose," my mother cried. "Whatever I did was for the best, for the glory of this proud girl who will be a queen—yes, a queen, and for your sake whom Pharaoh will advance and indeed already has advanced. Aye, and—for I will tell the truth—because I would be rid of her who has stolen your love from me. Did she not make you leave my house that you might live alone with her, and has she not built a high wall betwixt us over which we cannot climb, so that you, my only child, whom for years I thought dead, are now lost to me again?"

"If so," I answered, "in your hatred and vanity you have added to that wall till now it reaches from earth to heaven. For the rest, what you did was for your own sake and not for mine. What Amasis has paid you for this treason I do not know, or wish to learn. Perchance he has given you high rank such as pertains to the widows of kings who do not happen to be royal" (here she started, for this arrow had gone home), "or he has endowed you with great wealth and many titles. Let that matter be. Whatever you have gained, learn that you have lost a son. Were you not my mother, I think that I should kill you. As it is I leave you to be eaten up with your own shame. I do not curse you, because no man may curse the flesh that bore him; it is unholy. Nay, I do but leave you.

"Farewell, my mother, upon whose face I hope never to look again.

130

When as Pharaoh's concubine you caused me to be born, you did me wrong though mayhap that was decreed. But when you stole from me all I love, oh! what a crime was that! Perhaps, blinded by a greed for pomp and vanities, you do not understand, yet one day you will. I go to seek her of whom you have robbed me, and to find her or to die. Whichever it may be, for you already I am dead. In this life, or any other, we are for ever separate."

I turned to leave her with these awful words, now in my old age I know how awful, echoing in her ears. Suddenly she seemed to awake from her lethargy. Rising from her seat she sprang upon me, she cast her arms about me. Sinking upon her knees she dragged me down to her. She kissed my garments, she babbled words of remorse and woe, she called me her babe, her darling. I thrust her from me and went. At the door I looked round to see her lying senseless upon the floor. I wonder did ever mother and son bid farewell in such a fashion and for such a cause, or have ever a woman's jealousy and love of empty pomp done a more evil work. Thus we parted, little guessing where we should meet again.

That night in a place where we lodged, for to my own house I would not return, Belus and I debated long and earnestly as to what we should do. Already he had been at work and learned through secret channels that were always open to him, who had many bound to him by ties I did not understand, that Myra had gone down Nile and with Metep had left Egypt in charge of that same splendid embassy of Babylonian lords and ladies who had brought the daughter or grand-daughter of Nabonidus to be a wife to Pharaoh. It seemed that no Egyptians went with her for a reason that could be guessed. Had they done so they might have talked and given the Babylonians cause to doubt whether Myra were really a princess of the blood of Pharaoh, though she was beautiful, wore royal robes and ornaments and had a regal air.

"Yes," I said to Belus, "but Metep can talk and so can Myra herself."

"Who would pay heed to a serving-woman whose throat can be cut if need be?" he asked. "As for Myra, doubtless all these plotters think that pride and desire of royal place will keep her silent; also fear lest should she be discovered, she would be put to death or made a shame of as a lying cheat."

"Yet she will speak, Belus."

"Aye, without doubt she will speak and prove all she says. Therein lies her peril, or mayhap the peril of Amasis against whom Nabonidus will be enraged, or the peril of both of them."

I wrung my hands who saw many pictures in my mind. Myra doing herself to death rather than be shamed: Myra being butchered or tortured or cast to soldiers by a furious Eastern despot: Myra escaping from all but to fall into the hands of Amasis who would certainly kill her in his rage, if only to hide his fraud. Yes, and others.

"Truly the gods have set a snare for us," I said.

"That which the gods tie the gods can loose, Ramose. Have faith, for there is no other crutch upon which to lean. My spirit is silent; having spoken to me once on that night when the lily that Myra wore seemed to rot, then grew white again in the water of the bowl, it speaks no more. Yet then it said that all should end well. Have faith therefore in my spirit, as I have, lest you should go mad. Come now, let us make our plans."

Taking such comfort as I could from these high words, I gathered up my strength that I might think with a clear brain. For long we talked, seeking light. This was the end of it. There was but one hope of saving Myra—to follow her whither she had gone. That, as it chanced, we could do, having wealth at our command and holding Pharaoh's commission, though in it I was spoken of not by name but only as "the bearer of these letters."

Under this, it is true, we were ordered to proceed to the court of Cyrus wherever it might be, but Susa, his capital, could be reached by way of Babylon, though this was not the shortest road. Therefore, making no complaint to Amasis as to the fate of Myra, for who can reproach a king and live? and leaving it to Heaven to avenge that sin upon him, we determined to proceed at once upon our mission, or so to pretend.

To be short, this we did. In a few days all was made ready. My wealth was great and we took with us not only a large sum in gold in addition to that which Pharaoh provided for the costs of the mission, but also written letters from my agents which would enable us to obtain money in the cities of the East. For the rest, discarding an escort we travelled unattended in the character of merchants desirous of opening up trade with Persia and other Eastern lands, but having hidden about us letters from the vizier of Pharaoh to all his agents and officers throughout the East, commanding these to give us help as it might be needed; also the secret despatch for Cyrus of which I have spoken, offering him the friendship of Egypt. Lastly we took other names, I calling myself Ptahmes, that by which I had been known in Cyprus, for none guessed that the merchant of Salamis and the Count Ramose were one man, while Belus once more became Azar, a buyer of Eastern goods.

Thus armed we started upon our search, determined if we lived to follow Myra wheresoever she might have gone. The question was—whither had she gone? We learned that the Babylonian embassy to which she had been given over, had departed to Damascus because it was said that Nabonidus the King was in that city, making a study of its antiquities and religion, having left his son Belshazzar to rule in Babylon. So joining a company of merchants at Pelusium we set out for Damascus.

Here I must tell how I noted at this time that Belus seemed filled with a strange joy which in such an evil hour I thought almost unholy.

"How comes it that you are glad, when my heart breaks, Belus?" I asked of him as we left Pelusium.

"Would you know?" he answered. "Then I will tell you; it is because that call is come of which I spoke to you in past days. In Babylon I have an enemy who has wrought me worse wrong than any that you suffer. Now after many years of waiting God gives him into my hand; now at length I go to be avenged upon him. I know not how, I know only that I go to be avenged. Ask me no more, Ramose."

I looked at him marvelling, and there was that in his eyes which counselled me to be silent.

CHAPTER 13

Babylon

Behold us at length in Damascus after weeks of weary travelling delayed by many accidents, and of suspense that ate up my soul, only to find that Nabonidus had left this city more than a month before. As secretly as we might we inquired whether a royal wife from Egypt had been brought to him while he dwelt there, and by some were told one thing, and by some another. It seemed certain that an embassy of his, returned from Egypt, had waited on him in Damascus, for so we were assured by Pharaoh's agent, a subtle half-bred Syrian, but whether they brought with them any lady to become one of his household was not certain. At least on this matter none would speak—least of all the agent who, we could see, suspected us notwithstanding our letters, for the Babylonians and their subject peoples held it a kind of sacrilege even to talk of women appointed to the king. Indeed our inquiries, veiled though they were, brought suspicion on us and after we had left Damascus, disaster.

Now having heard that Nabonidus had departed for Seleucia and that the embassy which came from Egypt had either accompanied, or followed him, to Seleucia we determined to go, sending a false report to Amasis of our reasons for so doing. Yet we never reached that place, for when we were five days journey from Damascus, of a sudden our caravan was attacked by men who seemed to be Arabs. In the darkness before the dawn they rushed upon us so that resistance was impossible. In the confusion Belus and I were separated. I was seized, being felled by a blow on the head as I was about to draw my sword.

"Bind him!" I heard a voice cry in the Babylonian tongue. "Harm him not, he is the Egyptian spy who pretends to be a merchant."

So bound I was and lay there among my captors, thankful that my life had been spared.

The light came and showed the Arabs, if such they were, going off with their spoil. The merchants with whom we had been travelling were also departing in a great hurry with what goods had been left to them. Looking about me I could see no dead, which caused me to think that the attack had been made either for plunder only, or for some other hidden purpose. Everywhere I searched for Belus with my eyes, but could see nothing of him. Certainly he was not among the fleeing merchants. I was taken to a tent that had been pitched, led by two men who when they reached it, threw off their Arab robes and revealed themselves dressed as Babylonian soldiers. In the tent were officers also of Babylon, and a man whom from his attire I took to be a scribe or priest. There, too, was my baggage already being examined, though not that of Belus, here known as Azar.

The officers bowed to me courteously. Then the chief of them said in the Accadian tongue,

"You take much wealth with you, traveller," and he pointed to the bags of gold that they had found.

I answered haltingly in the same language, which I pretended to speak but ill, that I was a merchant journeying to Iran to buy goods from the Persians.

"Yes," he replied with a grave smile, "we know that you go to deal with the Persians." Then he nodded to the soldiers who began to remove my garments.

"It is not needful," I said with dignity, "I admit that I am more than a merchant. I am also an ambassador from the Pharaoh of Egypt to Cyrus the great King."

"Indeed," answered the officer. "If that is so, what were you doing in Damascus making inquiry concerning offerings from Pharaoh to Nabonidus, king of Babylon? Did Pharaoh, whose ambassador you say you are, order you to travel to Susa by way of Damascus and Seleucia? Seeing that Babylon is at war with Persia, it seems a strange road."

Now I pretended not to understand, whereon the officer said sternly,

"Will you deliver up your letters to Cyrus, if you have any, or will you choose to be killed as a spy? Here is the rope from about your baggage and outside stands a tree that will serve to hang you on, seeing that according to our law it is not allowed to shed the blood of an envoy such as you say you are."

Now I thought for a moment. If I refused they would either hang me at once or take me to Babylon to be tormented, as was the barbarous fashion of these people. Also they would search my clothes and belongings piece by piece, and find the letters. Further, I did not wish to die who sought Myra, and lastly, I had little scruple in betraying the secrets of Amasis which indeed I could not hide, who began to believe that Amasis was for the second time betraying me. So without more ado I told them where the writings were, since my hands being tied, I could not produce them—the letter to Cyrus written in the Persian language sewn up in my undergarment and the letters to Egyptian agents cunningly hidden elsewhere, how I will not stay to describe.

"You speak our tongue better than you did at first, Ptahmes the Egyptian," said the officer as he handed the writings to the priest or scribe.

This man scanned them swiftly, and said,

"The letters to the agents of Egypt throughout the East are the same as that which this Ptahmes delivered to Pharaoh's officer in Damascus which we have seen. The letter to Cyrus the king seems to be written in a kind of secret script that I cannot decipher easily. It must go to Babylon with the prisoner who perhaps may be willing to read it to us himself."

I shook my head, saying,

"I am not able to do so, for I have not studied it; it was given to me to deliver—no more. But if you will find my travelling companion, Azar, who is learned in all these secret writings, perhaps he can help you."

This I said hoping to discover what had chanced to Belus.

The scribe looked at the officer as though in question and in obedience to some sign, answered,

"If you mean the Babylonian who was travelling with you, know, Egyptian, that when he was seized and in danger of his life, by tokens which we could not doubt, he revealed himself to be one of high rank among our people although he has been absent for long from Babylon, a priest and a magician also whom it was not lawful for us to detain. Therefore we let him go lest he should bring the curse of Marduk upon us. Whither he went we do not know, but being a magician perhaps he vanished away."

Now I understood that these people would tell me nothing of the fate of Belus, but whether this was because they were afraid of him, or because he had been murdered, I could not guess. So I remained silent. After this an inventory of all my goods, and especially of the gold, was made by the scribe, a copy of it being handed to me. Then my garments were returned to me, but the gold and the letters were set in a chest which was sealed by the scribe and by three of the officers, each of whom rolled upon the clay an engraved cylinder whereon were cut the images of his gods.

Afterwards my arms were loosed although my feet remained shack-led, and I was given food. When I had eaten a camel was brought, upon the back of which were fastened two large baskets of woven willow twigs, hanging down on either side. In one of these baskets were placed all my goods, and in the other I was laid, the lid being tied down over me.

Thus I started upon my journey to Babylon, for thither the officer told me I must be taken to be examined by the king or his servants who, he added grimly, would know how to find out my true name and business. Three days did I pass in that basket, being lifted out of it only at night and to eat food, the most wretched days, I think, that I can remember.

Not only was I cramped and shaken, but my heart was as sore as my limbs. Everything had gone wrong. Myra was snatched away; Be-lus had vanished, leaving me alone, and, as I was sure and grew more so hour by hour, Amasis had betrayed me. Oh! now I understood. He had warned, or ordered his agents to warn the Babylonians of my mis-sion to Cyrus, and given me letters to carry which would be certain to make them wrath with me and perhaps cause them to put me to death as a spy. Moreover I could not complain, seeing that instead of travelling straight to Susa, I had followed Myra into Babylonian ter-ritory as doubtless he guessed that I should do, and there was snared. Therefore I must suffer whatever befell me in silence and had no refuge save to trust in God. For always I have believed that there is a God who watches over those who put faith in him, though he be not named Ammon or Marduk.

On the fourth day of our journey, when I was almost overcome by the heat in my basket and misery of body and of mind, the officers took me out of it and set me upon a horse. At first I thought they did this from friendliness, or perhaps because they feared lest I should die upon their hands, but, having grown suspicious of all men, afterwards I came to believe that they had another motive. They hoped, I thought, that I should try to run away, when they would be free to kill me, for which reason two spearmen and two mounted archers always rode on each side of me. Whether or not this was their purpose I cannot tell, but certainly I had no mind to fly who knew not where to go. Moreover I wished to reach Babylon whither, as I gathered from the talk of the officers, Nabonidus the king had repaired, knowing that if so Myra would be there also.

At last one day shortly after dawn the walls of the mighty city arose before us out of the mists of the morning that the sun drew from its encircling river. Wonderful was the sight, most wonderful as the light fell upon those towering walls and upon the huge stepped mound where stood the temples of the gods, and upon the thousands of houses that stretched around. Never had I seen such a city. Compared to it Memphis and Thebes were but as little towns, and at any other time the vision of it would have rejoiced me who have always loved such prospects. But now when the officers asked me what I thought of Babylon, I could only answer that the trapped bird cares nothing for the glories of its cage, words at which they laughed.

All that day, save for a long halt during the hours of noon, we travelled slowly towards Babylon through cultivated gardens where thousands were at work. After these were passed we crossed the great river in a flat-bottomed boat which held both us and our horses, for here the baggage camels were left behind, and with them the brute upon which I had travelled in my basket for so many weary hours. Then we rode through more gardens till we came to a mighty gateway in the enormous outer walls that towered over us like a precipice of bricks. Beyond these was another wall with another gateway, and here we were delayed for some time till gorgeously apparelled, black-bearded men whom I supposed to be servants of the king, arrived to escort us.

These men who stared at me curiously, led us through league after league of streets crowded with people who hurried to and fro, taking heed of nothing save the business on which they were bent. So it went on till darkness fell, through which we were guided by men with torches. At length in the gloom I saw before me some vast building upon whose walls and roof burnt cressets of fire, and guessed that it must be a temple or a palace. In fact it was the latter, for presently we reached its door, or one of its doors, where I and all my goods were handed over to a guard and to certain men whom I took to be palace eunuchs. By these I was led down many passages to a chamber, not over large but well furnished with a bed and all that was necessary. Here food and wine were brought to me by one who locked the door behind him when he went away, leaving me alone save for the guard whom I heard pacing the corridor without.

That night passed but ill for me who after the air of the desert felt stifled in this hot chamber, which was in fact a prison as I judged by the small window-place barred with rods of copper and cut high in the wall where it could not be reached. Also I was very troubled. At length I had come to Babylon but oh! what had fate in store for me at Babylon?

In the morning more food was brought to me and clean garments, some of my own taken from my baggage together with a long white robe of soft material beautifully woven. When I asked the jailer what it was, he replied curtly that all who appeared in the presence of the king must wear this robe, but would say no more. So now I knew that I was to go before the king, which perhaps meant that after I had been questioned I should be executed as a spy. Well, if so, soon my sorrows would be done.

A little later the door opened again and with a guard there appeared a barber who set to work upon my hair, which had grown long during the journey, curling and scenting it. Next he cut my beard square in the Babylonian fashion, one that I much disliked who always wore it pointed. Then he washed me carefully and trimmed my nails, till at last I asked if I were going to a feast. The answer was, no, but that all who appeared before the king must be purified, also that this was a day of festival at the court when they must be made even purer than usual.

Scarcely had he finished rubbing me with his scented unguents till I smelt like some perfumed court darling, when a fat eunuch, richly apparelled, appeared at the head of an escort and having examined me as though I were a calf being led to sacrifice, commented that although an Egyptian, I was a fine-looking man fit to take a lady's fancy, and bade me follow him. This I did wondering whether some court woman of high degree had chanced to cast her eyes on me, and groaning at the thought. It was not so, however, for after passing through many passages and across courtyards we came to a curious doorway with stone gods or demons standing on either side, and going up some steps, entered an enormous pillared hall. All the lower part of this hall was empty, but at its far end a man sat upon a throne while about him, though at a distance, were gathered many court officers, also great princes and nobles, and behind him was a guard of soldiers.

The eunuch and those with him, even while they were still a long way off, bent down till they looked like monkeys climbing along a bough, and thinking it wise, I did the same. Thus we advanced up the great hall till we came to that part where the court was gathered. Now I found opportunity to examine the king who sat upon the throne, for he had taken no heed of our approach, but was engaged in studying a stone statue set upon a table near the foot of the throne, and in talking about it eagerly to a thin, tall, noble-featured and quick-eyed old man clad in a black robe, whom I took to be a doctor or priest, though by blood neither Babylonian nor Greek, nor Egyptian.

As for the king himself, he was a little, withered man of about seventy years of age with sharp, bead-like eyes that reminded me of those of a mouse, and a wrinkled, but shrewd and kindly face. He was clad in royal robes and ornaments which I noted became him very ill and seemed to trouble him, for the head-dress with the crown on it was twisted all awry and his golden, jewel-encrusted cloak had slipped from his shoulders; also the false, ceremonial beard he wore had become detached from his chin and hung loose round his neck.

"Behold the King of kings and be abased," whispered the eunuch in my ears, in a voice in which I thought I detected mockery.

"I behold him," I whispered back, and went on bowing.

"I tell you, holy Hebrew," said Nabonidus shrilly, "that you may be a very good prophet; but you understand nothing about gods."

"True, O King," answered the black-robed man in a deep and solemn voice, "I understand one god only. About these idols," and he looked contemptuously at the stone image on the table, "I know nothing and care less. Now I would speak to your Majesty of a pressing and important—"

"That is just where you are mistaken, Prophet Belteshazzar or Daniel, for that is your real name, is it not?" interrupted the king petulantly. "These idols, as you call them, are extremely powerful. Why, I dug up that one there under the foundations of an ancient temple that I am repairing, and have brought it to Babylon to add to my collection of the gods of my empire.

"Well, what has happened? The whole province whence it came is almost in revolt; indeed it threatens to make common cause with Cyrus the Persian, my enemy, or rather the enemy of Babylon, for personally we are on quite friendly terms and write to each other about antiquities. All this, if you please, because I have brought away the image of a god that none of their forefathers can have seen for generations, since the tablets buried with it, written in old Accadian, show that it was set beneath the angle of the temple, probably in a time of danger at least a thousand years ago. Yes, although they do not know the name of the god and have only a tradition that it was buried there in the day of some forgotten king or other, they are all up in arms because I have removed it. Yet you speak contemptuously of what you call idols and want to begin to talk of some other matter, I forget what. It would be more to the point, Prophet, if your familiar spirit would tell us the name of this one which I burn to discover."

The prophet called Belteshazzar or Daniel glanced at the stone image and shrugged his shoulders.

"Can no one tell me its name?" went on Nabonidus. "What is the use of a crowd of magicians who know nothing? If it is revealed to anyone here, upon my royal word he shall not lack a reward."

Now I who had been studying the statue, was moved to speak. "May the king live for ever!" I said. "If it pleases the King to hear me, I say that this holy image is one of Ptah, a great god of Egypt; or perhaps of Bes, a Syrian god whose worship in Egypt began in the time of Amenophis III nearly a thousand years ago, or even earlier. Without examination I cannot say whether it be Ptah or Bes. But I know that both of these gods have been sent from Egypt at one time or another, to work miracles of healing at the request of the kings and princes of the East."

"Here at last we have one with wisdom," cried Nabonidus, clapping his hands. "But who is this man? A handsome one enough as I note, with the eyes and hair of a Greek."

The scribe advanced, bent the knee and whispered in the king's ear.

"Oh!" said Nabonidus, "I remember, that Egyptian spy about whom we were warned in a letter from—" and he checked himself. "Let me think. He purports and represents himself to be an envoy from our brother the Pharaoh of Egypt to Cyrus the Persian, our enemy. At least a commission was found on him and has been deciphered, which says so, though the name of the bearer is not mentioned, but probably it is forged. Indeed it must be forged in face of what we learn about the record of the man from Egypt. Also, if he had really been travelling to Susa, or wherever that dangerous Cyrus may be living at the moment, he would not have been found in Damascus, making secret inquiries about me, journeying not as an ambassador should with an escort, but disguised as a merchant. Lastly we were told that he is one of the greatest liars in Egypt, a man who cannot be believed upon his oath, and half a Greek, as indeed he looks."

Here the king brought his long soliloquy to an end and calling to a robed man whom from his ornamented head-dress and splendid broideries, I took to be a councillor or vizier, he said,

"What was it you told me ought to be done with this captive?"

"Spies are best dead, O King," replied the vizier coldly.

"True. Quite true. He ought to be sent to spy in the land of the gods where doubtless there is a great deal to find out. Yet it seems a pity to kill so goodly a fellow who is also no fool, especially as thanks to the warning, he was caught with his forged letters before he got away to Cyrus to report what he had learned in our empire, and therefore has not done us any harm. No, Vizier, I cannot be troubled to listen again to those wearisome documents and reports, especially as we have heard all about this evil-doer from Egypt. Is the Prince Belshazzar here? Oh! yes, I see he is. Come hither, Son, and give us your opinion. You are the real ruler of Babylon, are you not, which gives me leisure to attend to more interesting and important matters," and he glanced at the stone image on the table. "Therefore you should bear your share of the burden, such as deciding about executions, a business that I hate."

As he spoke, from the centre of a group of nobles who stood to the right of the throne, with whom he had been conversing carelessly while Nabonidus talked with the prophet about the image, appeared a splendid figure who wore upon his head something like a crown. He was middle-aged, for the hair upon his temples was turning grey, tall and broad, black bearded and eyed, hook-nosed and cruel-faced, with the thick moist lips of one who is led by his appetites. He came forward, bowed slightly to the king and looked me up and down, then full in the face. Our eyes met and at once I felt that this man was my enemy, one who hated me at first sight as I hated him, and was destined to work me evil. Yet I paid him back glance for glance till at length he turned his head, understanding, as I was sure, that I was no common fellow whom he could despise, and that if I had spied, it was for no mean reason.

"As you ask me, O King," he said in a thick, loud voice, "I agree with the vizier. This knave should be killed at once, or rather, tortured to death, for doubtless out of his agonies may come some truth that will be of service and value to us, also his real name, which for some unknown reason has not been revealed to us. Had I chanced to fill the judgment seat today, as it was settled that I should, if another matter had not brought you here, O King, such at least would have been my sentence."

My blood froze at these words, yet in some strange, calm fashion as though I were considering another's case and not my own, I was able to take note of all. Thus I saw the face of the prophet who was called Belteshazzar flush and his lips move as though he were uttering a prayer; I saw Nabonidus shake his head uneasily like one who hears counsel that is not to his taste; I saw the vizier smile in a cold fashion and the officer of the guard look towards the soldiers as though he were about to order them to hale me away, while the others glanced at me curiously to learn how I bore this hammer-blow of fate. Another instant and the king was speaking,

"You have heard, Egyptian," he said. "The prince yonder, who is really the judge of such matters, has spoken and it only remains for me to confirm his doom, as being in the judgment seat I must do according to the law before it can be carried out, for here in Babylon even the king is the humble servant of the law. Have you anything to urge upon your own behalf?"

"A great deal, O King," I answered; "more perhaps than you would have patience to hear. It is true that I am an envoy to Cyrus, sent to him upon business by the Pharaoh of Egypt, against my will, because Amasis wishes to make friends with all the rulers of the East. But that I am a spy is not true—"

Here Nabonidus held up his hand to silence me.

"Why waste your words," he said, "when you were found spying on behalf of Cyrus, and bearing forged letters which do not give your name; when, too, we have been assured from Egypt that you are the greatest of all liars? If you have nothing more to say I fear that I must bring this business to an end, as the vizier reminds me that another of more importance waits which also has to do with Egypt. So be brief, I pray you."

Now a fury entered into me that struck me dumb so that I could only answer mockingly,

"Then, O King, I grieve that I shall find no opportunity to examine yonder image," and I pointed to the statue on the table, "and to tell your Majesty whether it be that of Ptah or Bes."

"True," said Nabonidus, "and you understand about gods, do you not?"

"Yes, O King. I who am a philosopher and a student, understand about the gods of Egypt and their attributes; also about those of the East and those of Persia and of the farther lands beyond, as I could show you were the time given me."

"Is it so? Peace, Vizier, I know the lady waits. Let her wait. Am I of an age or taste to be in haste to marry again? Hearken, I will not be hurried. You need not frown at me, Belshazzar, for I do not heed you or anyone. I am still King of Babylon, the first Servant of Heaven with power of life and death. I refuse to condemn the man called—what is he called? Oh! Ptahmes, in this fashion. Take him aside to yonder gallery and keep him there, treating him well as a learned stranger. When the other business is finished I will speak with him again. Obey, lest some of you be shortened by a head. I bid you obey instantly," and he struck the arm of the throne with his sceptre.

Now his servants who knew well how these sudden furies of the weak but passionate old king could end if he were thwarted, namely, in the loss of their own lives or offices, sprang forward in a great hurry and led me away. We went through swinging doors and along a passage until we came to a stair hollowed in the thickness of the brick wall of the palace. Up this stair we climbed and at length reached a gallery set very high, near to the lofty roof indeed, and enclosed with a kind of wood lattice such as is common in Egypt, through which one could see without being seen.

The eunuch who accompanied me with the guard, wishing to please me lest by some sudden turn of the wheel of fortune, of a sort that often happens at the courts of these Eastern kings, I who a moment ago was about to be condemned to a lingering death, should become powerful and able to repay injuries, hastened to inform me that this was the place whence the ladies of the royal House were sometimes allowed to look down on ceremonies of state. He added that, whether by accident or skill, he did not know, it was so contrived that those who sat in it could hear all that was said below, whereas even if they were to shout, their voices would never reach those gathered in the hall.

I thanked him and seated myself upon a carved stool which he brought to me, in such fashion that through peepholes I could see everything that passed. As it chanced there was much worthy of note. The doors of the great hall had been thrown open and through them flowed a gaily dressed multitude of guests. Beyond these at the end of the hall, in that place where I had been judged, immediately beneath my gallery, many courtiers and officers were assembling before the throne, at the head of whom I noted the prince Belshazzar, he who had counselled that I should be tormented to death.

At first this throne was empty, for Nabonidus had left it for a while. When he reappeared I saw the reason, for now he was gorgeously apparelled and his head-dress and beard which had been disarrayed, were straightened, so that in his jewelled robes he wore the aspect of a great king.

CHAPTER 14

The Prophet and the Prince

For a while from this high place I watched the scene wondering idly what it might portend, as a man does who knows not whether he has another hour to live. Indeed it was not till afterwards that the chatter of Nabonidus as to marrying again came back to my mind, which at the time was full of all that I had heard as to the hideous methods by which Eastern kings did their enemies, or those who were condemned as malefactors, to death, with fire and water and hooked instruments that slowly tore the vitals out of them in a fashion that was not known in Egypt. Also it was full of rage against Amasis who, as now I saw clearly, although he did not guess that it would bring me to Babylon, had sent me on this mission that it might be my last. For had he not betrayed me to these Babylonians, naming me a spy to make sure, as he thought, of the death of one of whom for his own reasons he would be rid by the hands of others, thus leaving his own unstained?

But when there arose a cry of, "The bride comes! The royal Lady comes!" every word of that talk as to taking another bride came back to me and I felt my heart stand still.

What if this bride, this royal lady should chance to be my own wife—Myra? What if I should be forced to witness the giving of her to that crowned dotard whose foolishness had just saved me from death, if only for an hour?

I turned to the eunuch and asked him what was the meaning of this ceremony, but either he did not understand my question or thought it unlawful to answer. At least he remained silent.

Now through the open doors came a number of fair women singing and dancing. Then followed musicians playing upon flutes and other instruments, and after them heralds who bore gifts upon cushions. Next appeared a litter surrounded by a guard of soldiers. The lit-

145

ter was set down, the guard withdrew to right and left. Waiting ladies of the royal household advanced and drawing the curtains of the litter, helped her who was within it to descend. She came forward and followed by a woman of short stature dressed in a plain robe, walked to an open space in front of the litter. Now I could see her well for the light from a high window fell upon her.

It was Myra herself and her attendant was the old nurse, Metep! Yes, thus again I saw Myra from whom I had parted months before outside the temple of Hathor at Memphis.

She was royally arrayed and wore, as I noted, all the wonderful jewels that were her heritage, also the crystal pendant containing the little pressed lily that I had given her after Belus had seen visions in the bowl at the Happy House in Memphis. Upon her breast too was the emerald cylinder covered with strange writing which was among the gems in the bag her mother had thrust upon me in the tent on the battlefield; for all these, and others, had been sent with her from Memphis. Further, upon her brow holding her hair in place, was a little golden circlet from the centre of which sprang the royal *uraeus* of Egypt; even at this distance I could catch the flashing of its jewelled eyes. Thus adorned she glided up the great hall, staring about her like one bewildered who knew not where she was or what she did, a vision of such wondrous beauty that a murmur of amazement arose from the lips of the assembled company.

She reached the space before the throne where but a few minutes before I had stood, a captive condemned to death, and halted there. In the pause that followed I could see the courtiers and the nobles bend forward to study her loveliness, and especially the bold eyes of the Prince Belshazzar fixed upon her face. Next, stiffly enough, the old king Nabonidus descended from the throne and coming to her, parted the thin transparent veil that covered her from head to foot, and kissed her on the brow. Thereon all cried,

"The great King accepts the royal Lady of Egypt. May the King live for ever! May the royal Lady, his wife, live for ever."

The echoes of this formal shout of welcome which announced that Nabonidus had taken another wife in the presence of his people, died away and suddenly Myra seemed to awake and began to speak. She spoke low, yet, as the eunuch had told me, that hall was so built that every syllable reached me in the high-set, secret gallery.

"Touch me not, O great King," she said in a voice of music and using the Babylonian tongue which she knew well, "for I am not worthy."

146

"What do you mean, Lady?" asked Nabonidus astonished. "It seems to me that both in beauty and by rank you are worthy of any king who ever sat upon the throne of Babylon."

"I have no rank, O King," she answered, "who was not born of the royal House of Egypt. Nay, I am but a foundling taken from my dying mother's breast upon the field of battle in the time of Merodach. Amasis, the Pharaoh of Egypt, for his own purposes has deceived you, O King. He stole me away from my home because I am well-favoured, and palmed me off upon your envoys as a princess of the line of Pharaoh. This coronet I wear is not mine, O King," and with a sudden motion she tore the *uraeus* circlet from her brow and flung it away, so that her abundant hair was loosed and fell down about her.

From all who heard these bold words came mutterings and gasps of astonishment, for that such an affront should be put upon the majesty of the King of Babylon seemed to them impossible.

Nabonidus lifted his hand and they were silent. Then he said,

"If what you say is true, Lady, the Pharaoh of Egypt has done me a great wrong and one which many would seek to wash away in blood. But is it true? And even if it be true, well, I have accepted you and your mien is fair and royal if your blood be not. Though indeed," he added as if to himself, "to me who am so old, fair women royal or other now are naught."

He thought for a moment, then continued, "This is a tangled coil, but if you can prove what you allege, it still seems best and would do you least dishonour that you should enter the palace as one of the ladies of my household."

"It cannot be, O King," said Myra in a strained voice and I saw the pearls upon her breast quiver as she spoke.

"Cannot be! Why cannot it be?" he asked sternly, adding, "Great kings do not listen to such words."

"Because, O King, I am already wed and therefore unmeet for the royal household. Spare me, O King," and she sank to her knees, stretching out her arms in supplication.

"Already wed!" he exclaimed shrinking back from her, while some of those present in tones of horror echoed the words, "Already wed!"

For as I learned afterwards, for ages no such sacrilege had been known as that one who was married should be given to the Great King as a wife or as a member of his household.

"Let the woman be taken away," said a voice, I think it was that of the vizier who had interpreted the king's motion as an order of death.

"Nay," exclaimed Nabonidus, "I did not speak. If her story be true, namely that she was torn from her home and sent hither to me disguised as a royal princess of Egypt in return for my daughter given to Pharaoh, then the blame is Pharaoh's and not hers, and with Pharaoh we must settle our account. But I repeat—is it true? Though that a woman should lie upon such a matter, thus throwing away the place of Queen of Babylon, seems strange, unless love drives her. Lady, have you any evidence to your tale?"

Myra, still upon her knees, looked over her shoulder and said in the Egyptian tongue,

"Come hither, Nurse, and tell the king who I am and how I came here."

So Metep stood forward staring about her in a bewildered fashion, for she had understood no word of all this talk in the Babylonian tongue. Soon it was seen that she could only speak through an interpreter. After some search an officer was found who knew Egyptian, though not too well for he spoke it haltingly and with a foreign accent. At length he asked her whether it was true that her mistress was married.

Metep answered, "Yes, she is married, unless the priests of Hathor are all liars," and then began a rambling story of how Myra had been taken away from the Happy House by the servants of Pharaoh with whom came the great lady, Chloe, and how she had clung to the doorway pillars till they dragged her arms apart, a tale that caused me to grind my teeth with rage. Still it was one of which the king soon wearied, especially as the officer interpreted but ill.

"This old woman is a babbling fool," he said. "Let her be silent. Is there no other here who can speak of this matter? If not the lady had best be removed to the women's court and set among those to whom the King has bidden farewell, until our pleasure concerning her is known."

Then suddenly there stepped forward a man clad in the robe of a Babylonian astrologer, for on it and on his pointed cap were painted stars and other strange emblems. By the gods, it was Belus! Yes, Belus himself and no other, and oh! my heart leapt at the sight of him.

"Who is this?" asked Nabonidus.

"May it please the King," answered Belus, "I am one whom the King once knew well, before he was called to the throne of Babylon. Yes, I sprang from one who sat upon that throne before him. I was scribe and astrologer in the royal household; a priest also of Marduk and of Ishtar, the Queen of Heaven. In those days I, who am now known as Belus, or as Azar, had another name which the King may

148

remember. If not I will whisper it in his ear," and stepping forward he bent his head and said something that caused Nabonidus to start. Then retiring, he went on,

"The King will recall my story. I was married but had not lost my wife who left me with a daughter. That maiden was exceedingly fair. She was stolen from me, it matters not by whom"—here I thought that he glanced at Belshazzar who I saw was listening intently. "The maid was one of spirit and because she fought against fate, she was murdered. Her body was thrown into the river and found with a letter in her robe that told all the tale. If the King would see that letter, I have it here. I sought redress but found none. Therefore I left Babylon and went to dwell at the court of the Pharaoh of Egypt, leaving behind me my curse on those by whom I have been wronged."

Here again I thought that he glanced towards Belshazzar.

"Never have I returned to Babylon although I still have friends here to whom I write from time to time. These can testify of me, as can the masters of magic and the readers of the stars with whom I am ever in communion. Yet fate has brought me back to Babylon, as soon or late, I knew well that it would do. Now is the King satisfied that I am a true man, to prove which I have told him all this story?"

"I am satisfied and I accept the story which to my sorrow, I have heard before, O friend of my youth," answered Nabonidus.

"Then if the King will be pleased to listen, I will witness concerning this lady whom I have known from childhood. As she has said, she was taken from the arms of her dying mother when an infant after the great battle between the Egyptians and the Babylonians, in which the Prince Merodach commanded the forces of Babylon, for I saw her brought to his tent by the Egyptian captain who found her, and with her those jewels which she wears today. That captain who was my friend and with whom I dwelt, nurtured her to womanhood, all supposing that she was his daughter, till at length, but a little while ago, he took her to wife. Immediately afterwards she was stolen away by the Pharaoh of Egypt and, because of her great beauty and royal bearing, was sent in the character of a princess of Egypt to be a wife to your Majesty."

"A trick for which Pharaoh shall pay dear, especially as I have touched her with my lips and therefore accepted her as my wife," explained Nabonidus. "Yes, and my wife she must remain until I die, for is it not an ancient law that what the King of Babylon does in council before the people can never be undone?"

Now when I heard these words in my watching-place, hope left me, as I think it did Myra, for I saw her tremble and rest her hand on the shoulder of Metep as though she were about to fall. Still I set my teeth and listened on.

"What is the name of the man to whom this lady is wed, and what his station, O friend of my youth now known as Belus and travelling under that of Azar?" asked the king.

"His name is Ramose, O King, one who in my company follows after learning and holds high office in Memphis in Egypt. By birth he is a son of Apries, late Pharaoh of Egypt, having a Grecian lady called Chloe for his mother."

Now the vizier whispered something in the ear of the king, who nodded and said,

"Therefore one of whom the present Pharaoh, the slayer of Apries, would wish to be rid. Oh, now I see all the plan. The husband who sheltered the child as his daughter and afterwards made her his wife, is the bastard of a Pharaoh of the true descent and thus has royal blood in his veins. Hence she, the supposed daughter, is called a royal princess and as such declared to be a fit wife for the Majesty of Babylon. Truly a plot well worthy of the base-born venturer who sits upon the throne of Egypt."

He paused, his old hands shaking with wrath, then turned to Myra and asked,

"Much wronged Lady, what am I to do with you?"

"O King, I pray you give me back to my husband whom I love and who loves me."

"Where is your husband?"

"O King, I do not know. When I left Egypt in charge of your officers I heard that Pharaoh detained him at his court. Perchance Belus there knows, for never have they been separated for many years."

"If so, Belus may be wise to keep silent, lest Pharaoh should learn his answer," said the king warningly. "Listen, Lady, according to our law you are now my wife. The past matters not, I have touched you with my lips and you are the wife of the King of Babylon. Is that not the law, Vizier?"

"It is, O King," he replied, bowing. "Henceforward if any man ventures to look upon this woman, yea, even though he were once her husband, he must die, and if she shares his guilt she must die with him."

"You hear, Lady," said the king.

"I hear," she whispered.

"Yet," he went on, "be sure that you have naught to fear from me who do not wish to anger the gods by such a sin, and therefore lest you should be troubled on this matter, you shall not enter into my household. Nor can you be sent back to Egypt for many reasons, and above all for your own sake, for then Pharaoh Amasis would be avenged upon you who have betrayed his villainy. Where then must you go?"

"To the tomb, I think," she answered in a faint voice. "There alone are rest and safety."

"Nay," answered the old king looking on her with kind eyes, "you are too fair and over-young to die. Who knows what the gods may have in store for you? Yet what am I do to with you?"

Now I saw that black-robed, thin-faced, dreamy-eyed old man who was called Daniel or Belteshazzar and a prophet, step forward out of the crowd of courtiers. He came to Myra and studied her face. Next he dropped his eyes and stared fixedly at the emerald amulet which hung beneath the pearls and other ornaments upon her bosom. Then he turned to the king and said,

"May the King live for ever! It is revealed to me, O King, that this lady is by blood one of a captive people who dwell in this kingdom, that of the Hebrews, to which I too belong. Never before have I beheld her, still I say it is revealed to me. O King, it has pleased you and some who sat upon your throne before you to show me favour and to make me a ruler in your land."

"We know your story, O Prophet Belteshazzar," answered Nabonidus in a voice that was touched with awe, "and that you are favoured and protected by your God with whom you commune day and night. It is needless to repeat it before those who have seen your miracles. If you have any petition to make concerning this woman, speak on, remembering that having been accepted by me, under our law which may not be changed, she can be given to no other man who lives."

"I have a petition to make, O King," answered the prophet. "The King knows what I am and my manner of life. Let this lady and her servant be given into my charge till the will of God concerning her is known. Meanwhile I swear that during the King's lifetime she shall be visited or spoken to by no other man, and thus the law of Babylon as to those who have been accepted by the King, shall not be broken. Let officers be set about my house to watch the fulfilment of my oath."

Nabonidus thought a while; then he said wearily,

"I tire of this business. Scribes, write down my decree. I command that the woman named Myra, whom I accepted believing her to be a royal princess of Egypt given to me in exchange for that royal lady of Babylon whom I have sent as a wife to Pharaoh, but who it seems is already wed to another man and therefore unfit to enter my household, shall be placed in the charge of Belteshazzar, my servant, a prophet of the people of Judah, to hold in ward until my pleasure concerning her is known. I command that a guard be set by day and night about the dwelling of the prophet Belteshazzar, to make sure that this woman has no converse with any other man. If she is found in company or speech with any man save the prophet, let her and that man be slain. Now touch my sceptre, both of you, O Prophet, and Woman Myra, in token that you acknowledge my decree."

So saying he stretched out a little golden rod that all this while he had held in his hand, first to one of them and then to the other, thereby assuring them of safety and making his word unchangeable.

They touched the sceptre; the stern-faced, black-robed prophet bowed to the king and beckoned to Myra to follow him. A guard formed round them and they departed from the hall of audience by a side entrance. Myra, who seemed crushed with grief, leaning on the shoulder of Metep, for she tottered as she walked. Her path led her past the spot where the Prince Belshazzar, governor and vice-king of Babylon, stood surrounded by his courtiers. He bent forward and stared at her in a fashion of which none could mistake the meaning, then uttered some jest to the lords that caused them to laugh and the prophet to turn his head and look at him as though in rebuke. Next this Belshazzar advanced to the throne and said something to the king in a low voice which I could not catch. Whatever it may have been it angered Nabonidus, for he flushed and replied wrathfully,

"What I have said, I have said, who am still king in Babylon, and it shall go ill with any who defy me, yes, even with you, Prince."

In the silence that followed these threatening words, he waved his sceptre, thereby declaring the court at an end, left the throne and departed attended by his officers.

Belshazzar watched him go, then he shrugged and said in a loud and angry voice to his attendants,

"Even kings do not live for ever and their decrees die with them. Soon I will find yonder lovely one a gayer home than the cell of that black Hebrew wizard," a speech at which some laughed and others looked afraid, for it was treasonable.

****

The great hall emptied, the glittering crowd pouring through the doorways like a stream of gold and jewels. Soon they were all gone.

For a while I sat on in the secret gallery so overwhelmed with what I had endured that I could scarcely think. At last a messenger came who whispered to the watching eunuch. Thereon he touched me on the shoulder and led me away surrounded by the guard. I went, wondering whether I was being taken to my death. But it was not so, for presently once more I found myself in my prison where they left me alone.

CHAPTER 15

Ramose Finds Friends

They brought me food but I could not touch it, though of their strong wine I drank a goblet or two which gave me back what I seemed to have lost, the power to think.

Strange and dreadful was my case! I had found Myra but to lose her again for ever, although for the present she had escaped violence and was left alive in what seemed to be safe hands, those of the Hebrew prophet about whom such marvellous tales were told and who was feared of all.

I who was a student of the customs of foreign nations, well knew those of Assyria and Babylon, and indeed of all the monarchs of the East, namely that women were their chattels and that any who once had passed their doors and entered their presence, were sealed to them for ever and under pain of death might henceforward be seen only by other women and by eunuchs. The man who spoke to them was doomed, even though he were a brother; they were dead to the world. Such was the lot of Myra which perhaps she might have escaped, had she but spoken earlier before, moved by her beauty, the old king accepted her. Yet how could she speak who did not know or understand?

Stay! Belus whom I thought lost, had appeared again clothed with power and as a friend of the king, who it seemed had been a companion of his youth. In Belus there was hope. Yet what could Belus do? He might so work that my life would be spared, for which if Myra were lost to me, I should not thank him—no more. And that beetle-browed, fierce-eyed Belshazzar, that prince of evil fame, the real king in Babylon, who but for some chance, if there be any chances in the world, would have sat that day upon the seat of judgment—what of him? He had cast eyes of longing upon Myra, and what he desired soon or late he would surely take, as he had declared but now, unless indeed she escaped him by the gate of death. Oh! my strait was sore and I had naught on which to lean, save trust in God, if there were any god who paid heed to the miseries of us poor mortals and stretched over them the shield of justice.

Yet life still remained to us and while we lived all might be retrieved, for the last throw had not been cast. In my agony I prayed, not knowing to whom or to what to pray,

"O Power that made the world," I cried in my heart, "O Strength unseen, unknowable, that drew us out of darkness and set us on this gaudy, changeful stage, whence presently we must fall into Death's deeper darkness. O vast Intelligence that deviseth all, O Beginning and End that is no end; O Point of Time and Circle of Eternity, hear me, the mote of dust blown by thy breath. Help me and her thou gavest me who has been made the sport of vanity and statecraft. Save her from shame and of thy mercy give us who love each other, our little hour of light before we are borne back into blackness. Rob us not of the common gift that is poured upon beast and bird and flower—the joy they know beneath the glory of the sun. Or if this may not be, let us pass hence swiftly and hand in hand go to seek that which lies beyond the sun."

In some such words I prayed and as the last of them passed my lips, the door opened and a messenger appeared.

"Rise up," he said. "The Great King commands your presence."

A guard following me, I went with him to the private apartments of the palace. We passed through many that were gorgeous to a large plain chamber, well lit from the roof. Here upon a chair set against a table, sat a man whom at first I did not know, a little withered old man dressed in such a robe as workmen wear. Looking at him again I perceived that it was none other than Nabonidus the king stripped of all his finery and engaged in eating a meal. The food was simple. On the bare table were a jug of wine and a goblet or two, all of them, as I knew who collect such things, dating from ancient days. Then there was bread, and with it a bird cut up upon a platter, cheese made of goat's milk and a handful of onions. Such was the fare of this monarch of the earth.

I prostrated myself, but he called to me to rise, saying,

"We are not at court here. You are the Egyptian who understands about gods, are you not? Well, have you eaten after all that wearisome ceremony?"

I replied that I had not, whereon he added,

"Then come sit down and take some of this duck, if you can get your teeth through it, which I can't. And if not, the bread and the cheese are good and soft, and the country wine not bad. Don't stare at me, you fool of a eunuch! Of course I know he can kill me if he likes, but he won't, for learned men, and I take it he is one of them, who study and seek out the secrets of the past never kill each other—except with their tongues. Also if he did, I am not certain that I should be sorry. There is so much that I cannot learn in this world, that I rather look forward to another where if there are thrones, may it please the gods I shall not fill one of them. Out you go, Eunuch, and take that guard with you. I hate to see them watching me, and the shining of their swords, and to listen to the clatter of their armour. Swords to stab and armour to turn them, and war, war, war, these are the world into which an evil fate has cast me, and I weary of them all. Don't stand there stammering. Out you go! If he kills me, you can kill him afterwards, and we will continue our discussion elsewhere. But I tell you he won't."

So the eunuch and the guard went, unwillingly enough, staring first at Nabonidus and then at me.

"Now come and sit down," said the king. "There isn't another stool, or at least they all have things on them, but that old pottery coffin will do as well. I often use it myself."

"O King, I am unworthy," I began.

"By Marduk, or by Ishtar, or by Ammon of Egypt, whichever you prefer, that is for me to judge, not for you. Don't waste time, man. Look at all the relics I want to talk to you about," and he pointed to long tables on which stood a number of stone gods, among them those that I had seen in the hall of audience and trays full of inscriptions graved upon clay or marble tablets and cylinders.

So I sat myself upon the old pottery coffin which, I observed, still had bones inside it, and began to eat. For now, I know not why, my appetite had returned to me; perhaps hope was working in my heart.

"I did you a favour just now, Egyptian," said the king, with a chuckle. "When I told them to fetch you, they answered that they feared it was too late, as my son Belshazzar had issued an order for your execution in my name, perhaps because he thought I meant you to die after all, or because he wished to be rid of you, I don't know which. However, he won't do that again, for I commanded that his people whom he was sending on the business, should be seized and beaten on the feet until they can only crawl away upon their hands and knees. Really," he added reflectively, "it is Belshazzar who should suffer, not his servants. Only you see he is almost as much a king as I

156

am. That's the way of the world, isn't it? One offends and others pay for it. I daresay it works well in the end, as it teaches them and the rest not to have to do with those who do offend."

"I thank the King," I said, thinking to myself that it was not strange that my heart had been so heavy in my cell.

"Don't thank me for I owe you a good deal—take a cup of wine, won't you, and look at the carving on that goblet before you drink, for it is beautiful, of the third dynasty of Ur. See the lion. We can't do such work nowadays. Fill mine first that I may drink to show you it isn't poisoned. I have never poisoned a man yet, which is more than most kings can say."

I did as he bade me and we both drank.

"Now listen," he went on as he set down his cup. "Your real name is not Ptahmes but Ramose of whom, before you appeared here as a spy, I have heard as a scholar and a collector in Cyprus, for I know the names of all the really learned men. Don't deny it for I have just had a private talk with my old friend Belus. Of course I know that you are not a spy. You are a son of Apries, are you not, one of whom that dog, Amasis, wishes to be rid because of the blood in you which he and his son have not got; also for other reasons?"

"It is so, O King, yet of old days this Amasis showed himself a good friend to me because I pleased him as a soldier, though once since he became Pharaoh, when in his cups, he did threaten my life at my own table. Now if he would have me killed I think it is for another reason."

"Perhaps, Ramose. Who knows the reasons of such a low-bred man? They are as hidden as his parents. But this I can tell you. Through those who serve him in this kingdom he caused me to be warned that you were a dangerous fellow, believed to be the bearer of forged writings purporting to appoint you an envoy from Egypt to Cyrus the Persian, whereas really you were in the pay of the said Cyrus."

"It is false, O King. Let the writings that have been taken from me, be carefully examined and it will be seen that they are not forged. Also I was forced to this embassy; why I have learned today."

"Which if you had carried out you would have found an evil one, for doubtless Cyrus is also warned against you. Oh! your Amasis is a rat! He is afraid of Babylon and he is also afraid of the Persians, with more reason perhaps for I think their star rises in the East. Therefore he tries to play off one against the other and to pretend himself the friend of both. But tell me, Ramose. If you thought yourself an ambassador to Cyrus, what were you doing making secret inquiries in Damascus?"

"I sought one whom I had lost, O King."

"So I have learned. You and no other are the same Ramose who is the husband of that most beauteous lady who today was delivered to me as a wife, to bribe me to a friendship with Egypt, but who it seems was stolen from you by Amasis, pretending that he believed her to be your daughter and therefore with royal blood in her. Had I seen Belus first and known all the story, never would I have accepted her. But I did not until it was too late and she was so exceedingly fair that for a flash of time I thought myself young again, as old men do at moments, and received her in the ancient, accepted fashion, which perchance you saw."

"Yes, I saw it all," I answered with a groan.

"Therefore, Ramose, it is finished," he went on. "For even a king of Babylon with all his power cannot hand over to any other man a woman whom once he has publicly acknowledged as his wife, because if he did so, he would earn the curse of the gods—or of their priests—and bring contempt and mockery upon his name. Yet I have done what I could for you and her. I have placed her in the keeping of the holy saint who confounded one that went before me, and who is feared and honoured throughout my kingdom as a mighty magician; a half-god; not of it, but dwelling on the earth. With him she will be safe, for there are no men in his house where even the boldest dare not molest her, no, not Belshazzar himself—while I live," he added slowly as though to warn me.

"Still our case is evil, O King, who are wed and love each other, and yet under pain of death must always be separate."

For a while the old man went on munching the brown barley bread with his toothless gums and gazing at me. Then he said,

"Perhaps not quite so evil as you think, friend Ramose. Listen. I will tell you what I hide even from my physicians and astrologers. From the physicians because they cannot help me; from the astrologers because it will save them and their stars the trouble of providing favourable omens and interpretations that will never be fulfilled. I shall not be here long, friend Ramose, at least above the ground. At times my heart seems to stop, especially if I am hurried or angered, and I descend into a pit of blackness and walk upon the edge of death. It did so when I learned of the trick of Amasis and again now for an instant, when I grew wrath because Belshazzar for some dark reason of his own had commanded that you should be killed against my will. Well, soon I think I shall walk over that edge and there will be an end."

"May the gods forbid it! May the King live for ever!" I said earnestly, for forgetting its own troubles my heart went out towards this kindly old man to whom majesty brought so little joy.

"May the gods do nothing of the sort, Egyptian, for I think a fate is falling upon Babylon which I do not wish to live to see. While I have strength I cling to the throne that, if I can, I may shield her from the folly of those who refuse to make peace with this upstart Persian, Cyrus, who is yet a great man. When I am gone let Belshazzar and his young counsellors follow their own road to ruin. I read in your eyes that you are honest, also Belus has made report to me of you; were it otherwise I should not speak thus with a stranger, but it seems that after all you are only a flatterer like the rest with your—'May the King live for ever!' Being wise, you know that kings do not live for ever, unless indeed that is the lot of all elsewhere. Still I forgive you who being much shaken and afraid seek to speak smooth things."

"It is true, pardon me, O King."

"Let it be and hearken. When a king of Babylon dies the ancient and inviolable law is loosed and, within a year, the women of his household, save the mother of the new king, may marry and go where they will. Then will be your opportunity as regards this lady Myra, if you can win her out of the grasp of any who would hold her fast in Babylon, and especially of one whom I will not name who desires her and, as I hear, already has sworn to take her. Therefore you must stay on here in this city where your goods shall be restored to you with my pardon for all that you may have done. It is in the hands of the gods. May they give you strength and wisdom. Meanwhile keep to your false name of Ptahmes and, if you would live, let none guess that you are Ramose, the husband of Myra. I have spoken. Now let us talk about other things."

Then, dismissing my private business to which he had given so much thought in the goodness of his kind heart, he began to speak wisely enough of the old gods whose images stood about in this chamber, of their history and worshippers, of the cities where he had found them, of the temples that he had built or restored, and I know not what besides.

As it chanced of many of these matters I knew a great deal, having studied the attributes of the gods of many lands, comparing them one with another and tracing their rise and fall with that of the countries or cities which worshipped them, or how they changed their characters and names as it might suit their priests to make them do. So it came to pass that we talked on, as learned man to learned man, until at length the dusk began to gather and I saw that the old king grew weary, for he leaned back in his chair, put his hand upon his heart, closed his eyes and sighed. I watched him anxiously and especially a blue tinge which appeared upon his lips, not knowing what to do, who was sure that if he died when I was alone with him, it would be laid to my door and my life would pay the price.

Presently, however, he recovered and ordered me to strike upon a bell which stood near by. Instantly attendants and guards appeared who all this while had been gathered without, and with them one of his private scribes.

To this man the king dictated words which he wrote down. They were an order of pardon to me, Ptahmes the Egyptian, or rather a declaration of my innocence of all that was laid to my charge. Also a decree that I should be set at liberty, furnished with apartments in the palace and sustenance as the king's guest, and have right of access to the king at all times that he could receive me. This writing he sealed in duplicate with his own seal, and gave one copy of it to me, commanding that the other should be made known to all the officers and governors of the palace and of Babylon, and then filed in the temple of Marduk, that thenceforward I might be safe in my going out and my coming in and that everyone might do me reverence as the king's friend.

These things done he waved his hand, thus bidding me farewell and I was led away, no longer as a prisoner but with every honour, the soldiers saluting and eunuchs and chamberlains bowing down before me.

Such were the changes of fortune that I experienced on this, my first day in Babylon, and such were the strange happenings that befell me.

****

They led me to beautiful apartments high up in the old part of the palace that, as I was told, in the days of dead kings had served as the lodgings of envoys from foreign courts. Here I found all my goods, and with them the gold that had been taken from me, yes, to the last piece, and even the letters of Amasis and his officers, that should have brought about my death, though these were given to me later. Having been acquitted and honoured by the king, everything against me was forgotten; I was as another man. Palace servants waited on me, bringing delicate food and wine, palace minstrels played upon many strange instruments while I ate; even palace dancing girls appeared in light attire, but these I sent away being in no mood for their blandishments.

I ate, or pretended to eat, because I was ashamed to refuse the food with so many eyes watching me. I drank as much as I should drink, or perhaps more, because I needed the comfort of wine, and afterwards sat and brooded alone at an open window-place. Thence I could see much of the mighty city of Babylon over which shone the full moon, the towering temples, the gleaming river, the vast encircling walls, the palaces, the gardens, the populous streets whence rose the hum of a million voices, the flaring signal fires and cressets upon pinnacles and pillars, and a thousand other spectacles that were new to me.

But these moved me not, for always my eyes wandered over the sea of roofs, wondering beneath which of them dwelt that piercing-eyed old man, the Prophet Daniel, or Belteshazzar, of whom such marvellous tales were told, and with him, Myra, my heart's desire.

Now that I thought of it, Belus had spoken to me of this magician long ago, saying that he had interpreted the dreams of Nebuchadnezzar. Yes, even when the king had forgotten what they were, and thereby had saved the lives of all the wise men and seers whom, in his fury, the king purposed to put to death. Also, interpreting another dream, he had told him that because he thought himself greater than God, God would make him as a beast in the field, so that he would run about naked in his garden and eat herbs like a beast. This indeed came to pass, since before his end Nebuchadnezzar was smitten with madness. Yet he greatly honoured Daniel or Belteshazzar as he was named in Babylon, worshipping him as one divine, and promoted him to be the ruler of Babylon after the king, a rank that it seemed he still retained at least in name. Therefore Myra was more safe with him than any other. Yet was she safe? Remembering the devouring glance and the words of the fierce-eyed Belshazzar, the real king of Babylon, I asked myself—Oh! was she safe?

Why not—if this Daniel were the servant and minister of the true God and could throw his mantle over her? But was there any true god who had power in a world where dwelt so many devils? Alas! I did not know who for all my seeking, had never found him, though at times, it is true, I thought that I had kissed his feet.

There came a challenge at my door where it seemed a guard was set, a word spoken, the rattle of a sheathed sword and the clank of bolts. A man entered looking about him. As he moved his head the lamplight fell upon his face, and I saw that it was Belus! I remember that I ran and threw my arms around him, and that he kissed me on the brow as a father might do, for indeed he was the only true father I had ever known. Then, having made sure that we were alone, we sat down and talked.

161

"Fortune has not gone so ill with us, Ramose, or rather Ptahmes, for that name is safer here," he said. "When a while ago we were parted on that journey to Seleucia I scarcely thought to see you again living. They seized me and to save myself from death, I declared to the king's scribe who accompanied them, what I have hid even from you—my true lineage which is high enough, seeing that through my mother, the king Nabonidus and his son Belshazzar are my kinsmen. Also I showed my rank as a priest of Ishtar and one of the first of the College of Astrologers, and proved what I said by a certain writing and by tokens that I carry hidden about me.

"They bowed before those holy tokens and instantly I was hurried away in a chariot, that I might be brought into the presence of the king and my tale confirmed by the Councils of the priests and the astrologers at Babylon. I prayed earnestly that you might come with me but it was not allowed, which, had not my spirit told me otherwise, would have caused me to believe that you were dead, for of your fate they would say nothing.

"I reached Babylon before you, travelling very swiftly by the king's posts and though I could not see Nabonidus my cousin, because he was sick and might not be disturbed, I appeared before the Councils, among whom were men who had known me well in my youth. I was given back my rank among the companies of the priests and the watchers of the stars, which indeed I had never forfeited as the records showed, who had left the land by the leave of Nebuchadnezzar, to gather learning in other countries which I might share with my companions in Babylon, as I have done year by year. So very swiftly, as though it had been decreed, all went well with me and now once more I am a man of high rank and station in the great city, also as it chances, a relative by blood of that King of kings who today sits upon the throne."

"And how did you learn what had happened to me, and to Myra, Belus?"

"I made inquiry, but having so little time, could discover nothing because your fate after you were taken prisoner was not yet known, and of Myra who came to be wife to the king, if any knew they would not speak because of the strange laws of Babylon as to the women of the royal household. Not till early this same morning was I sure that you were in Babylon and, because the matter was urgent, would at once be brought before the king for judgment, also that afterwards the royal lady, as they thought her, who had been sent from Egypt to be wife to the king, would be presented to him in the presence of the councillors and nobles, that the friendship between

Babylon and Egypt might be thus publicly proclaimed. I strove to see you and to send a letter to Myra, but it was impossible, for both of you were too closely guarded. I strove to see the king, but this also was impossible for, having been sick, he was still asleep and would not rise from his bed till the hour came for him to attend the court, as by good fortune he had suddenly determined to do at the time of the uttering of judgments, to settle some matters concerning a holy statue about which there was trouble because it had been brought to Babylon. Do you know the rest?"

"Yes, Belus, for after my trial I was hidden away high up in a secret gallery of the women where I could see all and hear every word that passed. I tell you when I beheld Myra standing beneath me in her beauty, and saw that old king so moved by it that he forgot his years and weakness and, descending from his throne, embraced her, thereby receiving her as a wife according to the ancient customs, I thought that my heart would burst. Oh! why did she not speak sooner, for then, being good-hearted, he might have spared her?"

"Doubtless because it was so fated, Ramose, for her good—and your own. If the king had rejected her as some common cheat trapped out to ape a royal lady, she would have been driven from the Presence to fall into the hands of the first who chose to take her. Whose would they have been, Ramose?"

"Do you mean those of the Prince Belshazzar?" I asked.

"Yes, I do. Ramose, I have known him from his boyhood and I tell you he is not a man, but a tiger who loves to prey upon fair women; in particular upon those who hate and fly from him. You heard the tale I told the king. Ramose, it was Belshazzar who stole my daughter and afterwards murdered her, no other man."

For a while he paused and there was silence, for I knew not what to say. Then his withered face and quiet eyes seemed to take fire and he went on,

"Ramose, as you know, I am by nature gentle, one who can forgive and find excuse for almost every sin because I understand the hearts of men. But this prince I never can forgive who, as it chances, knows all the horror of his crime and what he caused that poor maid of mine to suffer before he butchered her. Towards him I am a minister of vengeance appointed by God. Aye, through all these years, while I dwelt so peacefully with you, I have awaited my hour, sure that it would come, and now I think it is at hand, though still I know not how. Doubtless he will try to kill me because he fears me whom he has so deeply wronged, but he will not succeed."

He paused again, then said,

"Let my troubles be a while; we will speak of yours, or rather of ours. As he dealt with my daughter, so will Belshazzar deal with Myra if he can. Having seen her beauty of which he had been told, he will surely try to take her; indeed at the court I read it in his eyes and heard him say as much after the king had gone."

"As I did," I broke in with a groan.

"Now," went on Belus, "when I learned these things from those who had been friends to me in the days of my youth, also that it was impossible that I could speak or write you or Myra before the sitting of the court, I went back to my chamber and prayed for help to the Spirit of Wisdom whom I worship. So earnestly did I pray that a faintness came over me and all grew dark to my eyes; then on the blackness, or so it seemed to me, appeared one word in the Chaldean writing, namely 'Daniel.' My mind returned to me and I wondered who or what was Daniel, till presently I remembered that Daniel was the name of a certain high-born captain of the people of Judah, he whom Nebuchadnezzar advanced to great honour, giving him the new name of Belteshazzar, by which thenceforth he was known in Babylon. Also I was sure that this man was brought to my mind because from him there might come help in my trouble.

"I went out and having inquired where dwelt the lord and prophet Belteshazzar, I ran as never I have run before, to his house which is near to the southern gate. As I reached it Daniel himself came out from the courtyard riding on a mule, for after all these years I knew him again. I craved speech of him and at first he answered,

"'Friend, I go to my garden without the wall, there to rest and pray. If you have business with me I beg you to come at another time.'

"'Lord and Prophet,' I answered, 'the business is most urgent.' Then seeing that he was still minded to go on, I added, 'It has to do with one of the blood of Judah.'"

"Why did you say that?" I asked of Belus. "Was it only because you thought he would listen to nothing else?"

"Nay, Ramose, it was because Myra, as I have long been sure, is of that race. Did not her dying mother tell you so? Is not her name that of a woman of Israel? Are not Hebrew characters, of which the meaning is hid from me, engraved upon the emerald amulet she wears, which her mother gave to you with the jewels? Is not her appearance that of a noble and beautiful lady of the Children of Judah, as you say was that of her mother before her? At least I did say it and the prophet hearkened. Dismounting from his mule he led me into the house and there in a small room where stood many written rolls upon shelves, I brought myself to his mind and told him all our story."

"'What would you have me do, Belus?' he asked when it was finished. 'It is true that I am still named Governor of Babylon, but my word does not run against the king's, and it is Belshazzar, the king's son, not Belteshazzar the prophet, who today has power in this evil city.'

"'I do not know,' I answered. 'Who am I that I should instruct the greatest seer in Babylon?'

"'You tell me that you prayed—to what god I am not sure—and that my name came to your mind, O Belus. Well, the example is good and I will follow it, asking for light. Wait here a while and be silent.'

"Then he went to a window-place that jutted from the wall of the room, and knelt down by the open window to pray, and watching his face from where I sat, I saw that it shone as it were with light from within. Yes, it shone like a lamp, so that I grew sure that his god was speaking to him. If this were so he did not tell me what he had learned, for when he rose from his knees all he said was,

"'I will not ride to my garden this day, though that is a sorrow to me who longed for its peace. Nay, I will attend the court and there abide what may happen.'

"'Cannot you see the king at once, O Prophet?' I asked.

"'No, it is impossible unless I am summoned. Moreover, no such counsel has come to me. You are an astrologer and a priest of Marduk, are you not? If so, go, dress yourself in the robes of your office or of your false god and, as you have a right to do, attend at the court where I think you will be needed.'

"'My false god,' I answered. 'Well at least he led me to you, O Prophet. Tell me then who is the true God. For Him I have sought all my life.'

"'Mayhap to find him at last to whom you draw near, for otherwise your prayer would not have been answered. But of these matters we will speak afterwards. Go now and do those things which your heart teaches you. Go, and swiftly, for time presses.'

"So I went and what happened afterwards, you know, Ramose."

CHAPTER 16

Ramose is Tempted

Now for a while in this story of mine little happened that is worth the telling. Belus and I dwelt together in the palace as we were allowed to do by the decree of the king. Of Myra we saw nothing for it was impossible to come at her. In this business the Prophet Daniel, or Belteshazzar, was as a rock that cannot be moved or pierced. By the help of Belus I saw and talked with him, though not in his own house, showing him how hard was our case, and praying him at least to carry a letter from me to Myra. He listened with a courteous patience, then answered,

"Noble Egyptian, Ramose, hear my counsel. First of all, forget for a while that you are an Egyptian; that your real name is Ramose and not Ptahmes, and most of all, that you have had anything to do with a lady called Myra, who chances to be in my charge as titular Governor of Babylon and a prophet beloved by the king. At present all this is not known, or has been forgotten, and you are thought of only as a stranger suspected in error, and one admitted to the friendship of the king because you are very learned in ancient histories and religions which it pleases him to study. At least they are not known to Belshazzar the prince and the king to be, who believes that the man said to have married the lady Myra before the Pharaoh tried to palm her upon Nabonidus, as a maiden of the royal House, is some noble of Egypt who still dwells in that country. Were it otherwise, I think that you would not live long, Ramose, for Belshazzar has many servants in whose hands are daggers and no longer does he cause his victims to be thrown into the great river unweighted with stones" (here he glanced at Belus who was with me).

"All these things may be so, Prophet," I said. "Yet why should I not see my wife in private, or at the least write to her?"

"Has not the king told you?" he answered sternly. "Then once and for all I will. Because I have passed my word that no man should do so while the king lives, O Ramose, and the word of Belteshazzar, still known as the Governor of Babylon, may not be broken. Well is it for you that this is so, and for the lady Myra also. Twice already has the royal prince, Belshazzar, sent his commands to me under seal, demanding that I should suffer him to capture this lady, by allowing her to walk abroad beyond the shelter of my walls which are sacred to the Babylonians, aye, more sacred than the sanctuaries of their own temples, or at the least that I should give him access to her. Both these commands I defied, thereby earning his added hate and threats of vengeance. Can I then grant to you what I have refused the heir to Babylon? Can I even allow writings to pass between you which, if they were found, would mean the death of both and my dishonour?"

"At least tell me of her, Prophet, for that is not against your vow," I said humbly.

He thought a while; then answered,

"I may say this—she is well and after a fashion happy, who has escaped great danger if only for a while; also for other reasons."

"What other reasons?"

"One of them is that she has learned with certainty of what blood she comes through her mother. It is high, for this mother, as she told you at her death, was truly the daughter of Zedekiah, the last king of Judah, who when he fled from Jerusalem towards Jordan, took her with him, a little maid. He was captured and brought to Riblah with a great number of the people of Israel. Here Nebuchadnezzar in his rage because he had rebelled against him, caused his sons to be slain before his face. Then he blinded him and brought him as a slave to Babylon, where for years he lay a prisoner in the dungeons of yonder temple till at length his misery was ended in death. But the girl was spared for she showed promise of beauty, and was afterwards given to the Prince Merodach. You know the end of that story, Ramose, for you saw her die in blood as her brothers died, and took away her babe and reared it."

"How do you know these things, Prophet?" I asked eagerly.

"In sundry ways, Ramose. When I was young I knew her mother and that she was killed in the battle between Merodach and the Egyptians in which you took part. Also I know the emerald seal she wears, that has cut on it the name of God in ancient Hebrew characters which I can read. It is an old seal and has a long history. I remember it when it hung about the neck of Myra's mother, as it did on that of her mother before her. Moreover the truth of all this

167

matter has been revealed to me. Without doubt this lady Myra is descended from Zedekiah the weak and the accursed and, as I think, is the last of his race left living."

"It seems that I have a wife of high lineage," I said. "Well, I heard as much before from the lips of the dying Mysia, but scarcely believed it who thought that perhaps her mind wandered."

"Aye, Ramose, too high for safety, who on both sides is of the race of kings. Still it has made her happy to learn the truth, because she thinks that this will please you who have wed one of whom you need not be ashamed. She is happy also because now I am leading her to worship the God of her fathers Whom I serve, and lastly because she knows that you live in this same city and believes that He will throw His shield over you and her and keep you safe. For, Ramose, day and night she thinks of you and prays to God for you."

Now when I heard this my heart melted in me with love and longing, so that almost with tears I implored the prophet that even if I might not speak or write to her, he would suffer me to look on Myra with my eyes. At length he yielded.

"Hearken," he said. "Behind my house there is a little garden through which runs a channel of water planted on its banks with willow trees. Beneath these willows Myra sits in the cool of the afternoon, reading or doing such tasks as please her. Now overlooking this garden is another house that the king gave to me together with that in which I dwell, where at times I shelter those of my race who need it. Today it is empty. Belus shall lead you there and from its upper window, hidden yourself behind the shutter, you may look on Myra, although she will not know that your eyes behold her. This you may do on one day in every seven, that which is our Sabbath, and no more, swearing to me that you will not attempt to call to her or show yourself, and this for your sake as well as hers, also for the sake of me and of my oath. Babylon is full of spies, O Ramose, and were it known that a man was so much as gazing upon a lady of the king's household who is in my charge, it would bring death to him and perhaps to her, with much trouble upon me. Swear now and leave me."

So I swore and went.

****

The fourth day from that of my meeting with the prophet who was called Belteshazzar, was that of the Sabbath of the worshippers of Jehovah, and until it came it is true that I scarcely ate or slept, because the desire to behold Myra burned me up. At noon on that day, when men rested in the fierce heat and few were in the streets save beggars and others who slept in such shade as they could find, Belus and I, wrapped in the cloaks worn by the poorer class of traders in Babylon, made our way to the house of which the prophet had spoken.

Passing to the back of this house which was set almost against the wall of an old and deserted building, once occupied by priests and therefore, for some superstitious reason, no longer dwelt in by others, Belus led me to a secret entrance that could only be reached through the wall and doubtless was used by the priests for their own purposes when they owned this house in ancient days. At least there was the narrow, hidden door that he unlocked with a strange key, and beyond it a dark and twisting passage leading to the cellars of the house whence a stair, or rather a ladder, ran to the floor above. Locking the door behind us we climbed this ladder and came to a stairway of brick that led to the upper rooms, for like many of the houses of Babylon where land was precious, this was built in several storeys.

Entering a room that was well but plainly furnished, we found in it a window-place projecting from the wall of the house, around which were fixed wooden shutters whereof the bars that were many, opened upon hinges to admit air and to enable those in the room to look out whilst they remained unseen from below.

Belus went to this window-place and tilting up one of the shutter bars, showed me that beneath us at a distance of not more than ten or twelve paces, lay an enclosed garden such as the prophet had described, of which the house formed a boundary wall. There was the stream, or rather ditch of water, planted with flowering lilies that floated on its surface; there were the willow trees with their weeping branches in which birds were nesting, and there beneath them were low cushioned seats and a rough table of wood.

Here in this chamber we waited a long while, till at length the great sun turned towards the west and the city around us, awakening from its midday sleep, began to hum with life. Then at last we saw white hands part the willow branches and a tall figure glide across a little bridge of planks and enter the green arbour, as we could do easily because the branches did not grow thickly towards the blank wall of our house where there was little light and no sun. It was Myra— Myra herself clad in simple white robes on which hung a single ornament, the lily-bloom enclosed in crystal, but looking more beauteous in them even than she had done when arrayed in jewels and glorious apparel, she was brought into the palace halls of Babylon to be presented to its king.

For a space she stood motionless gazing at the lilies floating upon the water. Almost was I tempted to call to her; indeed I think I should have done so, had not Belus, guessing my purpose, whispered in my ear—

"Remember your oath."

I bit my lips and kept silence.

She sighed—I could hear her sigh; then sinking down upon the cushions she bent forward and drew one of the floating lily blooms towards her as though to pluck it. If so, she changed her mind for she loosed it and taken by the current, it swung back to its place. Then she lifted the crystal from her breast, studied the flower within, pressed it to her lips and letting it fall, began to weep very softly, a sight that I could scarcely bear.

At length she paused and wiping away her tears, sank to her knees upon a cushion and prayed aloud but in so low a voice that I could hear little of what she said. Still I caught some words, such as—"God of my fathers. God above all gods, Thou that hast power even in mighty Babylon and over the hearts of its princes." . . .

Then came murmurings not to be distinguished, and after them, these words, spoken more clearly as though the weight of sorrow pressed them from her heart:

". . . Ramose my most beloved, he from whom I have been stolen, my husband whom my arms ache to hold. Oh! bring me to him or let me die. Let me not be defiled by the touch of this vile prince who seeks me. Nay, rather let me die clean and wait till Ramose comes to join me in the grave."

She ceased her pitiful prayer, pressed the crystal case passionately against her lips once more and drawing a roll from a satchel that she had with her, began to read.

Not for long did she read, for presently she threw down the roll, pressed her hands upon her heart as though to still its beating, and glanced about her wide-eyed, while the colour came and went upon her cheeks.

Then I knew that she felt me near to her. Yes, that love opened some door in her breast through which had entered a knowledge that her senses could not seize. In her agitation she spoke to herself in a low and thrilling whisper that floating on the still air, reached me faintly in the window-place.

"I feel Ramose near me," she said. "Is he dead? Does his loosed spirit speak with mine yet captive in the flesh? Nay, it is his living love that beats upon me, wave after wave of it filling the cup of my heart. I dream! I dream! Oh! would that the dream might last for ever, for in it his lips touch mine that hunger for them. Oh! Ramose my love, Ramose my own, come to me, Ramose, and not in dreams."

Such words as these she murmured and others that I could not catch.

Now I was gripped by mad temptation. A strong creeping plant from whose woody stems hung masses of blue flowers, climbed up the wall and past our window-place, by aid of which it would not be difficult to descend into that garden. In the fury of my great desire, honour and all else was forgotten. I would descend. I would be with her; if only for a breath I would hold her in my arms though my life should pay the forfeit. Might I not take my own? Already, staggering like a drunken man, I was at the shutter, purposing to push it back, when I heard the voice of Belus whisper:

"Remember your oath, Ramose. Shall it be written that you are a liar?"

"By the gods, no!" I answered huskily. "Let us go before I fall."

With one last glance at the passionate loveliness of Myra, who seemed to have taken fire from the power of her living dream and now stood glancing about her with parted lips and heaving breast, I turned, cursing my fate, and reeled towards the doorway. Behold! in it stood a man, the prophet himself! He gazed at me sternly, yet with a little smile playing about the corners of his thin mouth.

"You have fought well, Ramose, and gained a victory that one day should not lack for its reward."

"Not I, but Belus," I muttered.

"Nay, Belus did but give tongue to your own conscience. Learn that had you yielded, what you sought would never have been yours. Though none can hear her words, eyes other than your own, the eyes of women and of eunuchs, watch that lady always from a hidden place when she is unguarded in the garden, and had a man been seen to join her, she would have been dragged away to suffer the fate of those who are faithless to the king. Yes, to die by fire or water—or if his officers were very merciful, to be mutilated and made hideous, and thus cast upon the streets where you would never find her, for you would be dead."

I shivered, for Myra not for myself, because at that moment I thought death would be better than so much suffering. Then words came to me and I said,

"I have gone near to great evil. I pray your pardon for being but a man. Prophet, unless you bid me, I will come to this place no more, lest once again passion should lead me whither I would not go. If you may, tell Myra that I have seen her and aught else that you think wise, for it is not in the heart of woman to think the worse of one who has done wrong because he loves her overmuch."

"So be it," he answered, still smiling faintly, and thus we parted.

Thus it came about that until fate drove me there, I came to that house no more.

****

Now I have to tell of the death of Nabonidus. For many weeks I dwelt on in the palace and almost every day this kindly old king, save when he was too ill or too troubled with the affairs of state, sent for me, and sometimes for Belus his cousin also, to talk with him about such matters as the learned love. It was strange to see him, still one of the mighty monarchs of the world, caring for none of its glories, hating them even; turning his back upon high officers and lovely women; upon the pomp, jewels and worship which in the East are offered to the king, to give all his time and thought to the study of ancient writings or forgotten temples, and to the history and attributes of a thousand gods. Yet such was the pleasure of this shrewd but innocent mind, and to it I was a minister. Indeed had I chosen, I might have become great in Babylon, for he would have heaped on me any wealth and offices that I desired. But I did not choose who sought above all things to remain humble and unknown.

So under the name of Ptahmes, by which I had passed since I entered Babylonia, I remained in the palace, as did scores of others to whom it pleased the king to give hospitality in that vast building, which covered almost as much ground as does the Great Pyramid near Memphis.

Here I gave out that I was an Egyptian born of a Cyprian mother at Naukratis in the Delta, a man of independent means who followed after learning and in its pursuit wandered from land to land, desiring to see them and to study their customs and peoples that I might write of them in a book. This tale was accepted readily enough for since I had been acquitted by the king and admitted to his friendship, the accusation against me of being a spy in the pay of Egypt or of Persia was forgotten, as soon most things were in the vast metropolis of Babylon, a city where memories were very short, especially concerning those whom it pleased the king to favour. So I dwelt in peace, consorting only with a few other learned men, to whom Belus made me known as a friend of his with whom he had studied at Naukratis in Egypt. For now Belus had recovered the lost ties of his youth and was accepted everywhere as a noble of Babylon, a blood relation of the king, a priest of the gods and an astrologer of high degree.

Here I should say that shortly after I had seen Myra in the prophet's garden Belshazzar, the king's son and heir, left Babylon at the head of a great army to wage war against Cyrus the Persian who was threatening the empire, and while his enemy was away Belus was safer than he had been before. Therefore he too remained at peace in the city. Why he did so I was not sure, seeing that the place was still perilous for him. When I asked him, he said that he would not leave me and Myra with whom his lot was intertwined, and when I pressed him further, that he was commanded to bide here by the stars which he consulted after the fashion of the great astrologers of Babylon.

Yet all the while I knew that he was hiding his true reason. In those days there was something fateful, even terrible about Belus. Often I watched the old man pretending to read or to consult mysterious signs written upon skins or tablets and noted that his mind was far away. There he sat like a sphinx, his lips pressed together, his eyes, cold and fixed, staring out at nothingness and his face grown fierce as that of a lion which scents its prey.

At such times if I spoke to him all this would fall from him like a mask; the eyes twinkled, the face grew friendly and a smile appeared around the lips where it was wont to be, so that I wondered which was the real appearance and which the mask. Little did I know of the great schemes that seethed in the heart of Belus; of the mighty plots he wove in his cunning brain and of the terrible revenge he planned, or why at night he met many of the great ones of Babylon now here and now there, and talked with them secretly.

When I asked him of these meetings he answered that those great lords and priests came together to consult their stars, as indeed in a sense they did. To this I said nothing though I thought it very strange that men, however gifted, should be able to consult stars on nights of full moon when the sky was almost as bright as day, or as I knew sometimes was the case, in vaults beneath the piled-up mass of temples.

In the beginning I was vexed who felt that for the first time for many years Belus had drawn a veil between us, hiding his secrets from me, but after thought, I grew sure that this must be for some good reason. So it was in truth, for as I learned later, he held that there was much passing in Babylon which it would be dangerous for me to know, because those who knew might suddenly find themselves face to face with death.

On a certain day when, as was common, I had been summoned by one of his chamberlains to wait upon Nabonidus in the private chamber where he studied, surrounded by the statues of gods and other relics of antiquity, I found the old king much changed. In body he seemed weaker than I had ever known him. He could scarcely rise from his chair without my help, and to do so left him almost breathless for a while. I asked if he were ill and if so why he did not summon his physician.

"No, not ill, Friend," (for so he often called me now) "but only burning out. Physicians cannot help me and I will have no more of them. Indeed for the matter of that, I have seen Belus, my cousin and your companion, who having studied in Egypt among the Greeks, knows more than do most of those in Babylon, who doctor men according to their reading of the stars or the divinations of those who consult omens."

"What did Belus tell you, O King?"

"Nothing, Friend. He bade me open my robe and set his ear against my naked breast and listened to my heart. Then he shook his head and was silent and I knew that the day of my fate was upon me."

"May the King live for ever!" I murmured in the accustomed form, not knowing what else to say.

"Aye," he answered smiling, "so long as it is not in another Babylon beyond the Gates of Darkness. Friend, I must go as all these have gone," and he pointed to the statues of dead monarchs that stood about the room and to the writings sealed with their seals. "I will tell you the truth. I am glad to go, though I must be stripped of all my pomp and power and pass naked to whence I came."

He paused a while, then went on,

"Egyptian, they say that dying eyes see far, and certainly I see much woe coming upon Babylon, or at the least upon her kings. Have you not heard of Cyrus the Persian?"

I bent my head.

"And have you heard that this great man, for he is great, has but now defeated Belshazzar my son at Opis and threatens Zippar?"

"I have not heard it, O King."

"Yet it is so, for swift posts have brought the news. Doubtless soon his armies will threaten Babylon, aye, and as I think, take it, for both the people and the army hate the Prince, my son, and will fight for him but feebly, making an end of my House and its rule, and perchance of the ancient city, queen of the world, also."

Again he paused, and presently continued,

"If so, she has brought it on her own head, for I tell you, Egyptian, that Babylon is evil; aye, she is a bladder filled with sin and the blood of peoples, a bladder waiting to be pricked. Belshazzar, too," he added with passion, "my son who already rules the empire in all but name, is an evil man. From his boyhood up he has been turbulent, lustful, cruel and bloody, one who wades through death to his desires, a tyrant, a betrayer of his friends. Moreover it is too late for him to change who is past his fiftieth year. How long will the gods bear with such a man? Against our foes he might fight, for the empire still is mighty, but can he fight the enemies in his own house? I tell you the people murmur against him and the nobles plot to overthrow him when I am gone. So let me go where, being innocent, I hope for peace. Blessed are the dead for they sleep, or if they wake, of earth and its troubles they know no more."

Thus he spoke in a voice that grew faint and yet fainter till it ended in a kind of wail and died into silence, so that I thought he was about to swoon. But it was not so, for presently he recovered his strength and said,

"I talk much of myself as is the fashion of the aged, and of what I fear or feel, forgetting that others also have evils to bear and face. You for example, Friend. Let me think, what were they? Oh! I remember. That beauteous woman whom the dog Amasis tried to palm off on me as a princess of Egypt, but who, it seems, is a private lady and your wife, or so you and Belus swear. I hear she swears it also, but in such matters none can believe what comes out of a woman's mouth. The business is unhappy. Could I have my will, you might take her at once and welcome, but here I face a rock which even the king cannot move, namely the law concerning the ladies of the royal household on which one might think that the whole empire of Babylon was built. Moreover someone is at work in this matter, for when on your behalf and hers, that old prophet of Judah put it into my mind to try to find a way round this rock, all paths were blocked, I know not by whom."

"Perhaps by the Prince Belshazzar," I hazarded.

"It may be so; indeed it is very likely, for Belshazzar is always coveting this one or that, even though they be of his father's household, at any rate in name. Well, I say that the way is blocked and if I tried to force a path, the priests would stir as though an insult had been done to their gods. Yes, there would be scandals and talk of impiety by an unbelieving king, that would serve the purpose of the plotters against my House among the vulgar, and I know not what besides. So nothing can be done."

"That is sad for me and my wife," I said sighing.

"Yes, of course, though it is strange that it should be so. There are so many women in the world that it seems foolish for a man to break his heart over any one of them, when doubtless a fairer awaits him in the next street. Also there is hope in the case. Much trouble has arisen about this lady with Egypt against whom, because of her, Babylon has threatened war. Now Amasis the Pharaoh pretending to be insulted and believing you, the husband, to be dead,—I thought it well for your own sake to tell him that the man who bore forged letters to Cyrus of whom he warned us, had been caught and executed as a spy—demands that his daughter, as he calls her, should be sent back to him with a great present of gold. Yet this cannot be done for the reason I have told you, namely that she has been taken into the royal household."

"Then it seems there is an end, O King."

"Not so, for have I not told you, Friend, that even in Babylon kings do not live for ever. When I die my household is dissolved, at least after a time, and I shall die soon. Therefore because you are a brother scholar who has solaced my last months I have made a plan to serve you. As this lady and I have never met but once and that in open court, I have issued a royal decree that immediately upon my death she shall be set at liberty and sent back to Egypt with all her belongings and a gift. Moreover I have appointed that you, under the name of Ptahmes by which you are called here, for none know you to be her husband, and Belus shall accompany her, as you also wish to return to Egypt in safety, though if you are wise neither of you will set foot in that land while Amasis reigns. No, when you have crossed the borders of this country and are free, you will turn and fly whither you will, out of reach of Amasis and of Belshazzar.

"There, that is all. I am weary. The decree has been registered in due form, sealed with my own seal, and you will find a copy of it in your lodgings, for it was given to Belus only today that it might not miscarry. Farewell, Friend. Your theory of the beginning of the gods is most wise and pregnant; soon I shall learn whether it be true. Farewell and may all good fortune be yours. When you are as old as I am, think sometimes of Nabonidus whom they called a king, but who knew himself to be a ruler of nothing, no, not even of his own heart. Ho! chamberlain, take me hence, I would sleep."

CHAPTER 17

At the Western Gate

What Nabonidus promised me, he performed. In my lodgings I found Belus waiting with the writings under the royal seal, whereby he and I were given safe conduct to leave Babylon when we would and go whither we would, which writings all the officers of the empire were commanded to obey. In them, however, nothing was said concerning Myra. I asked Belus what this meant and whether I had been tricked. He answered no, for other writings had been sent to the prophet Daniel or Belteshazzar, as he knew from his own lips, commanding him so soon as the news of the death of the king should reach him, to hand over Myra, with her woman named Metep, to an escort charged to conduct her to the frontiers of the land and there leave her to await the coming of another escort from Egypt.

I listened and answered that I liked the plan little.

Where, I asked, must we meet Myra and how were we to know when she left the prophet's house? Also, even if all should go well, what would happen when we came to the frontiers of the empire, where perhaps she would fall into the power of Egyptians waiting to receive her, and I with her. If so, our case would be even worse than it was before.

"Ramose," answered Belus, "we wander in the darkness of night and must follow the only star that we can see. Like you, neither the prophet nor I think well of this plan. Yet if we do not act upon it, which way can we turn? It is certain that while the king lives, not even he can command that Myra should be sent from Babylon."

"Why not?" I asked angrily.

"I think that he has told you himself, namely, because he whose duty it is to administer the law, must not break the law. Moreover, if he gave the order it would not be obeyed, because under these same ancient statutes any man who touches or holds converse with a lady of the royal household, is criminal, an outcast to be slain by whoever can or will. Once the king is dead it is otherwise, for the edicts which he has signed must be fulfilled, unless indeed they are revoked by other edicts of the new king."

"Which will surely happen, Belus."

"Aye, it will happen—if there is time. For as I have heard from a sure source, Belshazzar when in his cups gave out that so soon as he had power he would certainly take this Egyptian Myra whom it was the pleasure of the king his father to keep from him, and whom therefore he desired more than any woman in the world. Indeed he is foolish about the matter, having been smitten by the sight of her beauty when she appeared at the court as though by a sword, and, as he says, wounded through the heart. Certainly had it not been for the law as to the King's wives, and still more because of his fear of the prophet in whose holy charge she is, already he would have seized and smuggled her away."

"Then this he will surely do as soon as the king is dead, Belus."

"Aye—I repeat, if he has time. But should Nabonidus die soon, Belshazzar is not in Babylon. With the remainder of his great army he is in Zippar that Cyrus besieges. There perhaps he may be killed or made prisoner, or many things may happen. Also Nabonidus is not yet dead. He may pass at any minute, or he may live for months, as men suffering from the heart sometimes do. Everything is dark and doubtful. Still we must be prepared to act at any moment. Therefore let us forget our fears and go straightforward, though for my part," he added darkly, "I do not believe that fate will take me from Babylon till a certain doom has been accomplished."

This then we did who could find no better counsel, putting our faith in the goodness of God, and trusting that we should find help in our need.

Having wealth at our command we bought swift horses and hired servants, faithful men of Israelite descent and free citizens who could go where they would and who desired to leave Babylon, which men and horses we kept at hand in a safe place near to the western gate whence we must start for Egypt. Also Belus devised a scheme which provided that Metep should hang a cloth from a window of the prophet's house, telling us when her mistress was about to leave so that we might be ready to start to join her. And many other things we did that need not be told.

****

At length Nabonidus died very suddenly. From the time that I had last seen him he had kept his bed, sleeping a great deal and paying no heed to anybody or anything that passed, till on a certain afternoon he rose, saying that he felt quite well again, and went to his favourite chamber, that in which I was wont to visit him. Here while he was walking up and down, some message was brought to him by one of the great officers, of which all we could learn was that it had to do with Belshazzar and the Persian war. Whether the news was good or ill I do not know, but this is certain, that Nabonidus said aloud,

"It is the will of God. My day of fate has come."

Then he set his hand upon his heart, fell down, groaned once, and died. Such was the end of this weak but honest and kindly man, a scholar of whom to his sorrow destiny had made a king over a doomed empire. In one thing at least Heaven was good to him, he did not live to see it fall.

Having bribed certain eunuchs and a scribe, Belus and I were among the first, if not the very first, to know that all was over, that is, save the prophet who learned it in his spirit as he learned many things. Instantly we rushed to the appointed place where our horses and goods awaited us, whence we could see the house of Daniel and watch. Presently at a window appeared a white cloth showing us that there too all was known and that Myra was about to start with her escort.

This was the plan—that we should stand to one side till she had passed the gate, and follow with our men to the first camping place, where we could discover ourselves to the captain of the escort who had been warned that we should join him. Having authority under the seal of the late king and his vizier that we could show, if there were need, this, we thought, would be easy, especially as the death of Nabonidus was not known in the city and perhaps might be kept from the people for hours—or days.

We came to the gate as the sun began to sink, and waited as though for some friend or other merchants to join us there, for we were disguised as traders. At length through the gloom, which gathered very quickly that night, because after some days of terrible heat the sky was full of thunderclouds which were about to burst, with beating hearts we saw a company coming down the street towards the gate that pierced the mighty wall of Babylon. A captain rode ahead of it, then came soldiers, a dozen or more of them, and in their midst mounted upon white mules two veiled women, one tall and graceful as a reed, the other short and thick in body, at the sight of whom my heart leapt for I knew them to be Myra and old Metep. After these followed other mules and asses laden with baggage, tents and so forth, and accompanied by servants. As they passed us I saw the tall lady turn as though to stare at me through her veil. Then I was sure that Myra had seen and knew me, and bent my head a little, which she answered by bending hers.

Tonight, I thought to myself with joy, we may speak together in some camp, if no more. Tonight our troubles may be over and our long separation ended.

At that moment, while my heart was filled with this happy dream, came the first flash of the storm. Like a sword of fire it seemed to strike the watch towers set upon the crest of the wall high above us, and in a line of blinding light passed down the pillar of one of the inner brazen gates into the earth, with a noise and a shock that caused the horses of the officer and some of the soldiers to wheel round and charge back among those that followed. Confusion came, and shoutings, for all believed that men had been killed by the flame from heaven, whereas in fact one or two had been unhorsed—no more. Then the clamour was covered and lost by the crash of thunder pealing overhead. It died away and for a little while there was silence, through which I heard the officer rallying his men with words of command; no easy matter, for they were entangled with the baggage animals whose drivers were frightened and knew not what to do.

Then I heard something else, namely, the sound of a horse galloping. The lightning flashed again piercing the gloom. It shone upon the gilded armour of a captain of the royal bodyguard riding at full speed who, as he passed me, cried,

"The King is dead. Ho! Warden, shut the gates that none may make it known to the enemies of Babylon!"

The officer in charge of the escort heard and strove to press forward through the long archway of the wall before he was cut off. Too late! With a great clashing, worked by their engines, the outer gates of bronze swung home in front of him. He called for the warden of the gates and showed him a writing which it was too dark to read. They wrangled together as Belus and I, who with our people had followed them into the archway, could hear. There was great disorder. Some pressed forward and some pressed back, for all who could had rushed into the tunnel to escape the lightnings and the heavy rain that began to fall. Men thrust, horses neighed and trampled, moving to and fro and mingled together. Presently I found myself by the side of a figure clad in white which jostled against me.

"Your pardon," said a gentle voice, and I knew it for that of Myra!

"Myra," I whispered, "it is I—Ramose!"

"Oh! my love, my love," she whispered back, and next moment I had bent down and was kissing her upon the lips, cursing the veil that lay between us. Yes, and she was kissing me. But one kiss and it was done, for we were thrust apart again.

The tumult and wrangling increased. The officer in charge of Myra's escort demanded that the gates should be opened and threatened the wardens. A loud voice cried,

"In the name of Belshazzar, King of Babylon, it is commanded that none leave Babylon."

Between the bellowings of the thunder I heard the clattering of horses' hoofs and chariot wheels. Again a voice cried,

"A woman of the royal household escapes. Seize her!" words at which my blood ran cold.

Another voice answered,

"They are here—two of them!"

Armed men rushed upon the mob. The escort gathered round Myra and Metep, whose white dresses could be seen dimly through the gloom and more clearly when the lightning flashed. I and my people did likewise. Swords were drawn; there was confused fighting. A huge black man in brazen armour seized Myra's mule by the bridle and began to drag it back towards the street; Metep screamed; soldiers cursed. I attacked the black man. He smote at me and missed, I thrust my sword through his throat and he fell, dead or dying. Others seized the woman; the scene in that narrow place as the lightning showed it, was terrible. All shouted, all smote scarcely knowing at whom they smote, while Metep still screamed long and loud. My horse was thrust back against the bars of the gate, plunging and kicking. Someone struck me on the head, I think with a club, causing me to drop my sword and almost stunning me. When my wits came again I was outside the archway in the narrow street whither my horse had borne me, following others.

The storm raged more fiercely than before and the rain poured down. Far up the street I saw soldiers retreating and in the midst of them two figures in white. The lightning showed them clearly, also many men in flight. In the darkness that followed the flash someone approached and a voice spoke. It was that of Belus.

"All is finished, Ramose," he said. "The guards of the household of Belshazzar have snatched away Myra. Come now quickly before we are known to have taken part in this tumult, else we shall be seized and slain. I have told our servants where they may find us."

Still dazed by the blow I followed him, who knowing the city from boyhood, led me through a maze of streets where none was stirring because of the great storm and the darkness of the falling night. After us came our servants, or most of them, and the laden beasts.

"Where have they taken Myra?" I asked with a groan.

"Doubtless to Belshazzar's palace," he answered. "Yet be comforted. He is not in Babylon. She has been seized because of commands which he left with his great officers who have watched the prophet's house day and night lest she should escape."

"A curse is on us," I muttered. "We are dogged by evil. Another hour and we had been free. Could not your spells have protected us for one hour, Belus?"

"The tale is not yet finished," he answered quietly. "Mayhap this evil has protected us from greater that we do not see. Mayhap it is appointed that we still have work to do in Babylon, whither I at least must have returned even if we had escaped tonight, though this I hid from you."

"Have done!" I exclaimed fiercely. "Myra is in the house of Belshazzar and who can save her now?"

"God," he answered and was silent.

"Whither go we—to our lodgings?" I asked presently.

"Nay, it would not be safe. We go to that house whence once you looked upon a garden. It is the prophet's and holy ground which none dares violate, not even Belshazzar, because he believes that to do so would bring a curse and perhaps death upon him. Had it been otherwise Myra would have been seized long ago."

****

So, broken in spirit for all seemed lost, once again I entered that Hebrew guest-house by the secret way, not caring whether or no I were dragged from it to my death. Indeed I was as a little child and did what Belus bade me, asking no questions. He managed all, finding lodging for the men in the outbuildings of the house, bringing food and I know not what besides.

That night the prophet came to us. I looked up from the stool on which I was seated, my head resting on my hand and saw him standing before me, tall, black-robed, thin-faced, dark-eyed, white-haired; more like a ghost than a man. I would have risen to bow to him, but he stayed me with his hand.

"You are weary," he said, "and smitten to the heart. Rest where you are and listen. All seems to have gone awry. The lady Myra, my ward,

182

has been snatched away and now, as I have sure tidings, is a prisoner among the women of Belshazzar, and in his own palace which once was that of Nebuchadnezzar the great king. Nor, good old Nabonidus being dead, can I take her hence, for none so much as reads the edicts of departed kings. Who prays to the sun that is set?"

"How did it happen, Prophet?" I asked wearily.

"This house was watched," he answered. "From the beginning Belshazzar, the woman-hunter, having once seen her beauty, determined to possess himself of Myra if ever she passed my doors which all Babylonians hold inviolate. When she went forth spies reported it to his officers, or perhaps the hour of her going was already known through some traitor. If so, here and now I call down upon him the wrath of God," and he lifted his hand to heaven, then bowed his head, muttering some words.

"At least she was taken, as you saw, for as is common the tidings of the death of a king, the guardians closed the gates, which they must do. Nor would it have helped if she had passed them, for she would have been followed and seized, and you with her. As it is, both you and Belus have escaped because you were not noted in the darkness of the archway as having fought against the guards of Belshazzar, aye, and slew their captain. Therefore you are safe here and in sanctuary where none dares to set a foot lest the curse of Jehovah should fall upon him, and here you must bide till all is accomplished."

"What will happen to Myra?" I asked.

"At present—nothing, save that she will be fed on sweet-meats, perfumed with scents and purified, according to the custom of these Babylonian hogs with women who are dedicate to the king. Then, at such time as he shall appoint, she will be offered to him, as a lamb is offered upon an altar, and if she pleases him, be set high in his household, perhaps upon the throne itself."

Hearing these horrible words I went mad. I raved; I cursed; yes, I reviled this Daniel or Belteshazzar.

"You are reported a great prophet," I said, "one who worships a just and mighty god that even the Babylonians revere, although he be but the lord of a conquered, captive people. Yet you tell me that such a crime will be worked upon an innocent woman because she is accursed with great loveliness, by a king who is but a brute in human shape. If your god and hers be a true god, as they say Nebuchadnezzar held he was, let him manifest himself and save her, his servant. Then I will worship him whom otherwise I name but another idol."

The prophet looked at me and smiled, a strange and quiet smile.

"Poor man!" he said. "What do you know of God and of His ways? This day by the gate you slew a gallant soldier who did but obey his orders to capture certain persons. He had committed no sin. He knew nothing of this business, yet God suffered that you should drive your sword through His throat and bring him down to death unavenged, for in that darkness none saw who smote him."

"Did you see?" I asked angrily.

"Perhaps, with the eyes of my spirit. Or perhaps I learned it otherwise. It matters nothing. At least God commanded that he should be slain, we know not why. So God has commanded that this woman of my people who is your wife, should be captured, we know not why. Yet it may please Him to save her at the last, or it may not please Him. Let the scroll of fate unroll itself at the appointed time and bow your head before what is written there."

Then he lifted his hand as though in blessing and departed.

****

So it came about that I took up my abode with those servants whom we had hired, citizens of Babylon but all of them of the Israelite faith, who, after what had happened at the gateway, thought that they would be safest here until they could leave the city with me, or otherwise. But although he often came to visit me at night, Belus dwelt elsewhere with friends of his own, now in one place, now in another. When I asked him why, all he would say was that it must be so, adding darkly that he was a marked man with many enemies, and now that Nabonidus was dead, if we consorted together I should be marked also.

For my part I was but little known and so long as I remained under the shelter of the prophet's roof, one who would not be harmed, unless by evil fortune the King's Council heard that it was I who had killed the officer of the guard while attempting to aid the escape of the beautiful Egyptian.

So guessing that Belus had other reasons as well as those which he set out, I let the matter be, though in truth my life in this place was very sad and lonely with no companion save my own thoughts which were black enough. I did not dare to go abroad for the prophet forbade it, and of the few learned men and royal servants whom I had met in Babylon while I waited on Nabonidus, none came to visit me. Indeed either I was forgotten, or believed to be dead, or to have departed.

In Babylon not many strangers were remembered even for a month among the thousands from all countries who came and went on the business of their trades, or to visit the temples, or study the wonders of the mightiest city of the earth. Also, now that Nabonidus was dead, his court was dispersed and his great palace in which alone my face had been seen, stood empty, for that of Belshazzar, the new king, was in another quarter of the city. Therefore I was quite unknown, for as Belus told me, the company that had captured us on our road from Damascus had, it chanced, been sent upon duty to a distant part of the empire.

From time to time the prophet visited me and we talked together. I told him the history of my life and in his grave and gentle voice he instructed me in many matters, especially in the faith and nature of the God he worshipped. Through His strength, he said, he interpreted dreams and worked marvels, which caused him to be feared of the Babylonians from the days of Nebuchadnezzar and, although they were jealous of his magic as they held it to be, bowed down to by the magicians and interpreters of dreams as one greater than they. So earnestly did he instruct me and with such power, that at length I, who all my life had searched for a true God and been able to find none, came to accept Him of Daniel, as indeed I think it was in his mind that I should do. Thus it came about that in the presence of certain of the captive Israelites I, although of another race, was admitted to the company of the worshippers of Jehovah. To that faith, rejecting all the multitude of the gods of Greece and Egypt, I hold today.

For the rest, thenceforward that holy prophet treated me as one dear to him, one to whom he could open some if not all of the doors of his secret heart. He gave me sacred books to read and expounded their mysteries. Filled with fire from Heaven he repeated prophecies, whether his own or those of other seers I do not know, that foretold the fall of Babylon, Queen of the world.

"Behold all this," he said, pointing to the glittering city that on every side stretched further than the eye could see, to its towering temples and its vast encircling walls. "I say, Ramose, that of it not one brick shall remain upon another; it shall be a wilderness where shepherds feed their flocks by day and the lions prowl at night; an abode of death for ever. The curse of God hangs over Babylon."

Once more I became a recluse as I had been at Cyprus, more so indeed, for then I heard the voice of the infant Myra prattling about the house and busied myself with my trade. Now I studied alone, or walked in the garden where once I had seen Myra and been tempted to break my oath, thinking and dreaming till, had it not been for a certain comfort which flowed to me from that quiet prophet and from the new faith he had taught me, I believe my heart would have broken. Even so I grew pale and thin, as he noted, for often I saw him watching me, after which he would speak hopeful words, bidding me to take heart because all that is hidden is not lost.

From Myra no whisper reached me. She had vanished into the secret courts of the frowning palace of Belshazzar where, when he was in Babylon, he held his orgies, and the world saw her no more. If the prophet knew aught of her fate he hid it from me. From Egypt, too, no news came, though much I wondered what had passed there and what had chanced to the mother who had treated me so ill, and to the plotting Pharaoh who had made a tool of me hoping that I should return no more.

So except for the rare visits of Belus, who to me appeared changed and bent down beneath the weight of hidden business of which he would not speak, and for the converse of the prophet who seemed more of an angel than a man, from day to day I dwelt quite alone, feeding my heart on hope that grew ever fainter and strengthening my soul as best I might with prayer.

CHAPTER 18

The Letter

One night when I sat brooding in my chamber at the guest-house of the prophet, playing with food that I could not eat, a servant opened the door and through it came Belus. With much joy I rose to greet him whom I had not seen for many days, for always I longed for his company in my loneliness, but without taking the hand I offered him, he sank upon a couch, saying, "If you have wine, give it me."

I filled him a cup unmixed with water. He swallowed it and asked for more which he drank also. As he did so his dark cloak fell open and I saw that beneath it his tunic was stained with blood and that a short sword thrust through his girdle, for its scabbard seemed to have been lost, was likewise still wet with blood.

"Whence do you come?" I asked.

"Out of the jaws of death," he answered. "Certain of my friends and I were supping together when the door burst open—doubtless it was some traitor's work—and a number of soldiers rushed into the room. An officer summoned us to surrender in the name of Belshazzar the King, calling out the names of most there present, and mine among them.

"'Would you work sacrilege against the gods and their priests?' cried one of us, for we were supping in chamber of the temple where none but the ordained might enter.

"'The King of the God of gods. Obey the King or die!' shouted the officer.

"He spoke no more, for a man of our company, I know not who, hurled a knife, or a sword, with such strength and so true an aim that it pierced that captain from breast to back and he fell down dead. Then began the fight. We were well armed and wore corselets beneath our robes, for we knew that we went in peril; also we were desperate who did not desire to die by torment.

"We cast the flagons and the stools in their faces, aye, and the burning lamps. We leapt upon them like lions. We slew them, though of us, too, some were slain. We hurled them, living or dead, from the window-places to fall a hundred cubits and be crushed at the foot of the temple towers to make food for jackals. Then we scattered and fled and here I am, bloody but unhurt."

"And what now, Belus?" I asked. "Do you seek sanctuary with the prophet?"

"Nay, I seek horses and men to ride with me, also a bag of gold, for my lodgings will be watched and I dare not return to them."

"These you can have, Belus, for they are here. But whither go you? Back towards Egypt?"

"Not so. I go—" here he bent forward and whispered in my ear— "I go to Cyrus the Persian who advances upon Babylon the accursed. I go to tell him that her gates will open to him and that if he will but purge her of her rulers and punish their iniquities, the millions of the people will welcome him. Do not stare, Ramose. What I say is true. Not in vain have I worked for all these moons to fulfil the decrees of God upon Belshazzar the murderer, and his evil counsellors."

"Oh! that I might go with you," I said.

"Nay, you must bide here where none knows what may happen. They say that Zippar is about to fall, but I hear also that Belshazzar purposes to desert his army and slipping away like a snake, to return to Babylon which he believes impregnable, hoping for help from Egypt and thinking that before its walls Cyrus and his Persians will certainly be destroyed. Therefore if Belshazzar comes to Babylon you must be here, for then who knows what will chance to Myra who is captive in his palace?"

"Who knows indeed?" I moaned, "and alas! how can I help her?"

"I cannot say, but doubtless there is a road. I read of it in the stars, though God alone can point it out. Now I go to speak with the prophet. Do you bid them make the horses ready—four horses and three men."

"How will you pass the gates?" I asked.

"The gates of Babylon are open to me," he said darkly and glided from the room.

****

Belus went out of my sight and knowledge. Day followed day, moons waxed and waned and I heard no more of him, nor whether he were dead or living, or had fled to some other land. Now I was quite alone and save my servants and sometimes the prophet, I saw no man. Of him I asked, what had become of Belus and if he had heard aught of the fray in the temple of which I have spoken. He answered that he did not know where Belus was, but he believed him to be still alive, for he thought that if he were dead some voice which have told him so in his sleep, a saying which comforted me who knew that this prophet was not as are other men, but one who communed with Heaven and to whom from time to time, Heaven gave tidings.

"As regards the fray in the temple," he went on, "I have naught to say, if I know anything. To all tales of conspiracies I shut my ears. Why should I heed them? Men think that they do this or that, but it is God Who works through them. Therefore I await the decrees of God and watch for the falling of His sword. What He reveals to me I know, to all else my ears are shut."

I bowed my head, being sure that to dispute with him was useless; as soon would I have attempted to reason with a spirit. Then I inquired of him whether I might now go abroad, seeing that all must have forgotten me.

He answered somewhat sternly,

"Did I not tell you, Ramose, that here and nowhere else you are safe. Here then bide and be patient."

So I obeyed him; only I did this, knowing that if it were not lawful he would forbid me. Finding that a steep and narrow stair led to the roof of the tall house, I went up it and often sat there, crouching behind the parapet in the daytime and leaning over it at night when I could not be seen from below. This house stood very high, being built upon a mound where once, perhaps, was a palace or a temple now long fallen except for some walls of which I have written. Therefore from its roof I could see much of Babylon; its great buildings, its open places, its gardens, its soaring towers, its embracing walls, Nimitti-Bel, the outer wall like to which there is no other in the world, and Ingue-Bel the inner wall, both of them held to be impregnable, its citadel rising from an enormous platform of dried bricks between the two; its temples of Enurta, Marduk and Ishtar with its lovely gate; its thousand streets where all day multitudes moved up and down, the great river Euphrates to the west and among its many royal dwellings, the vast palace of Nebuchadnezzar where Belshazzar had made his home.

It was on this palace that always I fixed my eyes, for I knew that up its steps guarded by statues of gods and demons, Myra had been borne and that somewhere in its courts she dwelt, lonelier and perchance more afraid, if that were possible, than even I, her husband.

Night by night I would watch the cressets flaring upon its walls, wondering what passed there and throwing out my heart to the captive whom they hid. But alas! no answer came. Had she been in Egypt, had she been in Hades, she could not have seemed further from me, or more lost.

In the daytime, too, I stared at the streets and places where people gathered, and noted, or so I thought, a change in the demeanour of these people. They seemed more hurried than they were wont to be; they stopped and spoke to each other, head close to head, like folk who tell each other tidings that must not be overheard; or they gathered into knots and crowds in the squares and open places and were addressed by officers. Then troops would come and disperse them and they fled sullenly, sometimes leaving certain of their number on the ground dead or wounded, whom slaves or watchmen bore away on stretchers. Certainly all was not well in Babylon.

Among the servants who were left to me after the departure of Belus, was a man called Obil, an Israelite by descent, though a citizen of Babylon, a quiet man who seldom spoke unless he was spoken to, but one to whom I took a liking and learned to trust, as indeed the prophet had told me I might do, for he was of his faith, that had become mine also. This Obil often went abroad in Babylon, especially at night, and having friends there, gathered much tidings.

When I discovered this I began to speak with him apart and learned many things. He told me that great fear had come upon Babylon, partly because of the war with Persia which, it was rumoured, went very ill, and partly because of the dark sayings of the magicians and astrologers who prophesied evil at hand—much evil, and the wrath of God about to fall upon the ancient city.

Listening to these tales I wondered to myself whether Belus had been one of the astrologers who spread abroad this prophecy. Then I asked what of Belshazzar and whether the people loved him as they did Nabonidus the Peaceful, although him the priests did not love because he meddled with their gods.

"Of Belshazzar, Master," said Obil, "the news is that he is still with the army at Zippar, yet not so closely invested by the Persians that he cannot send messages daily, sometimes by word of mouth and sometimes in writing, to his officers in Babylon; yes, even about small matters," he added with meaning. "I know it, for the sister of one of the messengers is a friend of mine."

"What kind of small matters?" I asked as carelessly as I could.

"Well, for example, Master, such as that which has to do with the

190

lady who came from Egypt to be of the late king's household, and who afterwards was sent to the prophet's house by the royal command; the same with whom we were to travel when the gates were shut upon us on that night of storm and there was fighting in the gateway."

Now my blood ran cold, but turning my head to hide my face I asked again,

"And why does Belshazzar send messages about this lady, Obil? Did your friend's sister tell you that?"

"Yes, Master, she did and the reason is very strange, though I who in my time have served in the households of the great lords of the earth and watched their ways, know that it is true. Kings and princes and others of their kind, Master, have everything at their command; power which some desire; wealth which most desire, and especially women whom all desire if they be really men. Therefore having all, they become sated like gorged brutes, and of the fair women that are offered to them continually few catch their fancy. Now and again, however, they see one for whom they would give half their kingdom, especially if it be not lawful that they should take her, or if they know that for this reason or for that she turns from them.

"Such it seems is what has happened in the case of Belshazzar and the lady from Egypt who is named Myra. He saw her at the court when old Nabonidus, the late king, being moved by her wondrous beauty, descended from his throne and publicly received her to himself. That was before this lady told Nabonidus, as I heard with my own ears being then a servant of the court, that she was no princess of Egypt; also that she was already married to a man from whom she had been stolen. Perhaps you have been told the story, Master."

"Yes, Obil, and I have learned that thereon Nabonidus committed her to the charge of our great prophet whose sanctuary none dares to violate, and we know the rest."

"That is so. Still, part of this story may be new to you, if my friend's sister tells it truly. Not even Belshazzar dares to violate the sanctuary of the holy prophet of Israel whom he fears above any man that lives, because like Nebuchadnezzar before him, he believes him to be almost a god. Yet he caused it to be watched by many spies and gave strict command to his officers, for which they must answer with their lives, that if the lady came out of that sanctuary, even by order of the king his father, she should be seized and carried to his palace, there to be given to him when he returns. This, Master, as you know, was done."

"Is this all that your friend's sister told you, Obil?"

"No, Master. It appears that Belshazzar who now is king, has been smitten with a madness concerning this fair woman, so that he thinks more of her than he does of the war with the Persians or any other matter, which madness has increased greatly since a rumour has reached him that the man to whom she was married, is not in Egypt but hidden in Babylon. This is his desire—to find that man and cause him to be tormented to death before her very eyes and while he lies dying, to appear and drag her away. For such, Master, are the royal pleasures of great kings."

"Does he know this man's name, Obil?"

"According to my friend's sister who seems to hear all secrets, he is not sure of the name, but he believes the man to be Belus, also known as Azar, an enemy of his own to whom he worked some injury in the past, and by birth a great lord of Babylon; he who appeared before Nabonidus and told a tale as to this lady being wed to a noble of Egypt. At the last, although he is not sure whether he be the man, he seeks everywhere for Belus, that he may capture him and put him to the question, or failing that, kill him outright."

"As nearly chanced the other day," I said.

"Yes, Master, but Belus escaped him and now has left Babylon with some of our people, upon a mission of his own."

"Why did you not go with him, seeing that it was Belus who hired you and not I?" I asked sharply.

"Perhaps because I was otherwise commanded, or because I thought I might be of more service elsewhere," he replied, bowing his head.

I thought a moment, then I turned and spoke words that seemed to be put into my mind.

"Obil," I said, "you know more than you pretend; you know that *I* am the husband of the lady Myra, not Belus, and all my case."

"Yes, Master, I know these things, for I have been told them under an oath that may not be broken if I would avoid death in this world and save my soul in any that is to come. We worship the same God and therefore he who betrays his brother, betrays his God."

"Who told you?" I asked.

"Belus told me. In his youth he was my father's friend, therefore he trusts me and hired me to go upon that journey which has not been accomplished. Afterwards, knowing that he might be called away, he told me all, bidding me to serve you and another to the death."

Now I bethought me that this Obil whom it pleased to play the part of a servant, was more than he seemed and that doubtless he had his share in the dark conspiracies of Belus, but of this matter I said nothing.

"Does the prophet know that you have my secret?" I asked.

"The prophet knows all, for God tells him."

I thought a while. For good or ill I was in this man's power no matter what I did or left undone. He had learned my secret from Belus or another, and if it pleased him, could betray me, or leave me unbetrayed. My crime was that I had married Myra whom the mighty king of Babylon desired, and for that, if I were caught, I must die; it could not be added to by aught that I did, or lessened by aught that I left undone. Therefore I would be bold.

"Can you help me, Obil?"

"How, Master."

"By causing it to come to the ears of a certain lady that a certain man still waits in Babylon hoping for the best, and by bringing tidings to me of her, under her own hand if may be, that I may know that they are true."

"It is dangerous, Master, and yet I have friends in the palace, aye, even among the eunuchs, and if you desire it I will try who am bidden to serve you in all things. Yet blame me not if aught goes wrong."

"I shall not blame you," I answered, "and—oh! no longer can I endure this silence. I must hear, I must learn, or I think that I shall die."

"I will do what I may," said Obil, and turned to go.

"Do so, Friend, and whether you succeed or fail, be sure that if ever I come safe out of this accursed city I will make you rich. Meanwhile take what gold you want. You know where it is."

"I thank you, Master, who desire to rest in some far land, at Jerusalem if it may be, and whose substance has been stolen by Babylonians because I am of a race they hate."

Then he went.

******

Four nights later Obil appeared as I finished my evening meal and slipped a clay tablet into my hand. I glanced at it who could read the Babylonian writing as well as I could the Egyptian or the Greek, and saw at once that it was but an ancient table of accounts, sealed by some priest, a note indeed of the delivery of a number of measures of corn into the store-house of a certain temple.

"What jest is this?" I asked.

"Let the Master press the tablet between his finger and his thumb, and he may learn," answered Obil in a dry voice.

I did so and it flew to pieces, being in truth but a hollow cylinder of clay that had been broken and cunningly joined together with an invisible cement. Within was a tightly rolled papyrus covered with tiny writing in the Grecian character, at the sight of which my heart stood still.

"There is your letter, Master," said Obil, "which I came by at great risk, how is best left unsaid, and at the cost of all the gold you gave me, aye, and more of my own."

"Recompense yourself with as much as you will, I will thank you later, Friend," I answered hurriedly, who burned to study the letter.

He went and standing under the hanging lamp, I undid the roll. On it were written these words:

"O most Beloved,

"The message has reached me, it matters not how, and I rejoice. Yea, I thank God, for thereby I learn that you are safe and well. Know, Beloved, that I feared, aye, and had it not been for my faith in God and my memory of a certain prophecy made by a true seer far away, I should have believed that you were dead. Immediately after that kiss in the archway, which in dreams still burns my lips, I thought that I saw you fall pierced by a sword. Now I know that it was another man and that the gloom, or the dazzle of the lightning deceived me. I was dragged away. I am a prisoner—you will know where— an appointed prey to a certain great one when he returns. For in an accursed hour—may it be blotted out of the Book of Time!— he looked upon me unveiled and found me to his fancy. Indeed it seems that although absent, he remembers me and rejoices that I am taken, as he planned that I should be. He has even written to me, vile things, to which his servants force me to listen, dragging away my hands when I would stop my ears. All his fair women whom I hate, praise my beauty. They scent me, they comb my hair with golden combs, they paint my eyes and lips, feeding me with sweetmeats, and if I struggle, they laugh, naming me a cat of Egypt and calling to the eunuchs to come to hold me while they appraise me inch by inch. All these and other things I suffer because I hope that God will be good to us and bring us together again, how I know not who am a bird in a golden cage. Learn this, my heart's desire, that the worst shall never fall upon me, for when all hope is gone I will die, as I have the means to do. Never shall that royal brute so much as defile me with his finger tip. I dare write no more, for I think that I am watched; here the very walls have eyes and ears. Beloved husband, I trust in God, do thou the same, for He is just. Aye, even if He does not help us here, yet I am persuaded that He is just and good, and in some other land far from Babylon and the cruel earth, He will unite us for ever. Yes, when Babylon is dust and quite forgotten, that lips to lips and heart to heart we shall look down upon the sands that shroud its palaces and the bones of its accursed kings."

Such was the letter that was unsigned. Indeed from the writing I judged that for some reason or other it was never finished. Still it was hers. This I knew from some of the Greek phrases more ancient and purer than was the common use, of a style indeed that I, who was half a Greek, myself had taught to Myra. Also those high thoughts and that vision of peace beyond the earth and every joy for those who had suffered on the earth, were all her own; indeed once when fears of the future took her, she had spoken to me in like words.

Oh! the letter was Myra's. Her hand had pressed it, her breath had breathed upon it, her eyes, perhaps, had wept upon it as certain marks seemed to show, and therefore to me it was a thing more precious than all the treasure of the world. And yet how dreadful was the tale it told. Myra a prisoner; pampered, petted, fattened, scented, that she might be made more acceptable to the jaded appetite of this filthy king, this royal ravisher who preyed on women as a rat preys upon cooped birds, seizing them, sucking their blood, casting them aside to die, and rushing at another. My soul sickened at the thought, my blood ran cold when I pictured her, my own, my peculiar treasure, my love whom I had always loved from her childhood and yet for long had never quite known that I loved in that full fashion, helpless in the hands of this crowned brute.

What a fool and madman had I been! Why had I not married her when first she came to womanhood? Then before ever these kings set their leering eyes upon her beauty, she would have been the mother of children and therefore one whom they did not desire. Then we should have passed our lives together in peace. But I thought to give her liberty, to let her choose some younger man, if so she willed, not guessing that with body and with soul, from the hour that she knew I was not her father, she had turned to me, and me alone. Therefore, because of my mother's pride and common vanity, all these evils had come upon us, and what was done could not be undone. Myra lay in her gorgeous den, panting and beating its bars of gold whilst she waited the coming of the wolf that would tear her for his pleasure, and I, far away and powerless, could stretch out no hand to save her, although her cry echoed in my ears.

She said that first she would die, and doubtless it was so, unless in their cunning way they robbed her of the means of death. Well, if she died, surely I should know it, surely her spirit would touch me in its passing, so that I might make haste to follow. Yet, what an end! One that was forbid also by the law which said that all torments must be endured for the pleasure of the gods. Yet if need were it should be faced.

I lifted the letter to my lips and kissed it; then I pressed it to my heart and wept. Yes, I, a man of full age and a captain of men, wept like a girl!

I felt a hand upon my shoulder and looked up. By me stood the prophet, the holy one of the People of Judah.

"Why do you weep, Ramose?" he asked gently.

I told him all and even gave him the letter to read, though in truth he scarcely looked at it but set it down as though already he knew what was written there.

"You have done foolishly and for the second time, Ramose," he said, "you who lack faith and patience. Have I not told you to wait and be content? And now, who knows? It is not easy for women of the king's household to send out letters unobserved, and if this one has been seen, what then? Well, it is too late to question. Let the matter be. Yet I pray you to promise me that you will send no more such messages and seek no more letters from a certain lady who lies hid in yonder palace."

"I ask pardon and I promise," I answered humbly. "Be not wrath with me, O Prophet. I feared lest she were dead, as you see she feared that I was dead, and the temptation was too great."

"Had she been dead, I should have told you, Ramose. Do you think that for no purpose I desire to keep you here in Babylon where you go in great peril day by day? If she were dead or lost to you beyond all hope, long ago I should have sent you hence. For the last time I say—be warned, and unless I bid you, do nothing in this matter save bide here and wait."

Thus he spoke, more sternly than he had ever done to me, and, seeking no answer, departed, leaving me afraid. What did he mean when he spoke of my going in danger day by day? I thought that here in his house I lay hid and safe from every peril, also that none knew that the Egyptian, Ramose, was in Babylon, or even that a certain Ptahmes dwelt on there. Yet if these things were not known, why did I go in danger? I say that I grew afraid, not for myself who have never been a coward, but for Myra. If evil overtook me, what would chance to Myra who then, save for Belus if he still lived, would be alone in the world?

Oh! I was afraid of this prophet about whom there was something unearthly, and even terrible. He seemed to walk the earth like a spirit or a god, knowing all, perchance directing all, yet holding his lips sealed and hiding his countenance. And he was wrath with me because I did not trust to him more utterly, forgetting that it is hard for men who are sinners to put all their faith and hopes in the hands of saints and prophets, seeing that to their knowledge such often deceive themselves and lead others to their ruin.

In what troubles was I snared and wrapped like a gnat in a spider's web! When the royal Atyra was murdered because of me, I had sworn that never again would I look in love on woman and holding down the flesh, for many years I had kept that oath and been happy. Then Myra the snow-maiden, of a sudden turned to flame and set me afire also, so that we burned upon one pyre which was like to be such as the old Greeks used to consume the dead. Well for me and well for her if we had gone different ways and our lips had never met in love!

Nay, it was not so, for even if we died, separate or together, still our lips had met, still that holy fire had been lit which must burn eternally. Oh! better to suffer and to love, than to live out fat, unanxious years in such peace as oxen know. For then what harvest can the spirit hope to bear with it from the earth to sow again beyond the earth?

CHAPTER 19

The Lady of the Litter

The weary days went on. As I had promised, I attempted to send no more messages, and indeed told Obil that I sought no further letters, for these were too dangerous. This saying, I noted, seemed to please him, who although he made no complaint and expressed no fear, to me now always appeared to walk like one who is straining his ears to listen, while continually he glances over his shoulder to see if he is followed.

Had Obil some secret cause for dread, I wondered uneasily, and if so, was I to blame? This doubt took a hold of me, so that more than once almost I spoke to him on the matter, purposing to ask him whether he would not do well to leave my service and hide himself. Yet in the end I did not, who in the words of the Egyptian proverb, though it wiser not to kick the sleeping jackal lest it should yap and call the lion. Also I believed that the prophet would protect him.

At last came a day when Obil brought some news and it was dreadful. Belshazzar the King had returned to Babylon that morning shortly after dawn. Obil, who had gone early to the market to buy our food, saw him come, driving furiously in a chariot and accompanied by other chariots and horsemen who seemed weary as though they had galloped through the livelong night. I asked him of this king and he answered that he looked fierce yet frightened, like to one who had an evil spirit sitting on his shoulder and calling disaster in his ear. His eye flashed, his long hair flew out behind him, and when an old woman carrying fish in a basket on her back, stumbled and fell, blocking the narrow road, with a curse he bade the charioteer drive over her. This was done, leaving her crushed and shrieking, with blood running from her, a sight that angered the people, for they muttered and some shook their fists after the king. Yet none of them dared to touch the woman whom he had chosen to destroy and who lay there till she died.

"It seems that the people of Babylon do not love this king of theirs," I said.

"No, Master, they hate him, who is the most cruel of whom history tells. Yet they fear him for he never forgets and his vengeance is very terrible. While Nabonidus lived they could appeal to him sometimes, but now that he is dead they can only appeal to their gods who do not listen."

"What news of the Persian war?" I asked him.

"None that is certain; indeed few talk of it because it is forbidden, but those who do shake their heads and mutter of defeat and captured cities. They say, too, that Belshazzar has escaped from Zippar or some other beleaguered place, and fled to Babylon because he believes it impregnable and hopes to hold it until he can win succour from other countries. It is even reported that an embassy has come from Egypt to treat with him on this matter. For so hardly is he pressed that he has offered to Pharaoh lordship over all the Syrian lands that Babylon still holds, and a great sum in gold, if only he will send an army to his succour."

Now when I heard this I marvelled. Only a little while ago Nabonidus was quarrelling with Pharaoh over the matter of Myra, and that Belshazzar should now be imploring help from him showed me that he must indeed be pressed. Still I said no more, thinking to myself that I would ask the prophet of the truth of this story. But when I inquired whether he would be pleased to see me I received a message which he had left for me, saying that he had gone to some hidden place to pray and would not return till after sunset, or perhaps not until the morrow.

So I sat alone in my chamber, consumed with such fears as may not be written, for were not Myra and Belshazzar the king now beneath the same roof? Aye, was she not as a bird in the very hand of the snarer.

Later in the day I sent again for Obil, thinking that I might gather more tidings. But a servant called Nabel came in his stead, much disturbed. He said that he and Obil had been walking in the street when suddenly guards pounced on them, seized Obil and dragged him away. Thereon he fled, fearing lest they should take him also, which they made no attempt to do.

"Where then is Obil?" I asked.

"Where the lamb is after it wandered and met the eagle, Master," answered the man grimly, "for those guards bore the royal badge."

"The motherless lamb is good to the eagle, but what is Obil to a certain bird that has a beak but no wings?" I asked.

"Doubtless food also, of one sort or another, or may be his entrails will furnish auguries," he answered in a cold voice that frightened me.

For now I was sure that Obil had been seized because he had to do with a certain message and a certain letter, and could say who sent the message and who received the letter. Still, all was well; Obil was an upright man, like myself a worshipper of Jehovah who would break no oaths.

Then I remembered that tyrants and kings have dreadful ways of dragging out the truth from the most secret soul, and shivered.

****

Later in that terrible day, between two and three hours before sunset, this same man Nabel entered the chamber where I sat brooding, bearing a covered basket of woven rushes.

"What is this?" I asked.

"A love-gift, as I think, Master; at least the women of Babylon, when they are smitten with desire for some man who has caught their eye, are wont to send such baskets adorned like this with the rich colours of love."

"Then it cannot be for me, upon whose countenance no lady has looked for months," I answered smiling.

"Yet it is always well to learn what is hidden in any covered basket," said Nabel meaningly.

Thereon I undid the silken string and threw back the lid, revealing ripe figs, each of them wrapped in a vine leaf.

"Take out the figs—but do not eat them," said Nabel and I did so, lifting the purple fruit one by one and setting them on the table.

At length I came to a package wrapped in linen. I undid this package, and behold! there appeared just such a clay cylinder as that which had covered Myra's letter. I took it, I pressed, it fell to pieces, and within was a little papyrus roll inscribed with tiny writing in the Grecian character.

Eagerly I read. It ran thus:

"Beloved,

"I am in a sore straight, but I have found a certain road of escape for both of us; what it is I dare not write. There is a feast tonight in the great hall of the palace, which feast you must attend. Array yourself in a dress of honour and come hither guided by one whom I send who is a friend to me. I dare write no more, but all will be made clear at the time appointed. Oh! fail me not. If ever you would clasp me in your arms and look again upon a happy house, fail me not now. Cast aside all

200

doubts and fear. Be bold and come, lest we be parted for ever. Choose then between joy and death. For learn, Beloved, that if you come not, this very day I must die to save myself from a more evil fate."

Twice I read this letter through from the first word to the last. Then I laid it down and thought, as perhaps I had never done before. Swiftly, fiercely I weighed and pondered all. Taking the first letter from where it was hidden, I compared the two. The encasing tablets were of the same sort, though the writing on them was different, for this second tablet purported to deal with the sale of a field in the reign of some earlier Babylonian king, reserving the trees in the field to the seller and his heirs, as is often done in the East. Moreover the broken fragments of the tablet had been joined together with the same sort of invisible cement. The papyrus on which both letters were written, also seemed to be the same, of an Egyptian make, as I who had used so much of it, knew well, and scented with a like scent; in the Greek character further I could find no difference though the ink of the second letter varied a little in colour from the first, being darker in hue.

Still, seeing that Grecian characters written by a good scribe are hard to know apart, I could not be sure that this Greek was written by Myra, though as in the case of the first letter, from its style I believed it to be hers. Lastly in both letters the writer spoke of ending her life rather than suffer shame, and in the second she called our house at Memphis by its name, which surely no one else would know. Oh! I could not doubt. Myra had penned this second letter as she had penned the first.

Then why did I not prepare to do her bidding, putting aside all doubts and fears, as she bade me? For one reason only—because of my promise to the prophet. Yet what was that promise? That I should attempt no more to send her messages and draw answers from her; one that I had kept to the full. For the rest, he had only bidden me to bide here in this house. But if he saw that letter, doubtless he would recall his words. Alas! that I could not show it to him! Alas! that now when I needed him so sorely, he was far away, where I knew not.

So it stood thus. On the one hand was Myra's letter which, if obeyed, meant escape and joy, and if not obeyed, meant her death that must soon be followed by my own. On the other, the bidding of the prophet that I should not leave his house, because if I did so I might come into peril. But could I hesitate for such a reason when Myra stood in perils a hundred times as great? I could not; I would put on the robe of honour that Nabonidus had given me to wear when I walked from my apartments to the royal presence, and go. Yet how was I to go?

She spoke of one whom she sent to guide me, who was a friend to her. Where then was this guide? I called the man Nabel who had brought me the basket and inquired how it had come into his hands. He answered that an old beggar-woman had given it to him as he stood in the street outside the door, and that she was now crouched in the shadow of a broken wall near by, as he thought asleep. I asked him if she had said anything.

"Yes, Master," he replied. "She said that she was commanded to lead the lord to whom the basket must be delivered, to where he would go and that she would wait until he was ready, which he must be by sunset."

I glanced at the sky and saw that there was yet an hour before the sun vanished. This was well, for in an hour much might happen. The prophet might return; the old woman might depart, in which case I could not accompany her and the problem would solve itself. Meanwhile I would make ready.

I washed myself, I trimmed my long hair and the square beard that I now wore after the Babylonian fashion, wondering foolishly whether Myra would prefer it thus or whether she would bid me shape it as of old when at last we were far away and safe; wondering also with what looks and words she would greet me, and many other such vain things as come into the minds of lovers. Then I put on the robe of honour, a rich garment embroidered with silver and having a deep collar that could be turned up to hide the face; such a robe as the Babylonians wore over their linen dress when they attended feasts, or at night when they went where they did not wish to be known, for then they raised this collar till almost it met the head-dress of folded silk.

By the time that all was done the sun's red rim made a path of fire over the broad bosom of the Euphrates and I knew that very soon it would be gone. I sent once more to learn if the prophet had returned, but there was no sign of him. Then torn this way and that by hopes and fears, I knelt down and prayed to God to guide me, as I knew the prophet was wont to do. I was not warned against this enterprise by sign or token or symbol, or by the stirring of my heart. Therefore I felt encouraged in it, who did not understand that already the first warning and the last had been given to me through the mouth of the great prophet who, as always, spoke with the voice of God.

The sun having vanished I gathered up my courage and called to Nabel who had brought the basket. In his charge I left the letter I had received with a message to the prophet, should he return, saying that I had obeyed what was written in the letter, having no choice for otherwise I must have gone mad. He learned the message by heart and said that it should be delivered with the writing, which I knew he could not read who had no Greek.

Then Nabel led me out through the secret door by which first I had entered this house, and along an old, broken wall of the building which was here before it, to a niche in the wall where perhaps once stood the statue of some king or god. In this niche wrapped in a tattered garment, crouched an old woman who seemed to be asleep. If so, she slumbered warily, for at the sound of our steps she scrambled to her feet, hobbled forward and stared at me by such light as remained.

"La!" she said, "so this is he to whom I bore the love-basket. A likely man enough, though no youth. But there, when I was in my flower and beautiful, always I turned to one of middle-age, perhaps because, being no fool myself, I sought wisdom as well as kisses. Come on, lover, and may the goddess of Love who, mind you, by whatever name they call her, is the greatest in the whole world, be your friend tonight."

Thus she babbled on, as I guessed to stop my mouth, so that I could not question her, all the while leading me by quick turns from side street to side street, till at length we reached a quiet, grass-grown place surrounded by tall houses in whose windows no lamps burned, either because it was too early for them to be lit, or because the houses were deserted.

In this place as the faint light showed, for that night was one of full moon, was a large litter resting on the ground and standing at its poles twelve black men dressed in uniform who neither stirred nor spoke; Ethiopian slaves they seemed to be. The old woman led me to the litter, whispering,

"Enter, lover. Nay, stop not to fee me who am already well paid and whose joy it is to bring together those who waste away apart. Enter and when you are happy, remember me."

So through the curtains which she opened, I stumbled into that dark litter, to find myself caught in a woman's arms and resting on a woman's breast. I thought—who would not?—that it must be she I sought, she of whom my heart was full, and no other. Therefore I threw my answering arms about her and drawing her to me kissed her on eyes and lips. Nor did she say me nay. At length she laughed a little and the laugh seemed strange to me. Then she said in the Babylonian tongue and in a voice that though pleasant, was stranger still,

"I have always heard, Friend, that you men of Egypt were warm-hearted and forward to attack, but never till now did I understand how faithful was the tale. Kiss on, Friend, if it pleases you, for kisses are cheerful and they leave no scars."

Now I shrank back gasping and amazed, not far it is true, for the litter would not allow of it, whereon my companion continued her mockery.

"Are you tired of love-making," she answered, "and so soon? Or do you fear that Ishtar has not blessed me? It is not so, I swear. Look now, I will draw the curtain a little and you will see that I am well-favoured enough to please most men, even if they be high-born Egyptians."

Thereon she leant forward, pressing her face against my own, and did so. At first I could see nothing both because I could scarcely move my head, and secondly for the reason that the moonlight was cut off either by a cloud or by some house. Presently, however, the litter swung round a corner, for all this while we were being carried forward, and for a few moments the light shone on her, showing that in her fashion she was very fair, round-faced, red-lipped and with dark alluring eyes. Also she was young and most shapely.

"So!" she said, letting the curtain fall again, "not so ill, am I, at any rate in this gloom where one might well pass for another? You, too, are better to look at than I thought, handsome indeed—therefore—" and again she pressed herself against me.

"Lady," I murmured, "I may not. I go to meet one to whom I am sworn and—I may not."

"Well, even so there is no reason to tremble like a leaf, or as though you found yourself companioned by a snake. You would not greet the lady by telling her how you came to her and with whom, would you? If Ishtar keeps her eyes shut need you open hers? Moreover," she added and now I caught a note of warning in her voice, "how do you know that you will find that lady, who perhaps also travels in a litter with another? Have you no proverb in Egypt, Friend, that says: 'Take what the gods give while their hands are open, for none know what they will withhold when they are shut.'"

"Oh! Lady, mock me not. I am in a sore strait."

She laughed a little, musically enough, and answered,

"So I can guess; indeed I am sure of it and therefore I forgive you, which, being vain, I should not do if I thought that you shrank from me because I was unpleasing to you. Poor man, be at peace! See, here is a cushion, will you not use it to cover your face? The warmest kisses cannot burn it through. Moreover it was you who began them, not I. I did but take fire from your torch."

Then she leant back and continued laughing, and there was something about her voice which told me that however bold she might be, she was also kind-hearted.

We travelled on in silence for a while, then she said,

"I will tell you something lest you should misjudge me. You can guess that I am girl whose eyes are not always fixed upon the ground, but I am nothing worse. I was sent to bring you as one from whom a man would not flee as he might do from another man. But by Marduk I do not know why I am sent who earn my fee and ask no questions. Believe me, Egyptian, I am not the bait upon any trap."

"Who sent you?" I asked.

"A eunuch as usual where such palace errands are concerned, and therefore I smell a love affair."

"Is it so? I thought perhaps that it was a lady."

"Without doubt, for there is always a lady behind the eunuch," she answered in the voice of one who wished to leave this matter undiscussed.

Then I remembered the words of Myra's letter, that she was sending one who was a friend of hers to lead me to her, and marvelled a little, for this fair wanton seemed a strange friend for Myra to have chosen. Only I remembered also that she was dwelling in a court and, it was probable, could not choose her friends, but must take any that would serve her turn, a dangerous one enough. Therefore I let that doubt trouble my mind no more. Presently the litter halted for a moment and a challenge was given which was answered by one of the bearers in words that I could not catch. Thereon he who had challenged laughed and we went forward again, from which I guessed that we had passed some gate. The lady leant forward and whispered in a new voice,

"Friend, we have passed the outer wall of the palace and are about to go down into—hell, for the palace of Belshazzar is hell indeed, as I know who dwell there with others of my kind. You are bold who being free, enter such a place where from hour to hour none knows what may chance to him. But doubtless you have your reasons which it does not become me to ask. Now I am going to make a request to you, to grant or to refuse as you will. It is that you will kiss me once more, upon the brow this time, not as a lover but as a brother might, and tell me that you forgive me my mockeries. For I would fain be kissed once by an honest man as I feel you to be."

Now I thought a moment. I did not wish to touch this woman again yet some voice speaking in my heart urged me to do as she desired. So I listened to that voice and kissed her, for which she thanked me very humbly. As the end will show well was it for me that I did so, thereby making her my friend.

Again we were challenged and this time the word of the bearers was not accepted.

"Lean back," said my companion.

Then she opened the curtains a little and spoke between them, at the same time thrusting out her hand on which there was some ring.

"Go on," cried a voice. "It is only Adna with one of her gallants, who carries warrant on her finger to pass where she will with whom she will on this night of festival when Ishtar reigns. Say, Adna, may I not share that litter with you three nights hence when my leave begins?"

"Aye," she answered mockingly, "if between now and then you will change yourself from a vulgar fellow into a gentleman of breeding who can tell the name of his grandfather, which is impossible," a bitter saying that caused the officer's companions to laugh.

We went on again through sundry courts, as I gathered by the cutting off of the moonlight, and at length halted in some silent place.

Adna, as I had now learned the woman with me was called, sprang from the litter that had been set down upon the ground, and running up some steps to a little door, tapped upon it three times, and after a pause twice more quickly. The door opened and for a while she talked with some one in a whisper, after which she returned to the litter and said,

"My task is done. Yours, whatever it may be, begins. Descend."

Now some cold hand of fear seemed to grip my heart, some sense that this place was unfriendly and dangerous to me, so that of all things in the world that which I wished the least was to enter there. A sweat burst out upon my brow; I became a coward eaten up of doubts.

"Can you not take me back by the road we came, Lady?" I asked.

"Nay," she answered. "You have entered by your own will and here you must stay, as the fish-god said to the eel in the trap when it learned that it was about to be skinned alive. Oh! why will men run so fast to catch women who are not worth it after all? Goodbye and may all the gods of all the lands befriend you, just for the sake of that one honest kiss."

Then servants, four of them all armed, appeared and handed me from the litter, bowing as though to a great lord. At the head of the steps I glanced back and saw the light of the torch they bore, shining on the beautiful face of the white-robed Adna as she stood by the litter watching me depart. Moreover, unless some trick of the shadows deceived me, I could have sworn that tears were running down that face.

Why and for whom did Adna shed those tears? I wondered.

206

Chapter 20

The End of Obil

The little door clanged to behind me and with a fluttering of my
heart I heard the bronze bolts rattle as they went home in their marble sockets. Then I was led down narrow passages, many of them that
turned and forked and turned again till I lost all count of how they
ran. At length I reached cedar doors before which stood guards. The
doors opened and out came other servants who took me from those
by whom I had been brought thus far, and led me into a lofty room
that was separated from an inner chamber by broidered curtains.

Here I stood for a space while, passing between the curtains, one
of the servants made some report that seemed to cause a man within
to laugh loudly. Then he returned and I was led, or rather pushed
through the curtains, on the farther side of which I halted bewildered,
being dazzled by the multitude and brightness of the lights. A voice
said in my ear,

"Down! Be prostrate before the King of kings!" but still I stood
bewildered, seeing no king.

When presently my eyes grew accustomed to the blaze of light
I perceived that I was in a large chamber, cedar-roofed and adorned
with gold-worked hangings. At the end of this chamber, seated in a
gilded and jewelled chair, was a large, hook-nosed, bearded man with
unwinking eyes that reminded me of those of a vulture, whom I knew
to be Belshazzar the King.

He stared at me with those bold, fixed eyes, then said in a voice as
soft as though his throat had been soaked in oil,

"Let him alone. These barbarian foreign lords do not understand
the customs of our court. If he does not prostrate himself of his own
courtesy, I say—let him alone who may ere long learn to mend his
manners. Bring him here. I would speak with him."

So I was led forward and stood before the king.

"How are you named?" he asked, eyeing me up and down with his vulture stare.

"I am called Ptahmes, O King," I answered who did not dare to give my own name, and I noted that a scribe who stood by, wrote down the words.

"Is it so? I think that I have heard otherwise. What are you doing in Babylon and what are you?"

"I am a man of learning, O King, of whom the late king, your father, was pleased to make a friend when we discussed the attributes of the gods. He gave me this robe in which I stand."

"Did he? Then a fool made presents to a knave," he replied coarsely, and the courtiers laughed. "Where are you living?" he went on.

"I am the guest of the prophet Belteshazzar, O King, he whom the late king Nebuchadnezzar made governor of Babylon."

"Indeed. Then as I suspected, that old Hebrew dream-doctor keeps bad company. By Marduk! he shall answer for it to me who do not fear his spells as did Nebuchadnezzar the Madman. Are you also one of the men of Judah?"

"I am a worshipper of the God of Judah, O King."

"And therefore an enemy of the gods of Babylon. Well, let the gods fight their own battles. I mock them all who have served me ill of late and chiefly this cheat of Judah, whose temple we have plundered and whose golden vessels are my wash-pots. He has cursed me, so say his priests, but as he has no statue to be defiled, I spit upon his name and will show him that the King of Babylon is greater than the Heavenly Cheat of Judah, as did the kings who went before me. What say you, man?"

Now when I heard these blasphemies I shivered, nor, as I think, were they pleasing to the ears of the courtiers, for I saw some of them turn their heads and make the sign that Babylonians use to avert evil.

"Is it for me to reason with the King, or to revile Him Whom I worship? As the King said, let the gods fight their own battles, which doubtless they will do," I answered slowly.

"So in veiled words you threaten me with this god of yours, do you? Yet I think that before long you will revile his name, and loudly, in all our ears. How came you here and for what purpose, O Ptahmes?"

"A woman brought me, O King."

"Her name?"

"I am not sure of it, but one of the guards called her Adna."

All those present smiled and Belshazzar answered with a brutal laugh,

"Oh! Adna. We all know the beautiful Adna. Did you then propose to use my palace as a house of ill fame?"

"Not so, O King. I was told that I was among those bidden to a feast because the late king Nabonidus had favoured me."

"Were you? Then learn that I do not pick my feasters from among my father's toadies tricked out in his old clothes," and he pointed to my cloak which I now noticed was of a different make and stuff from those worn by the officers around him.

I was silent, not knowing what to say. For a while he sat staring at me, his face alive with hate as though I were his bitterest foe. Then he spoke again, changing his soft voice, as he had the power to do, for one like to the roar of a lion.

"Let us have done with all these lies," he said, "for I weary of the play and time grows short. Captain, bring in the man Obil, that we may refresh ourselves with a breath of truth."

Now the officer addressed hesitated, seeing which the king struck the arm of the chair with his sceptre and shouted again,

"Do you not hear me? Bring in the spy Obil."

So sharply did he strike that the ivory sceptre snapped in two and the golden head in which was set a great emerald, rolled along the floor till it lay still between my feet. A gasp of fear at this most evil omen rose from those who saw it, and even the king's wine-flushed face paled for a moment. Recovering himself, he turned on them snarling and asked,

"Are you afraid? Do you think that the cheat Jehovah answers me by a sign worked upon this rod of power that all the gods of Babylon have blessed? I tell you that with half a sceptre I will hunt him out of heaven, yes, and shatter Cyrus, whom the men of Judah call his Sword. Aye, I will thrust it down the Persian's throat and watch it choke him."

"May the King live for ever!" said the courtiers bowing. "The King is greater than all the conquered gods of all the peoples!"

I saw, I heard, and for the first time some comfort crept into my scared soul as I set my foot upon that sceptre-head beneath the hem of my robe where it lay hidden, and spurned it. For well I knew that this beast king was but as dust before the breath of Jehovah the Holy One of Judah. Then I stepped back and showed the great jewel flashing on the ground like to a tiger's evil eye.

A door at the side of the chamber was opened and through it came four bloodstained black men, naked save for loin cloths, who bore a stretcher covered with a cloth.

"May it please the King, Obil is here as the King commanded," said the captain.

At a sign from the king he threw back the cloth revealing a hideous sight, from which even those cruel Babylonians shrank back. For there lay Obil, mutilated, torn to pieces, scarred with fire and bathed in blood. More I will not write; it is enough.

"Bid the dog speak, if he would not taste of a worse torment, and tell me what he knows of this man who bribed him to corrupt my servants and carry letters from a lady of my household," said Belshazzar.

"May it please the King," said the captain in a trembling voice, "Obil cannot speak. He is dead!"

"Dead!" roared Belshazzar. "How comes it that he is dead when I commanded that he should be kept alive?" and he glared at the black slaves who shook in their terror.

"May it please the King," went on the captain, "the scribe here whose office it is to be present at tormentings and take down the words uttered by the victims—I mean by the wicked sentenced to punishment, says that this obstinate man of Judah, Obil, snatched a heated knife from the hand of one of the slaves and drove it into his own heart. See, it stands there in his breast."

"And what said the fellow before he died?" asked Belshazzar of the scribe, who answered,

"May it please the King, he said nothing save that he believed this man here was an Egyptian of royal blood and that the King could never harm him as he was protected by the spirit of Belteshazzar, the great prophet of Judah. Naught else could be wrung from him by any torment that is known. Indeed with his last words he denied all the little he had uttered."

"Did he tell you naught of Belus or Azar, my enemy in whose pay he was, and whither he has gone?"

"Naught, O King."

"Take that carrion away and let those clumsy slaves await my punishment under guard, for I think that presently they shall taste of their own medicine," said the king, glaring again at the black men.

So the body of the steadfast Obil was carried off and as it went I prostrated my heart before him whom unwittingly I had brought to death, and blessed his spirit, praying its pardon and that of God. When it was gone and slaves had scattered perfume over the spot where the tormentors and the litter had stood, the king spoke again, saying,

"We have learned little of this man from that dead Hebrew, save that he is an Egyptian of royal blood, and even this he denied again before his end. Nor is it of any use to ask the fellow himself, except under torment, for doubtless he will lie as all Egyptians do. Yet if, as is reported, he be really of the blood of Amasis we must go softly, for at this moment Babylon does not wish to make a foe of Pharaoh. Now I have heard rumours concerning the man and I would put them to the proof, as happily I have the means to do. What say you, my counsellors?"

"The King is wise. May the King live for ever!" answered these reptiles, bowing like snakes before the rod of their charmer.

Then Belshazzar turned to a chamberlain who stood upon his right with a wand in his hand, and said,

"Admit those ladies who await an audience of my Majesty, and be silent everyone while I talk with them. Remember all, also you, Egyptian, that whoever speaks before I open his mouth, dies," and without moving his head he turned his flashing eyes towards the door through which the torturers had departed with their horrible burden, then fixed them threateningly upon me.

Presently the curtains that hung over another of the entrances to that great chamber were drawn and from between them appeared two ladies draped in long veils, of whom because of these veils little could be seen, except that they were tall and walked gracefully. After them came other women whom I took to be attendants because their heads were bowed. Also I noted that the pair who came first seemed to be strangers or enemies, for they exchanged no word and edged away from each other. Having made their obeisance to the king, they were halted by the chamberlain at a little distance from where I stood. Then they looked at me and I perceived that both of them began to sway and tremble like papyrus reeds beneath the weight of a breath of wind, seeing which I grew suddenly afraid. Indeed from the moment that they entered I had been afraid, because there was something which came from them to me that stirred my spirit and awoke memories of I knew not what.

"Be pleased, Ladies, as this is no public court, to put off ceremony and to unveil yourselves," said Belshazzar in his softest voice.

Thereon the waiting women sprang forward and loosed the wrappings from the heads of the two ladies whom I watched intently, wondering whether I should know them.

The veils fell and were snatched away and next moment I too nearly fell down. For before me stood Myra and my mother! Both of them were wonderfully arrayed and, as a man sees in a dream, I noted that on my mother's head was a royal ornament, at least from it, fashioned in gems, rose something that resembled the *uraeus* snake of Egypt, that only might be worn by kings, their spouses and their children of the true blood.

Myra bent forward as though to speak but in a stern voice Belshazzar bade her to be silent. Then addressing my mother, he said,

"Royal Lady, for so from our brother Pharaoh's letters I understand you are, who for your own reasons have been pleased to favour me by accompanying Egypt's embassy to Babylon, as, if you were so minded, I prayed that you would do; tell me, I pray, whether you know this man who stands before me, and if so, who and what he is."

These words the king spoke in his own language, but an interpreter who must have been waiting there for the purpose, rendered them in Greek.

"Know him!" she answered with a cry, using that same tongue, for indeed she had never learned any other very well. "Can a mother forget the child she bore? Great King, he is my own and only son begotten by the good god, Pharaoh Apries, when I was his wife. Yes, my son of the royal blood, a Count of Egypt and a governor of Memphis, whom having lost, by Pharaoh's leave I have travelled so far to seek, as you invited me to do through your envoy, O King of kings. Amasis, the present divine Pharaoh, sent him as an ambassador to Cyrus the Persian, after which he vanished, O King; wherefore, hearing from your envoy that he was rumoured to be still in Babylon hidden away, I came to seek him and—am here."

"Is he named Ptahmes, Lady?"

"Nay, O King, his name is Ramose," she exclaimed astonished.

"I thank you, Lady, for this makes certain what we had heard elsewhere, that Ptahmes is a false name under which it has pleased the noble but modest Ramose to hide himself in Babylon. Now, royal Chloe, as I believe that you are called, be pleased to tell me whether you know the lady who stands near to you?"

"Yes, O King, though I have not seen her since she left Egypt to be wed to the King Nabonidus, a marriage, I am told, that did not take place because of some falsehood that was published concerning her, although now she is to become your queen, O King, a glorious destiny indeed. Yes, the wife of the greatest monarch in all the world!" and she lifted her eyes as though in adoration of a god.

"You are right, Lady, and it is for this reason that we have petitioned of you to honour us with your presence here in Babylon if only for a while, that we may bestow upon you such gifts and titles as become one who is said to be the grandmother of a lady whom its king takes as wife. We beg you, therefore, to tell us here and now whether this is so, as in his letters Amasis, the Pharaoh of Egypt declares, because if I may say it, in your person you are still so young and beautiful, that doubts have arisen as to this matter."

Now I fell into an agony, or rather into a deeper agony, who knew not what words would come from the mouth of this foolish mother of mine in the madness of her vanity. I who remembering Belshazzar's terrible threat, dared not speak, fixed my eyes upon her face, as I saw Myra did also, striving to send a message from my heart to hers, warning her of my peril. But she took no heed. Indeed she only blushed and bowed, then answered in a pleased voice,

"O King, my son Ramose was born when I was still very young, nor is he himself so far advanced in years as might be thought from his face, that has grown lined with study of deep things I do not understand."

Now Belshazzar leaned forward and said in a measured voice,

"Then this lady is the daughter of your son, Ramose?"

"So I believe, O King, although I never knew her mother, as I told Pharaoh Amasis in the past. Years ago a queen named Atyra came from Syria on an embassy to Apries my lord, a beautiful woman who, I heard, fell in love with my son and—the King will spare me, for we in Egypt are modest and it is not our custom to talk of such matters to men."

Now able to bear no more I was about to cry out that she lied, when a eunuch who had drawn near to me, gripped my arm and handling his dagger, whispered in my ear,

"Unless you seek instant death, be silent."

Then I refrained my lips, bethinking me that while I lived there was still hope. In death there could be none.

"All of us understand, royal Chloe," said the king with a false smile; "indeed I remember hearing of this Queen Atyra, a very fair woman who went to stir up Egypt against us of Babylon and returned no more. So enough of her. Now one more question, my royal guest, and I will cease to trouble you. A man called Belus, an evil-doer who fled from Babylon when I was young because of some crime he had committed, appeared here not long ago and was pardoned through the foolishness of the late king, my father, to whom he was a cousin. This man having been reinstalled in his offices, for by trade he is a priest and a necromancer, stated to the king in my presence that the lady Myra yonder was not a princess of the royal blood of Egypt as

Pharaoh Amasis had declared, but the low-born wife of an Egyptian named Ramose, a son of Pharaoh Apries and the lady Chloe, believing which, my father publicly put away the lady Myra and from that day till his death never looked upon her face again. Is this tale true or false, royal Chloe?"

"How can it be other than false, O King?" cried my mother in a high and rapid voice, "seeing that for years Myra dwelt with my son as his acknowledged daughter, first in Cyprus and afterwards in Egypt, where she herself often spoke to me of him as her father and where he suffered suitors to ask her hand as that of his daughter? Moreover did they not live in my house at Memphis as father and daughter? Lastly, if this were not so, should I have told Pharaoh Amasis that she was my son's daughter when he sought for a lady of the royal blood to be sent as a wife to the King Nabonidus? Further, if they were wed, how comes it that I, his mother, was never asked to be present when he took her as his bride?"

Thus she spoke in a torrent of words until she ceased from want of breath.

"It is enough," said Belshazzar, when the interpreter had rendered them all. "I thank you who with the wind of truth have blown away certain mists of falsehood which perplexed me, who purpose both for reasons of policy and of love," here he devoured Myra with his fierce and greedy eyes, "to repair the wrong done in error to your son's daughter by my father Nabonidus, one ever easy to deceive, by taking her to wife, thus wiping away that insult with the highest honour I can bestow. Be pleased to withdraw, royal Chloe, till we meet again presently at my feast when these nuptials will be declared. In your chamber you will find certain gifts not unworthy of her from whom sprang a queen of Babylon, with which I trust you will adorn your beauty at the feast; also the decrees conferring upon you titles of nobility which in Chaldea we think high."

When these words had been translated, Belshazzar rose and bowed to my mother, and she—poor besotted creature, prostrated herself before him as in her youth she was wont to do before Pharaoh whose woman she had been. Then muttering thanks, she withdrew with her following, forgetting in her joy and triumph even so much as to look at me, her son, who, although she guessed it not, she had condemned to death.

When she was gone Belshazzar dismissed most of those who stood about him, so that there remained only a scribe, a captain and four soldiers, three eunuchs, big, fat fellows with villainous, wrinkled countenances who, as I heard afterwards, were the chosen ministers of his pleasures; and some veiled women attending upon Myra, who from the way in which they moved, to me appeared to be jailers rather than waiting-maids. They went and there followed a space of heavy silence like to that which precedes the bursting of a tempest. All there felt, I think, that something terrible was about to happen, for even the soldiers and the hard-faced eunuchs looked moved and expectant.

Belshazzar descended from his high chair and stood in front of me, glowering, his evil face full of hate and jealous rage.

"You have heard," he said in that horrible soft voice of his. "Now what have you to say, half-bred dog of an Egyptian whose mother was a Grecian strumpet, you who came to Babylon upon a vile errand? Before you speak, learn that all this while you have been known and watched, aye, even while I was absent. After you were taken spying for Cyrus under a false name, the king my father protected you because you have some smatterings of learning and flattered him. He died and you and the traitor who is known as Belus, strove to escape with yonder lady under an order that you had cheated from him. But my officers outwitted you. The lady was taken in the gate, though owing to a storm bred of the wizardry of Belus, you and he vanished, as I think after killing my officer. Then you took shelter under the robe of the Hebrew prophet who is called Belteshazzar, knowing that none dare touch you there because of the superstitions of the Babylonians who believe that his house is fenced by spirits from the underworld. There, perhaps, you might have stayed safe enough, had it not pleased you to make use of that poor wretch whose corpse you saw but now, as a go-between with the lady Myra.

"In answer to your messages she wrote you a letter which was seized, copied and then delivered by your tool, Obil. Today, another letter was forged and given to you to serve as bait to draw the jackal from his hole. You came out of your lair and were met by a woman, because to have sent soldiers to take you would have been dangerous in a city that is full of treachery, thanks to your friend Belus and others, though that woman, the wanton Adna, knew not why she was sent, thinking only that she played a part in some love business from which she would draw gold. So through your own blind folly at last you came into my hands, where there is no prophet to protect you with the magic of the devil that he worships."

He paused a while, glaring and gnashing his teeth. Then he went on, "And now from the lips of that vain painted hag, your mother, lured here for this purpose, we have learned the truth, or what will serve as well, for who can doubt a mother's testimony concerning the son she bore? The lady whom you pretend to be your wife, is certified by your mother to be your own daughter and you are a wretch unfit to live, as all here and in Egypt will acknowledge, yes, even Amasis himself. Therefore I doom you to die, who on the head of your private crimes, have piled that of making trouble between Babylon and Egypt at a time when Babylon needs Egypt's help. Do you hear that you are condemned to die?"

"I hear, O King, that like every man—even the King himself—I am condemned to die," I answered slowly, for these words came to me. "Yet before I die I would say to you what you know already, that all this tale is false. Whatever my mother may have told you in her vanity and delusion, yonder woman is not my daughter but my wife."

"Dog!" he answered, smiting me in the face, "will you also defile your own mother? Well, soon we shall hear another story from you. Doubtless you think to pass hence swiftly and without pain. It is not so. You shall perish very slowly, as a monster who would take his own daughter for a wife and who slanders his mother is doomed to do under our ancient law. There is much that I would learn from you ere you yield your breath, concerning the doings of your familiar Belus who is reported to have gone hence to plot against me and Babylon with Cyrus the accursed Persian. Soldiers, away with him to the torment!" and he clapped his hands.

Then Myra who all this while had listened immovable, sprang forward and threw herself into my arms.

"He is my husband, not my father. If he must die, let me die with him," she cried.

"Drag her away," said the king, and they obeyed him.

Yet as she was torn from me, she thrust something into my hand which swiftly I hid in my robe, guessing that it was poison.

"Farewell, beloved wife," I said. "Soon we shall meet before God's judgment seat, we and this king."

As the soldiers haled me towards the curtains the captain who had departed to give orders returned.

"O King," he said, "the King's command cannot be carried out on the instant."

"Why not?" shouted Belshazzar.

"O King, the tormentors, fearing the just vengeance of the King that he had promised to them because of the death of Obil, are themselves all dead. Yes, there they lie dead, the four of them, having, as I think, swallowed their own tongues after the Ethiopian fashion."

"Send for others instantly," said the king.

Then the private scribe prostrated himself, saying,

"O King, the business will be long, for such instructed, devilish folk live by themselves at a distance and it is almost the hour of the great feast. Shall we not behead this man at once and make an end?"

"Nay," Belshazzar answered, "for I would court this daughter of his to the music of his groans. It will be sweet!"

He thought a while, then added,

"Bring him to the feast and guard him well, placing him under my own eye that I may be sure of him, who perhaps is also a magician and can vanish away like Belus. When the feast is over lead him here again where I and my new-made wife will talk with him. Bid more tormentors await us here with their instruments and see to it that they are the masters of their filthy company. On your heads be it!"

CHAPTER 21

The Writing on the Wall

It was the great feast of King Belshazzar, given to celebrate his
coming to the throne of Babylon, to attend which had been summoned all the satraps, high officers and nobles throughout the empire.
From east and west and north and south, in obedience to the royal
command, they had gathered together in Babylon like vultures to the
carcase, and waited there until the king returned from war to hold this
coronation feast. The enormous central hall of the palace was filled
with their glittering multitude, seated at scores of tables all down its
length and even between the towering side columns that bore up the
roof. In the centre there were no columns because this roof did not
stretch from wall to wall and here the hall was open to the sky. Nor
was one needed at this season of the year when no rain fell.

The night was hot and the air so still that the thousands of lamps and
torches burned without a flicker; even the flame of the candles in the
golden candlesticks that had been taken from the sanctuary of the House
of God at Jerusalem, pointed straight to heaven like fingers of fire.

The king's seat was at the high table, and behind him, at a distance,
was the white wall at the end of the great chamber. All down this table
on either side of the throne were placed his noblest lords, his queens
and his concubines, flashing in jewelled robes. Among these women
on one side sat Myra, tall, pale, beautiful, adorned as a bride; and on
the other side my mother Chloe, wearing the royal *uraeus* of Egypt to
which she had no right, and covered with gems, among them, upon
her heart, those that Belshazzar had promised to her as his royal gift.
Below this table stood another occupied by officers of the royal household, and at this board I, Ramose, was given a place looking up towards
the king, so that I might be in the king's eye as he had commanded.
At my back stood armed guards, and on either side of me were chief
eunuchs of the household who wore daggers in their belts.

When the countless company was gathered, a trumpet blew, heralds cried for silence, and the king entered. All rose from their seats and prostrated themselves before his majesty, lying on the floor like to dead men. He waved his sceptre, not that broken sceptre I had spurned, but another which a eunuch told me had belonged to a dead king. Thereon they stood up again and the feast began.

I watched it like one in a dream, touching nothing of that rich food which to my sight was viler than carrion, although with cruel courtesy the eunuchs pressed it on me, saying that as this would be my last meal, it was wise that I should eat, drink and be merry. Then, after their beastly fashion, the chief of them who had been present that night at the audience given to my mother, described to me how horribly I should be made to die; also what Myra must suffer if she turned from the king, all too hideous to be written.

Much wine was drunk and soon it became evident to me, watching and listening to what, as I believed, were the last voices I should hear on earth, that there were two parties in that hall which hated each other. For here and there quarrels flared up suddenly, even blows were given, until the guards who were everywhere, put an end to them with heavier blows.

At length the king rose and spoke, and I who sat not far from him, could hear every word he said. He told of the war with the Persians, boasting much and saying that Cyrus and his generals were already as dead men, for though at first they had met with some small success, their armies had now fallen into a trap and would beat vainly against the mighty walls of Babylon, like little waves against a mountain side. Some applauded these sayings, whereas others received them with mutterings, especially those whose sons and brothers had fallen in the battles or been taken prisoners and sold as slaves.

"I have good news for you, lords, rulers, captains and people of Babylon," went on the king. "There has been trouble between us and Egypt, brought about by spies, mischief-makers and liars"—here, as I thought, he glared at me. "That trouble is at end. Pharaoh is our ally again and will support us with his armies in our struggle against the Persian dogs. To seal our pact this very night I take to wife a lady of the royal blood of Egypt," and he pointed to Myra who sat still as a woman carved in stone, whereon all who could hear him rose and stared at her, appraising her beauty.

"Fear not," he went on, boasting madly, "I will lead Babylon to such glory as she has never known; guided by our ancient gods, again I will make of her the queen of the world. There are no gods like to the gods of Babylon who have smitten those of all the peoples. Some talk of Jehovah of the Hebrews. Where is this Jehovah? Behold! we have pulled him down from heaven. Babylon has sacked his sanctuaries, slaughtered his priests upon his altars of sacrifice, and taken his treasures as spoil. Ho! bring in the vessels from his house, those glorious vessels that were holy in the sight of this fallen cheat Jehovah."

Thereon men who were waiting bore in the golden vessels; the cups, the ewers and the basins, the receptacles of sacrifice and the lavers that had been sacked from the temple at Jerusalem. They bore them in with ribald shouts and lo! in each of them decked with flowers, was set some image of a god of the empire of Chaldea; gods of stone and ivory and wood, grinning and triumphant idols. They set the vessels down on the high-table while half-naked women jeered and mocked at them and into one of the most splendid Belshazzar cast the dregs of his wine, crying,

"Accept this drink-offering, O Jehovah, conquered demon of Judah!"

It was done and he fell back upon his throne panting and rolling his fierce eyes, while he waited for the shouts of acclamation that were to follow upon his vile words.

But no shouts came, at first I knew not why till it seemed to me, while I wondered, as though some shadow was passing down the length of that hall, yes, a winged shadow that could be felt rather than seen. Then I understood. After the passing of the shadow followed a heavy silence, for all were afraid. All knew that Death was of their company.

The silence lasted while one might count a hundred. Then over against me, at the far end of the hall, the shadow reappeared and thickened. Yes, against the white wall that towered high at the back of the king's seat, it began to take form and the form it took was that of a great hand which held a pen of fire. Such at least was its fashion to my eyes.

More—that hand began to write upon the lofty wall. Slowly it wrote with the pen of fire, tracing strange characters that I could not read, letters of flame which burned more brightly than iron at its whitest heat and were, each of them, of the height of a tall man.

Those of the feasters who sat far off were the first to see this dreadful writing, which the king and those about him saw not because it was behind them. They stared astonished and terrified; in utter silence they sat still and stared. Heavy was that unnatural stillness and dreadful was the gloom which gathered over the lower part of the chamber, as though some mighty shape floated there, cutting off the light of the moon and stars. Yet the lamps shone on beneath and by them could be seen the white, up-turned faces and the staring eyes of all that multitude of watchers.

"What ails our guests?" asked Belshazzar, gazing at those white faces and those terror-stricken eyes, and his voice sounded loud in the quiet.

Now for the first time I noted that Myra had risen. Alone among the women she had risen from her seat and stood with her back towards me looking at the wall behind her. Yes, it was she who answered the king which no other dared to do.

"Behold! O King," she cried and pointed to the wall.

He rose. He turned. He saw the huge black hand that held the pen of fire and slowly, very slowly, drew letters of flame upon the whited plaster of the wall, where they shone and sparkled like to the coals of a furnace heated manifold. Then he sank down in a huddled heap upon the edge of the table, crying such words as these:

"What witchcraft have we here? Come forward, appear, all ye my soothsayers and magicians, and show me the interpretation of this writing. To him who can read it I will give a great reward, aye, and set him up as a ruler in Babylon."

Presently from this place and that among the seats allotted to their Fellowships and Colleges and elsewhere, gathered the soothsayers, the magicians and all who were reckoned the wisest among the Chaldeans in the arts of divination. They advanced to the dais; they studied the characters of flame which one by one continued to start forth upon the plaster on the wall. But of them they could read nothing.

Appeared a lady who wore a crown upon her white hair. She came to the king whose body shook and whose face was ashen with fear.

"O King my son, live for ever!" she cried. "Let Daniel, the prophet of Judah, be summoned, he who among the Chaldeans is named Belteshazzar, for in him is the spirit of the holy gods. He will interpret this writing, as he interpreted many dark visions to Nebuchadnezzar the king who went before thee."

So in his terror the king commanded that Daniel known as Belteshazzar, should be brought before him. Tall, thin, solemn-faced, black-robed, white-haired, he was led through the feasters to the dais. As he passed the table where I sat, he turned and looked at me with his quiet eyes as though in reproach and wonderment. Then he looked at the eunuchs and armed guards around me; also at Myra in her bridal robes upon the dais, and seemed to understand. He climbed the dais and stood before the king, making no obeisance.

Belshazzar lifted his face from the cloth in which he had hidden it, and spoke with Daniel in a low voice, as I think offering him gifts, but what he said and what Daniel answered I could not hear. At length the prophet stepped back to the end of the dais and gazed upward at the letters which flamed upon the wall, for now the hand that wrote them with a pen of fire was seen no more.

"This is the meaning of the writing, O thou King that mockest the Most High God and defilest the vessels of His house," cried the prophet in so loud a voice that all in the hall could here. "Numbered, numbered, weighed and divided. Yea, thy days are numbered! Yea, thou art weighed upon the balances! Yea, thy kingdom is brought to an end! The Medes and the Persians take it!"

Now the king drew near to Daniel, imploring the prophet to take away this curse, or offering him gifts, I know not which, for the groans of fear that rose from all who heard, covered up his words. But the prophet waved him back and turning, departed from that hall, looking neither to right nor left.

In silence he went, in silence all watched him go; then, as though at a word of command, suddenly there was tumult. A madness fell upon the company and the rage of terror. Women screamed, men raved and shouted, the king flung himself face downward on the table, rolling his head from which the crown had fallen, from side to side; a fainting concubine caught at a tall light and overset it, firing her robes, and rushed shrieking to and fro. Here and there men drew swords from beneath their cloaks and struck at the lamps, extinguishing them. As though their use was ended and their message given, the fiery letters upon the wall faded and vanished, so that at last the only light left in the great place was that which came from the moon floating over head. Then voices cried,

"Down with Belshazzar! Away with the tyrant! Kill the cruel dog who tears us and brings maledictions upon us! Kill the blasphemer! Shut the doors! Stab the guards!" and I understood that there was rebellion here.

Those for the king and those against him began to fight and die. Groans echoed everywhere. Belshazzar sprang up and accompanied by his court lords and women, rushed towards the private entrance behind them, seeking to escape, for they knew that the curse had fallen and the hour of doom was near. Some of that glittering mob were overthrown and trampled, among them my mother. I heard her scream my name; I saw her fall and vanish beneath the stamping feet. Forgetting everything I rose to rush to her aid, for was she not still my mother! None hindered me, for hoping to save themselves, the eunuchs and the guards had gone I know not where. I snatched up a jewelled sword that had fallen from some prince's hand; I leapt on to the dais and ran to the spot where I had last seen my mother.

There she lay, her fair face crushed, her splendid robes red with blood. Already a thief had been at work upon her jewels, one of the black slaves, for I caught sight of him slinking away with the necklaces glittering in his hand. More, he had driven a knife into her throat to still her struggles while he robbed her. She was dead. Yes, poor, foolish woman, such was the end of her and all her vanities!

I bethought me of Myra and looked round. At that moment the moon that had been half hidden by a cloud, shone out fully. Lo! there she sat in her place at the high table whence she had never stirred, so still that I thought she must be dead, so beautiful that I wondered for a moment whether it were she herself or perhaps her spirit.

Leaping over the fallen who lay, some quiet, some yet struggling, I hastened to her. She saw me and whispered,

"I awaited you. Let us away from this hell."

"Aye, but whither?" I asked. "The doors are closed."

She sprang from her chair, saying,

"Follow me!"

A man appeared; it was the captain of those eunuchs who had sat by me at the feast and told me of the torments I must endure and of the shame that would be worked on Myra. He tried to seize her, shouting,

"She is the king's!" for in his mad bewilderment the poor wretch could only bethink him of his duty and that he must guard the royal women.

I ran him through with the sword. As he went down his long dark cloak fell from him. I caught it up and threw it over Myra's gorgeous bridal robe, drawing the hood over her head. Then heeding him no more, though it would have been wiser to make sure that he was dead, we ran on, following the wall. Myra came to a screen of cedar-wood behind which serving-men were wont to pass bearing dishes, as she remembered who knew the palace well. She peered down the little passage to learn whether it were empty, and I glanced back at the hall. As Myra had said, it was a hell in which everywhere men were murdering each other and thieves plied their business fiercely, there being much to steal. Many, however, were trying to escape, rushing madly from door to door to find them barred in obedience to the command of the conspirators, most of them doubtless in the pay of Cyrus the Persian, who had hoped thus to catch and kill the king.

Yelling, they ran to and fro while their enemies, coming after, hacked them down and, ere the breath had left them, thieves from among the palace servants and even soldiers, who having no pay lived by what they could seize, robbed them of their finery.

Such was the end, or at least the last I saw of Belshazzar's mighty coronation feast, the greatest that ever had been held in Babylon; yes, these terrors and towering above them, white in the moonlight, the wall whereon but now God's finger had written His decree.

****

We crept down the passage and came to the court of the scullions, off which opened the kitchens and the quarters of the cooks, a village in themselves. We fled across that court and found another that Myra did not know, for many a city was smaller than this palace. Here beneath awnings and columned porticoes men and women were revelling on this festal night, for as yet news of what had chanced in the great hall did not appear to have reached them. From the look of these women and all that passed around us, I guessed at once that this was the quarter of the players and dancers, also of the courtesans who were making merry with their gallants.

While we hesitated, hiding ourselves as best we could, the tidings came, whence I could not see. The men thrust away their darlings and sprang up, drawing their swords and gazing about them suspiciously. Discovering us, after demanding their password which we could not give, certain of them began to hunt us, shouting that we were spies who must be killed. We slipped away from them and hid in the deep shadows of a portico while they ran about like hounds that have lost the scent.

A woman glided up to us and peered into my face.

"Ah! I thought it!" she said. "Now, Friend, if you would save yourself and that beautiful companion of yours, follow me, for I tell you that wolves are on your trail."

"Who are you?" I gasped doubtfully.

"How soon men forget the voices of those they thought fair enough to hold close not a sunrise ago!" she said with a light laugh.

Then I knew that this was the lady of the litter, one whom I could trust, and whispered to Myra that she must come. Our guide passed on through many gloomy passages, and we followed, leaving the shouts behind us.

"Who is this woman?" asked Myra suspiciously, "and whither does she take us?"

"Her name is Adna," I answered, "one in whom I have faith. Oh! stay not to question. She is our only hope."

"A poor one, I think," murmured Myra. Yet she obeyed me and was silent.

At length we came to a little door which Adna opened with a key that hung to her girdle.

"Hearken, Friend," she said. "This door has no good name, yet it may serve your turn, for it leads from the palace wall to the street that is called Great. Descend those steps, there are twelve of them, and turn down the passage to the right where I think there is no guard, and you will be in that street where no one will note you. Farewell, Friend. Thus I pay you and someone else for a certain honest kiss. Farewell, and may the gods who have forgotten me, always remember you, as I shall."

Then the door shut behind us. We ran down the steps. We followed the passage at the end of which, used as a shelter from sun and rain by the sentry who watched this gate, was a niche in the wall that now was empty, as Adna had said it would be, why I do not know. Watching our moment, we slipped out into the street called Great where many people were afoot, although the hour grew late. All of these were disturbed as was shown by their gestures and the way in which they chattered to each other; doubtless some rumour of the terrible happenings in the palace had reached them, or other news of which I knew nothing. Therefore, as it chanced, we were little observed, for when its inhabitants felt the cold shadow of the Arm of God stretched out over Babylon, they took no heed of one whom they held to be some court noble passing with a cloaked woman.

"Whither go we?" whispered Myra.

"Anywhere away from this accursed palace," I replied, as though at hazard, but all the while I was wondering where we could shelter? In one place only—the guest-house of Daniel—that was the answer. It was fortunate indeed that during the weary months that I had lain hidden in this house I had so often beguiled the time by studying the streets of Babylon from its high roof, for now the knowledge I had gained came to our aid. Following these as I saw them in my mind, I led Myra from one to another until at length before us was the mount crowded with dwellings, on the crest of which were the walls of the old temple that hid the secret entrance to the prophet's guest-house. To encourage Myra I pointed to them.

"Behold our refuge!" I whispered.

"Then may we gain it swiftly, for oh! Ramose, we are followed."

I glanced back; it was true! Two cloaked men were dogging us, spies I supposed, or watchers sent out when Myra was missed. Perhaps that captain of the eunuchs whom I had cut down gave the alarm before he died.

"Now run your best," I said, and clinging to my arm she did so, though all her finery and the heavy cloak weighed her down and cumbered her feet.

We reached the walls and rushed into them by the little twisting path. Now the men were not more than twenty paces from us and I must almost carry Myra. Yet in that dim uncertain light, for the moon was sinking low behind the city's great encircling wall, they lost sight of us, turning to the right whereas we had turned to the left into the mouth of the path. I stumbled on dragging Myra with me; we came to the hidden door. Then with horror I remembered that it was locked and that I had no key, also that at this hour of the night it would be hard to rouse the servants who slept far away. Oh! surely we were lost, for if we knocked or called, those men would hear us and return. I gazed at Myra and I think that even through that gloom she must have seen the agony on my face, for she panted,

"What now, Beloved?"

"Only this, Myra. If you still have that poison, make it ready, unless you would be borne back to yonder palace—where Belshazzar waits."

"Never!" she exclaimed and began to search in her robes, while I did likewise to find the bane which she had given me in the presence-chamber, that I might use it now, should the sword fail me.

Then when all seemed lost the God we worshipped spoke a word in heaven and saved us. Suddenly the door opened! We rushed through. It shut again and the bolts went home.

"Be silent," whispered a voice out of the darkness, "be silent and stir not," and I knew it for that of the man Nabel who on the afternoon of this very day had brought me the basket of figs which hid the forged letter.

We stood still as the dead and next moment heard footsteps outside the door.

"Perhaps they went in here," said a voice.

"Not so," answered a second voice. "Surely I saw them run the other way."

"Still ought we not to seek help and break down the door which we have no tools to do?" said the first voice, "It seems strong and is locked."

"Nay, let it be," came the reply, "for I have no mind to tramp back to that palace where all is drunken riot and fighting, perhaps to get a spear through the belly for my pains. Nay, I shall wait till dawn and make report to the captain of the inner gate, according to the established custom in the matter of palace fugitives. We have our clue; it is enough. Come, brother, I know a tavern not half a mile away where they don't quarrel with late comers and the mistress keeps good wine. We will go sleep there."

"So be it, for we have done our best, but be careful of that trinket," said the first voice. Then the pair of them tramped off wearily.

Nabel led us down the passage to a little chamber at the foot of the stairs, where a lamp burned, by the light of which he looked at us curiously.

"How came you to be at that door, Friend?" I asked.

"My lord, the prophet returned here a little while ago, Master, and bade me watch by it till daylight, and if I heard any without to open at once, and should it be you and a lady, to admit you and close swiftly. These things I did, and it seems at the right time, though how he knew that you were coming he did not say."

I stared at him who also wondered how he knew that we were coming. Then I asked,

"Where is the prophet? We would speak with him."

"You cannot, Master. He told me that he was leaving Babylon instantly and would not return before tomorrow, if then; after which he departed with some cloaked companions whom he met without. Will you not ascend? Food and wine are set in the eating-chamber, as the prophet commanded, and one waits you there. Oh! be not afraid. She is a woman and harmless."

Taking the lamp we crept up the stairs, I going first with my sword ready. On a couch in the eating-chamber sat a woman, moaning and rocking herself to and fro. She looked up and we saw that it was Metep!

"Oh! my fosterling," she cried in a thick voice, "my fosterling whom I thought dead, and your husband, the lord Ramose also, who those chamber-girls said had been taken to the torture-room. Alive— both of you alive! Oh, that holy man must be a god."

"What holy man?" I asked.

"The prophet. I was at the back of the hall when the fighting began and I fled screaming with other women—I know not where. Then suddenly the prophet appeared among us. He took me by the hand, he led me away, and I remember no more till I found myself in this place. Oh! without doubt that prophet is a god!"

****

227

We drank wine; we ate food. Aye, we ate and drank with appetite for never were meat and drink more needed. Then side by side we knelt down, returning thanks to Him we worshipped Who so far had saved us from such great perils. We rose and as we did so Myra, who had thrown off the eunuch's cloak, looked down at her glittering bridal robe and uttered a little cry of dismay.

"What is it?" I asked.

"Oh!" she answered, "my lily. I have lost my lily in the crystal case."

"Let it go," I said smiling, "for you have found him who gave it to you."

She looked at me and I looked at her, until the blood flowing to her pale face stained it red as roses. Then forgetting all, yes, even the dreadful end of my mother, I opened my arms.

Whispering, "Husband! Oh! my husband!" Myra sank into them.

****

It was morning. Metep called at our door awaking us from sleep.

"Arise," she cried. "Armed men are without. They break through the walls!"

We rose and clothed ourselves as best we could. I looked from the window-places. Soldiers were hacking at the door, four of them, while behind, urging them on with many oaths, stood one wrapped in a dark cloak whom from his shape and voice, I guessed to be the baulked Belshazzar himself, come hither mad for vengeance on me and Myra.

"What shall we do, Husband?" asked Myra faintly, for she too had seen.

"Fly to the roof," I answered, "and take your poison with you, Wife, to swallow if there be need. Or if it pleases you better, should the worst happen, leap from the parapet to the ground, after which no king will wish to look on you."

"And you, Husband?"

"I? I am a man who still have some strength and sword-skill, although my last years have been peaceful, and while I may I will hold the stair. Wait. Bid Metep call those two serving-men."

She obeyed and presently they came.

"Friends," I said, "this house, although it be the prophet's and holy, is attacked by a lord from the palace who desires to steal away my wife, the lady Myra, and with him are four soldiers, as you may see for yourselves. Now choose. Will you help me to hold it, or will you give yourselves up? Before you answer, learn what befell your companion,

Obil. He was caught by the servants of the king, and yesterday I saw his body at the palace, torn to pieces by the torturers. Such will be your fate also, if you fall living into the hands of yonder men."

Now Nabel, he who had brought me the basket of figs and opened the door to us, a sturdy fellow with a dogged face, said,

"I stand by you, I who was a soldier in my youth and would sooner die fighting than on the rack. I go to find my shield and sword."

The other man, a tall, pale-eyed fellow whom I had never liked, slipped away, nor do I know what became of him. I trust that he escaped, though when the soldiers broke into the house I heard a cry that he may have uttered.

Metep fled to the roof and Myra, before she followed, stayed to kiss me, saying rapidly,

"Husband, now I am ready for aught. Fight your best without care for me, for if it comes to it, I, who am all your own, shall go hence happy, to await you elsewhere. Never will I fall living into the jaws of yonder dog."

Then looking prouder, I think, than ever I had seen her, she turned to climb the stair.

I too went to the foot of that stair where I found Nabel awaiting me, a sword in his hand and a shield of bull's hide of an old fashion upon his left arm.

"I thought that you had gone with the other," I said.

He laughed and answered,

"Not I! With this sword and shield my great-grandsire fought the Chaldeans, and I too used them in my youth. Now I would pay back my grandsire's death upon their accursed race. Better to die as a warrior than as a dish-bearer."

"Good," I answered. "If we live, you will be glad of those words, and at the worst they may prove no ill passport to peace. Now get you behind me, and if I fall, fight on."

This he did though being brave, he would have stood in front, and we waited, I winding the fine cloak that Nabonidus had given me round my arm to serve as a shield, for I had none. Soon the soldiers broke in the door and reaching the foot of the stair, rushed up at us boldly for they were brave fellows also; moreover the king watched from below. I drove my sword through the throat of the first, and he fell. The second cut at me over his body. I warded the blow with the cloak, but his sword shore through it and wounded me in the head, causing blood to run into my eyes.

"Back!" cried Nabel, and I staggered past him up the stair to the roof. Nabel fought with the third man and it seemed, slew him. Then he joined me on the roof where Myra and Metep were wiping the blood from my face with their garments.

The other two soldiers appeared. We sprang at them and that fight was desperate, but God gave us strength and we slew them. Then, sorely wounded both of us, we reeled back to the parapet and stood there in front of the women. Belshazzar came and mocked at us, but attack he dared not, being a coward in his heart; also we still had swords in our hands and were upright on our feet though we could scarcely stir. Nay, he stayed by the mouth of the stair, waiting for help or thinking that we should bleed to death or faint.

"I have sent for more men," he cried, "and presently they will be here to make an end of you, cursed Egyptian. You thought you had escaped me and so you might have done, had not that strumpet of yours dropped her trinket as she ran from the palace, telling my watchers which way she went," and he drew from his robe the lily talisman set in its case of crystal and waved it in front of us.

Now he seemed to go mad; indeed I think he was smitten with a sudden madness like Nebuchadnezzar before him. He raved at us in vile words. He cursed the God of Judah Who, he said, had sent a lying spirit to write spells on his palace wall, and the prophet who had interpreted those spells and changed the company at the feast into ravening wolves. With a working face and rolling eyes he blasphemed, he reviled, he uttered horrible threats against Myra, saying that he would throw her to the soldiers while I died in torment before her eyes. He defied Cyrus and the Persians, vowing that he would burn them living, hundred by hundred he would burn them all; he beat the air, gnashing his teeth, till at last, able to bear no more, I strove to spring at him, but being wounded in the thigh as well as on the head, could not, and fell down.

Belshazzar drew a knife, purposing to finish me, yet in the end dared not because Nabel still stood over me, sword in hand, though he might not move. So he began to mock again and talk of the manner in which we should perish.

"Hark!" he said, "my servants come. I hear footsteps on the stair. Now look your last upon the sun, accursed Egyptian!"

I too heard a footstep on the stair and whispered to Myra to be ready to die in such fashion as she chose.

"I am ready, Husband," she answered in a steady voice.

At the mouth of the stair appeared a man. Lo! it was no soldier of the king, but Belus carrying a sword. Yes, *Belus*, come from I knew not whence, haggard and travel-stained, but with the fire of vengeance burning in his eyes.

Belshazzar turned and saw him. His fat face paled, his cheeks fell in, his whole frame seemed to shrink. He staggered back.

"Do you know me again, Belshazzar the King?" cried Belus. "Aye, you know me well. I am he whose young daughter you wronged and murdered long ago. I swore vengeance on you then and through the years far away I have worked and woven, till now at last the destined hour is at hand and you are in my net. Look yonder," and he pointed to a wide street of the city beneath us. "What do you see? Soldiers marching, is it not? Behold their banners. They are not yours, O King of Chaldea. Nay, they are those of Cyrus. I, Belus, have corrupted your captains; I have opened the gates of unconquered Babylon; you and your House are fallen; God's curse is fulfilled and my vengeance is accomplished!"

Belshazzar looked. He saw, he began to whine for mercy. Then suddenly he stabbed at Belus with the knife he held. But Belus was watching and before it could fall he drove at him with his sword, piercing him through and through.

Belus stooped; lifting the lily talisman that had fallen from Belshazzar's hand, he gave it back to Myra. Yes, there, amongst the dead, he gave it back to her without a word.

****

Thus died Belshazzar, King of the Chaldeans, Lord of the Empire of Babylon, by the hand of one whom he had wronged, he to whom it was appointed that he should be slain on the night of the writing on the wall.

****

Here ends the history of Ramose the Egyptian, son of Apries, and of Myra his wife, a daughter of the royal race of Judah, written at the Happy House in Memphis, by this Ramose when he and his wife were old, that their children's children might be instructed and pass on the tale to those who come after them, of how God saved them out of the hand of Belshazzar, King of Babylon.

LEONAUR

ALSO FROM LEONAUR
AVAILABLE IN SOFTCOVER OR HARDCOVER WITH DUST JACKET

THE EMPIRE OF THE AIR: 1 *by George Griffiths*—*The Angel of the Revolution*—a rich brew that calls to mind Verne's tales of futuristic wars while being original, visionary, exciting and technologically prescient.

THE EMPIRE OF THE AIR: 2 *by George Griffiths*—*Olga Romanoff or, The Syren of the Skies*—the sequel to *The Angel of the Revolution*—a future Earth in which nation states are given full self determination when the Aerians, the descendants of 'The Brotherhood of Freedom,' who have policed world peace for more than a century, decide they are mature enough to have outgrown war.

THE INTERPLANETARY ADVENTURES OF DR KINNEY *by Homer Eon Flint*—*The Lord of Death, The Queen of Life, The Devolutionist & The Emancipatrix.*

ARCOT, MOREY & WADE *by John W. Campbell, Jr.*—The Complete, Classic Space Opera Series—*The Black Star Passes, Islands of Space, Invaders from the Infinite.*

CHALLENGER & COMPANY *by Arthur Conan Doyle*—The Complete Adventures of Professor Challenger and His Intrepid Team-*The Lost World, The Poison Belt, The Land of Mists, The Disintegration Machine* and *When the World Screamed.*

GARRETT P. SERVISS' SCIENCE FICTION *by Garrett P. Serviss*—Three Interplanetary Adventures including the unauthorised sequel to H. G. Wells' *War of the Worlds-Edison's Conquest of Mars, A Columbus of Space, The Moon Metal.*

JUNK DAY *by Arthur Sellings*—". . . . his finest novel was his last, Junk Day, a post-holocaust tale set in the ruins of his native London and peopled with engrossing character types . . . . perhaps grimmer than his previous work but pointedly more energetic." *The Encyclopedia of Science Fiction*

KIPLING'S SCIENCE FICTION *by Rudyard Kipling*—Science Fiction & Fantasy stories by a Master Storyteller including 'As East As A,B,C' 'With The Night Mail'.

DARKNESS AND DAWN 1—THE VACANT WORLD *by George Allen England*—A Novel of a future New York.

DARKNESS AND DAWN 2—BEYOND THE GREAT OBLIVION *by George Allen England*—The last vestiges of humanity set out across America's devastated landscape in search of their dream.

DARKNESS AND DAWN 3—THE AFTER GLOW *by George Allen England*—Somewhere near the Great Lakes, 1000 years from now. Beneath our planet's surface tribes of near human albino warriors eke out an existence in a hostile environment.

LEONAUR

ALSO FROM LEONAUR
AVAILABLE IN SOFTCOVER OR HARDCOVER WITH DUST JACKET

THE COLLECTED SCIENCE FICTION AND FANTASY OF STANLEY G. WEINBAUM 1—INTERPLANETARY ODYSSEYS *by Stanley G. Weinbaum*—Classic Tales of Interplanetary Adventure Including: A Martian Odyssey, its Sequel Valley of Dreams, the Complete 'Ham' Hammond Stories and Others.

THE COLLECTED SCIENCE FICTION AND FANTASY OF STANLEY G. WEINBAUM 2—OTHER EARTHS *by Stanley G. Weinbaum*—Classic Futuristic Tales Including: *Dawn of Flame* & its Sequel The Black Flame, plus The Revolution of 1960 & Others.

THE COLLECTED SCIENCE FICTION AND FANTASY OF STANLEY G. WEINBAUM 3—STRANGE GENIUS *by Stanley G. Weinbaum*—Classic Tales of the Human Mind at Work Including the Complete Novel The New Adam, the 'van Manderpootz' Stories and Others.

THE COLLECTED SCIENCE FICTION AND FANTASY OF STANLEY G. WEINBAUM 4—THE BLACK HEART *by Stanley G. Weinbaum*—Classic Strange Tales Including: the Complete Novel The Dark Other, Plus Proteus Island and Others.

THE COLLECTED SCIENCE FICTION & FANTASY OF JACK LONDON 1—BEFORE ADAM & OTHER STORIES *by Jack London*—included in this Volume Before Adam The Scarlet Plague A Relic of the Pliocene When the World Was Young The Red One Planchette A Thousand Deaths Goliah A Curious Fragment The Rejuvenation of Major Rathbone.

THE COLLECTED SCIENCE FICTION & FANTASY OF JACK LONDON 2—THE IRON HEEL & OTHER STORIES *by Jack London*—included in this Volume The Iron Heel The Enemy of All the World The Shadow and the Flash The Strength of the Strong The Unparalleled Invasion The Dream of Debs.

THE COLLECTED SCIENCE FICTION & FANTASY OF JACK LONDON 3—THE STAR ROVER & OTHER STORIES *by Jack London*—included in this Volume The Star Rover The Minions of Midas The Eternity of Forms The Man With the Gash.

THE CRETAN TEAT *by Brian Aldiss*—The Cretan Teat is a wry and comic novel that interweaves its own fiction with an inner fiction about the discovery of a Byzantine painting of the Mother of the Blessed Virgin Mary suckling the infant Jesus and a fake ikon that becomes an instrument of Nemesis.

LEONAUR

ALSO FROM LEONAUR
AVAILABLE IN SOFTCOVER OR HARDCOVER WITH DUST JACKET

THE FIRST BOOK OF AYESHA by H. Rider Haggard—Contains *She & Ayesha: the Return of She.*

THE SECOND BOOK OF AYESHA by H. Rider Haggard—Contains *She and Allan & Wisdom's Daughter.*

QUATERMAIN: THE COMPLETE ADVENTURES—1 by H. Rider Haggard—Contains *King Solomon's Mines & Allan Quatermain.*

QUATERMAIN: THE COMPLETE ADVENTURES—2 by H. Rider Haggard—Contains *Allan's Wife, Maiwa's Revenge & Marie.*

QUATERMAIN: THE COMPLETE ADVENTURES—3 by H. Rider Haggard—Contains *Child of Storm & Allan and the Holy Flower.*

QUATERMAIN: THE COMPLETE ADVENTURES—4 by H. Rider Haggard—Contains *Finished & The Ivory Child.*

QUATERMAIN: THE COMPLETE ADVENTURES—5 by H. Rider Haggard—Contains *The Ancient Allan & She and Allan.*

QUATERMAIN: THE COMPLETE ADVENTURES—6 by H. Rider Haggard—Contains *Heu-Heu or, the Monster & The Treasure of the Lake.*

QUATERMAIN: THE COMPLETE ADVENTURES—7 by H. Rider Haggard—Contains *Allan and the Ice Gods, Four Short Adventures & Nada the Lily.*

TROS OF SAMOTHRACE 1: WOLVES OF THE TIBER by Talbot Mundy—55 B.C.--an adventurer set during the Roman invasion of Britain.

TROS OF SAMOTHRACE 2: DRAGONS OF THE NORTH by Talbot Mundy—55 B.C. —Caesar plots, Britons war among themselves and the Vikings are coming.

TROS OF SAMOTHRACE 3: SERPENT OF THE WAVES by Talbot Mundy—55 B.C.--Caesar is poised to invade Britain—only a grand strategy can foil him!.

TROS OF SAMOTHRACE 4: CITY OF THE EAGLES by Talbot Mundy—54 B.C.—Rome—Tros treads in the streets of his sworn enemies!.

TROS OF SAMOTHRACE 5: CLEOPATRA by Talbot Mundy—Tros and the Roman Empire turn to the Egypt of the Pharaohs.

TROS OF SAMOTHRACE 6: THE PURPLE PIRATE by Talbot Mundy—The epic saga of the ancient world—Tros of Samothrace—draws to a conclusion in this sixth—and final—volume.

LEONAUR

ALSO FROM LEONAUR
AVAILABLE IN SOFTCOVER OR HARDCOVER WITH DUST JACKET

THE PRISONER OF ZENDA & ITS SEQUEL RUPERT OF HENTZAU *by Anthony Hope*—Two famous novels of high adventure in one volume.

THE GLADIATORS *by G. J. Whyte Melville*—A Classic Novel of Ancient Rome—Three Volumes in One Special Edition.

THE COMPLETE CAPTAIN DANGEROUS *by George Augustus Sala*—The Adventures of a Soldier, Sailor, Merchant, Spy, Slave and Bashaw of the Grand Turk.

ORTHERIS, LEAROYD & MULVANEY *by Rudyard Kipling*—The Complete Soldiers Three stories.

SIR NIGEL & THE WHITE COMPANY *by Arthur Conan Doyle*—Two Classic Novels of the 100 Years' War.

THE ILLUSTRATED & COMPLETE BRIGADIER GERARD *by Arthur Conan Doyle*—All 18 Stories with the Original Strand Magazine Illustrations by Wollen and Paget.

THE OHIO RIVER TRILOGY 1: BETTY ZANE *by Zane Grey*—The land along the Ohio River is newly settled. Indomitable men and women—Col. Zane and his family, the McCollochs, Wetzel, the "Death Wind" Indian killer, among them—have hewn a life out of the frontier wilderness.

THE OHIO RIVER TRILOGY 2: THE SPIRIT OF THE BORDER *by Zane Grey*—Fort Henry still stands as a bastion for the settlers on the frontier along the Ohio River. More pioneers are now moving west to carve new lives out of the wilderness.

THE OHIO RIVER TRILOGY 3: THE LAST TRAIL *by Zane Grey*—This final volume of Zane Grey's Ohio River Trilogy is a gripping finale to a great series—another thrilling story of life and death on the early American frontier and a classic in the tradition of Drums Along the Mohawk.

THE NAPOLEONIC NOVELS: VOLUME 1 *by Erckmann-Chatrian*—This book comprises two linked novels—*The Conscript* & *Waterloo*—about the adventures a young conscript in the French Army. during the Napoleonic wars.

THE NAPOLEONIC NOVELS: VOLUME 2 *by Erckmann-Chatrian*—*The Blockade of Phalsburg* & *The Invasion of France in 1814*—the events portrayed in these two novels of the Napoleonic period properly fit in time between those of the first volume. They appear together here since each—unlike the other two in this series—is a stand alone work.

LEONAUR

ALSO FROM LEONAUR

AVAILABLE IN SOFTCOVER OR HARDCOVER WITH DUST JACKET

THE CIVIL WAR NOVELS: 1 *by Joseph A. Altsheler*—*The Guns of Bull Run &
The Guns of Shiloh*—the first and second novels of a series of eight adventures which
follow the momentous events, campaigns and battles of the great American Civil War
between the Northern and Southern states.

THE CIVIL WAR NOVELS: 2 *by Joseph A. Altsheler*—*The Scouts of Stonewall
& The Sword of Antietam*—the third and fourth novels of a series of nine adventures
which follow the momentous events, campaigns and battles of the great American
Civil War between the Northern and Southern states.

THE CIVIL WAR NOVELS: 3 *by Joseph A. Altsheler*—*The Star of Gettysburg
& The Rock of Chickamauga*—the fifth and sixth novels of a series of nine adventures
which follow the momentous events, campaigns and battles of the great American
Civil War between the Northern and Southern states.

THE CIVIL WAR NOVELS: 4 *by Joseph A. Altsheler*—*The Shades of the Wilderness & The Tree of Appomattox*—the seventh and eighth novels of a series of nine
adventures which follow the momentous events, campaigns and battles of the great
American Civil War between the Northern and Southern states.

THE CIVIL WAR NOVELS: 5 *by Joseph A. Altsheler*—*Before the Dawn: a Story
of the Fall of Richmond*—the last of a series of nine adventures which follow the momentous events, campaigns and battles of the great American Civil War between the
Northern and Southern states.

THE FRENCH & INDIAN WAR NOVELS: 1 *by Joseph A. Altsheler*—*The
Hunters of the Hills & The Shadow of the North*—In this three volume, six novel set the
story of the war, with many of its real life characters, is told through the adventures
of its principal characters, Robert Lennox, the hunter Willet and his Indian companion Tayoga.

THE FRENCH & INDIAN WAR NOVELS: 2 *by Joseph A. Altsheler*—*The
Rulers of the Lakes & The Masters of the Peaks*—In this three volume, six novel set the
story of the war, with many of its real life characters, is told through the adventures
of its principal characters, Robert Lennox, the hunter Willet and his Indian companion Tayoga.

THE FRENCH & INDIAN WAR NOVELS: 1 *by Joseph A. Altsheler*—*The Lords
of the Wild & The Sun of Quebec*—In this three volume, six novel set the story of the
war, with many of its real life characters, is told through the adventures of its principal
characters, Robert Lennox, the hunter Willet and his Indian companion Tayoga.

Printed in the USA
CPSIA information can be obtained
at www.ICGtesting.com
LVHW040528130224
771577LV00049B/155

9 780857 061614